World of Ashes

By

J.K. Robinson

Chapter 1

Ash fell like snow in July, blanketing the highway and trees. Ash, though, no matter how clean, never really looks like snow. It looks like ash, like the cremated remnants of the greatest civilization on Earth, the Roman Empire of her time.

In this case the ash was mostly from the city of St. Louis. Ethan Kelly had no idea how many people lived there when the plague reached unmanageable proportions, but likely there was no one left now. The great cities of the world were burning as the living-dead rampaged through the streets and all the armies of all the nations utterly unable to combat the viral outbreaks. Last-ditch nuclear strikes happened in China and India, but none of the traditional tactics mattered to this enemy. The plague was a juggernaut helped out at seemingly every turn by nepotism, corruption and terrorism. This new scourge skipped borders before some nations were even aware it existed. Rings of fire could be seen spreading methodically from space and anyone with a television got to watch it coming their way in 1080HD with nowhere to hide.

The roadblock down Interstate-44, just south of St. Louis, was a total failure. Reminiscent of the collective cock-up that was the President's darling "Comprehensive Defense & Control" bill. What curfews for adults, closing malls and restaurants, or making people wear a mask against a disease that clearly wasn't airborne did for the country was anyone's guess. From what Ethan could tell it was just Martial Law rebranded, a fancy show of force to make the locals feel safe while they evacuated those who mattered and abandoned the rest.

In one monstrosity of an executive power grab, the sitting president not only suspended the next year's election, but mobilized a force not seen since the height of the Vietnam War. The CD&C spelled out what was nothing short of the forced conscription of all able-bodied persons with any military experience, regardless of age or disability. It didn't matter if you were in your sixties, in a wheelchair, or on the verge of eating your own gun, you reported for duty upon penalty of imprisonment in an all or nothing bid to save the day. Even bad-conduct discharges, like Ethan, were being unceremoniously dropped back into the very units that had thrown them out in the first place, just to fill the gaps. Luckily, or at least serendipitously, Ethan's old unit had been wiped out at the Battle of Savannah. With nowhere to send him to but a local Front Guard unit, (*fancy speak for the Redshirts about to be sacrificed on an away mission by a less than scrupulous captain,*) his fate seemed all but sealed until just this very moment.

A noise to the right drew Ethan's attention and his M-4. The little day-glow orange arrow from the ACOG sight danced over abandoned minivans, empty Army tents and piles of junk. Everything from blankets to gold ingots, abandoned by refugees fleeing for their lives, lay strewn along the road. It was a snapshot from the Polish countryside of 1939, valuables covered in a fine layer of gray death. There were no threats, but at least he was alert enough to find one had there been, which was somewhat reassuring.

The younger soldier with Ethan started panicking at the sight of the helo's. "They left us? They left us! We radioed in, how could they just leave us!? Top said they were coming back for us!" he shouted in an octave unbecoming of a man. Ethan rolled his eyes as Derrek Roberts made an ass of himself. Taking his helmet off and slapping Roberts in the back of his helmet with it, a *Turtlefuck,* in military vernacular, Ethan made his feelings known. The kid stumbled forward, furious, but was too dazed to strike back.

"Wake the fuck up," Ethan held out the ancient brick-sized radio, "if you hadn't been so busy freaking the fuck out, you'd have heard me say the battery died almost an hour ago. As far as they know, or care, we're dead. What a fucking tragedy."

"Well… help me get a car started, or something… we can catch up with them at the next town," Roberts said, pointing at the dealership where the Command Post had been. Their unit had left the tents and anything that was too big to carry, along with some of the unserviceable trucks. If they could easily be fixed then they would already be rolling down the highway, far away from this place.

"Dude, you need to chillax yourself," Ethan sighed, gesturing back toward the theme park, and started walking. "There are land-lines back at the park's main office. We can use one to call home."

"Home? Home!? What are you talking about, Kelly? We have to get back to our unit! We can't go home, they're everywhere!"

Ethan had had enough. He reached around, despite his bulky and mostly useless body armor, and wrapped his hands around the shoulder straps of Roberts' vest. Lifting with more force than he'd ever put into anything in his life, Ethan nearly picked up the other man. Through gritted teeth and bulging veins he said, "I'm not going back, *PFC...*" Their eyes locked for what seemed an eternity, "and you shouldn't either. My home is about twenty miles from here, and I'm going to go look for my fiance and my family!"

Ethan let go and started walking away. The signature clicking of a weapon from safe to semi came from behind. "If you strike me down now, I shall become more powerful than you could ever imagine," Ethan's Obi Won Kenobi voice was not convincing, and he felt a little stupid saying it, but his brain was full of rage and anger at the stupidity of the whole thing.

"We need every soldier on the line, Private Kelly!" Roberts recited their first-line supervisor's favorite one-liner while holding his rifle menacingly, but not directly at Ethan. The guy he was quoting was only a staff sergeant and hardly an expert tactician at that. He was the kind of doofus that, a hundred years ago, would be extolling the virtues of charging over the top of open trenches and running into a hail of enemy gunfire. Provided he was the one in the friendly trench blowing the whistle, of course.

"Because that's what some pot-bellied office clerk with no overseas time says?" Ethan's tone was pleading for the younger man to not be so stupid. "Look, I get it. You joined the Army just about the time shit started going tits-up. I'm sure you miss Jody Rottencrotch back home and football and Twitter and Facebook and all that crap, I'm sure your cell-phone withdrawal is just horrendous, but you have to make a decision. Go chase down our unit and hope rear element snipers don't shoot you in the face, or come with me," Ethan gestured broadly to the silent ash falling around them in choking a gray snow storm. *Had no city, no nation, survived Judgment Day?* "Go back. Fine. Whatever, but one day your number is gonna be up and you'll be eaten alive... slowly from what I've seen."

Roberts hadn't actually aimed the rifle at Ethan, but his finger was still dangerously on the trigger like the unseasoned sack of meat he was. A figure appeared in the vanishing point of the mist and Roberts put his rifle back up to his shoulder. Standing there in the open like a toy soldier, ready to perform more riot control duties while Ethan slipped silently behind a car, the kid made an excellent distraction. Ethan had been watching the camera feeds from the Tactical Operations Center before he was assigned to the tower, so he knew the Antire Hill Checkpoint had been overrun even before he went up. No one, not even Ethan, had expected the inevitable wave of undead to get this far, this fast at a shuffling pace. *Even the runners should have burned out by now*, Ethan thought to himself.

Thinking quickly, Ethan let Roberts' dumb-ass be the bait while he prepared to pick the infected off from behind cover. If they were lucky, Ethan could use his rifle to "butt-stroke" the zombie in the brainpan from behind and not attract attention with gunfire. Unfortunately, this depended on the private not forgetting his training and not shooting before the ghoul got close. Startling the infected during the Rage Phase, the initial minutes after infection where the victim is driven insane with fever and an uncontrollable, illogical rage, was generally considered a bad idea. *In fact,* Ethan's inner monologue mused, *it was kind of like poking a badger with a spoon. Then imagine that the one badger's hisses drew in every other badger for miles so that in no time you were drowning in pissed off badgers.* On second thought, perhaps Roberts would know not to be so stupid after so many painful hours of PowerPoint presentations on the subject.

Roberts held up his hand and squared his shoulders like a wall, "Stop. Stay where you are," he said in a sufficiently threatening tone. The shape didn't respond and kept staggering slowly toward them, its footfalls muffled against the soft dusty layer that clung to his boots and lower legs like paste. Ethan listened for breathing, but wasn't sure if the "Vics" even needed to breathe. It was a shot in the dark listening for something that might not even be happening, but whatever compassion he still had in his blackened heart said not to just kill the stranger outright. Roberts repeated the warning even louder this time, which wasn't very smart. Finally, Ethan had had enough and walked from his safe place straight at the person with his M-9 drawn.

"What are you doing!?" Roberts shouted, chasing after Ethan and slipping on the moist ash. He fell on his ass with his gear clattering, finding out the hard way what it felt like to be a turtle on its back.

Ethan got close enough to see the man staggering towards them in detail. He was a fellow soldier in a medic's short sleeve tunic and regular duty trousers that were stuffed lazily into his boots. His green and brown mottled uniform had dark red stains all over the knees and most of his chest, but none of it looked like the black bile the infected would ooze.

"Dude, you okay? Ya with me, man? Give me a sign or I'll put you down, man," Ethan warned with sympathy.

The medic stopped walking and looked up at him. The moment of truth, would he be a zombie, or would he be alive? After an eons-long moment the medic smiled and sorta waved, something the undead had never done. Ethan cursed as he closed the distance between them, holstering his weapon. Upon closer inspection the medic was only a little beat up, lots of scratches on his face and forearms from running through God knows what, but no bites. The medic wasn't all there for sure, asking Ethan repeatedly if he was "at that one concert" before collapsing in their arms and coughing wet ash.

"Help me carry him over the barrier, he's in shock. There's a medical facility in the park, it might have an I.V. I can stick him with, get some water back in his system," Ethan ordered, checking the man's pulse and fingernails for signs of dehydration.

"What? The theme-park? No, man, c'mon. Where are you going?" Roberts whined as Ethan quickly escorted the medic back the way they'd come, trying to get him to walk on his own as he came to occasionally.

"I just told you what I was doing, fucknuts. Either pay attention or go do what you want, but I'm getting me and-" Ethan leaned over and tried to read the medic's nametape, but it was caked with mud, "-the Tar Baby here, out of harm's way." Though he complained to the contrary, Roberts wasn't really that upset to be getting away from the road. There were more helicopters, Blackhawks and Chinooks, thundering overhead than even a few minutes before. Like geese fleeing winter they were all heading south. Only mass evacuations warranted that kind of mobilization these days, even the Federal Government couldn't afford the loss in aviation fuel just to rescue a few people.

The walk through the parking lot was long and quiet, the *Looney Toons* characters atop light-poles marked the rows of abandoned cars. This ocean of random vehicles was left by refugees at the behest of the Army and not by patrons of the park. All the fuel had been scavenged from them, or that would have been plan-A. It was a disturbingly upbeat contrast to the end of all things. Roberts noticed they were leaving tracks in the ash and repeatedly mentioned that too.

Ethan looked back and thought about it for a moment, "Something tells me these shit-sacks aren't that smart. If they were, we'd all be gone by now."

"I hope you're right. I'm just saying, we've got about a hundred and fifty rounds each, plus our 9's. Not to mention, Kelly, you can't shoot for shit. I've seen your target scores, you miss twenty nine out of thirty because your hands never stop shaking, you useless drunk."

Ethan pointed to the Third Infantry Division combat patch on his right shoulder. For the Army, a patch on the right shoulder signified a serviceman has been in a combat zone. He seldom wore it, but had put it back on to irritate the same first sergeant who'd sent him to the checkpoint to die. The man didn't like any reminders that Ethan might have, at one point, been a well adjusted soldier. It was true, if Ethan put half the effort into his job that he put into alienating people, he'd be a captain by now. "*Hero-Patch*, got it? If I wanted to hit paper targets I could and would. I was trying to get the induction board to think I had bad eyesight, it was a strategy."

"You are a bitch-ass motherfucker."

The medic laughed and coughed hardily, soot mixed with the snot before it had even left his mouth, "You two are gonna be so much fun to spend my last hours with. How did I ever get so lucky?"

"You're a *Dark Side of the Force* kind of guy, huh?" Ethan smirked, handing him the straw from his own partially depleted Camelbak to drink from. They were almost out of water, but the park had plenty. When it was open, the park had had a dedicated private security force. Ethan's instinct was maybe people thought armed guards were still there and so hadn't ransacked it yet. He knew the security guards were all gone for weeks now actually, because he had been one of them. It had been his dead end job he was working; it was hard to do anything with a Dishonorable Discharge.

The sad trio dragged themselves through the ticket booths, Roberts going over the gates to help from the other side in case the new guy fell trying to push through the turn-styles. The counting devices were clearly designed in an era when people weren't as fat or wearing body armor. Ethan led them through a hidden service door next to the World's Fair ice-cream shop. That revealed a precarious and noisy flight of oxidized iron stairs which promised to lead inside a moldy, warped wooden building's second story offices. They finally made it to Ethan's security office and were further relieved it contained FEMA ration packs and stacks of purified water bottles. Roberts went to get medical supplies from the first aid hut next to the log ride, glad to be away from Ethan for a few minutes. In the meantime, Ethan and the medic watched him through several video links, the power miraculously and suspiciously still on.

*****

Roberts genuinely considered just leaving on his own once he thought he was out of view of the security office. As much as he'd love to leave these assholes to their own devices, he knew he was ultimately better than that. He and this new guy would eventually harangue Kelly into rejoining the unit and all would be forgiven.

Sparking up a cigarette he'd pretended not to have around Kelly so he didn't have to share what precious few were left, Roberts took in the sights around him while he detoxed from his companions. He was aware of the irony of sucking ash into his lungs when there was already so much in the air, but habits were habits and these smokes were calling his name. Trash was strewn everywhere, especially the plastic coverings to brand apparel that was only partially stored away from the elements. A storm had knocked many of the racks over and no employees had been back to pick them up. A small piece of him had the urge to pick the racks up as a courtesy, *but a courtesy to whom now, Grams?*

Strolling forward along the path the cartoon-style map had suggested, he had to pass a section of games meant to fleece parents of their hard-earned cash. From a certain angle you could tell the rims of the basketball game weren't a perfect circle, it was how the house rigged the game in their favor. Roberts fancied himself quite the ball player and had to try his luck. The under-inflated balls were slick with ash, but after rubbing the soot off with his undershirt there was enough grip to shoot.

He shoots, he scores! "You are a first time go at this station, Private," Roberts smiled to himself. He tossed the ball three more times, but missed by a mile. Seemingly he had used all of his luck in that one throw. Glad no one was there to see it, he finished his short trek to the medical hut, still mulling over the idea of abandoning Kelly and this new guy entirely.

*****

Back at the security office, the medic was doing much better now that he was safe and able to drink water. "I'm surprised the power is still on," the man said, trying to be conversational, after downing four bottles. He'd injured his left shoulder somewhere along the line and lifting his ruined uniform off was a chore, "When I got to St. Louis an engineer company from the Texas National Guard was moving through to fortify the non-nuclear power plants, so I guess they're having some success.... so, you're really not gonna ask me?" he pointed at the pile of bloody clothes he'd discarded, slipping into a *Daffy Duck* shirt and *Tasmanian Devil* shorts from the gift shop below. The newcomer looked ridiculous, but clean clothes can make all the difference to someone who's been through hell, "About Antire Hill, I mean? Or what my name is? I'm Sergeant Keith Brewer by the way."

"I wasn't gonna ask while I wasn't sure if you were still in shock, but I'm Ethan Kelly, E1-type," They shook hands. "We had hoped some of you guys made it, but after our shit-prick CO saw the trucks hauling ass from the roadblock and then the Apache's go in, he decided it was time to pack it in too. Me and Roberts were supposed to be picked up before they left, but you know how it goes these days." Tossing Sergeant Brewer another bottle of water from the employee mini-fridge, Ethan tried looking out the windows for Roberts, but didn't see him. "You must have been running for hours to get this far, Antire Hill is like ten miles from here."

"Yeah, I ran for a while, but they'd blown the bridges over the Meramec. I thought I was dead for sure, but then I saw a third bridge through a fog bank and ran for it. There was a rage-phase victim from the hill chasing me and this nurse. Turned out the bridge was just a skeletal frame nobody felt like dismantling. It didn't even have decking to walk on."

Ethan nodded, knowing the area well enough to instantly recognize the bridge in question, "It used to go to a town called Times Beach, but there was a chemical contamination of the topsoil and they tore it all down and incinerated the top two feet. This three-story industrial furnace was there for a couple years when I was a kid, burning off the contaminated soil. It's basically Missouri's Centralia."

Sergeant Brewer finished off his water, "That's where the coal fire is, right?" Ethan nodded, so Brewer went on. "It took almost an hour to get just halfway across, then a girl, maybe high school age, I don't know, tried to follow me and a couple others. I turned back to help her, but there was a ghoul just behind her and he spooked her and she lost her footing. She was too far away for me to even think about catching. All I could do was watch her fall into the river, the zombie belly-flopping in after her. I didn't see either of them come back up. The other two trying to cross slipped and fell too, I didn't think I'd make it."

"That's fucked up, man," Ethan gave up looking for Roberts out the window. "Do you know if they're still alive when they start raging?" he had to ask, the debate had never made it into *Stars & Stripes,* the only "authorized" reading material soldiers under Martial Law were allowed to have, besides the pointedly boring *Army Times.* It did leave a huge knowledge gap in the force and really that part might have been the most unforgivable. Fighting men can do a lot with spotty information, but it's impossible to work with nothing.

Brewer nodded vigorously, "Oh yeah, they still have a heartbeat for a while after symptoms present themselves, which is fast like a weaponized nerve agent. It's a strange thing, though, after they're done spazzing out they actually die. They flatline, no vitals, no breathing. The really sick part is their brain activity remains off the chart, like this thing feeds on something in the brain specifically." Keith took another swig of water from a bottle someone had left behind, "The CDC was supposed to have recorded which parts of the brain are affected the most, but who knows where that data went. Personally, I really would have liked to have known how fast-" and he stopped as gunshots echoed from across the eerie, fun-sized ghost town that had once been the DC Comics themed area. On the out of focus black and white security cameras Roberts came sprinting from the first aid station, turning as he ran to shoot back into the building behind him. Grabbing his rifle and giving the pistol to Keith, they rushed to Roberts's aid, Ethan in the lead. PFC Darrek Roberts was reloading behind a basketball game, his gunner's mesh uniform soaked with sweat from panic and made pasty by the ash.

Ethan looked up at the old-timey locomotive before they met Roberts under the arch of the bridge. The propane powered, narrow-gauge engine and its cars, as ghostly gray as the empty park around them, stood where it had plowed under a zombie in a very public incident. Police tape still marked the scene, back when they bothered to mark the scenes of "Infection Related Attacks." The incident marked the unceremonious end of the park's final season.

In those early, dreamlike days of safety and plenty only a few short months ago, zombies were still relatively few in number and not well understood. Nobody took the threat any more seriously than Swine Flu or SARS. Hell, gas prices actually dropped because people weren't traveling as much due to an unrelated downturn in the stock market.

"There's like three of those fuckers in there," Roberts

said, out of breath. "I shot one of them, but the other two are still in the office." Ethan had never seen a black man turn the color of a sheet of paper before (Michael Jackson notwithstanding,) so his own level of alarm increased. The ghouls must have gotten the drop on Roberts for him to be this upset.

Silently, Sergeant Brewer motioned for the two to surround the First Aid station. "Time to play soldier," Ethan whispered as they went in.

They found the zombie that Roberts shot trying to get back up. Keith put a bullet in the rotting man's face while Ethan put down the last two undead paramedics in the adjacent office. The irony that he would be in this place, doing these things, was breaking Ethan down as much as being away from home, yet he was so close by. He slung his rifle and took a cigarette from Roberts's pocket, the kid barely taking notice.

All three of them were out of breath now, but not from the physical exertion as much as from the adrenaline dump. Ethan looked like he was either about to cry or break out in hysterical laughter, but as Keith was beginning to see it wasn't Ethan whose behavior needed watching.

"Fuck!" Roberts shouted, gesturing wildly and flagging his buddies with the business end of his sidearm, "I hate this fucking shit!"

Ethan patted the kid on the shoulder, "C'mon Dee, let's go. I'll even let you carry the backpack."

"I outrank you," Roberts said in an uncharacteristically bitter tone, narrowing his eyes and stepping back to square off with Ethan. Dried spittle at the corners of his mouth was beginning to turn red and he was grinding his teeth audibly.

"No. You don't. I have more time in the latrine than you have in the field, you assclown noobie. Besides, I've already deserted. You couldn't give me orders if you were General of the fucking Army Petreaus," Ethan smiled his typically smarmy smile and stepped past Roberts with a wink of the eye.

"Fuck you!" Roberts smacked Ethan in the face with his empty hand, then set about kicking a stuffed bear like it owed him money. "Fuck you fuck you fuck you!" He shouted over and over again before, out of nowhere, Roberts stood ramrod straight. He then recited the first three lines of the Army Values before saluting with his M-9 to his temple. Keith had only a moment to turn away and pull his shirt collar over his face. Ethan pulled the spit-shield scarf under his uniform up in a practiced motion from repeated drills, almost at the same moment Roberts pulled the trigger. Brain and bone sprayed all over the wall of the first-aid station with a grotesque splatting noise. Ethan and Keith both flinched when the gun went off, closing their eyes and mouths and looking away sharply. After Roberts's body dropped like a sack of potatoes to the blacktop, Keith stepped away from the shadow he'd left in the spatter pattern. It looked like the silhouettes burned into stone by the blast of the first nuclear bombs, only in red.

Ethan, on the other hand, was frozen in place. Normally his fight or flight response was the latter, but this time he couldn't move. The splatter-guard, as it was called, a sort of reverse-hoodie worn like a dickie-shirt, dropped onto Ethan's chest as he watched the blood pool. It wasn't as red this time...

Disconnect; a flashback to a hotter place and a darker time.

They only had three months left to go. Three months and this rolling hell on wheels called Operation Iraqi Freedom would be behind them. Left in the dust the entire country seemed to be made of. The pervasive stench of the burn-pits a bad memory, the overall unpleasant odor of trash and dead soil a thing of the past. So, with only weeks left, why had she done it? Why had Ethan's friend put a gun to her head and pulled the trigger?

He didn't have answers for that, but he could tell you who made her do it. He knew in excruciating detail the kind of torment his sorry excuse for sergeants had put her through. It was perverse, if you could take a step back and look at it from a dispassionate point of view.

That word, "dispassionate", was a good way to describe Ethan in the aftermath. And why should that be any different? What was there to be happy about? Even when the platoon rotated back to the states and the powers that be did their half-hearted investigation, her abusers got off scot-free. They were systematically either promoted or transferred to another posting.

Ethan couldn't bring himself to celebrate a change in command. That spell was broken. He'd lost all faith, didn't believe in the mission anymore, didn't believe in the Army values anymore, it was all just a sick joke. Patriotism, esprit de corps, *it was all a delusion...*

Snap Back

Chapter 2

Brewer picked up a latex kitchen glove from a hotdog stand and lifted Roberts' right arm by the sleeve. "He had a bite mark on his wrist." Keith wasn't taking any chances with the blood spatter as he worked out how and when Roberts might have been bitten and he didn't like the math. "But before the grace of God go we..." he said under his breath, though silently he meant *better you than me.*

"It's that quick?" Ethan knelt down to the body, trying desperately to block the images of another friend he'd lost in Iraq and all of that blood. The circumstances were different, sure, but the mechanism of death was a carbon copy. It took very little imagination to see this action juxtaposed with hers. Ethan took the kid's patrol cap off and let the pile of mush that had been his head and face, now unrecognizable, settle to the pavement with a slop sound that made his skin crawl. He barfed in his mouth, a flood of unwanted memories searing the back of his eyeballs like staring into those damned halogen headlights.

"Yes, it is. Are you infected?" Keith leveled the pistol at Ethan. This was honestly the first time anyone had ever pointed a real gun at him. It wasn't as earth shattering as everyone said it should be, not to someone who was already dead inside. In a very real way Ethan hoped this seemingly random guy would put him out of his misery, that he'd misread the signs of life and draw that trigger back just a little bit more...

"No. I was behind the, the-" Ethan snapped his fingers as his mouth went dry with panic, the blood-stained cigarette falling to the ground. He knew Brewer was close to going into shock again, who knew how stable his thought process was.

Even in a moment that didn't call for laughter, the man with the gun managed a chuckle, "I wasn't gonna shoot you unless you started getting hostile. That's how it starts, man.

That's how you know."

Letting his breath go, Ethan rocked back on his heels as he knelt next to Roberts, "I put this kid through some shit. Made him think I could help him get through this. Maybe he should have chased after our unit." Ethan looked at his late companion, "I can't believe he killed himself so he wouldn't hurt us."

"If you think he was really being altruistic," Keith's tone verged on dismissive, "he was probably trying to scratch the wasps between his ears." Brewer shrugged, looking like a shaggy haired madman in children's clothing.

Clearly Ethan was appalled, but had little room to object. "He was just a kid, man."

"Look, I'm sorry about your friend, but he's dead, just like all of mine. So, either stay with him in this creepy-fuck fun land, or come with me." Keith started walking back to the first-aid station. He picked up the medical bag Roberts had been sent for in the first place and despite the pain in his sprained ankle he started searching the shack. "Where are you from, by the way?" he asked without looking back.

"Right here actually... Well, about twenty miles and a couple towns south. I used to work security here before all this," Ethan followed Keith, the adrenalin and guilt making for a jittery cocktail. He also realized his hands were sticky with blood and it was congealing in the hash marks of the pistol's grip.

"Really? That's amazing man. Most of us are from all over." Ethan had caught on that Keith was looking for toilet paper, the stuff was worth its weight in gold. "I can't imagine how bad Pensacola is now."

They climbed the stairs back into the security office after checking every stall in every restroom from here to there. They were both still a little numb from the experience, not knowing exactly what to do next, this was a good chance for them to decompress.

"So, if you're from around here, is your family still at home?" Keith changed the subject, basking in the glory of finding three full rolls of two-ply bathroom tissue. Things had gotten primitive in the months after InV-1 skipped the Nogales Quarantine. Mouth-breathing soccer-moms in America had bum-rushed the stores and bought every sanitary item possible, including the store's entire stock of toilet paper. Attempts to ration everything from latex gloves and surgical masks to hand soap nationwide were a half-measure and ended in complete failure when the supply trains stopped running.

"I don't know. I've been through Sullivan four times going to and from Fort 'Wood since the Army kidnapped me like a British press gang, but they never let me stop." Ethan took his ID tags out of his pocket, "*Stop-Loss*, or Conscripted Veterans, get red dog-tags. It lets our command know we're a desertion risk. I haven't had access to a phone in two weeks. I really want to find out what's going on with my fiance and my parents."

Keith pointed his finger like a gun at a dispatcher's desk behind Ethan, "There's a land-line right there, amigo."

Without hesitation Ethan picked up the phone and dialed his home. Cell towers had gone dark days ago, but rumors that some landlines still worked persisted. There was a ringtone and within three rings Ethan heard the voice of an angel on the other end. "Baby!? *Omagod*! It's me. I'm in Eureka. I'm coming home right now, stay where you are!" His face suddenly grew concerned by what he was hearing on the other end of the line.

Keith's brow furrowed. He could hear muffled shouts and gunfire that echoed like they were from inside a building coming from the phone. Ethan's eyes widened with terror, "Don't go with them! Tell Dad to block the door, stay in the house and lock... Nicole? Nicole! Hello? *Fucking shit!*" He threw the phone against the wall, shattering it. "We have to go. There has to be a car around here we can use."

"Ooh, can we take a Moon Car?" Keith was referring to one of the oldest rides at Six Flags, small buggies with single stroke motors that resembled the early Ford Model-A. It was basically a super slow tractor with no blades and a padded steering wheel to absorb those insane two-mile-per-hour fender benders, all on a guided concrete track so even your toddler can drive.

An explosion in the distance rattled the rickety buildings. They both looked through the window to see a squadron of Apache gunships blowing up anything that moved near the highway. Their guns chattered and wire guided missiles destroyed things the ash had previously hidden, in this case probably the bridges where I-44 passed over State Highway 109. The amount of debris and obstacles created by blowing the bridges might begin to slow the undead's progress down the interstate.

"I don't think we should be on the roads right now."

"Fuck!" Ethan shouted again and threw a dark computer monitor across the room, "If I don't get there *now* they'll send 'em to some camp with Private Pyle as a guard and then they're all gonna die."

"Well, my schedule is conspicuously clear for the foreseeable future. Let's do this," Keith said, flipping on a radio in the security office. It crackled with static as he scanned through the channels, looking for one he and Ethan could use exclusively if they got separated along the way. They eventually landed on an unused police band, the other channels a veritable cornucopia of screams and gunshots. Some asshole redneck reading verses from the bible that seemed irrelevant to the situation. His actions made an entire channel useless with an open mic, to hell with anyone who needed to use that airtime. Other channels had calls for help from people who couldn't be saved and perhaps even something more sinister, something undead mindlessly pressing against their buttons.

Quietly Ethan tried the phones again before they left, but there was no dial tone this time. The lines were completely dead. More explosions shook the ground from much closer targets. They became anxious to gather what few supplies there were and leave. Contemplating the loss he'd just experienced, Ethan's heart weighed heavier than he expected. If Nicole had never answered he might have taken it better when he got home and inevitably discovered an empty house, but not now. Now he had practically no time to get to his family before they were evacuated to the care of incompetents.

As they left the room where he'd once worked, filed paperwork and let drunks cool their heels in the miniature cell, Ethan considered that he'd never see the inside of this room again. *Good riddance.* Around the front of the building he pulled out the pack of cigarettes he'd pilfered from Roberts. Half the pouches on his gear had been for candy and tobacco and whatever other contraband he could find, even before he'd become "That Guy." The way Ethan figured it, by the time he'd have to use a 9mm rather than his rifle he'd already be fucked, so why carry extra ammo? Lighting the cancer stick he inhaled the smoke, something that pained him, but nothing else was available. This was going to be a long walk if they couldn't find a ride.

In silence they headed back to the first aid station. Roberts was exactly as they'd left him, much to their relief, but beginning to be obscured by the ash fall. They didn't have time to bury him either, the sun was setting and both were already a measure beyond exhausted. Ethan whispered the words to The Lord's Prayer over Roberts before they left, but that was as close to a funeral as the poor kid was going to get.

Keith, who was a much better mechanic than Ethan, spent some time inspecting the vehicles the theme park had in its parking lot, with the hope of finding something that could be hotwired. The most promising was a newer model Chevy Impala that still had the keys on the seat next to blood streaks where the occupant had been dragged out and eaten behind a pile of broken roller coaster cars. Ethan slid in and turned the key. Nothing and why should it, the damned door had been ajar for days now. Thinking quickly, he ran to a park service truck with a rusted-out door and popped the hood. A few turns with his Gerber and he came hustling back with a fresh battery while Keith pulled security on top of the Impala.

"That's too much juice, we can't replace-" Keith paused when he saw Ethan's look of exasperation. "Right, you're just gonna jump-start the car with that battery, not use it as the new battery." He admitted his own mistake and that he was more tired than he thought.

The car started without much coercion and they breathed a sigh of relief when cold, soot free air blew over them for a moment before the intake sucked in the noxious crap. Sadly, the car only had a quarter of a tank, but that was plenty to drive thirty miles if they didn't get too sidetracked. Keith loaded their equipment, minus the body armor, and Ethan slowly pulled out of the parking lot. Deciding to avoid the highway he made the fateful decision to turn right and travel the back roads, fearing as he should that he might be killed by friendly fire. That was perhaps not the brightest idea he ever had, though, as the ash was already so thick the car couldn't maintain traction up the steep inclines of Allenton road. It slid into a ditch and broke a fence at the top of the hill. The engine sputtered until it died.

They sat for a moment in silence in the car while both took a deep breath in frustration, astounded at the sheer idiocy of their situation. Ethan had learned long ago never to ask what else could go wrong, he might get an answer. As they were about to get out they saw movement in the mists. Ethan raised his M-4 through an open window and held very, very still. The shape grew larger and more defined and in a ghostly scene straight from the Iraqi oil fires of the movie *Jarhead,* a horse that someone had tried to saddle before "something" stopped them stepped slowly up to what were probably the first living people he'd seen in a while. The only noise was the horse's labored breathing.

Keith got out of the car and went up to the majestic creature, made even more beautiful by the stillness around him. There were no reports of the virus jumping species, whatever it was seemed to attack only people. A reigning theory was the virus was only attracted to higher brain functions. However, zombies would eat an animal, this was true, but only if there was nothing else. Keith petted the mustang and looked it in the eyes. Ethan kept his distance though, he liked horses even less than people, having been kicked rather severely by one as a child. He likened them to ornery, vegan dogs.

"Looks thirsty. I'll bet his trough is completely saturated with ash," Keith reached into the car and pulled out a bottle of water and poured it into his baseball cap. The horse drank the water like it may never see something so good again, then just as quickly as it had appeared, turned disappeared into the ashen storm across the hole they'd put in the fence. "Good luck, pal," Keith whispered as the horse faded from view.

"Let's check the house. The people might still be home," Ethan stalked up to the mansion-sized ranch house and thoroughly checked the outside through the windows before knocking on the front door. Minutes later no one answered and they tried the knob, just in case it was unlocked. There was a notion to kick it in, but in the last moment before Ethan let his foot fly Keith whistled to him and pointed at a window that was unlocked.

The soot covered men climbed into the house, a beautifully maintained, upper income home. The inside was a refreshing clean space, much better than a car that smelled like gas-station perfume and lip-balm. As if they were covered in mud, or maybe snow, the grubby looking men stood in the foyer for a long while, unwilling to pollute this pristine palace at first.

The kitchen was like something out of a magazine too and if the front covers framed on the walls were any indication, it was. The refrigerator still put out ice and cold water, humming quietly as Keith polished off a glass. Out in the garage, along with a glossy new off-white Dodge Ram 2500, was a corner devoted to horticulture, hunting and equestrian pursuits. Keith found the tiger striped fatigues the man had used for deer hunting and tossed Ethan the larger pair, probably meant for guests. If Ethan didn't have places to be, he might have spent a few days here. It was a real treasure trove of post-apocalyptic luxuries, the likes of which they might never see again.

"We look like South Vietnamese ARVN's," Keith joked, pulling out two boonie hats from the box of hunting equipment. The wide brimmed hats would be good for keeping ash and falling particles off their faces and out of their shirts, but first Ethan had to cut that stupid draw-string off so it didn't choke him. The fatigues' matching tops didn't appeal to Keith, preferring his Daffy Duck sweater despite the heat. Perhaps it was his way of maintaining a sense of humor, because Ethan knew damned well those sweaters were cheap, imported shit. The sun was already nearly gone, dropping the temperature drastically, but that shouldn't have been a problem for the now well-equipped survivors.

"Give it ten minutes in the open and these will look as bad as our Multicams," Ethan fiddled with his pockets to store his knife and wallet. He climbed into the truck and took a huge whiff. The inside of the truck still smelled of rich leather and pine overlapping that delicious new car smell. Ethan had to hand it to the previous owner, the man had had taste, assuming the past tense since no one was home.

"I just thought of something funny," Keith said before Ethan started the truck.

"What?"

"Before the Multicam uniform the Army issued ACU's. They were grayish blue and white and blended into absolutely nothing.... And now the world ends and everything is gray and white... and the uniform was recently retired."

"You think about some dumb shit," Ethan shook his head, "but I do agree, History will not be kind to that uniform." He started the truck, grateful yet again that the man had been so well-to-do he could afford a $40,000 truck and a full tank of $8 a gallon, highly rationed diesel. It did beg the question just who the hell the owner used to be, but they'd never get answers.

The garage door opened slowly while the men waited with some patience until they realized that in front of them stood the man who had owned the house, the horse and the truck. His chest was ripped open, a pacemaker dangling in a stream of blackened, gooey snot that swung from his exposed ribs. There was a child's arm in his hand, gnawed to the bone. The child he had mostly eaten stood behind him too, a good portion of her face gnawed away along with the arm. The poor thing was completely naked, a rubber ducky in her remaining hand and ashen mud that had hardened all around her where it had collected and dried kept the body modest. There was no sign of who'd infected them but surely that loathsome creature was nearby too.

The child dropped the rubber ducky and reached toward them with her one arm. Ethan slammed the accelerator down and plowed the two under with an incredible *whump*. Despite the initial adrenaline dump, hitting the two zombies kept the truck under better control by giving them traction on the ash where the concrete driveway met the asphalt. The truck slipped and slid through the back roads at a snail's pace until Ethan found Old Highway 100. By then visibility was low without headlights, but they weren't willing to risk attracting the attention of bandits or the Army. The roads weren't as bad farther from the city and they could actually do the posted speed limit if nothing obstructed their path. It wouldn't last though.

A military roadblock sat atop a plateau where the road curved around a steeply sloped farm. An old barn with a massive flagpole in the middle of the yard could be seen clearly despite the haze. The garrison flag at the top was tattered and faded, barely visible through the warm, gray, faux snow and waning light. No one was left to lower it and no anarchist scumbags had yet to cut it down. It was just another eerie reminder that their world was over.

No trucks or armored vehicles were at the roadblock either, no soldiers or FEMA workers in their stupid looking multi-colored mechanic's coveralls milling about. They'd looked like human Skittles to Ethan, working in every refugee camp like none of this bothered them. This checkpoint was only manned by a few infected, though. They were looking in the other direction from inside a cattle corral and never noticed the truck slip by.

For a brief time, the authorities had tried to jail the zombies themselves, the results being predictable. This corral was likely a local roundup and Ethan accelerated once they passed it, wishing he hadn't seen it at all. Keith opened the door to hit a stray zombie and laughed maniacally when the impact gave a satisfying *thud*. "I've always wanted to do that," he said when he was done laughing long enough to catch his breath. If that was what tripped his trigger, Ethan figured, let him have it. *There were probably worse ways to spend the end of days, like fighting for a lost cause or bearing witness to a documentary on sex change operations because you had the flu, couldn't find the remote and were too fever stricken to get up and change the channel, congruently.*

Checkpoints were at every overpass over Interstate 44 and the Gray Summit staging area was no different. It was now just as abandoned as any other, ash drifting in the wind but thinner as they got farther from the more developed areas. Ethan stopped the truck and watched through a hunting scope for hidden elements, dead or alive. They saw nothing and after their approach collected several green metal boxes of 5.56mm ammunition left in a supply tent. It did feel a little like a first-person-shooter game where your character must collect resources as they move through the map, the critically acclaimed *Half-Life* series being a prime example. Radios had been left on in the command post and made their eerie wailing sounds, computers displayed Blue Force Tracker information that Ethan paused to read, but basically it outlined that there were no more "Blue" forces in the area. Just Red. Just undead.

The speakers on the radios were either humming, hissing,

or broadcasting the moans of the undead operators on the other end. One radio, though, let them listen to an air traffic controller in charge of directing planes and choppers out of the Sullivan and Cuba regional airports to... somewhere. The destination was in code and neither knew how to decipher it. The evacuation wasn't under direct threat at least, so maybe not all was lost. Only every other word was audible, but "Green Zone" was repeated several times, giving some false ray of hope that galvanized Ethan to continue without further delay.

"We stop for no one we don't have to, especially not for other soldiers, I don't trust them not to turn us in or try to pull rank. We want to go back on our own terms if we have to, not because we're made too. Agreed?"

"Absolutely," Keith nodded, his eyes as wide as Ethan's while they listened to the dead consume their world. Ammunition loaded, Ethan continued driving through the remains of the various small towns he'd once known well. They didn't see a single living soul until the Twin Bridges Underpass that split from I-44 toward the college town of Union. Locals had already overrun and taken control of the Army's TCP there, using what had once been a Harley Davidson store and its dilapidated storage facility as a forward observation post.

How in the hell had the US Army lost accountability of so many weapons? Ethan wanted to ask, though he knew the answer. If they were willing to abandon living people, then weapons and ammo must mean next to nothing to them at this point. Things had to have gone from bad to worse to full-blown clusterfuck. The Army had been obsessed with keeping track of every weapon and every bullet for as long as Ethan could remember. He'd spent countless hours "policing" expended casings in grassy fields and foxholes that had been in the same place since World War Two. Punishments for misplacing a weapon in the Army Ethan was raised in were typically severe, up to and including courts-martial hearings, unless of course, you were an officer.

(Then, when the missing firearm, or night-vision device in question was found, everyone who'd been taken off their normal duties and ordered to search the immediate area, had to politely pretend they didn't know their leader had been masturbating in the porta-shitter. Furthermore, they had to pretend they didn't know he'd forgotten his weapon, blamed some random private for misplacing it and then later an unsuspecting civilian worker found the missing "sensitive item" in a puddle of piss and toilet paper while vacuuming out the septic tank. Not that that's ever happened of course.)

Unable to avoid the checkpoint now that they'd been spotted, Ethan slowed to a stop so they could talk to a gangly looking kid in fluorescent yellow "Sk8er" shoes and a douche-hoodie, one of those bland looking designer hoodies with tribal swirl-designs all over it. His hair was dirty and dangling in his face, white iPod headphones hanging from his neck, he clearly wasn't concerned with camouflage. The kid was armed with a .308 hunting rifle and an expensive scope he probably didn't even know how to use. Ethan was astonished at how brazenly the kid just walked up to the truck and stuck his face right into the driver side window. Even in the old world, approaching someone's car window like that was a good way to get shot in the face.

"They're letting people pass, but don't give 'em any shit," the kid said as if he'd already said it a thousand times and was bored. "Are either of you hurt?" he wasn't unfriendly, just not very good at socializing. "There's a doctor with the checkpoint if you are."

"No," they lied. Keith was still beaten up pretty good, but they didn't want to get stopped for some other medic to check him out. If Keith thought he'd make it, he probably would. Stopping was a good way to lose what items they'd already collected and in this world someone might just decide those weapons would be of better use to them. "We were hiding in the countryside. We found this stuff. The owner blew his own head off."

"Whatever, man, save your sob stories for someone who

cares. They'll probably try and bribe you to stay and help fight. They figure the corpses from St. Louis will follow the highway here in a couple of days," The kid jumped into the bed of their truck without asking. He didn't make any threatening gestures, he just didn't want to walk the quarter mile to the checkpoint and miss all the action if his people decided to blow Ethan and Keith's heads off.

"I have a bad feeling about this," Keith said in a low voice as they rolled forward. There were more and more local militia coming out of the woodwork it seemed, surrounding the truck. Were they really letting anyone through? The two had their doubts.

Guided to a halt in a sally port they were surrounded by bomb-proof wire baskets, each the size of a compact car called Hesco Bastions. These improvised walls had saved countless lives in Iraq and Afghanistan and that was only when filled with the crappy, sunbaked, flaky earth that existed over there. Filled with solid Missouri river clay the barriers could stop a small tank; their truck had no hope of running over it or breaking through. A woman approached the truck in woodland fatigue and they could tell she'd been a cop once too as she still had her shiny leather utility belt.

"Is this your truck?" she asked over the din of the diesel, patting the hood and admiring the beast of a vehicle before her.

"It is now," Ethan said, looking at the skill tabs sewn onto the lady's old uniform. Airborne, Air Assault, Combat Action Badge, 10th Mountain Division Combat Patch and a faded patrol cap with salt stains where staff sergeant's rank had been.

"I see. Does the legal owner know you have their truck?"

Keith froze, he didn't know what to say to that. Luckily, Ethan did, "Ask him if you want. Whatever's left is probably still stuck to the suspension. Let's just say he had a wicked case of the munchies and wasn't in the negotiating mood."

There was a brief moment where Ethan and the woman in charge of the traffic control point locked eyes. This was it, the game was up and they were going to be eaten alive in jail when the hordes made it this far, or shot. Probably shot. Then the woman burst out in an unexpected laugh that was horribly inappropriate in the dying world around them. Keith and the people at the checkpoint were mildly disturbed, but to Ethan it was a relief to meet someone who understood sarcasm and nihilism.

"So where are you coming from?"

"Wildwood."

She took a step back and looked at the tarp in the bed of the truck, "So what's in the truck?"

"Oh, you know Sarge, the usual: letters from home, a couple hookers I chloroformed, a box of duct tape, some Mike 'n Ikes in case we get hungry… oh and the full second season of *Scrubs* on Blu-ray. We're heading to his place for a marathon," Ethan said with a wide smile, putting his arm around Keith's shoulders.

"I don't know this psychopath," Keith tried to get lower in the seat.

"You two meet in the Army or something?" She said with a sly smile. Ethan shared the smile as Keith realized it was a gay joke.

After a laugh Ethan pointed down the road, "So what's it gonna take to get you to let us on through, Sarn't?"

The woman eyed the inventory in the truck, "Well, here's the thing…" She said, "You two know damned well what happens to deserters." Without so much as another word the truck was surrounded by rifle-wielding locals.

Chapter 3

"We didn't desert, we were left behind," Ethan protested while a man who reeked of stale cigarettes patted them down none-too-gently. "My company's fallback point is Sullivan, we're trying to get there so we can rejoin the unit," he lied.

The woman rolled her eyes, "Tell it to someone who cares." She unknowingly repeated the kid at the lookout post and pointed to a fenced in area around a commuter parking lot. There stood a poorly assembled JP-Medium tent, sagging under the weight of the ash. A few equally sad looking people huddled in corners around it, all wearing Army or FEMA uniforms.

Ethan and Keith didn't argue, they just kept their hands up and walked. These people weren't the military, hell they weren't even police. This was mob justice and there was very little scarier prospect. Keith said as much, eyeing the fenced-in area for ways to escape once their escorts had gruffly shoved them through the gate. "If they don't hang us at dawn, something tells me we just volunteered to be the tip of the spear."

"That's exactly what they're doing," a voice they didn't know yet said from atop a small crate of water bottles. It was a diminutive looking woman in dirty Army fatigues chewing absentmindedly on a travel-kit toothbrush. "They're gonna use us to clear out a safe haven, like a gated community or something. Heard them talking earlier."

It was stupid to think protesting to these people for pressing them into service would work, but that didn't stop Ethan from flinging a sizable rock at one of the guards. It hit a car window, shattering it and setting off the alarm. He then pantomimed for the guards to perform fellatio on him while they rushed to disconnect the battery. In the near distance a thunderstorm was coming, creating the unmistakable aroma of ozone. The supercell, silhouetted by lightning, stretched miles above them. Somehow it seemed more menacing in its appearance with the apocalypse raging below.

"I guess we're going to fight in the rain, too," Keith braced himself. "Are they even going to give us guns?" he asked the others gathered.

"Maybe, just before the end, when there's no time to run away," the woman atop the boxes sighed, but she was wrong. As the rain finally found them, huddling inside the urine reeking tent, the town's militia backed a dump truck up to the gates. The hatch came down and armed men told them to get inside. One man refused, a first sergeant from a battalion that had been wiped out in St. Louis, breaking the arm of a local before the butch woman who'd been giving the orders shot him twice at point-blank.

Turning to the others before his body even hit the mud, she aimed the gun at them, "You're going to get on this transport and you're going to fight like you should have all along." Thunder interrupted her for little other reason than dramatic effect, "You don't fight, I kill you myself. You secure our facility for us, maybe we let you stay."

Taking a deep breath, Ethan was the first one on the truck, "C'mon, if we stay in formation and draw them to us, some of us just might live through this." He reached out for Keith to follow him. Fifty men and women, most walking wounded and all in varying states of shock and dehydration, were carted off to the front lines of Union to die.

Lightning flashed as the motorcade of civilian vehicles staged themselves in the lowest parking lot of the community college campus. The sheriff, for lack of a better word, strolled around in front of the gathered condemned and postured for them all while the storm finally settled overhead. They were joined by two more truck-loads of sorry looking FEMA and army personnel, probably from other checkpoints. It was a brilliant strategy, really, if you were a psychopath. It seemed having the dead walk was bringing that side out in people more and more these days.

"We want this building as a shelter," the sheriff gestured at the castle-like structure before them, "but there's a bunch of Plague Vics inside. I don't need any more of *my* people dying because you pricks failed." She motioned for the nearest asshole to begin distributing weapons. They weren't even guns, just machetes and metal pikes for gigging mixed with the odd riot shield. Even in the hazy light of the parking lot's streetlamps Ethan and the others could see the blood stains on the shields, lazily cleaned by someone just before they were reissued. "Like I said, if you live through it you can stay with us, or fuck off. I don't really care."

"When the man with the rifle gets killed, the one with the bullets picks up the rifle and shoots," Keith muttered, quoting from the movie *Enemy at the Gates*. Whether or not Russian troops had really been sent across the Volga river with only one rifle per two men is still a topic of some debate, but it had its desired effect. Even if it was all true those poor bastards were still better equipped to handle the undead, or Germans, than this lot.

Someone from another group tried to run, a woman in filthy mechanic's overalls, but rather than shoot her this time a local woman with a crossbow put a bolt through the runner's neck. Ethan overheard her say to the militiamen around her that it was a lucky shot, because she'd been aiming for center-mass. The arrow had surely gone through the fleeing woman's esophagus, because nobody heard her scream as she writhed like an exposed night-crawler in the muddy ash. Now they all got it, now they knew why nobody was passing out shotguns, besides the obvious danger of doing so. The militia wanted to be quiet and the storm provided that ever-so precious noise cover outside. Indoors was another matter entirely, but Ethan had gone to Central Missouri College for a semester before classes had conflicted with being drunk all the time. He knew the inside well enough to know it could contain hundreds, if not thousands of zombies and just as many blind corners, but if cleared it really could be a fortress with little effort from the defenders.

To everyone's surprise Keith actually raised his hand like they were in class. For lack of knowing what else to do, the sheriff nodded for him to speak. "Do you have any idea what we're walking into? Anything you can tell us would help."

Their captor nodded, "You see any stray, undead villagers walking around?"

"No," Keith said like a disappointed child. Wordlessly the sheriff pointed at the castle of a campus. "Wouldn't it be safer to do this in the daylight, then?" he shrugged. It was an oddly personal exchange, like chatting up your executioner.

"Probably, but I'm not willing to wait that long," she admitted, then motioned for her minions to get the war weary and wounded moving toward the entrance. "You're going in through the theater department. Send someone out with a white flag when you've cleared the first building. Try to run, we kill you. Try to take the building for yourselves and we set it on fire. If we can't have it, then you sure as fuck can't."

"Fair enough," Keith tried to play the mediator, also realizing that at the ripe old rank of Sergeant, barely middle management as far the Army was concerned, he might be one of the highest-ranking servicemen there. He'd spotted an Air Force E7, but Airmen weren't typically considered "Combat Arms" in Army speak, implying they were of little use in a ground fight. Besides that, the man was wounded with a stained bandage around his head, he was in no shape to lead.

Thankfully he had someone by his side who, when not habitually drunk, might almost qualify as an adequate leader himself. Ethan turned to address the men, "Look, I went to school here because I'm from just a couple towns over. The theater department is a multi-level building with a lot of hidden nooks and crannies. We're going to take this slow, find some tools we can use as close-in weapons. We'll move in teams of four, one on point and the other three to support him. If you think you're too wounded to take on a zombie in hand-to-hand, don't be shy about saying so. You'll be our backup with the gigging rods."

"This is suicide," someone said, seriously contemplating running for it. The tree line was barely a hundred meters away.

Ethan steeled himself, "We're all already dead. We go into battle to reclaim our lives, but to be sure, today is a good day to die." There was a general murmur of agreement, some inspirational words were better than none after all, even if they were all plagiarized from various *Star Trek* series. *A little Jem'Hadar here, a dash of Klingon there and you got yourself a shake and bake speech,* Ethan thought to himself, hoping nobody else recognized the words.

The heavy metal doors swung outward, but didn't make any squeaking noises. They weren't chained from the inside either, what with security being conceptualized somewhat differently at a college than at a high school. Basically, colleges aren't prisons. *Imagine that.*

Props and sets for an upcoming play were in various stages of completion, tools lying about as much as raw materials. Ethan swapped his flimsy machete with a loose screw in the handle for a well-worn crowbar that had been repainted a lot of different colors over the years. Motioning silently for the others to break into their groups and start searching the building, Ethan and Keith chose to clear the main theater rather than risk the others people in their group. No need to have everyone die in one room.

Unlike the sweltering summer outside, this windowless theater was cool like a cavern and as clean as the house they'd found behind Six Flags. At the rear of the seating area was a control booth, a sleeping bag and some typical refugee trash was under the desk area. Someone had been living here, but it didn't look like they'd been back in a few days. Keith stumbled over one of the refugee's piss-bottles and they had to listen to the glass Snapple container roll all the way down the aisle to the middle row of seats before clanking to a halt on a rubber guide strip. The two other men in their group narrowed their eyes at Keith and shook their heads, but they kept quiet besides that. Forming up with the rest of the conscripts in the study area that served as the lobby for the theater, the group dutifully sent someone out to tell their masters. Ethan tapped his guys on the shoulders and they continued walking, knowing there were three adjoining buildings to clear. The militia knew this too and sent their conscripts back in to actually finish the job while they started moving their people in.

The four classrooms that made up the music department were empty, the rooms dark despite there still being power. On the level above that, the pottery, drafting and welding departments were also cleared by Ethan and Keith personally. A full can of Sprite, albeit room temperature, was sitting on a centralized secretary's desk in an office cluster at the far end of the Arts building. One of the men in their group scooped it up, cracking it open loudly before putting it to his lips. A zombie hurled itself at an office window behind him and headbutted the glass. Startled, he spat the soda all over Keith, dropped the can and ran for it. Keith grabbed him before he got himself shot, then they watched in morbid curiosity as the zombie struggled to get through tempered glass with a wire mesh inside it, all the while the door next to him was wide open. Finally, Ethan ended the ghoul's misery and stuck the tines of his crowbar in his temple. He removed the curved metal with chunks of skull still attached.

"I think I met him a few times," Ethan said, cleaning off the crowbar on the dead man's own shirt. "Guidance counselor or some such."

"If you're from around here, you must have a plan to get away from these guys, right?" the panicked man said, catching his breath. Ethan saw that he was easily in his late thirties and his uniform was messy looking too. The rank patch still sewn to his chest proudly displayed the mosquito wings of an E2, probably one of those first-round emergency "volunteers," this guy had surely never thought seriously about military service before the undead. Likely it was only just now dawning on him that joining the Army wasn't necessarily an easy meal-ticket in a crisis. Too late now.

"Sure do. It's called don't fucking die," Ethan said flatly, "but this is proof there are undead in the building. Someone infected him, so let's be on the lookout for that one and any friends he has lurking in offices too. Also, new rule, don't pick anything up until we've cleared the-" A loud, hollow smack sound that could only be a wooden baseball bat making contact with a skull and then the moan of the undead from the nearby stairwell, interrupted Ethan mid-speech. Someone out of sight was bitten, by the sounds of it a woman too and she screamed a blood curdling scream that sent chills down everyone's back.

Keith pointed to the sloping ramp that passed by an adjunct office and he and Ethan ran off for it while the other two men in their group threw themselves into danger on the lower level, acting on what Ethan called *Damsel in Distress* syndrome. Now separated from the main group, Ethan took Keith into a lecture auditorium and shut the door, bolting it from the inside.

"There's a door at the top level of the classroom," Ethan whispered, pointing. "It lets out on the second level right next to the handicapped elevator. We're going to make a break for the Gym & Cafeteria building, there are as many places to hide as there are doors to escape from. There's a loading dock at the bottom level, when they dropped us off I saw a Gator, one of those beefed up golf-cart thingies. That model runs on propane, I remember the janitors bitching about replacing leaking valves a while back, so maybe it won't be empty, assuming they fixed it."

"And then what?"

"And then we get back to Sullivan, man. Nicole, my mom and dad, they're all there. I have to get back to them before... it's over," he finished quietly, watching one of the other men look through the classroom door's window. After only a few seconds he turned around and rejoined his group, but their hiding place wouldn't last.

Slinking between the administrative building and the arts center, Keith worried about the footprints they were leaving in the muddy layer of ash. Ethan understood, but there wasn't much he could do about it. Motioning to crouch while crossing the skywalk that connected the courtyard to the G-C building, they went as fast as the awkward position would allow their legs to move. The doors at the far end of the elevated skywalk weren't locked, which made entry easier, but didn't bode well for the building being clear. Grabbing a dust mop from the corner of the foyer, once they were inside Ethan jammed the doors just in time for the rain to pick up and a duo of militia who'd spotted their trail to slam into the doors. Wet and infuriated, the smaller one, dressed like a cowboy with a worn leather Stetson that barely fit him, shot the glass with his sidearm, putting several small holes in the tinted panes. His lack of progress only made him madder, motioning with his finger that he was going to slit the soldier's throats.

Having narrowly escaped being shot, Ethan wasted no time in leading Keith through the third floor weight lifting room. Ellipticals and treadmills still glowed, waiting to count miles and be used by a world that was already gone. *Animals seemed to be jumping ship, did our technology know we were circling the proverbial drain too? How obscure that a treadmill might bear witness to the end of days.* On the far side of the weight room was a seldom used stairwell that Ethan liked to brood and get shit-faced in between classes. It went down all three levels and was used primarily for freight, so maybe it wouldn't be the first place the militia looked for them. They heard the report of a heavier gun, probably a twelve gauge and men shouting as they breached the third-floor door.

At the bottom of the second flight of stairs Keith, who'd taken the lead, stopped cold in his tracks. Ethan plowed into him and together they almost knocked over the first in a cluster of zombies that were all facing the doors toward the locker room. They had been FEMA workers mostly, but a sizable number were nursing students in the same light gray polo shirts with ID tags clipped to the collar and an even larger cluster in the center were just infected civilians, hundreds of them maybe. This was typical of almost any organized shelter, it only took one and the virus would rampage through the crowd. Before anyone had a chance to flee out of doors that had been barricaded against zombies getting in it would all be over. Above them the militia had figured out which way they'd gone and were closing fast. Thinking quickly, Ethan pushed Keith behind a billiards table the student council had installed. Up close the green felt still smelled of cigarettes and beer from the bar that had donated the table when it shut down, but now wasn't the time for reminiscing, Ethan decided.

Snatching the solid red "3" ball from a basket, Ethan tossed it up the stairwell where the militia was coming down and slid under the table with Keith like that sadistic little kid from *Home Alone*. Instantly there was a cacophony of musty smelling moans and the group of undead went shuffling up the steps toward the clattering ball and their next meal. The militia had made the mistake of not sending in their conscripts first and gunfire echoed like firecrackers in a soda can. Without much more warning the adjoining cafeteria emptied of the several hundred zombies that had been milling about in a dormant state just out of view. This explained where some of the undead locals were and why the militia was so worried about this building they'd started from the other end.

Wasting no time, Ethan dragged Keith toward the last set of stairs that would lead to the basement-level school store. They might have passed them quickly, but both saw the unfortunate hundred or so wheelchair bound bodies, gnawed to virtually nothing and sitting in a cluster by the far wall. Only one of the handicapped zombies was still able to move enough ligaments to reach for them, but they didn't stay to see it fall out of the chair and drag itself toward them.

The bottom of the stairwell was a noise trap the original survivors had attempted to set up, soda cans and stacks of chairs a dozen high were waiting to attract the horde now feasting above. Taking their chances Keith went first and did his best to play hop-scotch over the clusters. Ethan, being stockier and less nimble, made a complete mess of it and ended up with a soda can crushed perfectly around the center of his boot. Now with a loud crunching sound on every other footfall, they sprinted toward the door that would lead to the loading dock. It was chained and at least one zombie had fallen down the stairs to investigate the noise. Pulling off the can, Ethan grabbed a dolly and swung it like an ax into the glass doors. The pane he hit shattered into thousands of pieces and a gust of hot, moist summer air blew into their faces. Hearing zombies on the upper level throw themselves down a different stairwell they hadn't cleared, which was much closer to their current location, they left without looking back.

Jumping into the gator they knew it wouldn't have the keys in it. Ethan popped the gears into neutral and together they used their feet to get them going down the loading ramp. The beefed-up golf cart rolled down to the bottom parking lot before it ran out of inertia and there Keith set about trying to jump start what wasn't a terribly complex machine. Ethan turned and watched as his trap worked maybe too well. Like he'd hoped, most of the conscripts were making a run for it in the chaos, but just as many were caught up in the dying as the militia that had kidnapped them. Someone threw a grenade and it blew a dozen zombies and a few live people off the skywalk, but that was all he wanted to see.

The gator started with a sputtering purr, but a man was approaching at a staggering run that suggested he was still alive. Occasionally he'd hold out an arm for them to stop and wait. Readying his crowbar Ethan watched the man get less than fifty feet from them, then fall to his knees sobbing and coughing.

"C'mon, man, we gotta go!" Ethan forcefully whispered to the man as the admin building above them caught fire. Some idiot inside had a captured machine gun and was drawing the undead in so they could all die together in the fire, apparently, but it was good noise cover. Then Ethan noticed the man straighten up and look right at him, holding his hand out now in a pause motion to make sure Ethan stayed back, finally accepting that he'd been bitten somehow and would only endanger others.

"I didn't want to die in this place..." The man whimpered, blood dripping from the corners of his lips as he fought back the rage, finally understanding why there was so much hate in the eyes of the undead. *This hurt, a lot.* It was nothing short of being burned to death while you drown in an icy river and *fuck almighty the voices... like a collective of suffering...*

"Neither did I," Ethan said before he cracked the dying man over the skull with all his earthly might, unable to stomach the idea of hitting him more than once. He motioned for Keith to drive and sat in the passenger seat silently with his arms folded defensively over his chest. He only motioned with his hand when it was appropriate for Keith to make a turn.

Chapter 4

Just a few miles from home now in the dead of night, Ethan sat on the edge of his seat even though he was so tired his eyes hurt. The only physical picture he had of Nicole was one she'd sent him during basic training, back when neither of them were dating each other yet. It was meant platonically, but later it had meant more. Now it was priceless. Nicole sat on the daybed of her father's spare bedroom, relaxing against the backboard with the second *Twilight* book in her hands. The edges of the picture were tattered and fingerprints from oils collected across two continents stained the white backing. Even a footprint from the time he'd dropped it at the airport was still partially visible. Ethan normally saw the wear and tear of objects as character, but in this case it only blurred Nicole's features so it was hard to see even her eye color.

"Is that her?" Keith asked as they approached one of the few overpasses where no checkpoint had been established. Stanton was, a hundred years ago, a relatively large mining town. Now its only reason for existing was Meramec Caverns and a small zoo annex from a larger zoo in Branson. There was also the Jesse James Wax Museum, if seeing life-size human replicas was your thing. Ethan had always wondered why the wax museum and the caverns didn't just form a single company. The caves were, after all, always 62 degrees. *Was that not somehow perfect for wax statues?*

"Yeah... I need my guns and some supplies if I have to walk at any point," Ethan was dead set on leaving almost as soon as he'd gotten home, but he was also going to let Keith stay at his place. At this point it was hard to argue the man was anything but trustworthy.

Keith tried to be more optimistic, "Well, the weather's been shit, maybe they didn't fly anyone out. They'd have to wait for trucks or one of those armored FEMA trains, ya know?" Ethan's skin crawled to think of how people could willingly get into boxcars. The trains and convoys might be going to the same fancy Green Zone at Cheyenne Mountain, but the idea of being taken to somewhere like Auschwitz instead would never leave the back of his mind.

They stopped at the Stanton overpass and tried to look as far as they could down the highway. There were no tracks in the light layer of ash and grass from the last time MODOT sent out brush-mowers with riot cages over their pilot houses. This close to a major helicopter landing hub and an Army/FEMA forward operating base, mowing was still taking place so they could better see incoming zombies or refugees.

"The rain probably obscured the tracks. It would take them more than one night to fly an entire town away."

"There were only seven thousand people in town. The Army can move that many people on any given Tuesday," Ethan took the driver's seat and checked the gauges. They still had more than ¾ of a propane tank. This beat up looking John Deere Gator was a godsend to their cause, but it wouldn't hold his whole family. At least Keith would still have it.

"Best if I drive from here," Ethan said as the first signs of daylight approached. Supercells surrounded the Meramec River valley, but for now they were in the eye of it all. Still taking the frontage roads to avoid the serpentines and refugee debris, Ethan floored it until they reached the actual checkpoints at mile marker 226. The floodlights were off and the sentries were gone, the empty M-240 and the dead-lined Humvee it was mounted on were nothing more than lawn ornaments at the moment.

What they found in Sullivan proper, just beyond the checkpoint was far from what either had expected. There was no massive Army buildup, no Chinooks thundering overhead to whisk civilians away from the inevitable fighting. Instead, there were pickup trucks in parking lots with extremely well-armed children guarding them while their parents looted anything that wasn't nailed down. It was semi-organized chaos, but no one was shooting at each other, so at least they had that going for them. Keith snatched a flier printed on lime-green paper from a shrub. It read:

FEMA EVACUATION ORDER FOR TCP 226 AND GREATER SULLIVAN AREA: 0600 SULLIVAN REGIONAL AIRPORT. ONE CARRY-ON PER PERSON, NO PETS, NO EXCEPTIONS.

"An armed Society is a polite Society," Keith muttered, watching one of the children packing a short barrel 12 gauge walk up to a stray zombie and shoot it where the neck meets the shoulder. Its head rolled forward as the body went backwards, separated but for a single congealed artery. Before either side had completely fallen the child turned back to his older cousins, looking delighted. Holding up a package of whatever sadistic round was capable of severing a zombie's head, the scrawny looking crotch-goblins started peddling the munitions to passers-by for gold or food.

They moved quickly by that horrific sideshow and walked up to a truck with slightly older children guarding it, "Who's in charge around here?" Ethan asked, looking around in bewilderment at his childhood home. It had become more a scene from any run of the mill disaster movie than the serene midwestern hideaway it should have been. *Hell, they could have filmed The Wonder Years here when I was growing up,* Ethan thought. *Now it could be New Orleans after a tropical depression, or New Orleans under a broken fire hydrant, or New Orleans after an ICP concert, or New Orleans.*

"Like we know," a little girl with an overdramatized southern accent said. She was kind of chubby and filled her father's old Air Force uniform well, if she'd been six inches taller of course. "Everyone's takin' what we can. Like, for realz we got to keep an entire police cruiser from the Highway Patrol yesterday. Daddy says they have better engines than our cars and that we should keep it because the cop inside was *infected* and he wasn't gonna need it no more." She hissed the word *infected* for extra effect.

Keith smiled, even with the world ending children could still be cute in the most fucked up ways. "So there's no sheriff or police?"

"My daddy's a cop, but he says all them other chicken shit motherfuckers left with the Army. We all decided they can eat shit and rot in *hell*." All three kids made the sign of the cross over their hearts.

"Nice touch, *Lordess of the Flies*. Do you know where your daddy is?"

"I'm right here," they both turned to face a rather plump man holding a Ruger Mini -14 menacingly enough. "Who're you?"

"I'm Ethan, he's Keith. We're looking for family, Mike and June Kelly, they live out on Highway D just before it turns into Rock Road. Do you know them?"

"Never met 'em, but you stand a vague chance of finding them," the chubby cop relaxed his grip on his rifle and swatted away a bug. "Most civvies left along with the Army yesterday. Last soldiers we saw lit outta here around midnight. They promised another flight, but nobody's holding their breath. The guy directing incoming flights left too, so that was kinda telling. Were you guys trying to catch up with them?" The officer eyed them with some sympathy, "Because I'm afraid that ship has sailed."

"What makes you think we're part of that mess?" Keith pretended to be Ethan for a moment. It felt... well, not evil, but somewhere adjacent. Unclean at any rate.

"Because your body language, haircut and general demeanor screams soldier, although your friend there looks like he's tried to disguise himself as a dirty hippy."

"Thank you," Ethan curtsied almost too well. "I like to think my inner self shines through when no one makes me shave at 0500."

"Where are you going with this?" Keith didn't like the

direction the conversation was taking. The guy was still wearing a royal blue polo that read POLICE over his heart and a work belt loaded for riot control. Having just survived Union they didn't want any more contact with local lawmen on a power trip, but they hadn't found any weapons since then either. What could they really do if he got froggy?

"You misunderstand me," the officer smiled. "I've been hoping all morning there'd be some Army guys out there who weren't stupid enough to get infected, that some of you might wind up here. There's only three of us and a retired sheriff from Branson that thinks he's got the *winning strategy*," he rolled his eyes. "We could use some help keeping order."

"Is there some kind of government here?" Ethan was again surprised.

"Not really, not anymore. You can only be in charge of what you can patrol and that would be just three cops right now to cover a lot of hostile area. If you two are who I think you are, we could use you. Shit, we *need* you."

"Is there a meeting place?" Keith wanted to know. This was their final destination and these folks were actually asking, not demanding, so why not?

Ethan, on the other hand, couldn't have cared less. He was already antsy to leave and thinking about stealing a truck from a kid who only carried a large kitchen knife for protection. His heart was breaking at how empty his home town was now, there should be people and dogs and overfed squirrels and *life*... instead there was just trash and smoke from a house fire blowing in the wind. Stray cats fighting over scraps ruled the roost, easily running rough shod over the packs of shovel-faced dog breeds that had been forcibly abandoned by the Army as they took their owners away. Soon enough the bigger dogs would find the smaller dogs easy prey and so the circle-jerk of life would continue, just maybe without humans.

"We're meeting tonight at seven at the Police Station. You two gonna be there?"

"We hope so," Keith said before they turned to go back to their golf cart on steroids. "If we're not, don't send a search party."

The trip winded slowly through the older part of town on the east side of the tracks that paralleled Main Street. A dozen people on the roads were just wandering around in the middle of the overcast day, shock and disbelief disconnecting them from their new reality. Either these people had stayed behind because they couldn't bear leaving, or they'd been left behind because they couldn't get to the evac point in time. The latter idea Ethan empathized with on a very personal level. One man was even walking along the sidewalk next to the local head-shop with his cell phone out, looking for a signal that surely would never appear again. Even in the daylight the streets were a lot scarier than Ethan remembered as a boy, it was only a matter of hours or maybe days before these people turned on each other for the scraps of food left in pantries and the last drops of fuel in cars.

Deeper into the countryside it became river bottoms that faded into miles upon miles of identical trees and farms, stretching into oblivion. Keith was completely unprepared when Ethan swerved onto a gravel road with a single level house situated comfortably at the far end. After an insufferable amount of time on the dark, nondescript patchwork of gray and black county roads, they were finally home. As if a miracle there was a light on inside and Ethan was sure he saw the shadows of movement. He leapt from the overworked Gator before it had completely stopped and ran into the house while Keith was left to gather his wits.

The windows were all intact and the garage door was closed, so his hope soared that his family would be hiding in the loft bedroom or maybe in the potato cellar behind the house. Ethan grabbed the door knob and to his horror the door was unlocked and nothing barricaded it from inside. He ran through and cleared the house twice, the living room, furnished basement and loft bedroom and the hidden storage areas in the corners of the roof too. No one. His hands shaking, Ethan went to the closet in the furnished basement where he and Nicole shared the precious small space. Behind a few jackets he hadn't worn in years were two rifles he hadn't touched in even longer. When his grandfather passed back in 2006, Ethan's interest in hunting waned quickly, but being the sentimental type there was no way he'd let go of the weapons. A Remington .243 bolt action and a semi auto Remington 20 gauge shotgun were oiled and waiting as if they'd just been used yesterday, even if yesterday was more than a decade ago. The scattergun went to Keith, Ethan would either live or die by his grandfather's rifle.

"There was a note under the table, I guess it fell," Keith said, taking the shotgun from Ethan. Soaking up the scene for himself it didn't feel to him like anyone had been home too recently. Surely Ethan was clever enough to figure that out too, but there was no reason to pour salted lemon juice on an open wound.

Ethan bent over slowly, like he was finding one of his family's bodies, and gingerly took the folded letter that hadn't made it into an envelope. His whole family had left their own goodbye note just in case he made it home in this exact scenario. The world stopped while he read them, tears already rolling down his face as he read of dead friends and family, of things he couldn't have known while sequestered by the Army and finally of what the Army and police tasked through FEMA had done to get people to leave. Nicole's warnings were vague, as if she were afraid of someone other than Ethan reading it. Clearly though, there was a mortal, compelling reason for them to obey the Army when they were told to leave.

"Fuck!" Ethan threw a rather justified tantrum, "God fucking damnit!" A bowl of plastic fruit went sailing through the air. "Twelve hours! That's all I fucking needed was twelve fucking hours! If those fucking assclowns hadn't taken the truck..."

"It would have made no difference. The Army would have just recycled us to the front. You were never going to be able to join your family," Keith was getting the impression Ethan wasn't the type to take things sugar coated, so he didn't.

The shouting back and forth about sticking around or chasing down the evacuation continued until Ethan was exhausted. He collapsed into his old armchair, a complete wreck. Convulsions of pain from the anxiety of *not* knowing rippled through him over and over again. Where had they taken his family? *Why* had they been taken at all? The air conditioner kicked on outside. Aside from the whirring of the vents and the now unbearable, thunderous ticking of a grandfather clock, the house was silent.

Slower this time than before, Ethan began circling the house and touching things like he thought he might never see them again. Pictures of family on the walls, clothes his parents and Nicole wore, he stopped to smell a hairband she'd dropped behind the closet door. Vanilla and warm sugar, an aroma he could bury himself in and forget about the whole world. He must have been sobbing over the light blue strip of scrunchy nylon for a while because he didn't notice Keith until it had gone from romantic, to sad, to pathetic, to full blown awkward.

"It's six thirty. We should go," Ethan finally admitted defeat, watching the sun dip below the crest of the hill overlooking his serene farming valley. It wouldn't be fully dark for another hour at least.

His grandmother's Ford Crown Victoria was still in the garage, but barely started, it had been sitting for so long. His parent's minivan and Nicole's Jeep Patriot were nowhere to be seen, which meant for whatever reason they'd been allowed to drive themselves to town. One of Ethan's *Evanescence* CDs started playing, startling them both at the volume as much as that the radio was even on. The memories of better times the music brought back were too painful and Ethan ripped the removable faceplate off the radio and threw it into the garage somewhere. He had no idea what would happen at the police station when they arrived, but he sure as shit didn't feel like being in a good mood when he got there. Someone would surely be trying to take power, to be a king of their own shitty little fiefdom and he wasn't going to play that game. Ethan pounded a couple of Wild Turkey Honey shooters he'd taken from a stash inside the house and slapped himself hard on either cheek to wake up. Keith watched this sad ritual but said nothing, his only regret being he wasn't offered a shot too.

The station parking lot was almost completely empty. Only a couple of cruisers and a pristine, antique Cadillac were parked neatly by the door, but not in the handicap spaces. *Were there really any handicap people left? Wouldn't their medical needs have made them easy prey for the infected?* Even Keith wondered about this truism of the apocalypse, that few were willing to admit that in the end a lot of those not ambulatory were simply left behind. Ethan decided to park in the handicapped space and they went inside. In the clean, cool air of a relatively quiet building they found the portly cop from earlier, another male officer with a crappy bowl cut he must have done himself and a female cop who tucked her lower belly fat into her pants like it was somehow more natural looking that way.

"So now what?" Ethan said once everyone had turned to him.

"We were hoping you knew. You two are in the Army, right?"

"That's an ambiguous question," Ethan took a chair and sat in the semicircle with them. "We were left behind at different abandoned outposts when they pulled out."

"They left their own behind?" A man Ethan hadn't noticed was walking towards them from the break area's coffee maker. He wore jeans that might have fit fifty pounds ago, his gut hanging over a glittery rodeo belt. The pants had holes in the pockets with a circular bleach mark over a tobacco tin and a red and black plaid shirt proudly displayed a Winston logo. He carried an 1890 model Remington revolver in a leather holster strapped to his shoulder and a frosty cold Coors in his left hand. A cigar of the finest quality alternated between stubby fingers and his tobacco stained teeth. The Stetson on his head had a big fat Eagle Globe and Anchor pinned to the center. "Typical Army pukes." He smiled, making it clear he was joking.

"There were Marines there too," Keith said indignantly.

The old Marine harrumphed, "Look, Chief," he said to the fat cop, "we got problems. If it ain't the lootin' it's the dead and if it ain't the dead it's the gangs. At least that fuel ain't all been stolen from the truck stop, but that's only because they shut off the master switch. That action, whoever did it or why, might be our only saving grace this winter." It seemed to the two newcomers this four-person government was trying to hold on to at least some commodities for the looming winter. They already assumed they'd be on their own for the duration. If any order was going to be maintained, they'd need to act quickly and they'd need help.

"He's right," Ethan said without looking anyone in the eye. "We need to protect resources for the town."

"So, are we deputizing these guys?" The female officer gestured to Ethan and Keith, but didn't look at them either. "Can we trust them?"

"Can *we* trust *you*?" Ethan countered, feeling relatively drunk and enjoying the liquid courage. "I'm from here, lady, born and raised. You pulled me over two years ago for doing forty in a twenty-five on Church Street, so I remember you at least. To that end, I'm here and so are you. Makes sense that we have a common goal in mind, so get your complaints and or concerns out in the open now if you want my help."

"And what goal is that?"

"I want to find my family, dammit. I need to know where they were evacuated to. I need to stock up before I go get them and then there has to be a safe place for me to bring them back to. Helping you, in this case, is actually helping myself."

The cops and the old man shared glances. There wasn't any political deceit or malice in trying to find your family.

Finally, the fat cop spoke up, "I say tonight, while we still have electricity, we print out notices about a town hall meeting and then hold it at the outside stage in the fairgrounds so no one feels threatened or trapped. The Army was using it as a secondary landing pad for choppers. We can sweep the area around it first and all that." He cleared his throat, not used to cigar smoke in confined spaces. Ethan, for one, enjoyed the aroma. "Once we have the organized manpower, we start a door-to-door sweep for the infected. It grossly violates the Constitution, but we have no choice. Thomas Jefferson never envisioned zombies."

"Madison."

"What?"

"The Fourth Amendment was proposed by James Madison as part of the Anti-Federalist Papers," Ethan said without looking up from suppressing a terrible belch.

"We'll never be able to pull that off," the woman, Officer Liza Rowe, interjected. "Lots of people have infected family in their homes. Are we really talking about police entering private residences without a search warrant? Because good fucking luck, even these days. You'll be more likely to get shot than have them help you shoot someone they love. I don't even think most people here will consider us a legitimate police force anymore. Not after the Army abandoned us. Not after the things they did…"

Ethan agreed with a slow nod. "That's exactly what we're talking about. Big Bubba over there is right and so are you Miss… Rowe? It's going to be a nightmare to convince people to let us put a slug in their zombie kid's head, but they have to be made to understand they can't save them. We need Keith to tell them what the CDC knew. The civilian doctors aren't being told the truth, but he was at the Battle of Antire Hill, they got more information from FEMA and the CDC than we ever did."

"Thanks for throwin' me under the bus there, buddy," said Keith as he flipped off Ethan by subtly scratching his eyebrow, "but he's right. I can brief a doctor if you want, but

I was actually there. It wasn't a battle though... Not anymore than DC was a battle and I'm sure we all saw the footage of that..." Keith's speech slowed and his gaze came in and out from the thousand-yard stare, "It was a full-on clusterfuck of the highest magnitude. I'm sure you saw some of that here too. The big thing though, when we do clear the town, is that people are going to have to zombie-proof their homes at the same time. More than it would take to keep a man out. I mean strong, heavy boards and flat roofing aluminum so they can't get a grip on your windows in the first place. People are going to have to get used to guns too, baseball bats are only a half-measure, we need sturdy melee weapons for younger people or those who somehow can't handle a firearm. If there are any Army leftovers, namely guns, we should issue them to deputized citizens too."

"That obviously didn't work for the cities. Why should we expect any sort of cooperation out here?" Officer Rowe folded her arms.

Ethan smiled, "Because this isn't a city, it's our hometown. Because we're not going to get in each other's way, we're not going to be the crabs that pull the others back into the pot and because we know this area and we know each other. This is our home, what else could be more important? The infected aren't that smart, they can't strategize, their only saving grace is the ability to swarm our defenses." He sighed, thinking about another battle he didn't want to remember, "And maybe, if we're lucky, Union's fuckwit militia stemmed the tide. Manning the checkpoints and making sure the public knows everything we know as soon as we know it, will give those of us left behind a chance for cohesion. They'll respect those who take charge and respect some semblance of the rules if we play fair. Playing *Follow the Leader* hasn't completely left our collective psyche yet, we just have to prove we're the leaders to be followed."

The man in the Stetson puffed a giant smoke ring. It was competition level perfect. "You keep being useful, Mr. Kelly and I might have to appoint you to something when I'm elected mayor of this town."

"Elected? The dead have risen and you are... voting?" Keith was astonished.

"We're still Americans, aren't we?" The old man said.

*****

Around noon the next day, fifty or so people of all ages lined up to be deputized under the authority of the Sullivan Police Department. True, the SPD was a sad looking trio who rarely left the police station as swamped as they were, but it was an inch of authority that seemed to stretch a mile. Most new deputies were assigned to guard the remnants of the town's gas stations or the hospital. Others did what they could, anything from scouting the area for incoming packs of zombies, or to try to locate and secure warehouses that might not have been raided yet. Ethan's job was the last one, though it was true he had ulterior motives. He might be writing down the locations of useful supplies for his report, but it was on carbon paper meant for writing receipts, the pink copy was his to keep for a likely rainy day when all this went to shit and he had to fend for himself.

In the center of town, the day after that, members of the fire department's women's auxiliary served food at a free line in an attempt to raise morale. It did little to ease fears of abandonment to see so few people queued up for it. Instead, everyone wanted to top off their tanks before the electricity failed, assuming that this next disaster was just around the corner. Rolling brownouts were beginning to become a problem with all of America's nuclear power plants taken offline at the outset of the crisis to prevent a meltdown on top of zombies. Ethan remembered the President's famous line, *"Uh... There will be no... uh... Fukushima in America."* At the time he assumed it was just the Left trying to sell their latest Green Energy ponzi-scheme, but in these circumstances, it almost seemed, *dare he say it*, like a good idea?

One gas station didn't carry diesel, so Rowe bribed the

former attendant to man the station until the pumps ran dry. She made Ethan and some random deputy guard it for several long hours, but at least they had free reign over the tobacco left in the basement storage area. It had been a long time since Ethan had had fresh snuff. The line for gas stretched over the bridge and down a service road behind a bend, but at least the police could attend to more pressing issues with so many people distracted from stealing literally everything.

This was hardly a good use of his time, Ethan thought. He wasn't learning anything from the town's inner circle being sidelined like this and he wasn't making any progress toward finding out where his family was taken to. Hell, he hadn't even found their cars yet, but that was only a matter of time. Thousands of cars had been shoved together like sardines by heavy equipment to make room for more refugees and the sea of trash they'd brought with them.

After noon, when the various tasks of the would-be mayor and the legitimate cops all coalesced at the gas station Ethan was guarding, he finally felt better about being kept in the loop. Kelly's absurd car dominated an entire corner of the parking lot, making it hard for the last of the people in line to maneuver their regular-sized vehicles into the pumps. Kenly laid a large aerial map of the eastern part of Missouri out on his car's hood, using the longhorns bolted to the grill as a rack for his Stetson. In the south he may not have stuck out too badly, maybe not even in the "Las Vegas of the Midwest," but this close to St. Louis he really just looked like a caricature of a cowboy.

"...at a zoo-annex?" Kelly's voice carried over the din of car engines as Ethan made his way up to the gathered leaders, but he'd already missed part of the conversation.

"Yeah, just off the Stanton exit," Rowe nodded. "It's technically outside Sullivan PD's jurisdiction, so we didn't have anything to do with how it was shut down. I would have assumed they'd have euthanized the dangerous animals, but if what those refugees said is true..."

"What who said?" Ethan had to know now.

Kenly looked up, surprised Ethan was there, "I thought I had you guarding the truck stop?"

"Something must have been lost in translation," Ethan glared at Rowe, who naturally pretended the mistake was just that. He'd keep her secret that she'd disobeyed an order by placing him somewhere out of the way like this. Clearly, Rowe didn't fully trust him yet.

"Well if you're not there I can't imagine who's running that shit-show. Never mind, you feel like taking a cruiser and going up to Stanton? A family just arrived about three hours ago, said they saw a fucking *Liger*, a Lion-Tiger-thingy, one of those mutant-looking animals." Kenly rolled his eyes behind giant aviator sunglasses. He'd rant about it later over drinks, but his opinion on the cross-breeding of animals to create new ones was quite dour. Indeed, in Aaron Kenly's opinion, whomever created the Toy-Chihuahua had a seat reserved in hell.

Ethan's laugh sounded manic, but the idea of a poorly drawn, mythological creature from the cult-movie *Napoleon Dynamite* roaming the Missouri countryside tickled him some. "I'm sorry, come again for Big Fudge?" he snorted.

"Is that your new callsign?" Newton teased.

"Only if yours is Swarley."

Rowe narrowed her eyes, "Are you two fuckwits doing a bit right now?"

"Shut up, all of you," Kenly's tone was stern enough. "Until the existence of one of these designer-animals is confirmed, we'll need to make certain anyone leaving the gate is also aware of the potential risk. Worse-case scenario, we have to add a big-cat hunt to the daily roundup of undead."

"And if the people's reaction is like his?" Rowe gestured at Ethan with her thumb. "Some folks might not take the threat seriously."

Reynolds, who'd been quiet until now, was about to give his two-cents when the radios crackled a warning from the North Gate of approaching undead. The voice was that of

Keith Brewer, apparently answering Kenly's question about who was in charge at the truck stop. The leadership jumped in their respective cars, though Ethan had to bum a ride in Newton's cruiser if he wanted to go too. Despite his size and that of the car, Kenly and his El Dorado were surprisingly fast. Before he could tell the gas station clerk to pack it in, Ethan was nearly left behind and had to buckle up en route.

At the far end of the bridge a lookout claimed to see a person walking toward them. This close to nightfall and lacking effective backup, nobody wanted to be the unlucky member of Captain Kirk's away team and go check, though. This was the reason for the call for the legitimate police to show up. Keith turned on a set of thermal sights from the trunk of Reynolds' cruiser, thankful that in this rapidly devolving cesspool at least some modern conveniences were still available. Assuming it was another refugee at first, or at worse a stray group of a dozen or so zombies, he was disappointed to see that it wasn't.

"I definitely have movement," a guy in expensive looking, pixelated urban camouflage said from his roost between a bunch of sandbags. *What were those for?* Ethan wondered probably as much as anyone, did he expect the zombies to shoot back? The man on lookout reached to the forward grip of his M-4 and turned on an infrared laser that only specialized optics could see, painting his target. Those with sights witnessed the laser land with great precision on a figure's center mass. "I have one unknown at the far end of small arms range... Waiting for a kill order."

"We're not *killing* anyone just yet," Ethan warned, though he knew it was an inevitability. "Trust me, if the government does come back, we don't want to be the ones on record as having 'killed' infected citizens."

"Not that I disagree with you on that subject, but this guy's missing most of his left arm. I can see his tibia protruding from the flesh, man," Keith took his eyes off the lens, a red ring circling where the rubber had met his skin. "He's infected, Kelly. Let's just put him down. That was our mistake at Antire Hill, we let them get too close because we just had to flippin' know they weren't alive first." Keith gestured at the bottom of the hill with the military's favored *knife-hand* gesture, "In ones and two's they're almost harmless, but let them get five and six deep, let one person get bitten and that guy becomes the fucking Juggernaut..."

Keith's point was hit home when, minutes later, there were hundreds of undead shambling down the interstate, surely having overrun Union and St. Clair while Sullivan was still playing grab-ass about resources. It was a long way from St. Louis to Sullivan, but if you never paused to rest, never slowed your pace, walked all day and all night in search of the next soul to devour, distance meant little. A wind blew from behind them, whipping up pebbles and trash. For whatever reason the zombies in this one horrific scenario reminded Ethan of a short story he'd read in high school, the *"The Ruum"* by Arthur Porges, first published in 1953. In this short horror story, an alien device designed to collect living animal samples pursues a prospector at a slow, yet relentless pace through the wilderness. A creature could easily outrun it, sure, but that creature had to eat, drink, sleep, do all the things a living being must do. The Ruum, or in this case the Zombies, had none of those needs, no concerns about itself. Its only goal was *you*.

Reynolds blanched. He looked at the rest of the decision makers, "Should we shoot them all? Hell, can we shoot them all? Do we even have that much ammo?"

"Yes and we'd bettered fucking hope, respectively." Keith didn't back down on his beliefs that they had to act now, "I'll give the order myself," he walked to the middle of the bridge and looked at the dozen or so people gathered there. "We'll walk to the edge of the hill just forward of this position. There we will set up comfortable shooting positions and pick them off in the valley below. Those with guns in a caliber higher than .22 will try not to let them pass the road graters at the bottom. Take your time and fire selectively. If you need time to catch your breath or take a piss, just do it.

We're gonna be here a while. Those with .22's, crossbows or pistols need to be on standby to put down the zombies that make it closer to us. Some people, for example whoever thinks they're unprepared right now, should stay back until those who are ready right now start needing a break. Then we'll rotate until the job's done," Keith said loud enough to be heard by everyone without the aid of a megaphone. Reynolds had to admit he was a little jealous of that. Rowe had to admit she was a little turned on by Keith and Newton was using a lint-roller to remove ash from his uniform. *The town was truly lucky to have these three,* Kenly had thought on several occasions.

At first, several people refused to fire knowing there had been legal and political backlash to euthanizing the infected with what the administration had deemed "Illegal Weapons," (a dangerous term, as all firearms in the hands of the public are considered illegal under Martial Law.) The gathered men had no such reservations after Keith fired and hit the closest zombie in the leg with Ethan's .243. It fell to its knees, but continued to moan and drag itself toward the thin red line. Its head then exploded in the opening salvo as the others let loose their bullets, now sure that if someone were going to hang for this, they at least wouldn't be first at the gallows.

The one-sided gunfight started at dusk, but eventually drew the entire town to watch as if this were the first Battle of Bull Run. With any luck though, this time the spectators wouldn't be running away at the end of the battle, right behind the retreating troops. Given that Keith was actually a medic and not a combat trooper, the running of the firing lines fell mostly to Ethan. The rest of the leadership stayed on the overpass with a commanding view of the fight. A walky-talk, this time fully charged, let them tell Ethan where to direct his fire and that worked pretty well. He would order a ceasefire, wait for the wounded zombies to try to stand again or for the horde to bunch together a little bit more, rotate his shooters, reload and then with the waving of a red glowstick he'd let loose another devastating salvo of precision rifle fire. He'd been told there was a machine gun in the inventory the Army abandoned, but quite frankly his faith in that weapons platform when pitted against unfeeling corpses was limited. They'd burn through entire belts and maybe only kill a dozen in a hundred and then the crawling zombies would *still* make it to town. It was good to know there was a backup plan though and that might have emboldened him to fight harder, that and because he had been sneaking nips of whiskey all day and was still pretty drunk.

Chapter 5

Just as the tip of the sky was turning blue at the crest of dawn, the militiamen looked upon the devastation they had wrought. A pile of what would later be counted to be more than two thousand bodies lay at the bottom of the hill. The lifeless mountain of corpses didn't stop growing until it was full light, but by then only one man remained to fire, having sat out most of the evening's battle due to poor night vision. He was good at it too, once there was light and went to work picking off the stragglers with the methodical *boom*, click-clack, *boom*, click-clack, *boom*, click-clack of his Mauser K98. No one spoke, the entire experience so weird, so foreign to them they were to a man stunned to silence.

Except Keith, of course... *He'd seen this before, he'd been there when the checkpoint outside St. Louis was overrun, he remembered the last-ditch efforts to machine gun the horde as it pushed through the flimsy FEMA corrals, the black viscera of zombies mixing with the red of the freshly killed or still alive. The voices of the damned, of women and children as they were viciously bitten and clawed at by the raging undead still echoed in his ears. Then the guns opened up from atop the Humvees, loosing heavy caliber rounds into the teaming mass that couldn't be saved. Maybe it was the rounds themselves that broke the fences, or maybe the weight of the zombies crawling over their fallen confederates had finally bent the aluminum, either way they still got through.*

A massive fire was lit as a retreat measure, but the sound of the people shouting on the other side of the crackling flames could still be heard. Instead of having a million zombies being stopped by a moat of intense flames, they now had a million flaming *zombies already past the gate. Grabbing the kid he was treating at the time, Keith made a run for it toward the rear of what was then the largest traffic control point on the eastern side of Missouri. The sprawling encampment was practically a small military base itself, built right inside the valley of nearby Beaumont Boy Scout Reservation and encompassing both sides of the highway. Somewhere along the line, weaving in between tents and containerized housing units and a labyrinth of generators, he lost track of his equally terrified patient. As the fighting became more and more one-sided, Keith just kept running until he found the partially demolished bridge to* Where-ever-the-fucksville *and the rest was now still evolving history. He'd be damned if he would be running away from this town, though. Not this far into the game and not the least of which because there was literally nowhere else to go.*

"There were women and children down there too," Keith said under his breath, leaning on the overpass' railing. Whether or not he intended for Ethan to hear wasn't certain.

"There's always going to be women and children 'down there'. They're just as infected as the men and they'll kill you just as fast," Ethan sighed, feeling the fatigue hit him hard. It was like a cold he couldn't shake but still had to work through. "C'mon, let's eat, we have to clear the rest of the town. That Hillbilly Santa wants it done before nightfall."

"Why so soon?" Keith asked. "Most of 'em are locked in basements or closets and shit. Can't it wait a couple hours?"

"And what if all this gunfire compelled them to escape? Or before one of them causes a new outbreak in the middle of the night? This isn't lawful, it's survival and I have to survive long enough to bring my family home. We can hate ourselves for it later, because there will be a later. Nicole or my dad, they'll send an email or call soon enough, though, you'll see." Ethan handed Keith another energy drink. They were both too worn out to take an accurate shot anyhow, why not add some caffeine jitters to their mix of anxiety and fear?

Newton loaned Ethan the keys to his patrol car so he and Keith could go to the local VFW hall, where hot breakfast was being served under the protection of armed guards. It wasn't fancy, bacon that was going to expire if no one ate it and eggs from local farms. Almost everyone in town who had come to help brought their own supplies with them and with little coercion added those to the simple feast. Keith was so tired he barely pecked at his scrambled eggs, but Ethan tore into the food like it was sprinkled with crack. He was about to make a move on Keith's plate when they heard people shouting and a dozen more gunshots rang out from the roadblock. Without much thought they jumped back in the car and drove back as fast as they could. A bullet smacked the construction spotlight next to them as they pulled to a stop and took cover, unslinging their own rifles.

"Who the hell is shooting at us?" Keith wanted to know, taking a hiding position across from Newton. While all the other sleep-deprived deputies were hunkering down, the only licensed cop was still smoking a cigarette like this was when and where he normally had his morning death-stick. The crappy bowl-cut aside, "Newt" as Reynolds called him, was actually giving a semi-competent air of confident leadership ability, which right now couldn't hurt.

"Some assholes who took *Mad Max* a little too literally," Newton flicked the cigarette butt over the edge of the bridge. "I watched their lead rider hit a corpse and go flying just after you took my shop to go get food," Newton went on, trying to sound like one of the cops on TV by calling his cruiser his *shop*. "Pretty sure he's dead, because he still ain't got up, but I admit it's hard to make a prognosis this far away." Ethan laughed at the last quip, which pleased Newton that at least one person thought his jokes were funny.

"Well, the rest of them seem a shade of upset that we put those bodies down there in the first place, or at least that's what I've gathered in the last thirty seconds," as another bullet smacked the sandbags that made up the forward firing positions from the night's battle. "Case in point," Ethan muttered.

"Has anyone tried talking to them yet?" Keith asked.

"No, they just got here," Newton shrugged. "Besides, they'll be out of ammo in a few minutes if they keep this up."

"How very strategic of you," Ethan laid on the sarcasm like thick gravy.

Newton's radio crackled, "*John, you there? It's Liza.*"

"10-4," he responded, clutching the mic over his left shoulder. "Are you aware of the current situation?"

"*Affirmative, George and I are at the truck stop, can you make it over here?*"

Looking around at the others, Newton waited until he was reasonably certain those surrounding him were capable of moving if need-be, "Me and a few of the deputies can make a run for your position. We don't think these guys have any long-range stuff, just side-arms, but that might change without the floodlights to mask our positions, over."

Ethan grabbed Newton's mic, "Belay that, Counselor Troy. You need to get one of those LMTV's, the flat-nosed, tan colored Army truck with the turret on top. Bring it to us, I have a plan to bring these guys in alive. I don't know about you, but I'd like some answers rather than some corpses."

There was a pause, probably Rowe arguing with Reynolds. Among the three of them she was actually senior and likely pulled rank, "*George and I are gonna bring the less shitty one to you, standby for retrieval, over.*" The Army had left behind at least two of the armored cargo trucks, called LMTV's, among their stockpiles of other broken junk. A few minutes later the truck in question came lurching down the ramp from the truck stop, the bright-orange work order for the Army's mechanics still stuck under the windshield wipers like a ticket.

"What are you doing?" Newton demanded as Ethan climbed into the LMTV.

Ethan looked back, "What, you wanna play hero? Be my guest."

"Now that you mention it, no," said Newton, looking downrange. "So why are we bringing them back? Aren't they attacking us? I say fuck 'em," he was mostly talking to Rowe.

"Yes, fuck them. That makes total sense. Shut up, Newt," Rowe narrowed her eyes at the other officers. "George, you're in charge until we get back."

"We?" Reynolds flinched as another bullet from the bottom of the hill zinged overhead. It sounded slow, if you knew the difference in bullets heading *toward* you rather than away. It did remind everyone there was a limited amount of time before these guys got back on their bikes and then they'd probably come back with better weaponry.

Rowe pulled herself up and into the armored transport with little that resembled grace, but she at least didn't ask for help. Ethan handed her a headset plugged into the truck's radio so they could talk over the din of the engine. *"You know I was only offering options, I didn't necessarily have a good plan for the intake of a dozen prisoners."*

"You were right, I don't need more bodies laying around," Rowe folded her arms after buckling herself in. *"I also need to interrogate them. Are they part of a larger gang? Is it the same gang that's taken over Bourbon? Not to sound cliché, but I got ninety-nine problems, it would be nice if a biker gang wasn't one."* She motioned for Ethan to start driving after getting the thumbs up from Reynolds. Several more deputies had climbed into the canvas-covered bed and one scrawny kid climbed into the turret between Ethan and Rowe.

The second LMTV had been coaxed into motion too and was sent to join the circus of attention. Slowly, the two trucks crept toward the newcomers, rolling over corpses while the first truck's transmission refused to leave second gear. Bloating sacks of fat and gasses, stuffed full of flesh they'd eaten previously, popped and crunched like so much roadkill. Everyone vomited at least once, if not from the smell then from the sound, or the texture of the imploding human bodies. It's not a sensation you ever forget, like the squeaking of a cassette tape when the Play button isn't pushed hard enough. *Nails on a chalkboard, but for your soul.*

As soon as the convoy was within seventy-five meters, still just outside pistol range, Ethan got on the bullhorn, "Attention. Attention. This is the Sullivan Militia. Lay down your weapons and come out where we can see you and you will not be harmed. We're not your enemy, nobody wants to fight, we just want to talk."

There were glances shared among the bikers, likely about whether or not to fight, but the collective group of about twelve thuggish looking men eventually complied without a fuss. It was probably the machine gun in the turret that changed their minds, but whatever worked. Ethan and a few others dismounted, carefully approaching with their weapons pointed down, making it clear they weren't the aggressors here. A zombie that had been buried under the other infected groaned and reached for a deputy, startling him as he took his position for the encounter. A three round burst echoed across the valley as he shrieked, blowing its head apart in a cloud of sticky gray mist and ricocheting asphalt.

Confused and frightened, a biker grabbed a hidden shotgun from behind the seat and let loose at the deputies. Buckshot slapped the front of the first truck and nicked a deputy in the arm. Someone managed to hit another deputy in the calf, knocking him down and out when his face hit the pavement. This was all spiraling out of control before Ethan's eyes, despite holding his hands out to tell his men to stand down, it only got worse.

His experiences in Iraq had been harsh, but none of it had prepared him for what transpired in the next ten seconds. The machine-gunner, having seen it all from above and withholding his fire because his own men were below, took a buckshot pellet to the helmet. Recoiling from the massive impact to his head, which drew blood from slamming his face into the turret-well as he fell, the kid jumped back up and pulled the trigger, screaming like a wounded animal. Ethan could feel, in slow motion, the air pressure of each of the M-240's heavy caliber rounds as they broke the sound barrier directly over his head. Yet he didn't flinch, already so numb inside that this most recent tragedy somehow just didn't feel real. Blood sprayed into the air and mixed with cordite and Ethan had to stand in the center of it. His attention was so focused on the brass casings and black, metal belt links clattering the ground that at some point he didn't even hear the gun anymore. The screams were drowned out and only this clinking and clanking sound against the pavement.

Perhaps killing zombies from a distance was also something of a disconnect, like a video game that has no real consequences. Killing living people at point blank range was messy and brutal. It's a different experience entirely and unimaginably horrible. Viscera and the stench of disemboweled victims became an inescapable cloud that hovered over them. Ethan was still standing in the midst of it, just below the gun's defilade when the shooting stopped. The 7.62mm rounds had blown people almost in half, most of the deputies stopped firing after only a few shots, but the gunner hadn't. He was still screaming from the same breath when the gun finally jammed and the barrel drooped, white hot.

In this deafening silence where only your heartbeat can be heard, Ethan looked up the gunner, still clutching the trigger for dear life. Black carbon and cordite covering his face like a pilot from the Great War. A stream of dirty tears ran from his eyes and mixed with his own blood from a nasty gash to the temple. Ethan and the others saw the damaged Kevlar helmet when the kid sank back into the turret, holding his head and rocking back and forth.

"It's okay, kid," Rowe repeated, first to get to the boy.

Ethan took and then stuffed the damaged helmet in an empty duffle-bag for evidence, just in case someone accused the boy of murder. Maybe it was murder, maybe it wasn't, but for certain it was panic. What he'd done was terrible, but it might have saved everyone there. To be fair though, being shot in the head can have a profound effect on someone's thinking. Ethan wasn't going to let anyone use the kid as a scapegoat either, realizing only then how important it was to him to refuse to let his home devolve into the Wild West. Nobody was getting hung at dawn if it was up to him. *We were still better than that, right?* He and Rowe shared a significant glance when she saw him stash the Kevlar in a duffle bag.

Chapter 6

"What happened!?" Reynolds and Kenly demanded to know when the trucks lurched their way back to the overpass. Because of the rise of a hill the scene below was actually out of view from the town, but they weren't deaf.

"Probably the inevitable," Newton said under his breath, but everyone ignored him. Just because he was right didn't mean they needed to acknowledge him.

Keith held up his hand to prevent more hearsay, "They wouldn't come peacefully." He choked back tears, looking around at an even larger crowd who'd gathered to see the commotion. It wasn't every day one heard a machine gun rattling in suburban America, even during the apocalypse. Now there was no way to hide, or even downplay the incident. It might be a dirty tactic, but nothing distracted people faster than simply not acknowledging the incident. The authorities took the gathering as an opportunity to announce the news that the town needed to be swept and cleared of undead. The next night a bulldozer would be sent to the bottom of the hill to remove the bodies and bury them in a mass grave in a field, thugs and zombies alike.

More living-on-living shootings happened that day too; a mother shot her neighbor for euthanizing the infected son she was keeping locked in his room, a traffic accident involving a box-truck nobody had set the brake on and one person whose death was murder by stabbing. There were no witnesses to the murder and the body was found in a mostly abandoned area. Though he was exhausted and barely functional, Ethan went with Newton to record the scene while Reynolds and Rowe took the bereaved mother into custody. The town had only three jail cells in the basement level of the city hall and one secured interrogation room at the police station. Now they only had two jail cells, as it was unlikely they'd be able to release the woman anytime soon. It wasn't something Ethan wanted to think about, the long-term incarceration of anyone during this kind of crisis. Was it more humane to simply hang offenders and be done with it? These questions would continue to vex him in the quiet of sleepless nights.

At the scene of the second murder Ethan realized why there were no witnesses, just beyond the South Gate a natural blind spot obscured the area from the sentries. Newton interviewed the woman who'd found the body of a man in his late twenties, or early thirties. Ethan used a cell phone camera to document the scene, using the burst option to make quick work of it. Now was hardly the time to admit it, but Ethan's on-the-job experience as an MP wasn't what most people imagined and he felt horribly under qualified to be there. Sure, he'd taken a class on crime-scene procedure, but he'd only ever been assigned to work the road at Fort Stewart, Georgia once. That adventure hadn't lasted two weeks when, as if a cruel joke, the opportunity to do what he'd signed up for had been cut short upon receiving orders to deploy to Iraq in 2009.

Ethan had written a total of three tickets on the rural road that ran through a logging site behind post and been spat on by a colonel's fat little boy for no apparent reason other than he knew he could get away with it. The rest of Ethan's time in the Army had been spent getting acquainted with the unofficial term "Combat MP." For the layman it was tantamount to reducing specialized troops to Infantry-With-Trucks. With no actual law enforcing occurring in a nation where local law was "suspended until the cessation of hostilities," and all other offenses not covered by the Uniform Code of Military Justice simply weren't considered offenses, Military Police were all but useless. The most law enforcing Ethan had ever seen done in Iraq was when the MP's of 4th Brigade escorted then accused murderer Joseph Bozicevich back to the US for arraignment.

In another notable incident at Fort Stewart, Ethan had been assigned to a security detail at a fall festival held for the local high school's football team. That year's live entertainment featured the aged, if not still enthusiastic

Commodores. *Their music was... not Ethan's style, but using the police station's fleet of golf carts, adorned with lightbars, to have a whiskey-fueled race across the fairgrounds with the guys was a priceless memory.*

Ethan became lost in the darkness and anxiety and the mental haze that surrounded his time after Iraq. It felt like he was perpetually waiting for the proverbial hammer to drop from his chain of command's latest scheme to berate and bully some sort of discipline back into a unit they'd already lost control of. Ethan, like most of the men in his platoon, couldn't hold back how much he hated his superiors. *Not after what they'd done, or hadn't done in her case,* he thought. Third Infantry Division at Fort Stewart, Georgia was a posting considered by most to be the Army's version of *Hotel California: you can reenlist any time you like, but you can never leave.* Ethan wasn't paying attention to Newton anymore and didn't notice the cop creeping up behind him. Using his taser to zap Ethan from up close in the kidney, Newton laughed a little when his deputy fell forward onto the body like a flailing fish.

"I called your name like five times, Kelly. Find anything?"

"I haven't checked for ID yet. I was still taking pictures," Ethan wasn't even mad that he'd been zapped, he was distracted from an important job and that was on him. Putting on latex gloves, he moved the man's jacket to reveal the half dozen eye-slit shaped wounds. The blood was already a congealed maroon, the victim's skin as cold as the ground. The body's limbs were even stiff from rigor mortis, "You wanna call for a nurse to come check his liver temp? Because I forgot my rectal thermometer at home."

Newton handed the radio to Ethan, who'd proven he had no fear of it. "MC, this is Ghostrider, can you have an ambulance sent to Officer Newton's location for body retrieval. There's no sign of interference from the Infected or animals, so we're pretty sure the cause of death is Human-related."

"Deputy Kelly, I am never calling you Ghostrider," Reynolds responded over the radio. *"Keep the scene secure, we'll have a nurse sent your way with body retrieval."*

Returning their attention to the corpse with blue lips, they rolled him over to get a better look inside his jacket. Newton made certain to micro-manage Ethan through searching the body, but eventually stopped talking. He didn't stop hovering uncomfortably close, though, ready to take over or berate Ethan for failure.

"There's no wallet," Ethan finally confirmed, patting down each of the dead man's pockets several times over. "There's no anything-else, either. I'd expect a refugee to have lots of useful, or sentimental items. Hell, I still have fifty bucks in my wallet and paper money has been useless for weeks. This guy doesn't even have a folded dollar, cigarettes, keys or a tube of chapstick. I was only in the wild for two days and I found tons of useful stuff like that."

"Maybe he just found these clothes recently," Newton was actually being helpful. "It's not like you can't just walk into any store and walk out wearing new duds."

Ethan surveyed the scene again, trying to piece together where the body might have come from in the first place. *John Doe* had been here long enough that the unkempt grass had sprung back up from the direction he'd been dragged and blow flies were gratefully eating a corpse that wasn't infected.

"Look, I'm writing it up as probable refugee-on-refugee crime. The guy likely got robbed on his way into town," Newton was already scanning the horizon for the incoming ambulance. Like the local funeral parlors, the ambulances would only take a body if it wasn't bitten.

"Yeah, I got nothin' to add."

As the ambulance came to collect the body, Newton tried his hand at small-talk again, "Are you heading home after your shift?"

"Home may as well be haunted, at least for me," Ethan admitted. His answers were probably always weightier than

Newton was prepared for. "I'll probably try to get a couple hours of shuteye at the station, but I doubt it."

"Humans have to sleep," Newton said, totally oblivious to the amateurs manning the ambulance as they fumbled to get the body inside. The real EMT's, or at least the ones with any genuine experience, were all dead by now. "I could get Doctor de la Garza to give you some Ambien. It's what my mother used to take before she passed."

"Is she the one who taught you to cut your hair?" Ethan joked.

"Yes," Newton responded quickly, seemingly unaware he'd been insulted.

Ethan patted him on the shoulder, "Take me back to the Batcave, Alfred."

In the back of the police station, located on the edge of the city park, Ethan found a cot and the standard scratchy, green wool blanket with a bold **U.S.** stenciled on it. The cot was even missing the brace at one end, making the ensemble of knee and back pain a certainty. Hell, it almost made him nostalgic for his time in Iraq, or more specifically getting there. The series of corrals and waiting areas from Kuwait to Baghdad International Airport, or BIAP for short, was uncomfortable, boring, dusty, smelly and cramped. It was also the last time he felt like he was a part of something bigger than himself and not simply in its way. Anticipation hadn't devolved into anxiety yet. Ethan crashed onto the cot, his sidearm digging into his hip, but he was too tired to care.

The back of his eyelids were painfully dry when he closed them. Rolling his head so his left arm blocked the light from the hallway, Ethan wasn't sure when he actually fell asleep, but it was quick for the first time in a long time... *between this world and next there exists a link to both your past and present, when the actions you took make perfect sense in the clarity of future context. Then that clear view is obscured by fog. The primal fear of being lost and alone in the enveloping darkness... and then at last someone was coming for you, but not someone you wanted... the hate...*

hate directed at you because you weren't one of them, because you weren't like them... you were a threat to them more so than the enemy...

A deputy's handheld radio woke him mid-nightmare, just before the same hateful, gaunt face appeared as it always did. By then it was fully dark and nearing eight o'clock. It would be time for their would-be mayor's meeting to brief the townspeople on their immediate future and solidify his "elected" status. Sure, he didn't really need to have the three thousand or so people left vote for, or against him, (Retired) Sheriff Aaron Kenly basically had the reins already. The leadership was playing this pretty close to the chest, though and any degree of cooperation and legitimacy helped. Kenly addressed a gathered crowd from the podium at the fairgrounds as Ethan was just arriving.

Kenly was shorter than the singer Charlie Daniels when he wasn't wearing cowboy boots, though the resemblance was uncanny otherwise. His weathered face wore a white beard and a stained, older Stetson that had seen better days kept a graying *high & tight* hidden from sight. He smelled of tobacco, alcohol and probably some pot too, as if he didn't care anymore and Ethan empathized. Suddenly he was aware he hadn't changed his clothes since the mansion behind Six Flags, the tiger-striped camo looking more like one continuous brown blob than a series of jungle leaves. His nose was numb to it, but he imagined he smelled awful.

Ethan stepped up to the side of the patrol car Keith was sitting in. "Turn down your radio," he said, unbuttoning his shirt when the wind picked up. Another rainstorm was approaching and it felt nice, though the omnipresent smell of trash and burning buildings still assailed his senses. "I want to hear him speak."

"I think I should go back to the station and monitor the radio. There's been people in trucks with guns mounted on them testing our borders. A few refugees showed up too, one was infected..." Keith trailed off for a moment while the would-be mayor tested the microphone by harrumphing several times. "That little bedroom community up the road's been overrun by some One Percenters, probably the same ones from..." He trailed off again and yawned, forcing Ethan to do the same. Neither of them were doing well at this point, "Lots of stories of torturing people *before* they rob them and raping women."

Ethan's eyes widened, putting two and two together, "You think it's the same guys from yesterday? Does this mayor-guy know?" he gestured with his thumb at Kenly.

Keith shrugged, so Ethan scooted right up to hillbilly Santa Clause and pulled him close just seconds before he was preparing to begin his speech, "Look, Sir, we have a situation in Bourbon of the *Likely Friends of the Guys We Machine Gunned Yesterday* variety. I'm going to handle it, but given the mess it'll cause I don't think the legitimate police should be involved, you get me? So, whatever you do, don't publicly announce us sending men to check it out, I don't want to risk spies in the crowd before we have a better formulated plan."

The shorter man looked up at Ethan and smiled patronizingly. He reeked of liquor even worse up close, but then who really wanted to be sober right now? "Look son, I got this." He pulled away and stepped back up to the microphone. "My fellow Americans..." He began, smiling at his own innuendo. "My name is Aaron Anthony Kenly. I served in the Marine Corps for eight years, I was a Deputy for fifteen and Sheriff for another twenty. I share that experience with you because I want you to believe me when I say I can see a path through this.

"The second thing is, retrieval is never coming. We've lost radio contact with anyone from our police or fire departments sent to Oklahoma, but that is no reason to be alarmed. No news is good news in a situation like this, it means they're holed up somewhere working on staying safe from the undead. Soon enough there will be global communications again, but for now I want to lay out my plan to keep this town safe and whole until the Army can make a good comeback."

"Are they really Zombies?" A man shouted from the front row, cutting him off. "CNN's broadcast is still sayin' they're just infected, like the flu and that there's a cure in the works. Is any of it true?"

Kenly shrugged, "I'm afraid I've not spent much time sitting in front of a television hoping for miracle cures as of late, but since I'd like to avoid the same questions, I will recap," Ethan smirked as Kenly continued. "The undead people are as close to those voodoo zombie movies as any definition allows for. They're attacking people and spreading this rabies-like virus and at last estimates more than half the world's population is infected. The government ain't workin', the Army's retreatin' and in case you missed their pull-out the other day, let me be the first to assure you that we are well and truly on our own." A murmur rose from the crowd, some people were beginning to panic, but that was the intended shock effect of his speech.

"But this does not mean there is no hope!" Kenly suddenly bellowed, gesturing wildly in the air, "We are still here, my friends! And our men will protect us, train us to defend ourselves for the future. We will hold out until the United States of America can get herself back together and then, I swear to you all, we are going to give the zombies a whoopin' history will never forget, this I swear to you...."

Ethan felt Mr. Kenly might be an okay guy, though his Winston Churchill impersonation had something to be desired. He was also certainly no poet. Kenly finished his speech on why he should be mayor and stepped off the stage so Officer Reynolds could address the people on emergency services and the possibility of making the Walmart parking lot a marketplace. Another meeting for those interested in a farming and economic council was scheduled, a waste and body removal council were mentioned as well. This was all going to get a lot worse before it got better, but at least they stood a chance with an organized resistance of locals.

"What're we going to do about Bourbon? They're ransacking the neighborhoods on the other side of the highway and frankly we need the supplies in those buildings more," Kenly said as he came back to stand next to Ethan.

Raising an eyebrow, Ethan shrugged, "I didn't know I was in charge."

"You are the dumbass who raised his hand."

Ethan sighed, "For now, Sir, we've established a roadblock at the corners of 185 and H. I don't think random bandits are going to be a problem very often, though, not once they figure out the town is defended. As for Bourbon, Sir, we're going to handle it when the time is right. They're almost certainly the same gang we shot all to hell at the overpass and I, for one, think we need to hurry before they figure out what happened to their men."

Kenly nodded appreciatively, "People are going to start to wonder the longer the men stay silent about that. Someone's gonna need to make a statement at the next meeting or we'll lose legitimacy in a scandal. There's already a rumored petition for the police to arrest the boy on suspicion of murder."

"Over my dead fucking body," Ethan's eyes widened. "I will not allow my home to devolve into mob rule. If you lose control of the masses, or turn on him for political gain, I'll take the kid and it'll be the last time you see either of us."

Kenly smiled again and walked back toward the massive Cadillac he'd parked near the stage. The ridiculous set of longhorns bolted to the grill shimmered when the engine's torque rocked the chassis. Ethan walked back to the patrol car and stuck his head inside, silhouetted by floodlights and a lightning storm in the distance that was following the Mississippi river. Keith was glaring at him like an impatient child.

"What?"

"A girl showed up at the South Gate... *buck-ass naked.* Deputy Carlisle says she was covered head to toe in blood, shit and cigarette burns," Keith swallowed hard, thinking about the description he'd read on the patrol car's computer screen. "She's in stable condition in the E.R. What if this is a reprisal for the overpass? Could they know already?"

"We should assume so," Ethan climbed into the car Keith was assigned, the drive to the hospital taking only seconds as it too was attached to the city fairgrounds. "If it isn't some kind of revenge, though... then they're a bigger problem than I thought." He said largely to himself, though Keith was welcome to add his two cents, but he didn't.

Walking into the air-conditioned lobby, the shock of cold air felt amazing beyond words in the late summer's heat. A nurse was there to greet them as representatives of the police department, along with a chubby girl in her twenties wearing hunting camo and an orange vest that read Hospital Safety Officer. She was toting a shotgun she seemed very comfortable with, which was good since allowing guns in the hospital had become a gruesome fact of life. Restraints and sedatives meant nothing to the raging infected and what few nurses and doctors were left had to be safeguarded as if they were more precious than a newborn, because sadly they were at this point. The most eye-catching change to the regional hospital Ethan had known all his life were the large fiberglass dog houses that dotted the interior at each nurse's station bearing the label **Emergency Shelter**. Inside was a day's worth of food and water, a blanket to cover the wire gate so a zombie couldn't see you and an adult sized diaper because... reasons. Ethan felt it would be a good idea to ask citizens to copy these for every home and office in town, but now wasn't the time.

"She's alert," The nurse said, "but suffered massive dehydration, broken ribs and a fractured arm. She's not talking, so we don't have a name yet. We also ran a rape kit, it was very, very positive... and she probably has a hairline fracture to her pelvis too. Once she's got more fluids in her we'll take her to X-ray and be sure."

"Is she infected?" Keith asked, needing to change the subject from imagining the mechanisms of injury.

"With the Inviere plague? No, but what those bastards might have given her only time and tests will tell..." The nurse teared up, but it was only momentary in her continuous world of horrors. "I don't know how she made it all this way. My husband says they shoot at least three zombies an hour coming out of the woods, but somehow she walked right through the sentries and just sat in the parking lot by a patrol car until they found her."

"Can we talk to her? It could be a while before the regular cops can get here. We need her memory to be as fresh as possible," Ethan asked, letting a lot of the training he'd suppressed rise to the surface. He wasn't actually as incompetent as he let on, that was just a defense mechanism lest someone saddle him with real responsibility, like now. "We're not just run of the mill Joes with guns, we both have advanced medical training and I'm... I *was* a Military Policeman." Ethan corrected himself, not really knowing why. *It was difficult to have pride in an organization whose "best and brightest" killed your friend, covered it up and let you twist in the wind after you tried to do something about it. Snap out of it!* Ethan almost slapped himself in real life, but refrained. "We'll be as professional as possible, I promise."

The nurse, now having much of the authority of an actual doctor, nodded to them and they went into the victim's room. Machines bleeped and whirred, the girl was awake, but her eyes never met the newcomers. "I'm Deputy Keith Brewer. What's your name?" he asked, keeping his distance and speaking in as soothing a voice as he could. It was indeed silky, but she couldn't be stirred by it.

"Ma'am, we need to know what happened to you, otherwise nobody's getting what they deserve over this." Ethan's bedside manner had something to be desired, but his gamble that she might respond to an authoritarian voice paid dividends. Everyone was patronizing her, trying to be sympathetic, but nobody had yet tried being as angry as she was.

"They did," she said, holding out two worn red ribbons in her black and blue, bandage-covered hand. Keith took them and let Ethan inspect them too. They were the name-tapes from a biker club's "cut", one reading MASTER AT ARMS and the second too damaged to make sense of, but it was probably a name.

"Those fucking mid-life crisis cunt-wagons, *they* are what happened to me. The guy I was traveling with didn't have any food or drugs to give them as tribute, so they took me and shot Drew in the gut, left him to die in the street." Her tone was clear and calm, as if her blood had been replaced with ice water, "After I bit their leader's dick off, they stripped me and beat me until I blacked out." She remained steady, gray eyes piercing through Keith like nothing he'd felt before, "But they didn't finish me because... I guess why waste a perfectly good collection of holes to fuck?" She shrugged, trying not to let herself become lost in the fog of hate.

"I killed their leader, he bled out, all over the parking lot while the others watched," her grin was missing teeth, but it was broad and defiant. "That was where I got the ribbons and then his shit-stain protégé took over. My reward for helping him to the throne was being raped by him exclusively for two days, then he doped me and just shoved me out a two-story window into a pile of broken beer bottles. They let me wander off like I couldn't possibly have mattered less." The girl finally broke eye contact, "I just picked a direction and kept walking until I heard the machine gun, I thought maybe you were the Army so I walked toward it."

The irony struck Ethan hard, that such folly would be a clarion-call for someone who needed their protection. "If you have names we can go there and look for, it will make things simpler for us," Ethan offered. "We'll need evidence to bring them to justice."

Her look was incredulous, "Monsters don't get names, *Officer*," she said, laying back down and becoming almost catatonic again. "They're just the darkness, the abyss of what we've become. You either kill them or they'll kill us all, there is no middle ground."

Ethan and Keith left the room and headed back to the

station. "What time do you want to call it quits tonight?" Keith practically begged. Seeing the beautiful young woman so badly beaten had taken more of a toll on him than his own injuries. Ethan's couch was calling to him, like it was the Isle of Sirens and he was Odysseus. So soft, so bongwater and pizza soaked, the glorious wooden 1970's monstrosity could swallow him into its overused cushions like a plump Army wife's ample bosoms. He could die there and would have gone out a happy man.

"After we cook up a battle plan," Ethan was letting on how much the girl's state had upset him too. Keith was gathering that most of his new friend's reactions were of the delayed variety. A bomb could go off and Ethan might not flinch until debris started raining down. "I'm not letting this go. They raped her. The world is ending and they're fucking raping young girls to celebrate it."

"From what I've read, this is about how it looked when Rome was sacked," Keith changed the subject, disturbed as well.

"I can't know this right now..."

They arrived at the police station where about twenty off duty deputies were filling out reports by the light of a construction lamp. The station's air conditioner had given out, apparently due to mechanical failure unrelated to the apocalypse and the place was stifling in this midsummer's nightmare. A strong wind blew from the West, the smell of death and fire assailed them now that they'd left the antiseptic cocoon of a hospital. Ethan clinched his eyes, unable to prevent flashbacks to the desert where he'd been sent to rot by an Army he'd put entirely too much faith in. The stench of ten thousand years of death, violence, trash and oil was omnipresent in "the cradle of civilization." The winds in Iraq made you pray for a still day where only the ambient heat made your skin feel like it was on fire and not the powdered rock, glass and particulate debris of Iraq's topsoil being dragged across your skin like a sandblaster. This breeze made the apocalypse all that much worse, polluting the alluring cedar and mossy oak that characterized Missouri's woods with the sour stench of burning trash.

Newton walked up to them in his long-sleeve winter uniform on, oddly unaffected by the oppressive heat. *Must be nice to be skinny*, Ethan thought, *my thighs could start a friction fire*. Newton's hands were clasped behind his back like he was at parade rest, though still walking, his body language suggesting he was enjoying being the top dog for once. Ethan waved to him, thinking it better to get the impending awkward conversation over with, but the officer started talking first.

"We found a guy wandering through the woods about an hour before dusk. North gate didn't report it right away because the radio operator had diarrhea," Newton's tone was light and jovial, as if he were sharing a joke with close friends. "Anyhow, he says he walked here from Union and that it's gone now like you and Brewer said. Washington's been abandoned too. Also, he said there are men in U.N. blue on watercraft patrolling the river, but not helping refugees or engaging the infected. He said they're just watching like they know something we don't. Liza disagrees, but I say we go make 'em stop for us."

Ethan and Keith just stared at Newton like he was stupid. Ample evidence was mounting that he might actually be. "So, what you're suggesting is there's still an organized government somewhere?" Ethan prompted.

"Probably," Newton nodded.

"Uh huh. And your plan, in its entirety, is to go *make* them talk to us?" Ethan was trying not to be an ass, but he was failing.

John didn't appear phased by Ethan's attitude, "Liza and George are getting more from the guy because he's the only refugee we've seen in almost a week. He says he wants to be let go so he can keep moving South. Says he doesn't want to be here at all when the real horde shows up, that all them we shot last night was just the tip of the iceberg."

"We've no right to keep him," Ethan gestured with open

palms. He didn't know why he was having to tell Newton about civil rights, but then times had been especially trying for some people more than others. That, or it could have simply been his awkward way of making conversation, something Ethan already knew Newton wasn't good at. They were all distracted from the conversation when they saw fluffy, fresh ash falling from the sky again, collecting on their hair and on the shoulders of their shirts.

"I agree. I'll see to it," Newton walked off. Ethan got the eerie impression Officer John Newton was seeking permission from him somehow, but who the hell was he to give anyone orders? Was this a test of some kind? It had to be.

Chapter 7

It was three in the morning when Ethan opened his eyes again. He didn't remember coming home, but at least he realized where he was before he went into full panic mode. Nightmares that didn't involve zombies had already seen to his bed being covered in sweat, again. He reached for Nicole at his side, devastated not to find her there. Her side of the bed didn't even smell like her anymore. She'd been his only tether to reality most days, his sense of self devastated after his time in what he felt was the world's largest kitty-litter box. Ethan's eyes were blurry, the half pint of vodka he'd been drinking had tipped over and soaked the carpet, *again*. Not that it mattered to him now, his mother and father weren't there to complain about the smell or stains anymore. Looking around he saw a light on in the kitchen, Keith had passed out with a cigarette burned down to the filter between his fingers. Of course, there was also the methodical, infernal, ticking of that damned antique clock. The six-foot mahogany and gold-leaf gothic monstrosity hadn't been moved from next to the TV since long before Ethan was born, back when this was his Grandfather's house. He hated it as much as he loved it, even the thirty seconds of chimes at midnight and noon.

Rubbing his eyes Ethan pushed back the screen on his laptop, lamenting the nearly broken hinge on the left, he looked at his normally empty inbox. He missed the instant gratification of deleting spam, or replying to junk emails with pictures of the infamous *Blue Waffle*. Only this time it wasn't empty. There was a government address on the email, which didn't elicit much excitement from him at first. He'd already gotten two emails confirming that he'd been reported missing in action and a third confirming his absentee brother Lee's status as missing in action as well. A fourth was a "canned" letter of condolence to his family with the names of both brothers copy pasted in the wrong font size. *Apparently using a phone was beyond the Army's resources these days,* he thought bitterly.

Sparking up a joint, the last one in his old stash, Ethan clicked on it. Choking on the smoke like this was his first time, he read the email aloud just to make sure he wasn't dreaming.

"Ethan were okay at tulsa if you read this we love you
     stay safe
-Nicole"

One sentence, no explanations, just a location. The typos made him think it had come through on a cellphone because Nicole was a stickler for proper punctuation, but even badly formatted news was good news. He tried not to think about what she'd had to do to get access to a cellphone in a place rumored to be as heavily locked down as a FEMA camp and excitedly woke Keith up instead.

"They're alive!"

Keith sat up and launched himself out of his seat. At that exact moment the phone rang. Ethan grabbed it, "Hello!? Nicole?" The response he got was even more shocking than the email.

"...Thank God you're alive..."

"Lee?"

"I don't have long, I'll be back soon, I promise."

"Lee!?" Ethan shouted as he heard static on the line, "Lee! Can you hear me? Where are you!? I'll come get you!" The line was dead. *"Fuck!"*

"Lee's your brother, right?" Keith asked, but Ethan was beyond reasoning with now. He shouted and threw a coffee mug through the clock that had tormented his dreams, collapsing to the couch in near convulsions.

"Where's Lee, Ethan? Where is he?" Keith grabbed his friend by the shoulders, trying to snap him out of the panic attack.

Ethan gulped air, "They reassigned him to Tenth Mountain Division after Nogales," he choked out. "He was in Kentucky when I got drafted back." Ethan calmed down some when Keith brought a half-finished bottle of Jagermifter to him. Polishing off the licorice flavored swill in a chugging motion that made Keith ill to watch, Ethan hastily typed a reply to the email and started throwing clothing towards a vintage "ALICE" pack he'd had since his freshman year of JROTC, some ten years ago.

"What are you doing?"

"I'm going to Kentucky, I have to get Lee."

"I get that you're drunk, but are you fucking insane too? You won't make it to the next county. You'll be lucky to survive the next week without this town and what about Bourbon?" Keith pinned Ethan to a wall when he resisted the lecture, hitting his head on the thermostat. "You gotta stay here, man! If Lee is coming home you can go when he gets here, I promise I'll keep the lights on for you, but if your family is using the internet then there is electricity and computers and the safety to use them. They're okay for now. They're fine. They're alive... My family is not, I saw my dad die on live TV fighting the spread from Flagstaff, my mother died in a car crash when I was seventeen. You have to pull yourself together and recognize the gift in front of your face." Pushing Ethan down on the couch, Keith, flopped into the recliner across from him, "Sleep it off, we got a lotta shit to do come daylight."

In truth both men were still really drunk and it wasn't even light outside yet. Ethan didn't want to go back to sleep, but he passed out without struggling too hard to stay awake... *dreams are illogical. They're the random clutter of whatever the camera in your brain records, mixed with the unsynchronized emotions of a different track entirely and all played back like a movie with no director. Ethan's nocturnal phantasms were always in muted shades of blue, like Picasso's Blue Era, but literal in their aesthetics instead of expressionist. Most of the time his mind's wanderings were centered around one time and place, a singular moment overshadowed by the horrible sorrow of failure... of her death. It was a death he could have stopped, even if it had meant stepping in front of the proverbial bullet. This was his thought as he stood at parade rest behind a diesel-powered generator. It was the dead of night, his rifle shouldered as the squad waited to fire the three salvoes of the 21 Gun Salute.*

Trash.

Fire.

The smell of burn pits.

Air that felt like fire.

Don't flinch, you're a soldier, an M.P. This is what you do. The First Sergeant, the one who replaced the old one now under investigation, sounds Roll Call. She doesn't answer...

Keith woke up some time later to the microwave beeping, which meant the power had gone off again during the night. Ethan was gone from the recliner, which immediately startled his friend to action. Keith jumped up and ran outside. The side-by-side was still there, but the doors to the garage were wide open. Fearing the worst he ran into the old wood and stone shed and breathed a near gasp of relief that Ethan was still there. He was sitting on the hood of the town car that looked the worse for wear, a dozen empty beers laying all around it along with some rusty looking tools and a frayed jumper cable that had been taped over maybe just one too many times.

"I thought you'd taken off."

"That were the plan," Ethan exaggerated his accent like a cartoon hillbilly. Two more empty half-pint bottles of whiskey on the ground behind him suggested he must have been at this most of the early morning. Motion caught Ethan's eye and he looked past Keith towards the road, cocking his head slightly in bewilderment. A solitary zombie was shuffling along, her arm had been either gnawed, or ripped off and she was dragging most of her lower belly fat in a long trail between her legs. They both knew the woman, she'd been selling beer alongside Main street the last three days, even going so far to still check ID's. Nobody was left to enforce that, yet she was a good enough woman she didn't want children drinking alcohol. She didn't deserve this, nor her husband whose brilliant foresight to steal the Budweiser truck he drove had maybe saved them all from dying sober (the worst of all fates in Ethan's mind.)

"How in the hell?" Keith said to himself, posing like Superman while craning his neck back to look. Before he could ask Ethan what they should do, what felt like a cannon from behind him broke the dawn silence. Keith didn't flinch at gunshots anymore, but this one was danger close and he leapt backwards some. Birds in the country don't usually make much of a scene when a gun goes off, but this time a huge flock of crows sailed overhead, cawing as the mutilated zombie flopped down in a pile of her own juices. Looking back at Ethan, Keith watched him work the bolt of his Remington and toss another beer bottle down the driveway.

"I guess we gotta go check out her house," he tossed Keith the keys to the Gator they'd commandeered from the college. Apparently, the Crown Vic in the shed still needed more work still. "You drive, I'm pretty fuckered right now," Ethan wobbled on his feet despite just having made an expert headshot, through the ears, at no less than a hundred and fifty meters.

"Do you know where she lived?" Keith's ears were still ringing a little.

"Are you too stupid to follow a blood trail?" The point conceded, they were off on another gruesome adventure. They radioed the officer on duty, Reynolds this time and told him the address before dismounting the vehicle just behind the bend. Helena McMann had been his neighbor for almost thirty years and though she and his grandmother attended church together, the families at large weren't especially close. He did know most of them in passing though and that they lived in a three-story farmhouse on a rocky outcropping just above average flood stage. The less awful scenario would be that the old lady was bitten and wandered off during the rage phase, leaving her family in relative safety. Of course, that wasn't the case, otherwise this wouldn't be a horror story.

The scene around the house by the river flats might as well have been Omaha Beach for all the dismembered bodies lying between it and the water. Ethan and Keith were bonafide war veterans, they'd collectively seen and done some really bad shit that would haunt them for the rest of their lives, but even this wasn't anything they could readily grasp at first glance. It was even worse than what some people were already referring to as the "Valley Massacre." Word of what had happened when they'd confronted the roaming gang members had leaked quickly and a few malcontents were even considering starting a newspaper just to cover the one story. Most notably though, those were the people who hadn't actually been there. The precarious position of power the SPD and Mayor Kenly enjoyed over the town was being threatened from within as well as from outside, but that was almost to be expected. This war zone less than a mile from Ethan's home, was not.

The demise of this local branch of the vast McMann clan had met its end in a sad way. After a few minutes digesting what they were seeing, it became clear how. A goo trail from a torso-zombie had dragged itself out of the Meramec River, through the unkempt grass and toward the lanterns that had been left lit on the porch. It need only to have bitten one person to start the slaughter and now twelve more were undead. Whomever had been on guard duty had really dropped the ball, but this was of course assuming they'd followed municipal advice and had someone awake at all times. Even their dogs had been slaughtered, though thankfully never to reanimate. Children's out-door toys littered the yard as well, some covered in blood like macabre finger paintings. At least by now Ethan was becoming more desensitized to seeing dead children trying to eat him and kept his liquor down.

Since they hadn't been spotted yet, Ethan and Keith waited for backup to arrive. Half an hour later three police cars and a five-ton loaded with deputies pulled in behind them. Ethan made a show of letting everyone look through his binoculars at the scene and strongly suggested they work on response times. After the briefing the men set about using a tactic a young man had suggested after watching the all-night battle to save the town. They would send out a fast runner, someone who could outrun anyone still in the Rage Phase, to make a lot of noise and get the undead to come after him. Then, like a slaughterhouse, the men would practice clubbing each zombie to death. The children, of which made up about half the undead, were shot from a distance. It seemed wrong somehow to club the little bastards up close.

The rest of the day Ethan stayed relatively drunk, Keith more than willing to drive around even though occasionally Ethan would take the vehicle on his own to do whatever the hell it was he did by himself. Keith also warned the South Gate not to let Ethan leave under any circumstance, but luckily he never tried. Maybe he knew about Keith's orders, maybe he didn't. As badly as he wanted to go to Kentucky, he wasn't that stupid. Adding insult to injury, later that day the phones failed altogether, marking just six days since Ethan's unit had thrown in the towel. For now, their only contact with the outside world would be drifters and zombies.

Chapter 8

"We need to send a scouting party to the nearest power plant," Reynolds suggested at one of the senior leadership's nightly meetings. The AC unit had been replaced and so nobody had to work in the parking lot anymore. "If they are safe enough to run the plant then they've got to have good protection. Maybe they'd be willing to send some men to help us with the gang in Bourbon. They're going to attack eventually, I just know it. We also need to see why, specifically, Labodie is still in use. There's no coal coming out of the mines anymore, they must just be using up what was already processed."

"What about the nuclear plants?" Rowe asked.

"The closest one is halfway to Kansas City," Reynolds informed his colleague. "We may be drawing some power from it, if it's even still online, but I do remember the news saying the NRC was attempting to put our nuclear reactors into standby mode, or whatever it's called. It was top on FEMA's docket before the signals went dark, but in any case, I'd say most of our power is still local, given that we are suffering rolling brownouts. Some of it might even be coming from the Bagnel Dam at Lake of the Ozarks. If that's true, though, it begs a whole new set of questions, chief amongst them why were we left behind if there's still power? There's nearly four thousand people here and a defensible position. There'd have to be a good reason we were left behind like this."

"We're still being powered by Labodie for sure. If there wasn't so much friggin' ash in the sky we could probably still see the exhaust stacks," Ethan confirmed. "We need to take a scouting party and find out who and what we're dealing with for sure. Best case scenario we find what you're looking for, most likely they tell us to bugger-off, but worst case we just informed an unknown force that we're still here, ripe for the picking."

Keith nodded, appreciating Ethan's unique concern, "We'll take a Humvee. We need a gunner, but the fewer people the better."

"I'll go," a hand raised from behind the group of deputies who'd gathered for the meeting. It was the kid who'd been on the gun when the bikers had shown up. Ethan could hardly believe he was still around, if it had been him he'd have sneaked out of town during the night and taken his chances on the road. He knew a good railroading when he saw it coming, hence a desire to protect the kid by keeping the helmet with the bullet damage. If *he* had it, nobody else could make it disappear.

"What's your name?" Ethan asked in front of the gathered people.

"Allen," the kid said quietly, seemingly aware now he was being stared at by everyone.

"Well, Allen, if we run into bandits I expect nothing short of gratuitous violence from you. Understand?" Ethan said with an authoritative voice. Allen nodded and never broke eye contact.

After the meeting Reynolds pulled Ethan aside, "Are you sure about taking that Broadwick kid? I'm not saying he's trigger happy, but..."

"I need to get the measure of the man. He's what, sixteen, seventeen maybe? Too young to join but old enough to fight," Ethan took a deep breath, watching the gathered deputies leaving the meeting room slowly. "He probably saved all our lives, shooting those men, but I'm also hearing rumors the ones we killed were just the tip of the spear. If their buddies put two and two together, Sullivan will be in their gun sights. I can easily see us needing him again."

Starting his nightly binge-drinking routine on the way home, Ethan didn't remember getting there... *his nightmares were the same again that night. The blue hues, familiar and cold in his warped and fuzzy periphery. He felt compelled to hold as still as possible, even to the point of muscle strain. Anxiety was strange like that, but all he could consciously dwell on was finding Nicole, or was it getting back to her? He'd lost his sense of direction as much as his sense of self over there. In the hellscape and heat sand he'd lost everything.*

Then the urge to run...

Waking to his heart thundering, Ethan scanned the dark and eerily silent room. At first, he hadn't recognized that he was in the furnished basement he and Nicole lived in, even if it was never quite good enough for her. It was cleaner than the rest of the house and full of the girly things she'd brought with her. None of it, however, hid the fact that as recently as the 1960's the basement had been the house's underground garage. A ramp from the driveway down into the cement foundation still existed, the retracting garage door replaced by a wall that matched as closely as they could the normal exterior.

Nicole was barely able to hide her contempt for this place and the lack of upward mobility it represented. Despite appearances and the voice of desperation that clawed and howled at the back of his mind to have his old life back, Ethan just wasn't the same as when he'd left. The evidence that Nicole didn't, or more likely couldn't, love this new Ethan anymore mounted every day. Every backhanded comment and roll of her eyes felt like knives going through his heart. Then one fine evening Patient Zero took a bite out of her boyfriend in a crappy little hotel on the outskirts of Nogales and the rest was... well, not history. Contemporary maybe.

The power kicked back on and dust blew out of the vent. For a moment Ethan caught a small trace of Nicole's fragrance, brown sugar and warm vanilla from one of those ritzy stores at the high-end mall in St. Louis. It was all he could do to keep his composure while he dressed and ate the last of the cereal without milk. Keith was already outside by the car smoking a cigarette when Ethan left the house.

"You ready for this?" Keith flipped the butt into the yard, displaying with a broad gesture that he had succeeded in reviving the badly cared-for Ford, "because I'll be honest, I'm not. I've come to rather like this last corner of civilization, it would be a shame to die now."

"I've lived here for twenty-six years and I feel exactly the same way," Ethan threw his kit into the back seat, except for a tin of Grizzly snuff. While letting the engine warm up he packed a respectable amount into his lower lip.

"So, where's *your* car?" Keith asked, finding an expired insurance card being used as a bookmark in a novel under the passenger seat. Between the sappy Louis L'Amour book and the name on the card being Norma, he reasoned this wasn't Ethan's personal vehicle.

Ethan closed his eyes with some force, pushing down another unpleasant memory. "Rotting in a lemon-lot on Fort Leonard Wood, right where they made me and every other recalled sonofabitch leave their cars. Why, you up for a road-trip?"

Keith nodded his head like he was going to say yes, building a moment of confused, false hope before dashing it with a hard, "No."

The Crown Victoria town car started rough, but stopped its infernal chugging noise when Ethan put it in drive, though the transmission felt like it had just thrown off a pound of rust before slipping into gear. "When my grandmother passed, year before last, we put her car in the shed because neither me nor mom could bring ourselves to sell it."

"This was her house before your parents, wasn't it?" Keith guessed.

"The land, yeah, but she and Grandpa moved around a lot after they retired, she didn't move back home until he passed in back '06. The original farm house burned down in the sixties, I think my mom said she was nine or ten when that happened." He pointed to an outcropping of trees at the far end of the unkempt field. If one looked hard enough, a broken concrete foundation and a few capped off, rusty old pipes remained amongst the thicket. "Lee and I used to pretend it was the Alamo," he smiled, trying not to get misty eyed. He failed.

"He'll come back," Keith put his hand on Ethan's shoulder. "You said he was in the Army too, right?" he was recalling one of their boredom-driven conversations while on walking patrol around the fences. "An officer, even."

Ethan only nodded, driving recklessly as usual, "I was thinking about this mission, but specifically about the worst-case scenario," he changed the subject.

"And that is?"

"I can't stress enough that we can't let the wrong people know Sullivan is still here. You were just talking about that slice of paradise, well, I can't speak for you or the kid, but I'd die to protect it. As a matter of fact, I'd kill you both and then myself, if it came to preventing just that," There was no hint that Ethan had said any of this in jest.

Keith blinked incredulously, "Man, am I glad I followed you home."

At the truck stop on the north end of town they found the Humvee already staged and provisioned for three days. Allen Broadwick was just finishing mounting the same M-240B on the turret that he'd been behind when the bikers were killed. Keith walked into the outpost, set up in the looted-out convenience store, to use the pisser. Meanwhile, Ethan went about checking the truck and chatting up his new gunner.

"How old are you, kid?"

"Sixteen. I'll be seventeen in January, assuming we live that long," he said, straightening up his back after struggling some to click the retaining pin into the gun-mount. True, it was a little rustier than it should have been.

"And how is it a high-schooler knows how to mount and load a machine gun?"

Allen jumped down onto the Humvee's hood and sat, "My older brother was in the Marines. Chris wanted me to know how to use any abandoned equipment in case..." Allen gestured at the overcast sky of the ashen apocalypse. "... well in case of this I guess."

"So where is Chris?" Ethan immediately regretted asking,

knowing the answer couldn't possibly be a good one. Christopher Broadwick was a well-known local football star from the graduating class just after Ethan's. That he wasn't home already should have been telling, but per usual Ethan was too hung over to read a room.

"He's dead, Sir. Another soldier shot him on accident. The Corps sent my parents an email..." That part hit home with Ethan, having seen both his and Lee's death notices in his inbox. "Fuckers couldn't even be bothered to send a letter or someone in person. What gets me is, it happened at the Battle of Georgetown. That wasn't a month ago. It was-"

"... right when the infection skipped the quarantine lines," Ethan finished the kid's sentence. That was almost precisely the day he'd arrived at Fort Leonard Wood, smoking a fat blunt and acting belligerent, hoping that failing a urinalysis would disqualify him from service. Obviously, it did not. In their darkest hour the Department of Defense was willing to take back anyone who wasn't already infected, or paraplegic and probably that last criteria was voted on by a narrow margin.

"I'm sorry, man. I didn't mean to interrupt... There's a lot of that going around these days is all. I got a similar email, only it was declaring *me* dead."

Allen smirked, "No shit?"

"Yeah. I'd have loved to have seen the chaplain's face if they'd sent someone, though. Look, we'll bring you home. I promise. That way your little brother doesn't have to get a visit from the Deputies." Ethan pointed to the left breast pocket of Allen's outdated woodland camouflage uniform, "Don't stand in the turret above this line. It's called name tape-defilade. Keeps you from ending up like those German bikers in *Raiders of the Lost Ark*."

"God you're old," Allen mocked.

Ethan gave serious thought to slapping the kid, but refrained. Aiming a knife-hand at Allen, through gritted teeth he quickly hissed, "The nineties were awesome, you mouthy little shit," just as Keith returned.

Keith started the up-armored M1114. It had been undergoing routine maintenance when the Army pulled out, so they'd simply abandoned it rather than take the time to put the battery back in and refill all the fluids. Keith turned the switch and waited seemingly forever for the orange light to turn off, then he cranked the engine and let it run a little to warm the crew compartment.

"Have you ever seen a war-torn landscape before?" Keith asked Allen, who shook his head no. "It's a sight that will never go away, kid. I'd say you're better off staying home and sitting this one out, but now your home *is* the war zone, so you're just going to have to accept the nightmares and cowboy the fuck up like the rest of us."

"Cowboys aren't real," Allen caught Keith off guard. "They're just a marketing scheme that became part of Americana like Santa Claus, only Marlboro made them up instead of Coca Cola."

Keith just stared at Allen blankly, "Is everyone from Missouri this macabre, or are you and Ethan some kind of kindred spirits? Because I'm beginning to think there is something genuinely wrong with both of you." Handing out the truck's internal headsets, they all tested them with standard greetings.

"It's an extreme lack of parental guidance, I assure you," Allen's voice chirped over the headset now that they were situated. *"My parents haven't left Chris' room in days. I don't blame them, but Jimmy is twelve and he needs them to be parents again. I just can't stay there and watch them wish they were dead too, its fucking depressing."*

Keith looked over at Ethan, confirming that this was an unsolicited admission. *"Damn, kid. I take back all the things I ever said about Ethan's life being a sad, lonely and kinda depressing mess."*

Ethan almost pouted, *"You never said any of that."*

"I didn't? Well, I meant to."

Since he was the only one who knew where they were going, Ethan drove the first leg of the trip. It didn't take long before not only his knowledge of the area, but Allen's trusted machine gun were both tested. The deputies had done a fair job of keeping a rough parameter relatively zombie free, but they'd had less success with reducing the number of highwaymen and general thieves in the few miles around town. At the junction of Hwy-185 and H, a late 90's model Nissan pickup started following them. It was hidden behind a taxidermist's office, but it might also have been just coincidence, the truck pulling onto the road at the same time they were passing. However, when the two men in the back tried to stand up and shoot at them, all bets were off.

Allen swung the turret around and belted off a little under twenty rounds into the pursuer's engine. The truck exploded in a rolling dumpster-fire of screaming men and broken glass that quickly lurched to a stop when it hit the drainage ditch on the far side of the road. When the three men went back to survey the damage, they found only one of the six still barely alive. His legs were broken backward at the knees and the upper receiver of a Kolashnikov was lodged in his abdomen just below the right lung. He was clearly going into shock when Keith started triage, but unlike his medic buddy, Ethan had had enough of these bastards already. It was his assumption they were all part of a larger gang that was testing the town's borders.

"Well that was monumentally stupid." Towering over the dying man, Ethan drew the 1903 Colt semi-automatic his grandfather had handed down to him. "Haven't you dumb-fucks ever heard of a Humvee? They carry machine guns and pissed off soldiers with more guns. So now you and your friends are dead and for what? What is it you thought we had in that shitty Army leftover that you thought you needed to die for?" In the worst way he wanted to kick the man, not for being a thief or for shooting at them, but for being so stupid.

Blood bubbled from his mouth, but even up in the Humvee's turret Allen could clearly hear the dying man plead to be shot before the zombies got to him. Ethan raised the gun, but Keith stayed his hand, opting instead to stick the bandit with the suicide-cocktail he'd prepared for himself in case he was bitten. It was basically a heavy dose of heroin and the drug that killed Michael Jackson, which all things considered, was a much more peaceful way to go than most people could ask for these days.

"Do I want to know how long you've been packing that?" Ethan asked as Keith headed back to the Humvee.

"Want me to make you one too?" Keith offered. Ethan's contemplative face gave him his answer.

Through open countryside, beautiful in the late summer, they saw hundreds of undead people just wandering in the fields. None of them made much effort to go after the truck and most looked half rotted already, though looks were deceiving when it came to the infected. The smell of death and fire hadn't let up and flies could be seen in droves that blotted out the sun like birds. Shit eating birds. The sun was warming them fast and Ethan switched on the air conditioner, one of the few things that made the combat vehicle bearable on long trips. The seats were uncomfortable "floatation devices" (as if this truck wouldn't sink like a stone with you in it,) and his ass was already numb from sitting. *Maybe,* Ethan mused, he could take the seat out and weld something more comfortable in place, *like a medieval torture device, or a display-size dildo.* Anything was better than the standard green cushion, that despite temperatures was somehow never fully dry.

A shot pinged off the truck's armor and Allen put a burst into the wood line as they reached the nearly forgotten community of Beauford. The shots were not repeated, whether Allen had scared them or killed them, the effect was the same. They also encountered a dozen more abandoned Army checkpoints, some of the former defenders still meandering about with those pale, dead eyes, black goo dripping from every orifice. They stopped to investigate one checkpoint before entering the outskirts of Union again, but were disappointed to find the soldiers had destroyed their heavy weapons before taking off on foot to parts unknown. It wasn't lost on either of them that they might have met some of the people who'd been stationed at these checkpoints. They'd abandoned them, been caught by the locals and that's when they were forced to clear the college too.

The winding route to avoid the major known traffic snarls made a forty-five-minute drive last three excruciating hours. The Labodie river bottoms came into view slowly, overgrown in thickets of tall grass. Allen made sure not to shoot any infected, no matter how close they were, so as not to draw attention from the living. Ethan was preparing to turn around and go back to a second dirt road he felt might lead where he wanted when an explosion in front of them made him slam the brakes. A zombie he'd earlier decided to avoid had stepped on a land mine and was blown several feet into the air. It landed with a thud and with no more ceremony than an exhale of air it didn't really need, dragged its legless torso off into the reeds that grew wild in the river bottoms.

"They mined it?" Keith's jaw dropped, *"We gotta get off this road."*

Ethan took a swig of water, *"I have to piss. We're still out of view, we can find another road in a minute."* Clearly, he wasn't phased by much anymore.

They were on a small hill behind a dense thicket of young trees, all knotted together by tangles of American Bittersweet and reasonably well hidden from main roads or the power plant itself. Aside from the zombie who'd been blown up, there were no other undead around. The silence was deafening, not even the insects made noise. Not the squirrels or birds either. Ethan took his rifle and scanned the area, the thin black crosshairs dancing over dark shadows in the trees. The unshakable feeling that he was being watched made his hair stand on end. Could someone already know they were there? Absolutely, the rule of thumb being *if you can see them, they can see you.*

"Allen, stay with the truck. Make sure your turret never stops moving for more than a couple of seconds, I got my throat 'cut' with a red marker during a training mission because I wasn't watching behind me," Ethan warned. The memory of how embarrassed he was that he'd allow that to happen to himself had been a powerful learning tool. Of course, where were the two fuckheads assigned to pull security on foot, he could only have guessed.

"My ass is asleep," Allen complained, unzipping his pants to piss in a bottle.

"We'll look into a better gunner's seat," Keith promised as he set his backpack on the hood. "Let's go to the tree line and see what we can see." He pulled a machete out of a sheath, feeling like a badass with a sword. Together the two men walked to the edge of the dust covered forest, the ash clinging to their sweaty clothes. This region hadn't had a solid rainfall in weeks, not to mention the particulate choking out the sun. While the soft mechanical whir of the rotating turret faded into the background they used their gun sights to scan the area. Commanding little attention, except that it was nearly directly in their path, Ethan read aloud a red, triangular sign that had several languages stenciled on it in bold white lettering.

DANGER MINES
PELIGRO MINAS
GEFAHR LANDMINEN
警告地雷
مرحاض

Ethan could still read a little Arabic and tried his best to translate, just for his own amusement. The Arabic script read "Toilet" rather than a warning about mines. Some genius's idea of a joke and it worked. Ethan shoved his face into his arm to muffle hysterical laughter. This was the exact kind of schadenfreude that appealed to his inner spiteful nature. After all, he never claimed to be the good guy.

Keith didn't get why Ethan was laughing at first, but had to stifle his own when his friend translated for him. Keith put the binoculars to his eyes and leaned against a tree for stabilization. Ethan provided security and pulled out a camera to film the power plant. It had zoom and he utilized it to better effect than the idiots who filmed "*Cloverfield.*" He filmed every landmine on the road before the tall grass obscured them. Most mines hadn't been hidden at all because the undead were too dumb to avoid them, but later review of the footage might reveal hidden anti-vehicle mines too. The explosives probably went all the way up to the main parking lot before the Hesco bastions came into view. The entire place had been fortified and a Sally Port for trains stretched half a mile stretched half a mile in either direction. It was a drastic change to the power plant Ethan had toured with a school group as a child. Construction equipment and workers were finishing the final few concrete sections that would effectively turn the plant into a castle, though now they'd taken a break for lunch and couldn't be effectively observed.

"This is insane," Keith said softly. Another mine blew up on the other side of the property. None of the visible guards pacing along the power plant's roof bothered to investigate with more than a casual glance.

"Its government run, as far as I can see. As long as we know where they are and they don't know where we are, I don't see any reason to bother them. We're deserters, remember? Who knows who they ultimately answer to."

"Yeah," Keith sighed with some disappointment. Then excitedly pointed to the right of them, "No fuckin' way."

"What?"

"Zoom in on that guy in the guard tower. This is some straight-up Orwellian shit man."

The camera zoomed in and recorded the soldier lazily smoking a cigarette, "Dude, that's the Texas state flag."

"Is Texas an independent nation now?" The implications were profound, but there was more to see. Ethan pointed out a zombie chained and bound by a leather dog harness meant for police K9's, "Look at that poor motherfucker."

The camera panned down to a zombie trapped knee deep in ash turned to mud, a wire fence around the pit and a sign that read **DO NOT APPROACH. SENTRIES WILL OPEN FIRE WITHOUT WARNING.** The Texans were monitoring this zombie's decay, seeing how long it would take them to rot without killing it first. "They're watching him to see how long it takes a zombie to get from the point of infection to putrefaction."

"That's... Just really fucked up, man."

"We should do the same."

"What?"

Ethan shrugged. "Why not?"

"Think about what the gangs in Bourbon are doing to the infected. We can't cross that line," Keith shook his head. "I guess if you're gonna do it... Just leave me out of it."

"You can do anything you want as long as you word it right on the paperwork. One of my previous sergeants-major taught me that," Ethan stepped back, having already turned the camera off before speaking. Keith raised a finger to ask for more about that story, but Ethan cut him off. "I've got everything we need. Halliburton is up to its usual, subtly creepy nation building with the military as their muscle and the rest of us are caught in the middle... so really nothing has changed, except the zombies," Ethan shrugged. "I say let's get back to town and take care of those fuckers in Bourbon while we can still come home to a hot shower and Central Air. I can't imagine these guys sparing resources for a local problem."

Keith wanted to gather more intel, but he had to admit Ethan was right when he suggested they had more important things to do than rock the proverbial boat with this bunch. The part about Halliburton was just one of Ethan's tin-foil-hat theories being vocalized. Allen voiced his own opinion that they'd basically wasted an entire day putting a permanent crease in his ass from the gunner's strap, so Keith was kind enough to volunteer to take the seat on the way back. Ethan had already flipped the ready switch to turn the Humvee on when they heard a train in the sally port pull forward with a loud series of clangs. They watched, impressed at the scale as the next few cars were cleared to unload their coal. It was a process that ran smoothly and efficiently, apparently not a lot more time consuming than it had been during peacetime. The Texans were already running a finely tuned machine and since it was benefiting them, it felt like interrupting these fine folks was just a variation of biting the hand that feeds you. Turning the Humvee around like a pro on the narrow dirt road, Ethan headed back toward home with due haste.

"*So what do you want to tell them?*" Allen asked, enjoying having a solid seat behind him on the ride back.

"*There's not much to tell. We can analyze the video later, but it's a safe assumption they're only working on the supplies that are left. Eventually it'll run out of coal and they'll shut down their operation,*" Ethan mostly guessed. "*Who knows what they'll do when they don't have a reason to be here anymore.*"

Chapter 9

The Longest Day

The sky was uncharacteristically clear for this stage of the end times and for once a reasonable amount of patchy sunlight lit the roads between the trees. Officer Rowe was on duty when they got back to the station, the mayor's car was just pulling away.

"You'd think he'd want to hear about the mission," Keith mused to himself. Finding out why the man had left in such a hurry would wipe the smile off his face.

"Seven more girls were found wandering outside of town, between here and Bourbon. Three more were infected and were clearly chasing the others. They said the men there gave them a head start and bet on who'd get tired first." Rowe made it obvious the Texans, as well as the zombies, were a close number two on the list of shit on her mind.

"After attacks like this, the town will rally behind us. We could invade and wipe them out," Newton suggested and Reynolds agreed.

"Not a chance," Ethan shook his head. "It's held by a coordinated, initiated and motivated biker gang. I'd bet dollars to pesos at least half of them are combat veterans and the other half are just violent psychopaths looking for an excuse. We go assaulting them with two soldiers and a bunch of incensed idiots who are *maybe* hunters at best, some vets even... My point is, the bad guys would probably win through sheer violence and what would that mean for those left behind? For these girls? How many do we risk leaving defenseless here? We risk giving them more prisoners, new equipment and worst of all, an excuse."

"Well, what's your brilliant plan?" Rowe quipped.

Ethan ignored her implied insult, partly because he was too tired to care and largely because Rowe's opinion meant precious little to him at this point, "We do what Gunnery

Sergeant Carlos Hathcock did to a company of North Vietnamese. Two snipers go in, pick a location on a hill and wipe 'em out methodically until they're either all dead or scattered," Ethan explained. "We need only risk two."

"So who's the sacrificial victim, you and...?" Keith almost laughed, looking for others to disagree with the plan. When none did, he knew he'd just been volunteered. "For the record Ethan, I hate you. I just wanted you to know before we die, that I hated *you* the most."

Ethan smiled, "Ya know, a Sergeant Major by the name of Campbell said something remarkably similar to me once, except we were in Iraq and zombies weren't real yet."

"Kenly wants this kept quieter than before," Reynolds said, sipping cheap smelling coffee and making certain no unwanted ears were nearby. "Four more people got infected trying to gather supplies in St. Clair and another five were shot by rival looters over what was left in a Dollar General. The last thing we need is bad press, folks barely respect our authority as is. We can't afford a breakdown in the faith these people put in us. They're very close to simply giving up on any kind of unity, especially if we can't protect them. If you fail to stop the gang, we can't be associated with it."

Keith shook his head, mulling the problem over, "Let us deal with Bourbon tonight, then you can start organizing official scavenging parties with armed escorts when we get back." It did strike him as optimistic to say "when."

"I'll make up some flyers to recruit from the Deputies. Nobody wants to make leaving the town an order, at least not yet," Reynolds folded his arms, breathing heavily. The humidity wasn't doing him any favors, but through this whole *running for your life* thing he'd already lost a good deal of weight.

On their way home he and Keith visited the girls in the hospital. There was apparently no limit to this gang's depravity and it set a mood among the nurses and deputies assigned to patrol the building. A blonde girl in her late twenties had lost an eye, another had actually been flogged with a bullwhip. Yet another miscarried a fetus somewhere down the road and almost bled to death as she was forced to cut the umbilical cord with a knife she'd found. With no fire for sterilization she'd had to abandon her stillborn before her infected sister could chase her down and kill her too. It wasn't said aloud, but in the report the only qualified psychiatrist still alive noted that "had the infant's corpse not been distracted by the mother's infected sister, the zombie likely would have chased them down and killed her." A taller girl caught Ethan's trained eye and he realized *she* was a formality.

Pulling *her* off to one side of the larger bay area, Ethan drew the curtain so no one could hear their conversation, "You'll have to forgive my coarseness, it's been a long apocalypse, but I've seen what they've done to women who were born women. I know how large groups of psychotic alpha-males behave, so how is it you weren't killed outright when they discovered you're trans? I've arrested men for beating a prostitute they didn't know was only moonlighting as a lady and they were just a couple drunk lance corporals... How did you live through... *them?*" His expression lightened, trying not to come across as unsympathetic.

"Crass," she said, her voice feminine, but more like that of a prepubescent boy with so much stress put on a practiced octave, "but you're not wrong. They figured me out after a few days locked in that damned train car they keep us unfortunates in. Most of the ringleaders have done hard time, so girl, ladyboy, actual boy, it really doesn't seem to matter to them. What was it the big one said, 'butt-pussy's still pussy.'"

Ethan had nothing for that. He tried to say he was sorry but she cut him off, "Now, in case you're wondering, Deputy, there's nothing down there anymore, which gave them all sorts of things to laugh about... and shove up in there..." She started crying. "I had breasts, before *them*, Deputy. *I was a fully defined woman.*" Ethan noticed the chest bandages under her shirt for the first time. Unable to do anything but lean into this shitstorm, he actually reached out and hugged her. What else could he do?

All of these poor women had been savagely beaten and raped, patches of hair torn or cut away. The first girl they'd met, before the mission to Labodie, was talking to the one who'd lost an eye, trying to make a prettier bandana to encompass the eye-patch. The one-eyed woman had been homecoming queen once upon a time, startlingly beautiful, though that wasn't to say she had lost any of her visual appeal. Scars had a strange beauty to them, suggestive of a strong person to make it through brutal injuries. She sat in total silence for now though, eye wide and unblinking at a mirror, unable to comprehend why she was made to suffer like this.

"I'm glad you guys came back," the first girl said, a nametag stuck to her chest read "Hello I'm PAULA." She'd started talking again, if only to be there for the other victims. "So, when are you going?" She seemed excited by the idea of Ethan and Keith dealing revenge and death on her behalf. "I mean, you are going to go kill them *all*, right?"

Ethan was about to talk about gathering intelligence first, but Keith took Paula's hand and kissed it gently. *"All of them."* He said, his eyes never leaving hers while the other victims watched. They left and didn't discuss Keith's gesture, because it wasn't a gesture. It was a promise that they would make into reality. There was no way Sullivan could let the gangs controlling the lawless little town next door remain in control of even one block, one building. How long would it be before they attacked in force if the two men failed? How many more girls would suffer at their hands, how many were suffering even as they spoke? *It was time to parole these shit-lickers straight to Jesus*, Ethan thought.

It was nearly dark when they headed for Bourbon, not a wink of sleep between them. The mission was kept a secret from Allen, lest he try to join. It was one thing to let him guard an armored truck that could be sealed like a pillbox, but they weren't bringing one of those. Inventorying all the weapons the Army had neglected to take or destroy, most stored in a modified 5-ton labeled Mobile Arms Room that was difficult to break into. A welder had to get the hinges off and not destroy the contents of the truck and that was no small task by design. They'd been delayed finding all the right gear for a prolonged sniper attack too, some of the Army's connexes were improperly labeled, or not labeled at all and there was no time to wait for that mess to be cleaned up. Though there were surely machine guns they could have taken with them, those were in one of the unmarked containers. The guns that were already set up would have to stay in town in case the worst happened.

Instead of the most current load carrying vests and body armor systems, they had to settle for Vietnam era gear from the back of a pawn shop, augmented by Ethan's personal collection of random military junk. He took his grandfather's Remington .243, a Mossberg 500 tactical and his antique Colt in case he needed to blow his own brains out rather than risk capture. Keith's standard loadout of medical supplies was left in town, so he carried an M-4, two M-9's and extra ammunition for all of their guns. Tonight, he wasn't saving lives, he was going to take as many of them as he could before what he considered the inevitable. There was probably a good quote in there somewhere about dining in hell or Valhalla. Sadly, Ethan was perpetually too hungover to quote things he'd only heard once and Keith didn't know that much about Norse mythology. They settled for somber silence.

Around 9 pm, just after dark, they crept along the South Service Road with their lights off, barely going above twenty. Choosing to travel in a nondescript, blue Chrysler Voyager from the early 2000's, was a calculated risk. It had no armor and the engine was capable of all the get-up and go of a heavily laden oxen cart. On the bright side, it didn't make the kind of noise a Humvee did and attracted little visual attention from the norm in its mildewed and partially rusted-out state. With random suitcases and totes lazily strapped on top of it and a missing handle on the outside of the wrong-colored passenger side door, they would easily be mistaken for an abandoned vehicle, even before the zombies.

Ethan parked outside what was left of several houses in a speed trap zone the Bourbon PD constantly stalked, once upon a time that is. When FEMA evacuated this berg, the houses at the edge of town were looted first, stripped down to virtually any part that might be used to further fortify someone else's property. The quiet bedroom community more resembled a war-zone than some actual war zones.

Keith had the idea to put the van's jack under the front bumper, raising it just enough to make it appear someone was working on it. The rear wheels were still on the ground, so they could get away in a hurry if they reversed. Donning face paint and their gear, the two men worked in even more intense silence than before, trying to keep their breathing quiet even. Ethan's inner thoughts dwelled on how he felt it was better they do this deed than someone who didn't yet know the evil of murder, didn't have to live with a living man's blood on his hands. Keith's motivations, on the other hand, were entirely about chivalry and his sense of justice. He wanted to punish these wicked men and he was utterly uninterested in their version of events. There would be no quarter.

Staying low, the two men all but crawled along the road now. They had to stay out of the grass unless they needed to hide from a random biker, what with zombies still being a threat and all. Stray dogs were everywhere and the cats in the town were breeding like rabbits with fangs already. The animals avoided the two men, used to being chased and abused by the man-cunts who'd taken over. Ethan could smell campfires and see the flickering of flames from the burned-out mayor's office. The scene was a nightmare from a poorly written, 1980's Mad Max-style grindhouse flic. Bearded men danced around bonfires with booze, guns, motorcycles and what looked like a free basin of cocaine and crushed pills that one could walk up to and take a hearty snort from. They had equipment that was clearly meant to be some kind of drug lab already set up out of a U-Haul truck. Ethan thought how best to explode it for them, wishing any of the weapons inventoried back home had been an M-203 grenade launcher.

Neither had put on mosquito repellent for fear the smell would give them away, but now they regretted it as there was nothing they could do except let the insects buzz in their ears and eyes. Nothing, except maintain the highest level of discipline. All the bikers had guns and indiscriminate use of black leather was the local uniform, making some of them hard to see in the flickering light of the fires and scattered street lamps, but with a little effort the two identified three separate encampments with clustered targets silhouetted by fire.

"This reminds me of a meme I saw," Ethan whispered. "Tired of both Neo Nazi wannabes and Muslim-Foot-Lickers, Statler and Waldorf plan to resurrect the glorious, *authentic,* German Empire by inviting both groups to the theater and gunning them all down with a *Maschinegewehr '08!*"

Keith just stared at Ethan for a second, a mosquito taking up residence in his ear, "Well, did you bring a machine gun?"

"No."

"Then shut the fuck up, Carl." Keith was maybe more amused at his meme reference than Ethan was with his.

After another thirty minutes of spying, it was also clear who was who among the gathered sociopaths. Two full-fledged Hells Angels, sporting their cuts and making a show of being the only legit "One Percenters" there, were hard to miss. About a hundred wannabes milled about, worshiping the ground these two human turds walked on. The uglier of the two and the worst dressed with tasseled chaps, motioned for everyone to get closer to listen to him while two piggish men hauled a "fresh" girl from the train car the woman Ethan had talked to had mentioned. Too defeated to fight back, she was dragged onto a fine oak dining table that had surely been taken from someone's home. Knife marks and blood had replaced the tablecloth and candles on this ornate antique with unfathomable depravity.

What they were planning to do to this poor girl was so evil it was almost beyond imagination, *almost*. Clearly, she was about to be a sacrifice of sorts and in that moment the snipers realized tomorrow was too far away, five minutes from now was too far away. The girl was already bound and gagged on the table, helpless like livestock she would be used and abused by every sack of salty shit in the square if they didn't act just right the fuck *now*.

Ethan took aim. This was the first time he'd actually have to kill a living person, not just be in charge when others killed on his behalf. Despite all the bravado and air of competence, Ethan's gut sank and he wrestled with that little voice in his head that replayed what every combat vet and cop who'd ever pulled trigger had said to him. Collectively it went something like: *Once you cross that line, once you take a life in anger, you change. You can act the same and appear fine for the sake of others, but you'll never forget the eternity long moments between making up your mind to pull the trigger and actually doing it.*

In their hearts, neither man believed this was what a benevolent God would have wanted, but then that was an issue they could take up with their creator when the time came. The simple black crosshairs of the aging hunting scope danced slightly as Ethan controlled his breathing, ate a mosquito on accident and honed in on his target. The biggest, ugliest motherfucker he'd ever seen tossed his beer aside and tore the girl's dirty, blood stained pants off like they were made of paper. They couldn't hear her screams over the cheering and music from crackling, damaged speakers, but surely it was bloodcurdling.

The pops of celebratory gunfire directed into the air were mostly what helped them do the deed, more so even than the tropey classic rock every biker gang seemed obsessed with. Keith spotted targets and Ethan eliminated them. The man about to rape the girl took a high velocity round, meant to drop full grown deer, to the back of the head, It exploding it into pink mist and clumps of hairy skull matter that rained down on the already traumatized girl. His body flopped forward on her too, possibly shielding her from the carnage about to unfold.

The crowd stared in disbelief as another round impacted the headless man's second-in- command in the lower gut. He would be dead momentarily, but for now he held his entrails as if they were so much tangled rope, horrified by his fate. The men who'd seen the shooting scattered, but the others were too messed up to even notice as their friends started dropping in the ensuing chaos. The Remington rifle Ethan carried wasn't silenced, in fact, to be downrange of it was like standing near a cannon, but he'd built up a mound of brush to conceal the muzzle flashes and wasn't spotted through two painfully long reloads. Likely, Keith killed more of them with the M-4 than Ethan did with the bolt-action, but the power and precision of the rifle was devastating. That it belonged to him personally before the zombies was powerful symbology that the world might never know about, but it made Ethan proud.

Dropping more and more "road-warriors", targeting specifically those who were shooting back or making for their bikes, the two men lost track of time. A few shots had been sent back to Ethan, but generally the men were too drunk or high to target his already hidden muzzle flashes. Able to squirm out from under the dead blob on top of her, the intended sacrificial girl ran away early in the fight and they lost track of her, but continued to harry the gang until their ammo was expended.

With all but the most inebriated enemies scattered, Ethan and Keith swept the area for more captives. They found the boxcar but nobody was left in it. Satisfied that they'd done serious damage and still wanting to escape, the men egressed as quietly as possible. As a last measure to distract not only the enemy, but the undead that were beginning to arrive they both threw flashbangs far to the left of their position and ran for it. Since he hadn't had a reason to commit honorable hari-kari, Keith left two claymore mines lazily rigged in the street, assuming rightly that someone on a bike wouldn't see it in time. One went off before they made it back to the van, the other must have been a dud.

The trip home took until dawn because of a hair-raising experience hiding from the few sober gang members that had started to search for them and because of a small swarm of hidden zombies that tried to tip their vehicle when their first hiding place was compromised. Keith only just managed to manually roll the window back up before the first pair of marbled fingers could force it back down. By the time they reached the South Checkpoint they were exhausted, hungry, dirty, covered in bites and completely out of ammunition. Ethan had taken two full boxes and a partial into battle, all bought by his grandfather before the turn of the millennium. The good news was he hadn't missed very many times and the better news was the rifle would look fantastic above the mantle now.

Kenly, Reynolds, Rowe and Newton all arrived at the station shortly thereafter. They finished breakfast before Kenly waddled up to ask what had happened, knowing full well he wouldn't hesitate to interrupt their rare sit-down meal.

"I'm pretty sure we killed anyone with anything to do with the girls, but let's prepare for a counter attack," Ethan rubbed his temples. "Unless we get any more problems like this, I suggest we start minding our own business. The less attention we draw the better for now..." There was more to say, but his head hurt.

"The deputy is absolutely right." Newton's nasally voice irritated Ethan, even though he was agreeing with him. Ethan envied John and thought maybe it was time he reconsidered hating the apocalypse too.

"We finally got into them connexes the Army left and did a full inventory while you were gone," Reynolds ignored Newton and changed the subject. "There's MRE's and solar generators. We might actually stand a chance of not starving this winter."

"That's kind of amazing," Ethan was genuine. "I expected unlubricated condoms, Halal meals and wet-weather ponchos, because you know... *Army*."

Reynolds laughed from deep in his potbelly, "On to the good shit then; after we stopped hearing from DC, HAM operators and hackers holed up somewhere in Alaska crashed the Martial Law blackouts on 'unapproved' news sources like *Reddit, MeWe* and that *4Chan* site. You know, the one for the really sick fucks."

"Ah, the *Tin-Foil Hat* people," Ethan smiled. Internally he was forced to admit that most of his time on the internet had been thoroughly wasted watching porn, YouTube and then even more porn. Using forum sites ruled by American Otaku with neurosis out the ass hadn't appealed to him. He would never have thought to check those sites for activity as he was really only aware of them through memes that filtered onto the insidious, cornflower-blue *Facebook*.

"Yeah, but through them we're starting to see the scope of the damage. It's worldwide, just like the news said, but worse. The real problem is the internet is slowing down with each server and satellite lost. If more satellites go dark, so will the net. A popular theory circulating right now is that it came from China, all that fucked up Nazi-style experimentation they claim they never do."

"It's not going to pan out with obvious facts that it started in the U.S." Ethan countered, looking for a way to escape this conversation.

"The other theory, believe it or not, is the Affordable Healthcare Act *you-know-who* bullied through Congress back in Twenty-Ten is truly to blame. This *Reddit* user theorized the AHCA caused people to go to Mexico for their meds because doctors and prescriptions were in short supply," Reynolds' political beliefs were not uncommon in an area made only poorer by high gasoline and food prices and an ever-vanishing industrial base. Anger at the slow FEMA response and uncoordinated military actions against the Undead had won the President no favors in the rural areas of the Midwest. People around there wouldn't bat an eyelash at confirmation their government had caused this entire mess, intentional or otherwise. After all, the Soviets had let Chernobyl happen, why shouldn't the US create its own world-shattering event? "They're saying some fake meds the Mexicans cooked up to sell to us Gringos started all this."

"That's an adorable theory," Ethan rolled his eyes and downed some black coffee, "We all saw the news. The homeless camps were where the outbreaks started. Filthy conditions, hard drug use, no law enforcement or medical services readily available. It's a wonder the Black Plague didn't make a comeback first." *They could raid the supplies from every neighboring town so that there was a surplus of peanuts and coffee of all things, but no one could be bothered to grab sweetener?* Ethan's internal monologue was becoming louder as the fatigue pulled at him like increasing gravity. It also bothered him that something as pointless as having peanuts, but no sweetener bothered him. He had so much more to worry about he didn't need to be burdened by the little things anymore. "I'll be at home if you need me."

"I need to sleep for a week," Keith groaned his favorite complaint, following Ethan out of the overpass checkpoint. They drove past a farmer bringing in supplies he'd looted from who knew where, his "employees" in the back of his wagon. They all looked exhausted too, blood stained their clothes and their expressions said they'd slept about as much as Ethan and Keith had. *Even these people knew more about the world around them than we do*, Ethan thought.

"Those poor bastards…" Keith turned his head, watching them pass by.

"I don't know how much longer I can wait for Lee," Ethan's reply was a little off topic, but not unexpected.

"Don't be stupid. You'll wait for him as long as it takes." Keith pointed to a new plume of smoke in the sky, almost absently asking, "Hey, isn't that Meramec State Park?" He'd been studying the local geography and was quite proud of himself for it. Ethan nodded, spotting the plume for himself. His eyes widening as he realized what was going on. Slamming the brakes on the rickety Crown Vic, they both craned their necks back to look at the smoke. It plumed black as night, so it wasn't a brush fire, at least not yet.

"Yeah, it's the park," another plume rose into the sky in that brief time. "Fuck," Ethan turned the vehicle around and raced back toward the police station. Apparently everyone in town was as observant as they were and a 5-ton was already being loaded with whomever was nearby and willing. Most anyone around had figured out by now that if the town didn't defend itself, they'd all be picked off one by one by zombies or raiders. Cooperation was becoming unexpectedly high amongst the survivors.

"No rest for the wicked," Keith jumped into a patrol car with Officer Rowe. Ethan took the passenger seat of the 5-ton to man the radio and a gun. Truth be told he was probably too delirious to drive anyway.

"Master Control, this is-" Ethan looked over at Officer Newton in the driver's seat for their call sign. Newton shrugged, so Ethan made it up, "MC, this is QRF Six. Any radio traffic from the state park?"

"*Negative, QRF. The area was supposed to be abandoned. Break.*" There was a pause, Ethan didn't speak. "*Proceed with caution, if radios fail return to higher ground.*" Reynolds came through clearly, at least for now.

"Wilco, MC," Ethan pulled out his walky-talky, which should be a different radio band than the one in the truck. "Officer Rowe, we're ready to rock 'n roll."

Without an answer the patrol car crept forward, several pickups with lift kits and gun mounts spot-welded to their beds followed. Someone used window chalk to mark the trucks with numbers so they could be identified over the radio, which was definitely good thinking but looked lazy. There were a few military vehicles laying about, but those were at the I-44 checkpoints as the town's only real defense.

With any luck, the trucks they had could survive a small zombie horde and maybe give scavengers pause before trying their luck.

"Forgive me for not asking earlier," Ethan had to say a little louder than he wanted to in order to get Newton's attention over the din of the engine, "but why exactly did you, Rowe and Reynolds stay when all the others popped smoke?"

Newton gazed ahead with a smirk, "Liza and I got in trouble before the Army pulled out, so we weren't exactly high on the list for a spot on the evac flights."

"Oh?" Ethan loved a good *So No Shit, There I Was* story. It was his personal belief that some people, himself chief amongst them, existed for little other reason than to serve as a warning to others. In fact, this was almost verbatim what his last *legitimate* First Sergeant (as in someone who wasn't promoted just to fill a dead man's boots) said to him during perhaps what was their last "Nic and Ethan" time. It was something 1SG Nicolas Casey liked to do with troubled troops, call them into his office and take both their rank patches off. As long as you weren't disrespectful it was basically the same as attorney/client privilege. Ethan hadn't treated that man fairly, he felt in hindsight. Taking out his rage against a chain of command that had already been relieved, on the relief.

"We were assigned to keep the crowd at the middle school's FEMA camp under control. It was two cops against something like a thousand people, a real no-win situation if things turned ugly and they did. We used OC spray on a dozen people who were really out of line, turns out one of them was pregnant and another was some mucky-muck from the State Department," Newton laughed. It was a weird laugh that sounded like he could repeat it syllable by syllable if he needed to. "Long story short, he threw the mother of all tantrums in Chief Winslow's office and we were suspended until review. Of course, as you know, that review never came."

"That's epic, bro," Ethan shook his head, bracing himself when they made the turn toward Potosi. "I never got to mace a Commie, but I have been maced for training and that shit *suuuucks*."

Newton raised an eyebrow like Spock, as if he'd never considered that getting OC-spray in your eyes might not be pleasant. Had he enjoyed it or something? "When the Army and the rest of the people left, Liza and I were still sitting at our homes waiting to be hung out to dry for doing our jobs. George, on the other hand, is a reserve officer. He didn't even get activated until after I was suspended, but I don't know that the two things are related. I am, however, glad he stayed. It would be difficult to do our jobs with just the two of us."

"I can empathize. My last unit was a cobbled together headquarters company made up of a dozen different job titles with no surviving senior leadership to fill in the gaps. They conveniently forgot me and this guy in my platoon, Roberts, at our lookout post. He's dead now because of that..." The inner monologue in Ethan's head shouted *because of me!* "It didn't take two days and my parent's email accounts got an automated letter that says the Army thinks I'm dead too. Probably put us there just to shut me up."

"Really? What could you have said?"

"Well, I'm not the kind to kiss and tell, but since I wasn't the one getting kissed, fuck 'em. I caught my sergeant major getting a B-J from a female E3 and snapped a picture with a cell phone I wasn't supposed to have. It was my plan to extort him into letting me leave on a medical discharge, but suffice it to say I didn't get away with it because there's no Judge Advocate General or Inspector General to turn evidence over to anymore. My clever hiding place was found and I ended up drawing every shit detail for the next month... then I was assigned to a watchtower with my bunk-mate," Ethan sighed as the convoy turned for the hill down Highway 185. "Bottom line, John's death is on me. I got him stuck up there with me, I sent him to the first aid station where he got bit... It was all me."

"I think it's for the best the Army left you behind. Now you're here to protect us." Newton couldn't have known that Ethan had long ago sworn off notions of fate, so being reminded this was exactly what a believer would argue made him want to punch the strange little man in the face.

All conversation abruptly ended when the source of the smoke turned out to be the tallest hill in the park. The last thing they needed was a damned forest fire. The town's entire regular fire department had either left with the Army, or more likely been infected in the one-by-one obliteration of the emergency responders during the outbreak.

"MC, QRF. Can we get a couple fire trucks out here?"

"*Standby*," Reynolds' unmistakable baritone responded, cutting right through the static. They waited a moment while the convoy came to a stop in the visitor's center parking lot. "*We're working on it. Not a lot of firefighters to go 'round.*"

"Understood. Make this is a priority, MC. We'll keep you up to date," Ethan dropped the mic and nodded to Rowe, who was looking at him from her car window, probably enjoying the air conditioning. A sandstone lodge at the top of the largest hill had a connecting hotel normally reserved for wedding parties. Ethan surmised someone must have set fire to it. It was really the only structure in the park that could burn so long and so intensely. Speeding up when no sentries showed themselves, the trucks climbed the hill until they saw their first zombie. A man in a suit you'd never expect to see in the middle of the woods, his chest torn completely open as if he'd experienced open heart surgery from an Aztec priest, was stumbling toward the fire. He was just behind a dozen other piles of half-rotted, bloating crap-sacks wearing moldy sneakers and tattered jeans.

He motioned for all engines to be cut and grabbed Allen from the back of the truck, "Here," Ethan handed the young man a heavy hatchet with a crowbar on the other side of the head. Together they walked up to and dispatched the closest three zombies. Keith stayed back with the convoy, his medical skills an asset they couldn't afford to lose if there were living hostiles too. It's not that he wouldn't have hesitated for a moment to tangle with the undead, he just knew now wasn't the time.

Ethan could hear the crackling of the fires ahead by now and as they got closer saw something no one expected. A group of survivors had fortified the entire hill crest where the lodge and adjoining parking lot made a decent enough retreat. The problem with this strategy was that they set up a series of moats filled with punji-pits and oil coated straw. Like so many people across the world they clearly didn't understand their foe and now they had flaming zombies too.

"Keith, bring the convoy forward," Ethan said into his handheld, "I can see survivors on the inside of the fence at the lodge. They're on the roof and I could be wrong, but I think they're out of ammunition because I don't hear any gunshots. That, or they're all high as shit from the fumes," Ethan felt a strong chemical high already, like he was using undiluted Killz in a room with no windows, not a good sign for the people trapped behind the walls. The oil fires were sucking all the oxygen from the air like napalm, the heat intense enough to keep the rescuers at bay for now.

"How many infected?" The radio crackled back.

"About fifty or so," Ethan grabbed Allan, who was lazily keeping a badly decomposed child at bay with the bayonet of his M-4 like an outstretched hand. Every so often he'd give it a poke with the blade and reset its progress. "We need to get out of the way, this is gonna be messy."

Allen shot the child-zombie and they climbed to a small hill off to the side of the road. Every pickup in the convoy came roaring around the corner, guns blazing wildly into the pack of burning undead. The zombies that were already on fire had gathered in a corner they couldn't navigate and burned down a section of fence just large enough that the trucks weren't damaged as they plowed through. After they were inside the perimeter, the 5-ton and the patrol car followed, picking up Allen and then Ethan just as a couple of recently infected zombies came after them from the wood line. A gun-truck moved in between Allen and the pursuing zombies, cutting them down with a makeshift brush-scoop welded to the bumper.

What was worse than oily smoke, Ethan thought, o*ily smoke mixed with necrotic flesh.* It was being boiled away, sizzling like bacon but creating a smell not unlike the toxic burn-pits of the Iraq and Afghanistan Wars. Most of the world was covered in this horrid stench now. Ethan had been certain he'd escaped this *aroma* after leaving the Army. Everything was a flashback now, except it was happening right in front of him, not a memory in hues of blue and black with equally muted sounds, eerie and far away. Nothing was far away anymore, it was all right here, right now and there was nowhere to run to this time, no bottle deep enough.

The people on the roof of the buildings, about thirty in all, jumped down and started running toward their rescuers almost before it was safe to do so. "They're coming up from the river!" a woman tried to explain frantically, catching Ethan off guard and smearing his arms with soot when she grabbed him.

It seemed a small refugee camp further up river had become overrun. The undead then floated or walked downstream until they spotted the people on the hill gathering water. An army of soggy zombies then followed the holdouts to their as-yet incomplete fortress some time the day before. Keith asked why they hadn't just come to town, knowing Sullivan was still there. It wasn't surprising when they said they were avoiding civilization, fearing the military would open fire on them. *From the lack of armaments these people carried, they were probably from Illinois,* Ethan thought bitterly. *Besides New Yorkers and Californians, who else would face the undead without guns?*

"How many we looking at?" Keith asked. It was more or less rhetorical, the exact number meant nothing, but he wanted to prove he was still listening.

"Enough that we're gonna be here a while," Ethan pulled

out a couple energy shots he'd been hoarding and handed one to Keith. "I guess we can sleep when we're dead, right?" It went without saying, but Ethan did anyway, "I get bit, you end me, got it? Don't trust me to pull the trigger on myself like Roberts and I won't trust you to do the same."

"I guess if we were Marines I'd say 'Semper Fi,'" Keith tried to take a deep breath, a real chore in the smoke, "but thank God my IQ test came back positive and I got in the Army."

Ethan snorted, trying not to laugh, motioning for some of the older veterans to gather so they could hear his plan of action, "The five-ton and the patrol car will take the refugees back to town and report on what we've found, but I intend to hold this hill. It could prove a strategic stronghold in the future and I'm not willing to give it up." Most people agreed, others had no opinion so long as they got to keep shooting people and not go to jail for it. Just one of the perks of being a survivor in the land of the Free & Well Armed.

"We're gonna stay here as long as those fuckers keep coming up the hill." A machine gun's chittering interrupted Ethan and ripped a cluster of three zombies into maroon paste. "Gird your loins, fella's. It's gonna be a long night."

Turning to Rowe, Ethan suggested she take the survivors and leave. She was a cop, not a soldier and her pants fit as if a donut shop were next door to the station. Rowe had no place on a battlefield and she knew it. The people on the hill were all too happy to go with her, knowing they'd been rescued by the good guys for once.

Ethan smiled, unable to help but say what he said next, *"Hold your fire 'till you see what's left of their eyes!"* It crossed his mind he might have sounded a little too enthusiastic with that one, like some lunatic reenacting Bunker Hill with a raging patriotic boner and a belt-fed weapon. The line seemed to have a rallying effect on the men though and some shouted OOH-RAH and HOOAH back. You'd have never caught Ethan repeating the Army's battle-cry, he was entirely too demotivated for that, but he appreciated the sentiment and didn't take the moment away from the others.

Raising his hand for all to see, Ethan threw it down, signaling for the clearing of the hillside to begin. Clean kills, every one of them, the men taking their time as instructed. This next part really was just like the movies: one army climbing slowly up a hill toward a fortification they clearly should have avoided and gets mown down by the defenders for their efforts. The fight almost resembled wars of the distant past; stand in lines, shoot the enemy, hope you don't get hit back, reload and repeat. Luckily this enemy's only weapon was their own rapidly decaying bodies and modern weapons had never been more efficient.

"One shot, one kill!" Could be heard from deputies all along the line. The moans of the undead thirsting for flesh cast an eerie background to the battle, staccato bursts of gunshots echoed through the valley. One deputy had the presence of mind to climb on the roof of the buildings and look down the hill. Along the path the refugees had built to gather water from the river, at least a thousand undead climbed toward them and yet more were floating down the river like so many turds.

"Are you sure we have enough ammunition for this?" Keith asked while Ethan reloaded the older model M-16 he'd taken from the gun rack on the 5-ton. He looked and felt odd without his granddad's Remington bolt-action, but it was well and truly out of ammunition.

"We should have plenty if we keep up this pace," Ethan took a deep breath, "Really wish we had a helicopter in town, airlift would be nice for supplying ammo and water. Harper said the faucets aren't working here anymore, probably park services shut the mains down."

For some six hours the men were still at it. Any zombies coming up the trails had been eliminated, but some infected were still wading through the immobile carcasses of the others. A siren at the gate heralded the arrival of two fire trucks and more ammunition, food and most importantly, fresh water.

"Are we going to start down the hill?" Kenly had come along with Reynolds to see the battle after being relieved by Rowe. The Mayor was at least armed, but his choice of a Colt Python .357 was a study in overcompensation, Ethan felt.

Ethan looked at Kenly as if he'd grown a dick out of his forehead, "Are you high?"

Kenly smirked, "Only on days that end in Y."

"No, we're not going *down* the damned hill," Ethan seemed disgusted at the very suggestion. "What if we didn't kill all of them? There could be dozens of undead fuckers who aren't completely gone and I'm not risking one more person to find out. Besides, Mr. Mayor, I've decided we're occupying this hill for the foreseeable future. Call it an executive decision, you can take credit if you want, but I think this place is a perfect fallback zone for the town if we get overrun again."

Ashing his cigar off to one side, Kenly nodded his approval, "You keep being useful, Kelly, and I might promote you."

"Please don't," Ethan snapped back in earnest, never considering he might be closing a door before it was even open to him, "you can do better."

Keith and Ethan didn't even bother driving home, instead they crashed in the lodge's main lobby for an all-too-brief couple of hours before Allen would come barging in like he'd gotten a good night's sleep or some shit. Ethan certainly wasn't having a good night, Keith had watched him toss and turn, the consternation on his face spelling out a plot that couldn't have been good. So far, he only knew bits and pieces, Ethan being fairly elusive about his past.

Ethan's aloofness was almost assuredly because he was ashamed of something and because he saw in Keith a leader he could respect, though who was leading whom was debatable. The Army must have really chewed Ethan Kelly up and spat him back out for him to remain virtually silent about his career, but what was the offense? Through little bits and pieces Keith had surmised Ethan's problem wasn't *Failure to Adapt*, the most common reason young soldiers were separated from the military, but more like he was drummed out.

The nocturnal self-torture Keith felt was probably relatively normal in this day and age, dwelling on current events, but Ethan was clearly living in the past before zombies. Keith's nightmares were of his aunt and adopted cousin Gabbi. *They were trapped in the seemingly endless traffic snarls between cities with nowhere to run or hide. They'd been fleeing Orlando, talking to him on the phone before service went down. He heard Gabbi shout that there was an Infected in the minivan in front of them, heard his mother curse that they were blocked in, someone outside their car was shooting...* Allen drew back the curtains as he burst into the lodge's foyer just as Keith had drifted into a deep enough sleep to be considered restful. He instinctively threw a bottle of piss at the kid, but sadly the cap was on tight.

"Is Ethan up?" Allen asked in a chipper voice, likely not gathering that it wasn't a bottle of lemon-lime sports drink he'd just dodged.

"No, I think he's down for the count," Keith motioned to Ethan, curled up in a ball on a worn-out mattress. "What's up?"

"We might have a problem."

Keith rolled his eyes and scratched the red stubble that was covering his face, "Kid, right now I got ninety-nine problems and you're *all* of them."

Allen got the joke, glad someone else could speak internet meme besides him, "There's a Humvee with a Texas flag on it. They're holding position and won't answer the radio, or our signal flags."

Keith groaned, "How long ago was this?"

"Right now."

Keith walked over and poked Ethan with a shoe, "Hey, get up. There's another crisis your yokels can't handle without us. It's Babysitting time again."

Ethan wasn't a morning person. He flipped them both off as he climbed out of bed and put the same grimy clothes from the day before back on. They still hadn't found the water main to turn it back on and so they hadn't been able to wash during the night. *Brushing my teeth before I die would have been nice*, Ethan thought, *but that was entirely too much to ask.*

Outside in the bright morning light the area already looked cleaner. Children were policing up spent brass so it could be reloaded back in town, their contribution to the war effort it seemed. Allen had gotten his hands on one of the cars from the dealership across the highway and was driving the newest model year Ram 2500. He wasn't a very good driver and the truck was a manual, which made everyone sick by the time they reached the top of the hill, lurching and grinding gears all the way. Kenly and the rest of the lieutenants were already at the North overpass. Someone handed Ethan a set of binoculars while Keith went about trying to raise the truck on the radio.

"What do you suppose they're doing?"

"Staying out of small arms range," Ethan felt that much was clear. "Assume there are more of them in the woods and near our other checkpoints too. They want us to know they could overpower us if they wanted to."

"I'll bet they're also getting firing solutions on our checkpoints," a man with a Vietnam Vet's hat said. "If we piss 'em off they could call in artillery and mortars."

"Are these the people you guys saw at the power plant?" Kenly asked.

"Probably, it's not like we're hard to find if you can read a map."

"He's right," Ethan said, turning to Keith, "anything?"

"I'm getting bits and pieces, but our radios aren't synchronized. I doubt they could talk to us if they wanted to. Hell, we're using MBITRs routed through a fucking SINCARS radio. They might have satellite phones for all I know," said Keith, tossing the mic down.

Kenly looked over at another deputy, "Write our frequency on a board and hold it up. Let's see if they answer then." He used old gas station price numbers to make the sign and as soon as it was ready two men held it up. A few seconds later Keith nodded that there was someone on the other line, but that they weren't talking, only listening.

"Maybe they're not authorized to talk," Deputy Carlisle suggested.

"Yeah, right..." Kenly took the microphone, "This is the Sullivan checkpoint to the Texan patrol on top of the hill. Please respond." Nothing. "This is Mayor Aaron Kenly, please respond." Again, nothing. "Be advised, if you cannot respond via radio, flash your lights so that we know you have received our signal. We are not, I repeat, *are not* hostile. We're all Americans here."

Without flashing lights, or any other signal, the truck backed slowly beyond the horizon and was gone. "We really need a fucking helicopter," Ethan and Kenly said at the same time.

"There's one at the airport," a teenager who'd been in the Civil Air Patrol interjected. "It's not anything special, just one of those little bubble canopy private choppers. You know, the ones that everyone keeps crashing."

Kenly nodded, "I see. What about the fixed wing aircraft? Any of them still work?"

"Well, I'd assume all of them, Sir. The Army shut the airport down to civilian traffic, including us, but they didn't destroy the aircraft already there, just pushed them out of the way. We haven't been out there to check on it because you guys haven't cleared it yet."

After eating something Ethan went with the bulk of the deputies to check out the small regional airport just west of town. There were vagrants in the office portions, people who weren't helping the town and had no intention of doing anything other than meth, prescription pills, fornicating and copious amounts of drinking. The floor of the lobby was covered in sticky beer cans and those wretched airline bottles of honey whiskey. A couple of them were armed and claimed the property as their own, but it only took the town's convoy of gun trucks showing up to convince them leaving was the right thing to do.

One of the smaller hangers had been made into a makeshift field hospital by the Army, abandoned just as quickly as the soldiers could leave it; there were even plates of moldy food and partially dehydrated cups of Kool-Aid sitting on the tables. The junkies had made use of all the fun drugs in the medical center's lockers, but left most of the equipment alone. It was like watching Keith find presents that hadn't been under the tree the night before.

As soon as the deputies had seen the vagrants disappear over the hills, the majority of the gathered men returned to town. A spotter on the water tower reported more smoke from St. Louis' general direction and the newly elected mayor had to leave the checkpoint to calm some of the people who feared this signified another wave of zombies. Keith, Allen and Ethan and a few others chose to stay for a little while, exploring the small regional airfield. The Civil Air Patrol officer, now a deputy, showed them the building the Air Force Auxiliary used for its Boy Scout-esque meetings. It now smelled of backed up toilets and a half-burned meth lab that would take weeks for the two HAZMAT trained firefighters they still had to clean, but the building would be worth the effort in the future they assumed.

The Army and FEMA had divided the runway in half, part of it being filled by containerized housing units, little white cracker boxes that could comfortably house two at a time, or four if your leadership didn't like you very much. The airfield was shortened yet again by temporary canvas hangars that had once housed half a dozen Apache gunships and twice as many Blackhawks. Now only one Blackhawk remained and it had obviously been cannibalized for parts. For no reason other than he was a giant nerd, Ethan had an impulse to keep the skeletal helicopter at his place, if for no other reason than it was really neat. It would make a perfect centerpiece for his "Mizzerah Court Yard," a euphemism his father used for the standard collection of rusted-out clunkers that decorated rural yards throughout the great state of Missouri (,and for whatever reason they're usually 90's model Camaros.)

"Should we even try to get a helo in the air?" Keith asked Ethan, looking around at the collection of crap the vagrants had left behind.

"I don't think so," another deputy said, pointing to a dust covered monitor still powered by a solar panel on the roof. "This is a radar screen for local airspace. Look at that," he used an ink pen to point to something crisscrossing a vague outline of Franklin County. "At twenty thousand feet we've got air cover. Speed and formation could only be military and I don't see anything else in the sky."

"That doesn't mean anything," yet another deputy argued.

"Angelico is right. We shouldn't put anything in the air if there's still an Air Force to enforce no-fly zones put in place during Martial Law. A time of war would be grounds to shoot down a kite," Keith said, ending the argument. At least, though, they had the airport, an area of maintained, fenced-in land that could have all sorts of future applications. For it being the longest day, it might also have been the best, or at least most successful day thus far.

Chapter 10

"We're running out of time before fall comes. I'm running out of time..." Ethan said quietly one day while sitting around for his lunch break. "This fence is taking away manpower from scavenging food and setting up personal greenhouses for the winter."

"What if we just asked those guys at the power plant for aid?" Kenly suggested, puffing on a pipe, a habit Ethan thought he wouldn't mind taking up because it smelled fantastic to him, allowing access to all sorts of memories from his childhood he'd forgotten. Most of his grandfather's friends were pipe smokers. He remembered the living room of one man who'd kept all his kid's old toys. He remembered playing by the fireplace while it snowed outside, but being too young to remember their conversation, though it was friendly and inviting. "They certainly haven't been hostile, it might not be the worst idea we ever had. If they can provide coal for power and their own protection, surely they can help fellow Americans with food and medicine."

"What if they *are* hostile?" Rowe shook her head. "I think we can just live without them, personally. If they haven't bothered to contact us by now then I think they're not interested in us at all."

"We should consider looting some of the larger towns," Allen changed the subject. Keith had been teaching the boy and his brother Jimmy how to look and act like officers and gentlemen. Their parents didn't seem interested in parenting anymore and hadn't left their house in months. The depression of losing their first born had wrecked them. Personally, Ethan had little sympathy for them as they still had two sons who needed them, but simultaneously he understood the illogical mental fog that described depression intimately. "We haven't gotten any refugees from the North in weeks. I think they've all fled the St. Louis urban-sprawl by now, which means there are supplies they abandoned during The Panic. Logistically it's almost impossible they ate or burned everything."

"Or they've all hunkered down, same as us and they'll defend their stockpiles just the same as us," Kenly said, unaccustomed to children being given a voice. "Look, boy, we're busy. Find something else to do and let the adults handle this."

"I don't know who the fuck you think you are, you simple fat fuck, but you had bettered show Deputy Broadwick some fucking respect." Ethan's glare was intense. He wasn't beyond punching the mayor in the face with the brass knuckles in his pocket. It was quite plausible to smash a zombie's skull with them as a last resort, especially if a piercing end were welded on.

Kenly didn't say anything. He just puffed on his pipe and walked away, satisfied that he could trust Ethan to stick up for those under his care, or maybe he was just bored with the conversation. Either way.

"We'll check the larger towns soon," Keith offered, trying to distract Ethan from opening a can of whoopass on Kenly. "For now, let's keep working on shoring up our defenses."

The next night at shift change at the police station, Kenly arrived to give new directions to his men. Some were assigned to protecting the town, maintaining law and order while others were tasked with planning raiding parties to loot local towns for winter supplies. Keith, Ethan and Allen were given the very specific mission of returning to the Labodie Power Plant to gather more intelligence and possibly make contact if the opportunity arose. Early in the morning, long before the sun came up, they prepped and fueled their truck. Allen, having recently gained a girlfriend, kissed her goodbye out of earshot and climbed into the turret where, as promised, Keith had gotten some welders to install a bucket seat from a car.

Ethan watched Allen's love-scene and couldn't help but let his jealousy rage inside. Probably he would never hold

Nicole again, smell her hair, hear her voice. He'd take an argument with her if only he could see her one more time. How horrible would that be, to spend every night alone in the cold for the rest of his predictably shortened life?... *why haven't I done it already...* he'd think... *she's not coming back, none of them are... I shouldn't be here anymore either.*

The trip back to the power plant didn't take as long this time because Ethan decided to direct Keith to drive along the railroad tracks. There were very few zombies on the back roads and, most roaming the open highways and traffic snarls or wherever people had gathered. What was most disturbing was the ever-decreasing signs of living people.

Around a corner Keith almost plowed headlong into a freight train that was stopped and hidden behind a row of trees, effectively camouflaging it. It was also blocking their path along the tracks. Unwilling to give the train's location over the radio, lest someone overhear them, they marked it on a map and drove around it. The Humvee almost became bogged down in a small creek and hedge row because Keith wasn't a spectacular driver, but they made it.

The dead, their vacant and glossy eyes always watching, led Ethan to a mental image of rotting corpses driving a locomotive. It made Ethan giggle out loud, but the engine was too noisy for Keith or Allen to hear him. Those zombies who could still use their ears, if they hadn't been eaten off or already rotted away, would turn toward the sound of the Humvee's engine as they passed, but didn't bother to change direction. The virus, though unaware of itself as a microorganism, seemed to instinctively know its hosts were dying out and so saved what energy the bodies contained for their final attacks. Perhaps that was one of the key features that made it so deadly though, the hosts would only attack to spread the virus when it detected an available body. Only one Zim on the trip had been fresh and instead of making noise with a gun Keith ran the college-age kid over with a thud noise they were no strangers to. The truck's brush guard would be a real pain to wash off later, the guy's skull having become wedged between the guard and the grill.

Ethan looked over at Keith when he heard laughing over the radio, *"WTF, Over?"*

Keith smiled and laughed even harder, *"Fuckin' Emo Kids, man. You'd think I'd hate all zombies equally by now, but no, here I am hunting effeminate dorks even after they've already died,"* he laughed yet harder. *"It seems my work is never done."*

"You're my kind of sick," Ethan smiled a little too, wondering to himself where the kid had been hiding for so long, only to become infected now. The reigning theory for fresh zombies were people running out of supplies and being killed while scavenging. Not everyone was fit to survive in a world without their iCrap telling them what to do and when they had permission to do it, (Introducing a new smartphone app for Surviving the Zombie Apocalypse; *Tips and tricks to avoid the undead and keep your bunker's living space looking fresh and fun!)*

The railroad tracks led where they wanted to go, even though it was mid-afternoon before they arrived shaken, not stirred. Empty train cars littered unused tracks, some tipped over where bulldozers had shoved them off the lines to make room for more cars. The massive amount of derailed hoppers blocked the best ways in, but provided almost complete defilade from the guard towers now. They could see through binoculars the dirt road they'd taken originally had been cleared of trees and brush, exposing the entire area to a machine gun nest on top of the power plant. It would be unwise to take that route again, who knew if the Texan's actions were because they somehow knew they were being spied on from there, or whether or not it was just an educated guess. They'd probably planted more mines too.

Dismounting the vehicle, the three men waited until the next train left the sally port. The locomotive was a yard-dog engine parking a train of fifteen or so empty cars on a spur-line. A few railroad workers and a soldier, all with brightly colored Texas flags on their uniforms, got out to uncouple and check the empty coal cars before leaving. This was when the trio made their move. Allen pulled a gun on the workers while Keith put their protection into a chokehold until he passed out, gently laying him on the gravel.

Ethan slung his own rifle, "Lower your gun, Allen." He turned to the terrified engineers, "We're not gonna hurt you, we just wanted to avoid a confrontation we couldn't control," he gestured to the soldier, knowing the young man would have raised the alarm. "We just want some answers. Like why are you keeping the power on and why are you wearing Texas flags and not U.S. flags?"

"Because there is no more United States of America," The lead engineer said, solemnly. He had faded Navy tattoos down both arms, indicating he'd been an American patriot all his life and missed his nation too. He had also been fat before the zombies, but no longer. "Texas and Alaska are the only state governments still functioning last time we heard," he added, trying to give the three the most pertinent information despite knowing little himself.

"What about the rest of the world?" Keith asked, making sure the young man would be comfortable when he woke up.

"Sometimes we hear from England, Norway, Iceland and Greenland, but mainland Europe, Asia, the Middle East and Africa are all dark."

"'Dark'?" Allen needed more.

"Gone. No way to sugar coat it, kid."

"We're still here…"

"So again, why keep the power on?" Ethan asked again.

"Because this shit ain't gonna last forever," the other engineer shrugged, feeling comfortable enough to lower his arms. "The infected are rotting. The vast majority will be too far gone to move by the end of next year, especially if next summer is like this last one, so the Governor refuses to abandon the Continued Energy Effort until, in his own words, 'we've emptied the last tank.' As long as we can keep the lights on, that's just that many more people we can help stay alive."

"Are Texas and Alaska friends with one another?" Ethan asked the next logical question.

"Well yeah, but there's three thousand miles of infected wilderness between us and them. We're on the offensive against the undead as we speak and Alaska's hunkering down, waiting for winter to freeze 'em."

"Will that work?" Allen asked.

"*General'ny Moroz,*" Ethan said in what would pass for a really shitty Russian accent. "*General Frost.* Russia has historically relied on its bitter-cold winters to defeat invading armies while they marshal their forces." He repeated like a robot, either unaware, or not caring that people thought his vast knowledge of strange shit to be extremely off-putting. (True story: While sitting in the break-tent during his deployment in Iraq, Ethan overheard part of a conversation between two sergeants where one loudly exclaimed, "What is the purpose of Drill & Ceremony?" Likely to express his dislike for the tradition. Without hesitation, as he thought he'd been asked a direct question, Ethan blurted out the definition from a JROTC leadership textbook, "To move troops efficiently from one location to another, to instill discipline and *esprit de corps* and to allow troops to regularly handle individual firearms." After that and the expressions on the other soldier's faces, it was really all downhill from there.)

"Do you speak Russian?" Keith glared, realizing there was more to Ethan than a layer of grime and boozey sweat.

"No, but my brother does," Ethan saw Keith's glare. "I can speak German though," he volunteered.

Keith sighed, "Because of course you can."

"*Ich bin auch nicht schlecht darin.* If the Zims are dead they're no longer exothermic," Ethen continued without acknowledging when or why he'd learned German when his brother had learned Russian. "Which means, kinda like a package of hamburger, they'll freeze when the ambient temperature is below zero for any length of time."

Keith eyeballed Ethan and then spoke for the rest of

them, "Most days I'm certain you're a burned out drunk with questionable access to guns and schedule-1 narcotics and other days I'm pretty sure you're a *genius* burned out drunk with questionable access to guns and schedule-1 narcotics."

Ethan looked back at Keith with a pleasant expression, "*Danka meine freund.*"

The engineers were more relaxed as the soldier started to come to. He blinked several times and immediately looked for his M-4. Keith had disassembled the weapon to its smallest components and laid it all neatly next to him on a towel from the man's own cleaning kit. It was a military faux-pas to toss another man's gun in the dirt, the idea being that it would take the kid long enough to reassemble the weapon that they'd have time to make a clean getaway.

"Specialist Tuft, who's your commanding officer?" Keith asked.

"Specialist Richard Z. Tuft, service number-"

"Dude, shut the fuck up. You're not our prisoner, we're all still Americans- we think. We're from a local town you guys have sent a recon party to scout recently. We tried to contact you, but no one spoke to us."

The soldier remained silent and glared like he wanted to set them on fire.

"For fuck sake, Ricky, these boys ain't the badguys. They're the people we're keeping the power on for," the conductor said.

"My unit is the 56th Texas Combat Engineers, Alpha Company, First Battalion. I'm not authorized to tell you more, so please don't ask."

"That's… great…" Allen shrugged, obviously unimpressed, "How many more units are there?" Tuft said nothing.

"It's okay, Specialist, you don't have to tell us anything," Ethan took a look around, fearing they'd lingered too long. "Just, if you could, tell your superiors we're not hostile. I don't think it'll be too hard to figure out where we're from. We're going to trust you, Specialist Richard Z. Tuft of the

Texas National Guard, to tell the truth. We're running low on ammunition to keep fighting the hordes coming from St. Louis and Columbia, so if it's possible we'd appreciate some help. Tell your superiors the Sullivan checkpoint is still functioning under the flag of the United States of America, but we could really use some allies. Surely there's a trade to be made here." He handed Tuft a piece of paper with the town's radio frequency on it. They left after that. Specialist Tuft didn't try to put his weapon back together right away either, he seemed to be waiting for the engineers to back him up or tell him not to obey. Ethan had taken Tuft's radio and tossed it into a coal car for extra time.

Ethan drove as fast as he could back to town where word spread about the train full of supplies faster than wildfire. In the morning over a hundred people went back for it, organized and protected by the Deputies. No one knew how to start a locomotive except a retired engineer who hadn't been behind the controls since 1985. There was a bit of a learning curve, but the locomotive started moving before long. Slowly, almost too slowly, the mile-long train headed down the tracks, armed men covering every car. There were no major delays, except removing a tractor-trailer full of McDonalds toys the train had hit in the first place. How that had come to pass was anyone's guess, because there were no zombies in either cab. There weren't any crossings Ethan could think of before St. Louis, so it boggles the mind where the truck had come from originally.

Keith was standing inside a box car that had mounds of mail in it with a dozen or so other people, enjoying a cigarette as they rolled through the countryside at a painstaking ten miles per hour. No one bothered to shoot any zombies, hitting a moving target in the head was practically impossible anyhow and they had a finite supply of ammunition, even with reloads.

It took a minute or two, but eventually Keith realized one of the gunmen was a girl in a desert camo uniform that would have better fit him. He recognized her as the girl named

Paula, the one who'd told them about the rapes and murders in the first place. She sat with her feet dangling over the edge of the train, watching the trees and enjoying the quiet between clacks of wheels on the tracks. He went and sat by her.

"Hey," he said, setting his rifle down and offering his hand to shake.

"I recognized you an hour ago," she said sarcastically. "Not so clever, this one." Paula was teasing him. "I heard from a girl who was there that night that it was like watching the wrath of God in motion," the way she described it was far more romantic than the truth, but she didn't need to know that.

Keith nodded at the macabre description, surprised Paula was so forthcoming. Rape victims were delicate to deal with, but perhaps getting her revenge had bolstered the woman's confidence. "I deplore unnecessary violence," he said. "It's why I'm a medic, but I don't regret what we did. I think Ethan would agree, some people just need killin'."

Paula smiled wide, "We're all fine now, thanks to you two." Keith noticed some of her teeth near the back of her jaw were still missing. Once upon a time she'd had an expensive smile, perfectly aligned by the best braces insurance could buy. There weren't a lot of dentists left anymore and it made him a little sad to think she'd lost her beautiful smile for no reason. "Some of the other girls are still in the hospital, they got beat up a lot worse than me, but-"

"I wish there was more we could have done."

"Unless you could time travel, or bring their dicks back in a bag as proof, I don't think there would be much else you could do. I mean, the world fucking ended, man and I'm still alive." She drank from her canteen like it was a celebratory shot, "...and I am... still alive."

"Kinda wish I had thought of the dick-bagging," Keith pouted. It was purely sarcasm, but then that was the basis for their conversation in the first place.

Paula's smile faded, "The world is never gonna be the same, is it." It wasn't really a question. "I mean, I was going to go to Mizzou this very summer. I was already enrolled for Security Protected Dorms, as if any of this could ever have been contained..." she trailed off but found her thoughts again. "It was just a way for the college to scam more money from my parents. Money we could have used to fortify the house, for extra food. Now I'm orphaned, a hundred miles from a home that probably doesn't exist anymore and I am literally robbing a train. Sometimes it feels so surreal, ya know? I almost expect to wake up at home to the smell of bacon and eggs, my mom's hairspray clouding the hallways, Dad not talking until he'd finished his coffee. Mom always used too much hairspray, stuck in the 80's I guess. I really miss them and it hasn't been three weeks since..."

Keith explained that most of his family was dead now too, offering her a sincere hug afterwards. Then Paula threw him a curveball, "So you and Deputy Kelly... are you two, you know... 'together'?" She did the quotation marks in the air with her fingers, a band aid on one hand and a Halloween pumpkin ring on another.

Stunned for a moment, Keith struggled to respond without laughing, "No! Neither one of us are gay. Why? Do we come across as gay?"

"No, but your face was priceless."

Keith narrowed his eyes, she'd gotten him good. "I guess I hang out with him because, as you pointed out, there's no place left to go," Keith gestured at the farmland, now growing wild like the untamed Missouri prairies of the last century. "I had never been to the Midwest before all this shit started. I'm from Maine originally, though I've lived everywhere but here it seems. I joined the Army back in '16, when my parents were living in Florida. Ethan, though, is from right here. He was in the Army prior to the Panic and got drafted back in when the shit hit the fan. He won't really talk about it, though I just know he really, really, really doesn't trust the Army. I can't say's I blame him at this point."

"At least he's back home. I'm from Springfield, my parents were trying to get to my aunt's in Kansas City when our car was clipped by an Army truck. The bastards didn't even stop for us. We walked to a town called Cuba and that's where my parents were... and then..." Paula didn't finish her story, there wasn't any need to. She'd lost her entire family like almost everyone else, but for some reason Keith felt sorrier for her than most.

"We're still kinda hoping that maybe Ethan's brother will show up. Before the phones and internet became unreliable, he called and said he was heading home." Keith sighed, "I'll be honest, though, I'm not holding my breath. It's a long way from Kentucky to here, especially for someone on their own."

"I wouldn't want to be out there, even if I were Dwayne Johnson," Paula shivered at the thought, but let slip her real crush.

Keith felt... *small* by comparison, but let it go, "I wouldn't mind having a few pro-wrestlers on our side right now. We're certainly not alone out here," he said with regret. "Eventually there's going to be a war between the factions of the Living, once the Undead have rotted away. People are going to fight over all of this. It'll be a second Manifest Destiny, but with machine guns and drones."

"Why? Before we left the news said more than half the Earth's population was infected. There's going to be plenty of room for everyone, if *anyone* makes it."

"It's cute that you're so naive. Texas is going to take it all. No other state really stands a chance. They've got the military reserves and the oil to fuel them," Keith was only theorizing about a worse-case scenario, but it was probably also the truest.

"I hope not. Maybe they'll just help us get back on our feet?" Paula was disgustingly hopeful for someone who'd witnessed hell and who was all alone in the world. The train made it to Sullivan without a hitch, but this time there was no free-for-all with the supplies like when the Army pulled out. Everything was inventoried, including anything useful that was in the mail cars. There would be enough dried goods to last the town through winter for sure now and the task of locking these supplies safely away was given to someone besides Keith and Ethan for once. They were starting to wear their fatigue on their sleeves and anyone with half a brain could see it.

Ethan, as usual, spent his free time at home waiting for an email or a phone to tell him something, staring in silence with a bottle of Southern Comfort in one hand, a blunt in the other. Most of the town was waiting for a response from the Texans as well. Keith took the opportunity afforded by the lull in activity to bring Paula to some semblance of a movie night, organized by a few parents, that was meant to keep restless children from living in a hellish world of fear all the time. The local theater had been shut down since the Army rolled into town and it was still too far out of town-proper to be protected anyhow. Instead, the high school gymnasium was used since it was still in town and had a projector with a decent surround sound system. Happily, they watched a marathon of *Star Wars* movies in the order they were released. Keith wasn't the biggest *Star Wars* fan and neither was Paula, but at least it was something to do besides hear gunshots and smell the acrid scent of death that permeated daily life. The gym smelled of rubber and cleaning agents and maybe even of the cheap perfume teens seemed to hose themselves down with. A marvelous change of pace to be sure.

"So what will Ethan do if his brother shows up?" Paula asked, sipping water from her canteen again. There was plenty of soda and beer still available, but she didn't want any. She was never without her canteen and something told Keith it was likely a safety blanket of sorts. As long as she had water she felt like it all was plausible she'd be okay. He'd have to explore that with her one day, see if he could help, maybe find out why she valued water so much. Before the first cases were reported Keith had been studying psychology to learn more about battle fatigue, or PTSD. Everyone these days, it seemed, had some form of Post Traumatic Stress or another and how could they not? When his generation was thirteen they'd watched three thousand people die on live television and literally nothing had gotten better since then. One day it would be his job to help mend people's minds as well as their bodies. That was, of course, all on hold for now, but Paula made him think about it again.

"I have no idea," Keith said as the credits rolled on *Episode II*. "I think he wants to go to Oklahoma and look for his family. They were taken there when the Army left."

Paula looked away, "He does know most of the refugee camps spawned the largest infected hordes, right?"

"If you thought your parents were still alive in one of those camps, wouldn't you go look for them?" Paula accepted the answer while a kid changed the DVD to *Episode III*. Most people got up to use the restroom and get food. Plenty of concessions were on a lemonade stand from the theater department. Fresh popcorn was a real treat, too. Keith traded a pack of AA's for a large bucket of it and two sodas. Paula said she didn't want one when he returned and with a wounded expression he teased that they were both for him anyhow. Later in the movie he drank them both anyway, so it wasn't totally a lie.

"I guess there's still no word from Texas then either? Lots of people are here just waiting, I think, wanting to know if there's somewhere warmer to fall back to," Paula was trying to make small-talk while the computer techies complained about something tech-related involving the speakers, but it really wasn't important to Keith.

"I don't know that we'll ever hear from Texas. They know who and where we are though, so I can't imagine it will take forever if they want to talk, of course," As the movie played Keith found that he hadn't even noticed Paula's head resting on his shoulder until she'd been there a while. He didn't think it was very comfortable because she had a boney face and he was mostly skin and brawn too, but she was asleep before Anakin discovered who the Sith Lord really was and he decided not to move her. Finding the third movie more fun than the first two, he stayed for the final duel, but had little interest in the predictable ending. He carried Paula to his truck and buckled her in.

Paula stayed in a previously abandoned residence with six other women, none of which were refugees like her, but more like some of the single women in town banding together to be more irritating in packs. The other girls thought it was "cute," and vowed to tell Paula all about it when she woke up. The largest clucking-hen wouldn't let him take her all the way up to the room she shared with another girl, so he left her on the couch and was glad to get away with his manhood intact.

On his way back out to Ethan's house Keith started feeling the last few weeks catching up with him with a vengeance. While Ethan was probably already passed out, Keith's eyes felt almost too heavy to keep open and the vehicle started to drift from one side of the narrow country road to the other. Snapping his head up again when he realized he was falling asleep, Keith slammed headlong into a zombie wearing an Air Force uniform with body armor. The '99 Dodge Ram he was driving might have been mighty, but almost three hundred pounds of immobilized flesh and Kevlar with ceramic plates was still a force to be reckoned with, much like hitting a waterlogged tree stump, or Roseanne Barr. A loud bang and a sudden stop later Keith stumbled from the truck in a daze. Cars torn to shreds by moose or horses didn't look, or smell, this bad. One of the zombie's hands was torn off at the wrist, still gripping the slats in the truck's grill as the radiator started to hiss steam. The legs were tangled into the driveshaft too, being practically cleaved off at the bumper and the headlights now pointed inward like crossed eyes that projected into the misty night.

"Aw… That's fuckin' nasty," Keith groaned to himself,

realizing just how exposed he was now that he felt the wind on his back. The zombie's torso, squished between the ceramic sapping-plates, was thrown down the road a good twenty feet from where the truck had been stopped. Fluids from both the truck and zombie leaked out all over.

Grabbing his M-4 Keith climbed into the bed of the truck, wishing he'd acquired one with a hard-shell camper. Flipping on a search light, he held his breath, expecting to face down a horde by his lonesome and lit up a field completely devoid of more infected, or even wildlife. Breathing a sigh of relief and chuckling to himself about how there was a lone zombie in the middle of nowhere and he just *had* to hit it. *Go figure.* The zombie's head, neck and most of the right arm started stirring some when the light stayed on it. Sighing again, Keith raised his M-4 to shoot it when a figure moved, almost as fast as an infected person in their rage phase, just at the edge of his vision. Before he could move the gun, it ran across the road and split the snapping skull in half with what looked like an angled machete.

"Halt! Identify yourself or I will open fire!" Keith shouted, putting the light on the figure. Instead there was just the Air Force zombie's corpse, no other person to be seen. The truck's springs started bouncing and Keith found himself face to face with an even more haggard looking version of Ethan, only with blondish hair instead of brown.

"Lee?" Keith guessed.

A blood-soaked Ka-Bar was suddenly at his throat, "How do you know my name?" The grizzly man demanded, his breath smelled worse than a corpse, tattered clothing and grime all over didn't help the argument that he might have been a civilized human once. Lee wore what was left of an Army uniform, the camouflage pattern beyond recognition with so much mud and blood all over it. He also hadn't shaved in so long twigs and clumps of dirt pocked his scraggly, patchy red beard.

"Your brother's been looking for you," Keith tried to remain calm. "We're not far, man, everything's cool."

Lee took Keith's M-4 and backed away some, "There's only seven houses on this road. Where were you going?"

"Back to Ethan's, man! I don't know the address, that's kinda unimportant these days, don't you think?" Keith was suddenly just glad to be alive, "Jesus H Christ, dude! You about gave me a heart attack. Ethan's gonna freak when he sees you!"

"He's still alive..." Lee allowed himself a brief smile, his right front tooth was chipped and his teeth were completely yellowed.

"Yeah, man," Keith breathed a sigh of relief. "C'mon, let me get you home."

Ethan was extremely drunk when they arrived, trying to calm his fear that his only remaining friend might have been eaten without him there for backup. When Keith came back he was elated, but when Lee followed, despite his odor and mud caked clothes, Ethan jumped up, fell over a foot stool and into his brother's arms for the strongest bear hug in the history of brotherhood. The family reunion was only broken up by Ethan strongly suggesting Lee take a shower and put on clean clothes. Reluctantly he did so, a grooming process that clogged both the shower and sink. An hour later, when Lee didn't emerge, they found him passed out on the toilet with clean boxers and one sock halfway on. Since he'd at least taken the shower first, they left him in there with a blanket and a pair of their mother's house shoes. The well-worn pink bunny slippers Lee had always hated, to be exact.

"So now what?" Keith asked, the only other sound in the house was the AC vents.

Ethan popped the lid off a beer, "I don't know. That'll depend on what he has to say when he wakes up. He looks like shit, though. I can't imagine what he's been through out there. Things were bad for us, but we weren't alone for long."

Keith had something witty to say, but a scratching at the door stopped him. Before either could reach for their weapons a gunshot rang out from the bathroom. Lee, still in his underwear, jumped out of the bathroom and fired two more shots from the hallway with a compact pocket pistol they didn't even know he had. The back door had been breached and Lee was the first to hear it.

"There's a whole shit-ton of 'em!" He shouted, firing twice more. "They're coming from the back yard!"

Ethan flipped the safety off his M-4 and shot the zombie pawing at the patio window. Three more immediately took its place, vying for room to squeeze through. It was the same story all over the house and Keith, thinking quickly, was already on his walkie calling the police station to get a truck of Minutemen to come and save them. There was no answer.

"I guess the undead flyboy I hit had some friends in the woods," Keith said as a motion light near the shed came on, exposing dozens more infected. Lee pulled a pair of pants on, then pointed, each of them slack-jawed as they saw just how many Zims there truly were. It was possible they were in for a fight worse than the battle for Meramec State Park, if only they were at the fortress now.

"I'm trying my radio," Ethan set the radio on the table and started calling for help. "Mayday mayday mayday. HQ, this is Ghostrider," a call sign he'd personally picked out. "Kelly residence is being overrun. Break." He took a breath, "Need gun trucks and retrieval. Break. Area crawls!"

A response came quickly, *"That's a negative there, Ghostrider. Attacks all along the border are tying up all available resources. Suggest going to the rooftop and waiting for morning. Break. Will send rescue when and if, possible. HQ out."* Their words were like a death sentence, an entire army of the undead was attacking the town right now and they were stuck at home. The only good news was they were prepared.

"Lee," Ethan hugged his brother again. "Welcome home. Now, let's get as much shit into the attic as we can before they break down the other doors."

Lee sighed, "Yeah." He was exhausted, but at least there wasn't much to take upstairs that Ethan hadn't already done.

Making sure the faucet in the attic room was still working, they pulled the drop ladder up and dug in and by "dug in" that meant Lee passed the hell out on top of it almost as soon as the trapdoor was shut. For good measure he flopped a mattress down on it before letting himself slip into a near coma. He didn't snore. People who snored got eaten in their sleep. If you snored, you learned not to.

"Well this is just fucking great," Keith rolled his eyes and started pacing. "I gotta get out of here man, I gotta make sure Paula's okay."

Ethan felt his stomach drop. Had he really been so busy that he'd never noticed Keith had a girlfriend? "I hate to ask, but-"

"How long have we been together? Kinda just tonight, so you're off the hook," he read Ethan's mind. "She's staying over by the library in one of the abandoned houses with a few others. I'm really fuckin' worried about her, man, those stupid women she lives with couldn't fight their way out of a wet paper bag, unless that bag were another Women's Studies Major," The joke might have been better received another time.

Ethan reached over and flipped on his father's old radio, a layer of dust came off on his fingers. His dad hadn't used the upstairs in a long time, a hip injury making climbing difficult for Mr. Kelly in his senior years. Flipping through the channels he didn't pick up anything on FM. Out of boredom, or maybe curiosity, he switched to AM and caught a weak signal. It was, unfortunately, another religious zealot. Ethan was about to turn it off when Lee reached up and grabbed his hand.

"No... I haven't heard a radio in forever," he shut his eyes and laid back down on the clean side of the pillow that had been left on the studio couch.

Ethan looked at his clock, "Two hour watches?"

Keith shook his head, "What for? It's not like they can reach us. Lee's passed out on the hatch. They'd have to chew the house out from under us." The brothers and their friend began drifting farther into sleep. They all listened to the zealot speak his mind, as twisted as it was and were grateful when a man taking the roll of a newscaster interrupted him.

"Good morning America and all the ships at sea..." he began. *"And there are a lot of you out at sea, or on barges on the rivers and lakes... In attics and behind Green-Zone walls... I'm sorry for those of you expecting rescue, but at this point I think we can all agree that that kind of hope may no longer be warranted. The only thing I can do is try to educate you, pray with you and say good luck."*

"Cheerful," Keith muttered, but Ethan threw his boot at him.

The radio continued after the announcer cleared his throat, *"I'll read to you a combination of reports we've managed to gather, some from the CDC and others from unverified, but likely credible sources. As before, warnings to stay inside and away from anywhere where people gathered in large groups during the initial outbreaks, stand firm. Cities with a population over one million prior to the plague are a prime-examples of where you don't want to be right now. I understand that that's also where the food is and where the tools to defend yourselves are, but I can't emphasize how important it is to ration what you have and minimize your time exposed. It's not just the undead that can kill you, septicemia works just as well. Bandits, or those who would do you harm for a variety of reasons, might be the second largest killer in the world right now, next to the Inviere plague of course.*

"For those of you who haven't heard, Inviere is Romanian for Resurrection, a moniker given to it by its discoverers, Elisabeta Argetoianu *and* Georgi Haralamb," the announcer slowed down to pronounce the names properly, but was likely still wrong, *"students at the University of Arizona Santa Cruz on a scholarship..."*

The radio went on for some time after that, but they were all asleep despite the haunting wails of the undead, pleading to devour their flesh. By morning, as the first light cracked over Ethan's eyes, Keith and Lee were already on the roof using an old Wrist-Rocket slingshot to peg zombies in the head. They had taken a supply of beer with them and were more or less making a sport of it, the only travesty being this was Ethan's last case of Budweiser Select. After this, there was probably never going to be more, but he let it go because he was so happy Lee was back and because he still had pot stuffed in an old ammo pouch and tequila and whiskey and some Perc-5's he'd hidden in the attic in a hollowed-out dictionary months ago.

"Can we see any fires from town?" Ethan asked, picking up the binoculars and pressing them to his sunglasses after he'd lit a poorly rolled joint. The light was unusually strong today, that or he was massively hungover.

"Only a couple, but if I reckon direction right, they're at checkpoints where bodies might build up in front of gun-nests," Keith pointed lazily towards the Northeast, offering an already opened beer in trade for a toke from Ethan's sloppy joint. Rolling papers were a skill Ethan had yet to master, what with having only joined the dark side when being one of the good guys wents tits up for him. "We've been hearing machine gun fire from The Hill too, so I think most people fell back there."

"Fuck," Ethan flopped down on the slightly angled roof, choosing his footing wisely. "How many are around the house?"

"Oh, a hundred or so. We've certainly got enough ammunition to take care of them, but fuck dude, that's a lot of bodies to clean up. We've just been shooting the ones that are too close to the doors or windows. but maybe we can draw them to just one side of the house..." It was then that Keith noticed Ethan hadn't been talking to him the entire time.

"Where's Mom 'n Dad?" Lee wanted to know.

"Oklahoma. Nicole's there with them."

Lee's heart sank and he tipped his tattered, filthy patrol cap forward over his eyes. For a moment he tried to control himself, but he broke down into tears anyway. Ethan moved to comfort his brother, but Lee would have none of it.

"No. Leave me alone! I failed them, I was supposed to get here but I didn't. Our lines fell... My platoon never had a chance!" They waited for Lee to calm down as he went into a violent shouting fit, shooting wildly at the zombies with an underpowered .22 revolver. Once he had to reload he seemed to revert to a calmer state, "There's maybe one safe zone per every couple of states, Ethan... There's rumors of holdouts in the Rockies and the higher Appalachians, but nothing the Army knew about for sure. Texas and Alaska seceded and took whatever troops they had with them, then the internet went dark for us; cyber warfare between the factions and overseas they said. The whole grid is trashed. I... I don't..." the glass of straight whiskey in his hand shook some.

"When did you leave the fighting and how?" Ethan pressed for more.

"Ethan, c'mon. He's been through enough for a while."

"After the Tactical Operations Center was overrun. My company was on the outskirts of Chattanooga, trying to clear a college campus so we could use it as a staging ground. That was when we heard the Battalion XO on the radio recalling the other companies to rally on his location. There was a well-armed, unfriendly local militia to their north and the whole of infected Chattanooga to their East. So the undead killed all of them, the gangs, the battalion staff and the airlift squadrons stationed there too. There were no armored units close enough to protect them, not that they would have fared any better with no useful weapons to fight corpses. We were given the order to disperse and seek refuge by whoever was left at Division HQ, a polite euphemism the fight's over and we lost. It's the last thing I heard from en-high."

Ethan took his weed back from Keith, "Mom freaked the fuck out when you were reassigned to a front-line unit."

Lee looked down in the direction of the zombies, "Well, she should have. After our battalion HQ fell we were cut off from any kind of support. We didn't have any radios with enough power to call for air evac, not that it would have come in any event. This gung-ho captain we'd been babysitting gave the order to finish clearing the campus we were in, get the antennae on top of a dorm and start squawking for help. Why we needed to clear the entire campus I don't know, but it cost every platoon dearly."

"Who would have come if you could call out?"

"I have no idea. I was company XO, so I pulled a Captain Kirk and pretended I didn't hear his orders. I sent the platoon I was with to shut and barricade the doors to the closest building. It cut us off from the rest of the company, but then that's what saved us, you see. Captain Corcoran was a high-speed motherfucker. Reckless even when he was fighting the Taliban, even worse when it came to clearing IED's in Iraq. Kind of a George Armstrong Custer type, ya know? Anyhow, Corcoran ordered snipers and sharpshooters on the rooftop of the building he was in to start shooting anything that came within three hundred meters. Naturally all the gunfire just acted like a dinner bell and they swarmed the whole quad in maybe twenty minutes."

"Why am I not surprised that speaking in colorful metaphors is a family trait?" Keith interrupted, but Lee continued after a brief smile. He'd had all morning to get to know the stranger living in his childhood home and he approved.

"So many, so closely packed, the sheer pressure of bodies pushing on the doors was like a rotten-meat grinder, the sounds of that... I'll never forget it, the cracking ribcages, popping like corks." Ethan shivered at Lee's description, remembering with no fondness the first time he'd run over a body. "Eventually they just poured in over the second story bay windows by piling on top of one another. We could have delayed them from our building, we had lots of ammo, 249's too, but then we'd only have suffered their fate."

"How did you escape? If there were enough zombies to push in double steel doors, the place had to be swarming..." Keith was enthralled by the story. He suspected his own battle at Antire Hill had not been an isolated incident, or even the bloodiest and this just proved his theory.

"Like I said, we didn't open fire. We stayed hidden for almost four days. After we'd eaten everything in the dorm, our own rations included, we found we couldn't even get birds to land on the rooftop so we could trap or shoot them. The smell of fresh zombies carrying around britches full of shit, that noise the undead make is so Goddamn loud no one could sleep." Lee pinched the bridge of his nose, which was more pronounced than Ethan's by a childhood injury. (If we're being honest, it was a homemade lightsaber to the face.) "The shortwave still worked and we talked to some poor kid from Custer's platoon holding out in a utility closet, but he shot himself before he could starve to death."

"Dude, that's rough," Keith commented while Ethan inwardly berated himself for not simply waiting things out at the theme park with Roberts. Sure, he wouldn't have found Keith, but then he wouldn't have been responsible for John's death either.

Lee barely nodded, "I don't blame him at all, there was nothing we could have done for him then and there was no reason to think our situation would change. Later we also got the attention of a passing CH-53, just around dark when signal is better, but he was laden with Marine wounded already. The pilot promised he'd call in our position, but made it clear there were maybe thirty other distress calls before ours. The odds were not in our favor."

"How long before someone came for you?"

"They didn't," Lee took a deep breath and cracked open the last beer. It was lukewarm, but hit the spot. "We got lucky or we might have starved too. A house near campus must have run out of supplies about the same time we did, because they took off on motorcycles. Loud and noisy fuckers, they drew the hordes away long enough that we opened the doors and just fucking ran for it. Everyone stayed together long enough to get out of Chattanooga, even though we lost Green and Chun.

"When we were finally safe I turned around to address the survivors and instead got to face a mutiny, because fucking why not," Lee laughed at his own words. "See, the men were aware there was no United States left, let alone a U.S. Army. They wanted to go home and who could blame them, so instead of me getting a bullet in the head I told them I was heading for Missouri, invited anyone who wanted to come and started walking."

"How many followed?"

"None. I haven't seen any of them since," Lee crushed the can and threw it at a corpse, but missed. "I know the boys who were from Texas took off for home together, but the rest just kinda went where they wanted, scattered to the wind. I think two of them shot each other, actually. I heard gunfire after I saw McCord and Troy walk over a hill. They'd been harboring grudges against each other for months, ever since Troy's buddy bought the farm while McCord ran for it."

"Wow. How did you survive out there?" Keith wanted to know more, ignoring the undead as they milled about, as if in a drunken stupor themselves.

"When did you call, Lee and how?" Ethan interrupted.

"I was recovering from a nasty gash to my arm, got sliced up pretty good by a rusty shard on a car I slept in." He pulled his sleeve up to reveal mostly healed stitches. "A retired waitress, Rosalie, found me trying to boil water in a pot that had a bullet hole half-way up one side. I was camped in a burned-out Target store, the only building in the area with doors I could barricade even though it didn't have a roof anymore," Lee trailed off for a minute.

"Rosalie took me in and I called you from her home," Lee made eye contact with Ethan for the first time that day. "The phones went down because a house-fire nearby burned the pole, I just got lucky I called you when I did... Rosalie uh, she had a heart attack about a week later... Ran out of medication for her condition, it was why she was in the Target store to begin with, hoping beyond hope. Instead, she found me. Poor consolation prize, I know. There were just too many dead in town for me to get to the pharmacy, God how I tried though. I set fire to half the other buildings trying to distract them, but I never got through. I was out of ammo and the people in her senior-living community weren't allowed to have guns."

Before Ethan could say anything else, Lee did offer a ray of hope, albeit a gruesome one. "The infection doesn't spread quite the way we thought it does. See, a guy I met along the way got bit on the left hand. Before I could turn my gun on him his friend chopped the hand off with a hatchet. Blood sprayed everywhere, but it was arterial spray going out, not infected blood going in, get it? After we got a bandage on it we started a fire and cauterized the wound. For the next three days no one slept, I promise you that. We just watched Nick suffer and suffered he did, don't get me wrong, but without the original infection site to continue spreading the infected material he pulled through. He might even be alive today, we separated outside Cape Girardeau."

Keith's attention turned to a sound on the wind, something like a motor or wheels crunching gravel and screeching around turns. In seconds he could hear a truck coming over the hill and a flatbed with a crane extension came into view. The truck pulled into the yard and Allen climbed from the cab's sliding rear window onto the cherry picker's boom. In a minute or so, after Allen had knocked over the house's old free-standing television antennae with a wide swing of the crane, they were able to get off the roof one at a time. None of the zombies were fresh, so none could make a serious attempt to climb the truck.

Once on the road Allen started laughing, though it was drown out some by the wind, "No one's gonna fuckin' believe we just did that!" Jimmy, Allen's thirteen-year-old brother, thrust his fist out the open window and started to hum the theme song to the Lone Ranger on the way back to town. The truck passed by the one Keith had destroyed the night before. There wasn't much left of the zombie or the truck and Ethan poked Keith in the ribs and teased him about driving like a woman.

"So what's town like now?" Lee asked as he shifted to sit next to his brother. "And who're these kids?"

Ethan appreciated that Lee might as well be stepping into an alien world, "Remember that baseball player who was behind us by about two years, the one who wrecked his Mustang just before graduation like a good little stereotype?" Lee's eyes lit up with recognition, "Those are his little brothers, but town's nothing like before. The buildings are the same, but none of them are used like they were when we were kids." That led Ethan to another talking point, "What did Keith tell you about how he and I ended up here?"

"All of it."

"Oh..."

Lee nodded with a deep respect for what his brother was capable of, if properly motivated, "You had a lot of tough choices to make, but the one I'm most proud of you for is that sergeant you put out of his misery." The image flashed through Ethan's mind, projected from his pupils onto his eyelids so he could never forget. "It's triage, Ethan and I think it's the part of the job you didn't grasp before."

"Combat losses are one thing, Lee. What *they* did to *her* was above and beyond the call of sociopathy."

"I can't disagree... I'm sorry I washed my hands of it... of you. I was a careerist dick and you deserved better than to be run over by CID's fake-ass investigation."

In all honesty Ethan was neither prepared for, or to, accept anyone's apology. Hell, he hadn't even forgiven himself for letting so many people down. In an older, more civilized time he would rightly have been expected to fall on his own sword, "I can't, Lee. Not right now." Ethan changed the subject, "You should know these guys in charge are going to try to give you a job, hell they'll probably deputize you on the spot."

"Is that what they did to you?"

"I was using them to help make it safer here. Not sure if I've succeeded really."

"The Mayor keeps trying to promote your brother, but Ethan keeps saying no." Keith joined the conversation since he'd been eavesdropping anyhow.

"Mayor Atwood stayed?" Lee actually laughed. "That Klan-loving cunt doesn't leave his timeshare in Florida unless it's *time* to campaign again. Mom said he telecommuted to the last two town hall meetings. Did FEMA threaten him or something?"

Ethan smiled, "New guy, some fat old Marine from Branson, you'll love him. Personally, I like giving him shit because he's about as pop-culture savvy as Grandpa was. He's doing good work, though. I think he can hold the fort down while we go get Mom and Dad and Nicole."

Lee didn't express his true feelings on his brother's plan, not yet at least. As they rolled into town, like Keith's truck, it too was a mess. The main battle was already over and people were just sitting in small groups to rest, weary and dirty from the fight. The undead hordes they'd encountered before were just small packs in comparison to the infected tsunami that had washed over the town. They had been wandering out of St. Louis for a month now, some massively wounded by military attacks but still quite mobile.

The sight of miles of putrid chunks of flesh and clothing stretching down the highways, an image nobody who saw it could ever forget. Had there been no plans to draw the zombies away with sirens and other distraction techniques while people hunkered down, more than a cursory three people would have died. They couldn't help but wonder if similar million-zombie-marches were heading down I-70 and I-55, the two other major highways in the state and how long before those herds found their way here too.

"I wonder why the Stanton outpost didn't say anything," Reynolds was saying to the other leaders as the rescued men entered the police station.

"We have an outpost in Stanton?" Ethan narrowed his eyes at the officer. "I thought we'd consolidated everyone."

"We had to know if anyone was coming from the North,"

Reynolds defended the decision, not that he had anyone to answer to.

"Well the men you sent there are dead now," Lee said flatly.

"Thanks, Captain Obvious," Reynolds' tone was testy.

"It's First Lieutenant, actually."

"I remember you," Newton pointed at Lee. "I pulled you over in that hot-rod 88' Mustang next to the Chinese place a couple years back. You had more beer in your trunk than a Budweiser delivery truck."

Lee smiled, remembering the night fondly, or at least the parts he could remember. "Yeah, she's in a parking lot in the middle of the graveyard that used to be Fort Drum. She was a good car though. I'm Lieutenant Lee Kelly, Ethan's brother," he stuck his hand out to shake, Newton and Reynolds both accepted.

"Where'd you come from this late in the game?" Newton asked. He seemed suspicious, but he was the only one who felt that way.

"I walked here from Chattanooga."

"Oh. Okay then," Reynolds didn't really have any more questions about that. The timeline made sense and this new guy looked enough like Ethan.

Newton and Reynolds went back to their conversation. They were discussing body removal, just another task on a to-do list that never ended. Mass graves for the infected corpses had become the order of the day, because there was no other choice. Most funeral homes had stopped accepting anyone bitten, no matter if they had been euthanized before the virus took hold. The Easton Funeral Home was silent as they drove by, the people who'd taken over from the original owners had a strict *Natural Causes Only* policy. All the dead from that night had been bitten and so none were accepted into the immaculate building. An incensed relative of someone came by and used red house paint to write *WHAT IF IT WAS YOUR CHILD?* across the funeral home's clean white walls. No one had a good answer for that, but why should the morticians be expected to take such a risk? This was no run of the mill virus after all.

Daylight crept through holes in the ashen clouds. The dead who'd come into town were sluggish, not as prone to chasing people with excitement as before. Keith was on a warpath for Paula's house now that they'd checked in and no one, dead or alive, was going to stop him from getting to her. Lee and Ethan were following, providing cover and arguing with each other about all manner of shit.

"I don't want you to sign up here. These people are nice and all, but we don't owe them shit," Ethan said to Lee as Keith roundhouse kicked a zombie in the head. It fell into the side of a train car full of silica sand and a small quantity of it poured down the chute and onto the zombie's head, burying it 'alive.' It didn't move again. As impressive as the move was, Ethan continued, "We need to gather supplies and head for Oklahoma. I figure if we drive in shifts, we can be there in a couple days, a week on the outside."

"And why would we do that?"

"Because our parents are there! My fiancé is there!"

"Look, it doesn't matter, Ethan. We can't go to Oklahoma."

"I got an email from Nicole the same day you called from Rosalie's house. They're alive and I'm going," Ethan made the statement seem final.

"Yo, Keith, we'll catch up," Lee said over his brother's shoulder. Keith didn't even turn around. He knew what Lee was about to do and right on que punched his brother in the face. "No, you're not. None of us are and that's final."

Ethan got up and acted like he was going to accept Lee's judgment, then headbutted the scruffier looking man. It was not a very tactical thing to do, because it hurt Ethan every bit as much as it hurt Lee and the brothers both staggered back in pain. Soon they were rolling in the gravel, swinging wildly at each other until Keith turned around in a fury. He only did so because they were attracting zombies and that might delay them longer. Pulling out a bottle of bear-mace he shook it and aimed it at them, "Knock it off!"

"Whoa whoa whoa! I'm done, we're cool," Ethan quickly surrendered to the power of sticky capsicum oil.

"Pussy," Lee sneered, certain he tasted blood.

"Have you ever been OC sprayed?" Ethan used a train car to pull himself back up to his feet, "because fuck you, I'd rather get shot. We'll talk about this later."

In the residential part of town, just past Main Street, most people had cleared their own property of zombies. A family in a recently restored town house was performing last rights for a little girl, presumably their daughter, not more than six. Her mouth was gagged and her body bound while she squirmed and snapped angrily at the people gathered. The parents wailed in grief as a relative prepared to put their little girl down for good. They turned the corner and heard the gunshot, the mother screamed louder.

Even in the darkest days of the Black Plague there were more people left alive than now. There'd been more chances to accidentally keep from contracting bubonic plague in medieval Europe than there was of protecting yourself from InV1. Had people in the Dark Ages even a rudimentary concept of public sanitation, the Black Plague may never have taken hold in Europe in the first place. But *this* epidemic, Inviere Virus: Strain 1, or InV1 for short, was just sadistic. How could a benevolent God allow such a thing to be created, some might wonder. Ethan would have suggested that, just because God had a plan, didn't mean you'd like it. Strangely this wasn't just cynicism, as Ethan was a firm believer in Intelligent Design. He, however, also firmly believed that the Almighty was much less like a personal shepherd of all mankind and infinitely more like a kid with an ant farm. Just like Tywin Lannister, he might believe in (the Gods), but that didn't mean he liked (him) very much.

At the door to Paula's house a handful of zombies were banging slowly on the door, moaning and smearing their blackened paste-blood all over what had been relatively new whitewash. Pulling out an illegally modified Tech-9 Keith had taken from the now unused and unguarded evidence lock-up, he mowed the zombies down on full auto. Then he cracked the last one in the head with the piping hot barrel just because it wasn't falling down fast enough.

Keith dropped the weapon after he'd finished, jumped on a railing above the porch and climbed up to the balcony that connected to the upstairs windows. Ethan and Lee stood in the yard, Lee dabbing blood off his nose and Ethan's eye beginning to swell. They bore witness to Keith's display of parkour prowess and romantic overture. The women in the house looked the worse for wear, the battle overnight kept them from their beauty sleep, but they too watched with jealousy while Keith pulled Paula out of the second story window and onto the roof for a movie-moment recreation of the V-J Day kiss.

A stocky looking woman in hockey armor was riding a bicycle nearby when Keith tore the zombies down and rescued his girl. She was a photographer/journalist for the first daily newspaper since the Army retreated, albeit printed on 8 ½ x 11 computer paper and stapled together by lamplight. Her camera clicked a dozen times during the eons long kiss and the image would be on the front page of the paper by the next day.

"I'm gonna be a little busy today, but I'll catch ya for dinner, okay?" Keith said to Paula, who was too absorbing it all to speak. He helped the love of his life back inside her house and hopped down off the balcony to greet the Kelly brothers, "Dafuq you two staring at? Carry on." He smiled, pretending to be someone special.

Chapter 11

The Winds of Change

Bringing Lee to the party was, as Ethan found, just like bringing the younger, more attractive and better socially adjusted brother to any party. The town's leadership immediately loved him and if Ethan wasn't wrong, Office Rowe might actually have swooned. Late that afternoon, back at the police station, Lee went into Kenly's office for a debriefing. The only person who didn't seem to hang on Lee's every word, besides Ethan, was Newton. They were still within earshot of the Mayor's open window, but both were standing under a smoker's pavilion as it began to rain.

"How the fuck did we not see this herd coming?" Ethan made small-talk. He wasn't necessarily better at it than Newton, but at least they could be awkward together.

Newton took a long drag of his cigarette, as if giving the question genuine consideration. "Normally they follow the roads, but this one came from the woods. If I had to theorize their eyes are too glassy to see the roads clearly anymore, but the lights from town? Well, they can still see those from miles away." He threw the butt into the grass, ignoring the bucket for them, "Did seem a little serendipitous though, that they'd find the one section of fence we hadn't even begun construction on yet."

"Nature's been trying to kill us since we unleashed Pandora's box on Nogales."

Newton craned his neck, "You really agree with the nut-bag zealots? That Zim is somehow divine retribution, or nature's wrath?"

"*Zim?*" Ethan hadn't heard that one yet.

"They turn a little green and they want to destroy mankind, so *Invader Zim,*" Newton explained, as if the correlation were apparent.

"Nice, I'm using that from now on."

"So why aren't you in there with your brother?"

"Why aren't you?"

Newton lit another cigarette, "Because I already know what's out there. Anarchy, destruction, carnage... hell we got that right here," and a back-hoe carrying bodies passed the station, interrupting, yet adding depth to the cop's words. "I don't think you should leave, Deputy Kelly. I think, if your family is at the OKC-FEMA Camp, it may not be comfortable, but they are safer there than they would be here. Those smote by the gods will be gone in a year, maybe two. Then the camps will empty and you'll get your family back. Your concern should be helping your brother make certain they have something to come back to, a new world for only the worthy to survive and inherit."

"Tell ya what," Ethan sensed Lee's story coming to an end by the laughter of those listening to him. "I'll start acting like I like it here when you get a real fucking haircut." It was true, Newton's already badly done home-job was growing out and looking even worse. Certainly, he still showered, because he didn't stink, but maybe *Newt* wasn't washing his hair as thoroughly as he once had and it clung to itself with a few days of light grease.

"Careful not to let your little brother eclipse you," Newton ashed the cigarette. "Nobody thinks about the sun, only the shadow cast by the moon."

"Thanks, Confucius," Changing the subject, because his brother wasn't one of his favorites, Ethan decided that, if they were waiting it out in Sullivan, then he should actually try to make it a safer place. "Say, you hear any more about a Liger from refugees coming in?"

Caught off guard, Newton almost dropped his smoke, "Oh, that? I think it was just a rumor. That zoo probably put all the dangerous animals down, I know that's what they did in Chicago just before the mayor called it quits and shot himself."

For some reason thinking of shooting anything in a cage, albeit an apex predator, didn't sit well with Ethan. Probably, he thought, it sat even less well with the zookeepers themselves. Then it dawned on him, maybe it *really* didn't sit well with some of the smaller zoos. Maybe some said *fuck it* and let the beasts go, assuming the end was nigh. Before Ethan could fully flesh-out his theory, Lee and his new cadre of admirers left the building for a smoke break.

Lee walked directly up to Ethan with his overconfident and heavy foot-falls, putting his hand on his brother's shoulder, "Big things are coming Bro."

"I'll take your word for it," Ethan was a little dismissive. As much as he loved his little brother and was overjoyed that he was alive, part of Ethan was realizing he had just lost the limelight. Another, nearly forgotten part of himself was also very clearly asking, *did I want it in the first place? Because it didn't feel bad.* "There's a thing I think we should talk about, it may be nothing but it's at least worth a look."

"Speaking of having a look, I want to see this fort you commandeered," Lee was clearly talking about the hill-top at Meramec State Park, but it took Ethan a second to catch up. "Putting concrete road barriers around it in place of the wooden fence was a great idea."

Unused to being complimented by Lee, at least not in the last four or five years, Ethan struggled to realize he wasn't being torn down. "Yeah... uh, I thought it would be a good fallback for everyone in case of- well *this.*"

Taking Ethan off to the side, Lee gestured to the town before them, "Has it not occurred to you that you are, relatively speaking, First among Deputies?"

"It's not like there was anyone else for them to turn to."

Lee laughed a little, sparking up a big fat cigar that Kenly had given him, "You're a fuckin' dumbass, but I love you, so I'm gonna spell it out to you. The three cops that stayed are going to be taking on the position of deputy mayors until a more functional city council is established. They want to offer you the position of Sheriff, but you keep saying no before they can finish their sentences."

"So they offered it to you instead," part of Ethan's heart

actually sank. This wasn't the first time he'd sabotaged himself, in fact he'd made an art of it since his downfall. What would Nicole think of him now that he'd just fucked it up *again*?

"Well, duh, but I said no."

Now Ethan was really confused, "So then you wanna go to Oklahoma with me?"

"Wow you're dense. No, I counter offered that we should instead double-down on the organization of this town. We have the manpower that we can separate the law enforcement deputies from those who go outside the wire. Those guys I can train and organize into a more effective fighting force of expert cavalrymen-" and then it was lights-out for Lee when Ethan sucker-punched his brother in the temple with all his literal might. The others stared in disbelief. Ethan cracked his knuckles and didn't give them the satisfaction of knowing he already regretted what he'd done.

Part II

One Month Later

Chapter 12

"What, our place not working for you anymore? Because you can have Ethan's room. He passes out on the couch most nights," Lee smiled, putting his gloves on for work. Winter had come early, the amount of ash in the sky had reduced the season of fall to barely a week of semi-enjoyable weather.

"I don't think Ethan would appreciate a crying child at all hours of the night," Paula caressed her not showing stomach. She could have just been full of food for all Lee could tell, but he wasn't going to say anything.

"Where is the Devil, if we're speaking of him?" Keith had to ask. It had been at least a day since he'd seen his best buddy.

"I sent him and that kid Allen on a scouting mission. They took a couple four-wheelers yesterday."

Keith narrowed his eyes at Lee, "And what are they scouting?"

"The other towns."

"For what?"

"For everything and anything, but mostly because Ethan won't drop this *Liger* thing, so I had to do something with him. In this case he'll see there are no big, mix-breed cats and we can finally get some real work done."

"And who gave you the authority to give orders around here?"

Lee smiled, "Take a ride with me today, Sergeant Brewer. I have a job offer for you too."

Paula stepped in. "What does it pay?"

"Um..." Lee wasn't sure how to answer that. Money was still something the town had no use for and they couldn't exactly promise gold if they had none to exchange. "Well, you want your own house, right? If Keith accepts my offer, I can surely swing one of those town-houses near the hospital. Mayor Kenly wants to start dolling those out to refugees and I think you both more than qualify."

"Deal."

"You don't even know what he wants. I might be the town's new professional escort," Keith rolled his eyes at Paula.

"Well you certainly have the ass for it," she said through gritted teeth, pawing at her fiancé in a way that made Lee intensely uncomfortable.

Pretending Paula hadn't just done that, Keith motioned for Lee to continue. "Bootcamp for the Cavalry volunteers is two weeks in and I need a medic."

"I think Ethan would be pretty butt-hurt if I left the deputies."

"He's going to be butt-hurt no matter what I do. He's had an exceptionally low opinion of all things military since-"

"Since what?" Paula had to know, "What? I've been living with you guys for three weeks and I know nothing about Ethan besides he acts like a bigger asshole than he really is. What did the Army do to him that made him hate it so much?"

"Covered up a murder," Lee said frankly. "There's an article in *Maxim Magazine* that was almost a carbon copy of what he saw over there, '*Love and Death in Iraq.*' He sent me a copy, but I didn't read it for... too long. I guess I didn't want to know, didn't think the source was that credible, I don't know."

"I'm confused, did he cover up a murder, or did someone in his unit?"

"Them, definitely. My brother is a lot of things, but a woman abusing sociopath that's adept at covering his tracks, he is not."

Keith nodded, "He does lack a certain... finesse."

Lee agreed, "You should see him try to play a video game that requires being stealthy. I swear he invented the

'*Leeroy Jenkins*' before it was even a thing. Anyhow, Ethan tried to blow the whistle on the whole deal, wrote letters to congressmen and lodged some pretty damning accusations with the Inspector General." Keith winced at the notion of raising such a fuss. As an NCO he was well aware of how whistleblowers were treated post-blow and it wasn't pretty.

"Snitches get stitches, huh?" Paula guessed.

"Something like that. I'm sure he could give you more details, I admit I tried to insulate myself from his inevitable downfall." Lee was becoming aware, while saying all this out loud, that just maybe he should have listened more and hung up the phone less. "It's not that I didn't try at all to get him out of there. Once his unit made it back state-side I had a friend in another battalion, who was putting in a request for more MP's anyhow, slip his name into the pile of 'random' soldiers whose serial numbers were drawn for the assignment."

"Well that was clever," Paula didn't seem to see the subtext.

"Oh, yeah and it cleverly fucking backfired. I was there when the liaison from Third Infantry Division told Cassy that she needed to stay in her own lane and dropped Ethan's paperwork into her trashcan with that stupid fucking bull-dog mascot stamped over the cover."

There was silence for a moment, "Does Ethan know you did that?"

"Yes and maybe it's the only reason he doesn't disown me, but it only made things so much worse for him. They'd already busted him down to E-1 for some bullshit involving an iPod in a secure area, because contacting your congressman isn't technically against the rules, but of course any dissention in the ranks has to be extinguished."

Keith wasn't very surprised, just disappointed, "Once you're a marked man there's virtually nothing a unit won't do to ruin you further. I've seen the *Fuck-Fuck Games* take down the best of us."

"Hence his overactive sense of justice and morality, but

it's also the very reason he lost faith in the first place, started drinking and popping pills, smoking weed, the whole nine. Personally, I think he needs professional help, but not the patronizing kind and definitely not the kind I can give him. That bridge has effectively been burnt," Lee motioned to the black eye that had only just faded from casual view.

"Then we'll build a new one," Paula said, putting words in Keith's mouth. "When he gets back you pin that star on his chest and act like it was never an option to begin with. These two men," she petted Keith's hair some, "did what an entire army wouldn't and it was all your brother's idea. He's the type, that if you saddle him with responsibility, he will rise to the occasion. However, if you treat him like a child he'll show you a child."

Lee popped the lid on a flask he'd stolen from Ethan, "I can drink to that."

Chapter 13

Elsewhere

"Explain to me again why I followed you out here?" Allen jumped to the hood of a car. It was wrecked into a ditch near the long-closed *Toy & Truck Museum* in Stanton, which was as far as their scouting mission had made it. "I mean, how many big-game hunts have you been on?"

"Three."

"*Game*, not man-hunts, I know you get those confused."

Ethan narrowed his eyes, "*You don't know me.*"

Allen laughed and seeing nothing he jumped back down to the street, "So what's your plan, exactly, if we do find a fucking Liger?"

"Not here to do anything to it, I just want to rub it in Lee's smug fucking face that there was one."

"And if there isn't a Liger?"

"Then I got to go hunting with my lil' buddy," Ethan tried to noogie Allen, but the kid was quick and dodged it. "I just gotta get away for a little while. The worst thing I'm expecting to find is-"

"A naked body?"

"Jesus, no."

"No, I mean there's a dead, naked guy in that parking lot," Allen was pointing at a building that had once been a successful hotel with an attached steakhouse. The whole thing had gone belly-up multiple times before Ethan was in high school, but vague memories remained. Indeed, though, there was a dead man laying splayed out in the parking lot like he'd been there all along, no clothing or a means of transportation readily in sight.

Taking out his phone, Ethan started recording video and handed it to Allen. Ethan turned to talk to the camera, "The time is 1552-hours, we're approaching an old motel in Stanton and have discovered what appears to be a recently deceased, black male." He pointed for Allen to record the body as he approached with rifle raised, "Keep a look-out around us, I don't want to get ambushed."

"By a Liger?" Allen rolled his eyes.

"By anything, asshole," Ethan cleared his throat. "The deceased is approximately thirty to forty years of age, I can see what appears to be an entry-wound to the left side of the chest just off center mass. No visible bites by infected or animals and as we can see the subject is, for no reason I can readily discern, completely nude." Bending down, Ethan pulled a small LED light from his pocket and started looking around the scene. "I don't see any trip-wires or alarms, I'm going to try to look underneath him."

"Ever think you might be paranoid?" Allen chimed in.

"It's not paranoia if someone's actually out to get you," Ethan reminded his young padawan. "The wound has been cleaned, I can smell soap. I'm going to roll him." He did so and was greeted by a clean surface but for some pebbles. "No exit wound, so it's still in there. No drag marks either, this guy either fell here, or was placed here."

Allen heard something to the side of him and turned to face an empty field, although the hair on the back of his neck was standing on end. Someone, or probably some*thing* was watching them.

"Does your radio work?" Allen asked, trying not to sound as nervous as he was while he put the otherwise useless cellphone away.

Sensing Allen's tone, Ethan did a radio check with town. What bothered him wasn't that they were out of range, because that he assumed, but that he was getting the same low hum on all channels. The only way that would happen is if someone were broadcasting silence from several radios at once, like a homemade jammer. "We need to get back to my car."

"My thoughts exactly," Allen wasn't certain, but he felt like one of the shadowy places in the unkempt grass wasn't where it was when he'd looked last. "So, Mr. Knows A Lotta

Dumb Shit... Is it true you shouldn't turn your back on a tiger?"

"Yeah, that's why people in India wear... wait, really?" Ethan raised his rifle at the grass, "Are you sure?"

"Nope, but then again I'd rather be called a coward than That One Guy Who Got Ate By A Fucking Tiger," Allen started backing away slowly. Ethan's Crown Vic was just around the next corner and if they ran for it the beast might only get the older man's fat ass before Allen was able to make it inside the protection of the car.

"How many big-cats did the zoo have, do you remember?" Ethan tried to calm Allen by talking to him as they slowly headed toward the car, circling one another for better cover.

"A couple, I don't know, I wasn't a zoo-person."

"Well, I don't mean to alarm you, but I think we interrupted feeding-time."

"That body?"

Ethan nodded, aware that he was being set up to be the hunter from the first *Jurassic Park*, the one who says, "*Clever girl*" right before he gets eaten. "Take the keys off my belt-loop and go back to town for reinforcements." This time he actually saw the hips of a large-cat move between two overgrown shrubs and almost opened fire.

"Why am I driving? I don't even have a license."

"Because I'm staying here," Ethan didn't turn around, he knew exactly where that animal was now. "Go get my brother and maybe a bigger gun."

"I'm not leaving you here."

"This is not the time for bravery, Allen. I'll stay hidden in a building, but I can't let these animals take that body. There's a bullet inside him and I want it."

"Your funeral," Allen snatched the keys and sprinted for the car. If this were a movie one of the cats would have made a move for him, but in real-life they didn't attack on que.

Hearing his "lil' buddy" drive off with his grandma's car, Ethan wasn't certain he'd made the right decision. Not by a long shot. Now all he could hear were the cicadas and the wind. Putting his ear-plugs in just enough to dampen the deafening muzzle blasts of an M-16, but not the rest of the world, Ethan started approaching the sheds. He stayed in the clearing of the leaf-covered road and fired three rounds in a perfect quarter-sized hole through one of the rusting tool sheds. Even though he could hear the brass shells clanking to the pavement, he didn't hear, or see the animal drop.

Switching the abused looking M-16 from semi to three-round burst, Ethan lit the building up with a sick grin on his face, determined to regain his status as the hunter and not the hunted. Before the magazine was completely empty he dropped it and slammed another into the magazine well with the practiced fluidity of a salty soldier. He had, however, only brought this one spare and so now his count was down to thirty one. Staying on the road, Ethan headed back up the slight incline to the abandoned motel and the body. A stray zombie, looking the worse for wear, found her way into the immediate area and he shot her too, though with a wall to his back for cover.

Flies were starting to gather in droves around the dead man when two patrol cars and an ambulance showed up to retrieve Ethan, albeit almost a full hour later. Lee, of course, had to tag along and why not? Ethan had failed to produce the proffered Liger and it was basically Lee's duty as a brother to rub that in his face.

"Um... Ethan," Lee was clearly going to tease him as he exited the car and pretended to be confused by the scene. "Do we need to go over basic animals with you again? Mom said you couldn't pronounce hippopotamus until you were five. I only say this because this is not a Liger. That is a human. Can you say hoo-*man*?"

"Clever. Eat any good books lately?"

Lee laughed, "You know I only eat-"

"Show some respect, a man's dead," Ethan cut Lee off. "I think they were going to feed him to a big-cat."

"Did you actually see a big-cat?" Lee lit a cigar, his

signature move for zoning out when he wasn't interested in a conversation.

"Yes."

"The whole thing? Like you could tell me what color it was and everything?

Ethan's glared, "Now isn't a good time to be poking holes in my story. I'm not fucking around, Scout's Honor." Lee was taken aback that Ethan would invoke such a thing. Given that they were both Boy Scouts once and that he'd never done this before as a joke, Lee paused with the comedy material.

"Alright. Let me see what Reynolds wants to do and I'll help you process the scene." It was good, or at least serendipitous, that both brothers would have a background in law enforcement. Since Reynolds was busy helping to train the next generation to bolster the Fire Department's numbers, he handed Lee a role of police tape and wished both men the best of luck before returning to his pupils. Ethan noticed Reynold's chubby little girl was among the ranks and for whatever reason that made him smile.

Using a now worthless one-hundred-dollar bill as a base for measurement, (because fuck it why not,) Ethan began a more thorough investigation of the body. It took about ten minutes to photograph everything within a few inches, then he motioned for the trainees to collect the body. That part was all Reynolds, so Ethan took Lee to explore a building neither had been in since early childhood, long before the restaurant closed. Built in the 1940's the "Delta Motel" was exactly the right fit for a time when *Route 66* was the main thoroughfare for the country. Thousands of similar strip-motels dotted the road, but this one was perhaps a little more unique than most with the lighthouse-esque restaurant built into the second story of the primary building. By the early 2000's the motel was by-the-week apartments and then abandoned, but what remained cut a striking figure in a one-horse town.

"I've always loved urban exploration," Lee admitted,

following Ethan through the unsecured front door. The unpleasant atmosphere of mold was only offset by the sourness of urine from refugees and the junkies before them.

"I think you meant to say you've always enjoyed trespassing," Ethan teased back, trying to show he was at least a little grateful help had arrived. The lower levels were little more than a rundown office area. There were no signs of recent inhabitation, except that the employee bathroom seemed to be where those hiding here overnight threw their refuse.

Using an ion-lithium powered "flashlight," basically a phased-laser from the future meant to blind deer and melt enemy spaceships, Lee scanned the whole lower level before they moved up the gently curving staircase to the restaurant above. Precious few signs remained that this level had ever been more than storage, but these included booths for diners and a large coffee machine. It was all covered in cobwebs and bird nests, especially near the large bay windows. One was shattered and the plywood covering it had long since begun to rot, letting in all sorts of vermin. This was also where most people stopping for the night chose to barricade themselves before pushing on to Sullivan in the morning. Given the view of the highway that made sense, except that some of the trash was fresh, yet no new refugees had arrived in more than a week.

"So why do you think he's naked?" Lee made conversation so they could hear something besides their own breathing.

Ethan shrugged, "I couldn't venture to guess. It's too cold to not be wearing something right now. Normally I wouldn't discount an overdose of some kind and the hospital will be able to tell us more after they autopsy him, but the gunshot wound is kinda telling." Dumping the contents of a child-themed backpack, it revealed mostly empty water bottles and dirty clothes for a woman who clearly wasn't a child anymore. He didn't find any ID's, but there was more clutter to look through.

"I'll be downstairs," Lee blew a truly crappy smoke ring and was entirely too proud of what he'd made. Ethan took the stogie and wiped off Lee's slobber like it was a dog toy, giving his brother a disgusted look.

"You're nasty," he commented, then drew in a mouth-full of smoke before showing-up Lee with a ring that was not only passable, but that lasted for almost three seconds before dissipating.

Lee narrowed his eyes, "If the zombies don't kill you, I will."

"Learned that playing dominoes with some lovely mercs in Iraq. Those Blackwater boys know how to party, lemme tell ya." Still feeling the urge to explore after Lee tossed the cigar and went back downstairs, Ethan rounded the far corner to see what kitchen equipment might still be left. He was a little dismayed to see there was nothing but a singular long sink piled high with an animal's nest that had fallen from the ceiling tiles. One last thing caught his attention though, which he had assumed was just a water heater, but that was before it lunged out from the corner and struck him in the face with the butt of a rifle.

True story: *During basic training there is an event popularized by Hollywood. This event is known as Pugils and it's meant to simulate using your rifle in hand-to-hand combat in case of a malfunction, or if you feel like breaking a perfectly good rifle over someone's head. The weapon looks like a giant Q-tip and if you have ever pretended to be Darth Maul with his double-bladed lightsaber you're already ahead of the curve. Having readied himself since the release of* Star Wars: Episode I *for exactly this, Ethan was a proficient, perhaps even deadly duelist. Amidst a crowd of cheering and jeering soldiers, he donned his padded helmet, put the mouth guard in place, adjusted his groin cup and stood relaxed with the enormous padded stick in his hands. Ethan could practically hear theme music playing in the background, a whisper on the sweltering Missouri winds that gave him the impression he was destined for greatness.*

On the other side of the court was his opponent, two hundred and thirty pounds of brick-shithouse with the IQ of a watermelon, PVT Macey was a prolific thug and a Drill Sergeant's pet. He was the kind of useful tool the Army desires above all others and the polar opposite of the one hundred and eighty five pounds of pale hillbilly that was PFC Ethan J. Kelly. Drill Sergeant Baker, a rabid fan of Bill O'Reily and MMA fights, had rigged it so that the know-it-all former cadet would face off against his dynamic opposite. Ethan wasn't worried though, because he was the ace in the hole and besting Macey at something physical would be a badge of honor to wear until graduation.

The whistle blew and Macey charged with a roar, the pugil in one hand like it was luggage and not the intended primary weapon. His heart only just beginning to race, Ethan prepared a graceful pirouette and spun the stick effortlessly around him in a display of prowess. Naturally, (because fuck his life,) that was when the one-size-fits-all helmet slipped forward and completely blinded Ethan. There was no time to react, not even to pray, let alone use The Force. It was like knowing your car is about to get hit by a semi and there's only that fraction of a second to acknowledge the inevitable.

The impact of PVT Macey, because there was no evidence he'd ever used the pugil, was a lot like being trampled by a horse. Ethan was aware of his brain staying in place like a cartoon while the rest of his body was smashed to the ground and stomped on for good measure. The only thing that hurt worse than the actual impact was hearing Drill Sergeant Baker's thunderous laugh and the collective mutters of shock and disgust of the other soldiers at Macey's display of calloused violence against an obviously helpless nerd.

Chapter 14

The pressure building in his sinuses was instantly more painful than the hit itself and as tears filled Ethan's eyes he saw the shadowing figure make a run for it. Choking on blood and snot, he wasn't able to call for Lee, but his instinct to reach for his sidearm remained and he pulled the trigger twice into the ceiling. Having your nose broken by the stock of a rifle would make anyone momentarily murderous, but more than anything Ethan wanted to interrogate this person. It was notoriously difficult to get dead men to talk.

Lee ran back up the stairs and burst through a row of boxes like the Kool-Aid Man, gun drawn, "Where's Zim? Are you okay?"

"No dombie," Ethan couldn't pronounce his Z's just yet and spat a wad of bloody snot while pointing frantically at the rear employee exit. "Man ran dat way!"

Reynolds and a few of the other men weren't far behind Lee and while one of them helped Ethan to his feet the rest chased after what they could only assume was the murderer. It did cross Ethan's mind, though, that if this was the murderer, why not just shoot him and make a run for it? There were more questions here than answers for sure.

It took less than an hour, but Ethan was already bandaged up and perfectly lucid when Reynolds and Lee decided to call it quits on the crime scene. It was getting dark and after much searching nothing new could be found about the mystery assailant, or why their vic was nude. During the ride back to town, Ethan and Lee rode in the ambulance with the body. For Ethan this was the moment he cemented his change of heart and asked Lee if the offer to be sheriff still stood. For Lee this was a watershed, not to be unreasonably optimistic, but the only thing he wanted out of all of this was to see his brother be himself again.

Ethan was actually so distracted by thinking about who the assailant was that he didn't really come out of his daydream until Kenly was halfway through handing him a badge on the steps out front.

"... we do hereby appoint *Sheriff* of the Provisional Territory of Sullivan, with all the rights and responsibilities afforded thereunto," Kenly finished by pulling back the felt bag in his hand to reveal an antique looking sheriff's star. Ethan took it slowly and studied the Missouri State Seal in the center, then flipped it over and read the engraving on the back. Though worn, it still clearly read *Aaron R. Kenly.*

The others dispersed as, to them, this was just an overdue formality, but Ethan remained next to Kenly on the station's sidewalk. Lighting a celebratory cigar from Lee, Ethan stared off into the overcast night, "Did the doctors find anything?"

"Why the fuck should I know? I'm just the mayor," Kenly mouthed the stub he was still smoking. "But yes, they're cleaning the bullet now. Sadly, Doctor Ramesh thinks we won't get much in the way of ballistics. The round was mostly sandwiched between two vertebrae, whatever striations present will be distorted."

Ethan sighed, "I was hoping for more." His face still really hurt and he couldn't breathe out of his nose, which made the cigar seem somewhat wasted. He'd have a black eye for a couple weeks, but the nose wasn't fully broken at least. Lee had broken Ethan's nose twice since middle school, this was just a love-tap compared to an air-hockey puck to the face. As teens they'd been banned from two separate arcades when the staff realized they weren't actually playing the game, but trying to injure one another with the puck. On more than one occasion passersby were caught in the crossfire, thus netting them their final ban from the local bowling alley.

"We don't have any suspects," Kenly winced as he watched Ethan adjust the bandage over his nose. Something inside the younger man's skull made a cracking noise that sent chills up the old man's spine. Ethan looked ridiculous, but at least he wasn't dead. "Besides, you said it yourself, we can't incarcerate someone for a capital offense. We'd be forced to hang them just to prevent future escape."

"I'm glad you used to be a sheriff," Ethan admitted. "I can't imagine being able to do this if I had to string you along with all the *Why's* and *Do's* and *Don'ts* of policing."

Kenly's laugh was deep and throaty, "That's what your over-ambitious brother is for."

"In another world Lee could be president one day... that, or the type who'd be rejected from Hell as a Takeover Risk."

Pulling away Ethan's cigar, as he was nursing it like a plebe, Kenly had thoughts to share. "I got shot on my very first solo patrol," Ethan's eyes widened at the opening to the story. "It was 1992, I was young and dumb and completely distracted by a pair of tits that looked like two moons glowing in a sparkly sequined dress."

"And she shot you for looking at her boobs?"

"No, asshole, the prick that used her face as a punching bag shot me," Kenly showed the scar by lifting his Marlboro promotional shirt to reveal a through-and-through just above the liver. "The point is, we all get blindsided sometimes. Sure, you got lucky the vagrant didn't shoot you too, but you were already trying to solve the crime of your own volition. This isn't about revenge, you just want the truth and that's the kind of shit I expect from you from here on out. Got it?"

Ethan smiled, thinking he'd be clever by quoting the movie *Starship Troopers*, "I guess I'm your man until I die, or you find someone better."

Mayor Kenly's brow furrowed, "There's no need to be so melodramatic, *Sheriff*. We'll have elections again in a couple years." Clearly, Kenly didn't get the joke, a dynamic that would come to define their relationship going forward.

Being Sheriff, though, wasn't as exciting as the job description made it out to be. For weeks the daily routine was to arrive too early, do too much work overseeing the rebuilding of a police department before lunch, skip lunch because Deputy Blah Blah was sick and someone had to man the gate, then take over Deputy Fragile-Ego's patrol route because they were bogged down with a citizen complaint, try to eat something for dinner, go to meetings with the town leaders even though they had little to nothing to with him, go home, get stoned, rinse and repeat. If he was being honest, though, Ethan hadn't felt this alive in years. If only Nicole was there to see it, oh how she'd love him again then. Soon, he told himself. Soon the undead would be dead again and the gates would open up and she'd come home with his parents and his insipid fantasy would make a lovely Hollywood story.

Twice in the coming weeks he'd been roused from sleep by the night shift reporting sightings of who they suspected were the Texans from the Labadie Power Plant. Their Humvees would sit almost out of sight and simply watch the town, to wit Ethan's standing order was to alert the Cavalry via radio and continue their regular duties. Lee, for his part in the situation, had always ordered his patrols to avoid the Texans to prevent any misunderstandings one way or the other. They'd talk when they were ready.

The citizenry at large, those from town as well as newcomers, seemed to respect Ethan's brand of law enforcement. He clearly wasn't there to hem anyone up on bullshit charges, though he was notoriously quick to let drunks spend the night in jail. Any illicit narcotics, like crack-cocaine, heroin or methamphetamine, or the obvious chemicals and equipment to manufacture them, were confiscated and destroyed. The person(s) in possession of them likely sent South and told not to come back.

There were those who argued such a practice was barbaric, including one of the former deputies who'd quit the force around the time Lee's sweeping changes took effect. Vincent Bass was always kind of a strange one, even back when Ethan and Lee had met him in high school. He was a religious fundamentalist too, though that was hardly what made him weird. He would hand out flyers about church events with a 9mm strapped to his hip, or take up collections to help notorious (reformed) African Warlord "General Buck Naked" raise funds for a new church. Seeing him at a town hall meeting berating the department seemed personal to Ethan somehow, sure he'd done better than the archetypes Vince so despised. He wasn't about to change the way he treated meth-cookers though.

As the winter drew closer most people resorted to living in a communal setting. Neighbors staying with neighbors, or in sheds where wood and coal-fire stoves still existed. Once, just before Thanksgiving, Ethan beat the fire department to a house fire that had already claimed the lives of eight people, including three children. Unable to save anyone inside, he was relegated to keeping nearby friends and onlookers away, despite their screams of protest to save the younglings. The coroner's report cited smoke inhalation and that most, if not all of them were dead before neighbors ever noticed the orange glow across the street. Knowing they didn't feel it didn't really make him feel better about it though.

It was a bitterly cold morning just days after the fire that saw Ethan overseeing five "Frequent Flyers," as he called those whose antics put them in his path more often than most. Today they were digging graves for the victims of the fire and one unrelated suicide. The four boys and one girl, none over the age of eighteen, were war orphans. Collectively they were of the opinion that it was just shy of their duty to enjoy all the finery and debauchery Mankind had left to offer before it and they were gone. The boys wore thousand-dollar suits taken from the office of a banker and the girl a prom dress with combat boots and an all-black field jacket. They fancied themselves a "secret" society of refined individuals who would be the Observers, (again their words), of the Fall of Humanity. That was good and all, but busting them drinking expensive scotch, smoking weed and shooting paintballs at road signs while grinding the gears of a 1957 Jaguar in a round-about at 02:10 in the morning, was hard to overlook. Ethan considered the demise of that car to be a loss to history and therefore he was almost happy to be their supervisor on this detail.

"We're sorry, Sheriff," one of the boys said during a

water break, trying to speak for the others.

Ethan, who was comfortable in his patrol car with the heat on, simply nodded, "That car survived sixty years, was treated like a princess the whole way... and then you idiots came along and trashed her in a night. Tell me, any other artifacts you'd like to destroy? Use the Mona Lisa as toilet paper, maybe?"

"It's not like that, Sheriff," said the one named Mike. Ethan remembered from the paperwork only because he'd had to resist making a ginger-joke.

"Then what's it like? Enlighten me," Ethan turned the radio down.

"Man, c'mon, nobody was ever going to drive that car again. It would have been left in that garage until weather and nature crushed the whole thing. This was its last chance for a joy-ride and we're honored to be the ones to take her on that ride."

Ethan smirked a little, "And what do you think Mr. Stratman will think when he gets home, about how you dicked-up his beloved Jaguar?"

The kid's face went from repentant to disgusted that Ethan would even go there, "Nobody's coming back for their old shit, just like nobody's coming back for any of us. They're all dead already. We've heard the traffic on the H.A.M. radios, there's fewer of them broadcasting every day, especially out West. Nowhere is safe, not even in those FEMA zones. How's the saying go, *the end is extremely fucking nigh.*"

That was an interesting exchange, at least in Ethan's mind and he said as much at dinner with Keith and Paula. She was really showing now and Keith had taken to pranking her by leaving needed items on the floor. For those who may not have lived with a pregnant woman, *down* is the one direction they cannot bend. Lee hadn't been staying at home anymore, preferring to set the example by sleeping in the "barracks" with his men. Really it was just the regional airport's primary hangar and adjoining office building, but

Ethan had to admit it really did resemble a functional military base at this point. Soon, if the winter didn't make the roads impassable, work would begin on the hilltop fort they'd rescued months earlier. The plan was to turn it into a secondary cavalry post that could function as a fallback point for the entire population of the town. It had, in a way, fulfilled that function during the last horde to pass through, but that incident only highlighted the fortress' deficiencies. Not enough food was stockpiled, barely enough for more than a twenty-four-hour siege at this point and the toilets backed up easily, but crews were working on both.

Ethan set the skillet on a cooling pad in the center of the table. Paula turned visibly green and ran for the bathroom when she saw the bacon he'd prepared, "I take it she doesn't like it crispy?"

"Morning sickness should be called *Just Sickness*," Keith sighed wistfully, unsure how he could love that woman more than he already did. "We're thinking about an official marriage ceremony at town hall, but we can't agree on who should officiate-" A crashing sound followed immediately by a gunshot sent both men flying down the narrow hallway to the back of the house, just like when Lee had first come home. The passage seemed to stretch on forever like *Rose Red*, but Ethan actually out ran Keith and was first in the master bedroom where Paula had her hand around a zombie's throat. Its left hand was clasped tightly on her right, so she couldn't get a shot and the right hand clawed at her shirt.

Without hesitation, or even slowing down, Ethan tackled the zombie out from Paula's arms and together they crashed through the thin drywall that separated the bedroom from the laundry. The zombie hit its head on the dryer, which sort of stunned it, but the whole fiasco opened the barely healed wound in Ethan's nose and the blood flowed like a river. Even though the zombie, whom Ethan felt he recognized, was already in the secondary phase of the infection, its attempt to get to him only intensified at the smell of fresh blood. Whatever little energy the virus could muster it used to try to spread in a last-ditch, wild-eyed effort.

"Shoot him!" Ethan shouted, pushing the snapping jaws up from below the chin. Even with laser-assisted aim, Keith wasn't sure he could make the shot without hitting his friend too, so he went to herd Paula into another room. Even if Ethan died, she had to live for the baby. It was a choice Ethan would have made too, so it was no hard feelings.

Knowing he was temporarily on his own, Ethan shoved a rolled pair of socks in the Zim's mouth and punched it for good measure. He then used the precious spare moments before the socks were spat out to find something more useful. His choices in a room full of soft, fluffy laundry, were limited to say the least.

An antique iron, the kind you had to wear oven mitts to handle, was on a recessed shelf as decoration, surrounded by horseshoes and cobwebs between the washing machine and dryer. Thanking his grandmother from beyond the grave for never throwing the heavy chunk of metal away, Ethan reached it with the tips of his fingers just in time for Zim to claw the socks out of its mouth and keep coming. The iron almost came off of the shelf on the first try, but Ethan had to elbow the zombie in the face to keep it at bay one last time before finally giving it one more good lunge. Bringing the unbelievably heavy appliance down point first, a happy accident as he hadn't been looking, Ethan sank it to the Sears & Roebuck emblem.

It made the same *schlock* sound as tearing off a turkey leg and for the first time the noise made Ethan momentarily want to vomit. Keith returned with a shotgun so he wouldn't miss no matter what and probably because he'd left the 9mm with Paula.

"Give me a sign or I'll put you down, man," Keith was deadly serious, but that was word for word the first thing Ethan had ever said to him. For no reason whatsoever Ethan started laughing at the irony of it. Since Keith had been pretty banged up at the time, he likely didn't remember their initial encounter.

"I'm fine, my nose just opened up again is all," he assured his friend.

"You'll forgive me if we wait it out."

Ethan nodded in agreement, but took one of Keith's clean shirts off the nearest pile and wiped the blood from his face with it, just because that was the Ethan thing to do. "I recognize him now."

Leaning in, but not through the door, Keith eyed the body, "Deputy Harper, from the South gate."

"He's cold too," Ethan felt of the man's skin, "Like outside-cold." As if on cue a wind moved the backdoor just enough to make a creaking noise. Keith went to investigate and realized there was a strip of tape over the knob's catch and the deadbolt was retracted. Across the bluish haze from a full moon, Keith saw another figure in the trees overtaking the backyard. He took aim at what he assumed was another zombie, only this figure recessed itself further *into* the woods and attempted to hide.

"There's someone out there," Keith set about tearing off the tape and resetting the locks. Rather safe than sorry, he checked all of the other doors and windows while Ethan rode out his five minutes of quarantine in nerve-racking anxiety. It was a little harrowing clearing the converted basement, as the door built into the bricked-over garage entry wasn't the most expensive door Grandfather Kelly could have used back in the day, but it was unmolested.

Keying the radio attached to his work belt, Ethan called the station for backup while he shook drywall out of his shirt sleeves. This far into the valley it was a crapshoot for signal, but it was the best they had for now. Maybe in the future he'd get a flair, or the damned Bat-Signal.

"Get Paula into the loft and pull the steps up after you're settled in. I'm going to shut off the lights and see if I can spot someone outside."

"Better idea, I should fire a couple shots in a second, it'll make whoever's still out there think another one of us had to be put down. Then, if they do come in to finish the job, they'll only expect one man and a pregnant woman." Ethan nodded in approval, returning to Keith his bloodied shirt, "...I liked this shirt..." Keith lamented.

Explaining the plan to Paula and that there was still someone out there, she voluntarily pulled the ladder up behind them. Ethan cut the cord and now the way upstairs was all but invisible. Returning to the body of Harper, Ethan shot it twice more while Paula let out a blood curdling scream that would easily be heard outside. Their trap set, Ethan kept low and skulked into a corner behind an enormous, aged TV that took up the entire corner of a room. The bulbous set had stopped working a decade before most people even owned a VCR, but had proudly served as the ready-made stand for all the television sets to follow.

For almost twenty minutes nothing happened and Ethan strongly considered Keith might have just been seeing things, but then he became aware of the sound of muddy boots on the hardwood floors. *This was actually happening!* Ethan's heart began to thunder and his mind raced with possibilities when he remembered his radio was still on. Clicking it off just in time, he heard a garbled transmission come over the spare set charging in the kitchen. The intruder fired through the false wall separating the dining room from the kitchen-proper and charged another shell into the chamber of his shotgun before going in to see who he might have hit.

Sure that he had a clear line of sight, Ethan stood up and knocked the newest television off the old one by accident. The clatter alerted the intruder to what was the matter and even as Ethan emptied all eight rounds from his .45 into the wall, the intruder ran back out the door he'd come through and into the night. Reloading and clearing the house again, Ethan secured the door and turned on every outside light that still worked. The radio in the kitchen, which hadn't been hit at all, chirped again and Ethan went to check it.

"Is anyone on this line?" he said into the little black box.

"*Sheriff, is that you?*" It sounded like Allen, but there was static.

"Affirmative, break, I need backup at my residence immediately. I've been attacked by live intruders. One male, unknown size and description, one Infected. No new infections." Dropping the mic back into its holster, Ethan went to check on his friends.

The trapdoor in the ceiling dropped a little, "Did you get him?"

"No, but we're all locked down. Unless you smell smoke, though, don't leave until backup arrives, even if I have to go get them."

"Did you at least see who it was?" Paula stuck her head into view.

"Yeah, it was fucking Santa Clause and he's pissed I left him warm cheesecake and half a blunt last year," Flashing red and blue lights appeared through the windows and the deep whooping sound of the siren was a welcome relief. Ethan considered it only a matter of time before their attacker decided to burn the house down with them in it.

A thundering knock at the door and Allen's muffled voice actually startled all three of the would-be victims. He and Deputy Charlie Whigg came in to secure the scene and were both surprised to see Harper's body. It was made all the stranger because he was supposed to be on duty right then.

"Did my transmissions get through?" Ethan wanted to know, finally letting himself absorb the scene from a dispassionate point of view.

Allen nodded, "You should move closer to town, man. It was only an educated guess that it was you calling for help." Like hell he was going to abandon his home this late in the game, but Ethan could see the logic in it. For certain he'd have to install a hardline telephone, but that might be an inevitability for the entire town.

Whigg, one of the more responsible and older war orphans who'd been unceremoniously adopted by the Department, helped Paula and Keith down from the narrow stairs to the attic while Allen and Ethan went about making solid contact with town. The next person to arrive after the cruiser's more powerful radio made it out of the valley, was Deputy Mayor Newton. He was all decked out in police gear since he'd been taking a rotation as the Officer In Charge while Ethan was off duty.

"Is Miss Brewer alright?" was the first thing he wanted to know.

"Yessir," Ethan reported, even though it was arguable Newton didn't outrank him anymore. "I'm sending her back to town with Deputy Whigg and her husband." Ethan turned his attention to Whigg, "Charlie, take Keith and Paula to the Cavalry barracks. Tell the sentry at the gate these are my direct orders; wake Captain Kelly and inform him in person that the Brewers are to be put under armed military escort until further notice. He can contact me on Channel Nine when they're safe. Until then it's radio silence, even through the town gates. Flash your lights in Alpha Sequence and they'll let you through without challenge."

"Yes, Sheriff."

"We're not helpless, you know," Keith protested.

"Of course not," Ethan handed Keith his utility belt, gun and all. "The real person under protection is your child. I expect her to outlive us all." Keith paused, mouthing the word *Her?* but there was no time to explain it was just a guess. Whigg piled his wards into the patrol car and went sirens blaring toward town.

Arming themselves with weapons from Newton's patrol car, the three men prepared to go on another manhunt. With the moonlight, it was relatively easy to follow the trail of the inept assassin. He wore smooth-sole cowboy boots and slipped in the bloody snow where he'd kept Deputy Harper tied up during his rage-phase, the decapitated zombie head used in the murder was jammed onto a broken sapling nearby. A lot of preparation had gone into making it look like an unfortunate zombie related accident, but the perpetrator seemed to not expect anyone to be armed inside their own homes. There were a lot of plot holes that made this look like the bone-headed idea of a rank amateur and not the machinations of a professional operator. Using Newton's car as a repeater they stayed in contact with town while stalking the trail. It came to a road that paralleled the Meramec River for about a quarter mile and there the boot prints ended with entirely new prints.

Allen turned on his flashlight to check something he suspected, "Horseshoes. The guy had a horse waiting here."

"Why a horse?" Newton looked confused.

"Because they're quiet," Ethan theorized. "At least quieter than a motorcycle or an ATV. I dunno, it's all pretty fucking elaborate, but dumb at the same time. I mean, why with all the smoke and mirrors? There are more efficient ways to kill someone"

"Like a nine-millimeter to the chest?"

"I got no proof they're related," Ethan debunked Allen's theory, "but if roles were reversed and assuming the zombie in my house was just meant to draw me out into the open, this would be a good place to shoot me. It's where I'd do it, for sure."

Newton holstered his sidearm, "Yeah, that would have been smarter than taking off on an animal we can still track. He at least should have left a trip-mine."

"Well, thank God this fucker hasn't figured out how to build an IED," Ethan started down the road in the direction the hooves led. The 12 gauge from Newton's car had no sling and he wished his .243 still had ammo left, if only because the leather harness was soft and well formed to his shoulder. Just after midnight, Lee couldn't take it anymore and asked to join the hunting party with some of his men. Ethan wouldn't have it until he figured out where this guy had gone, or until he lost the trail entirely. Besides, there was no way a squad of heavily armed soldiers could sneak around as well as three men with their ears to the ground. Ethan also wanted more eyes and guns surrounding Keith and Paula, even if there was no proof either of them were the intended targets.

By six in the morning, nearly ten hours since the attack,

they'd tracked the horse in an arching loop that took them, first, along the river's edge. Then the tracks made an abrupt turn up the seldom used Rock Road before turning on State Highway FF toward town. With snow flurries beginning to obscure the way and stick to the wet ground, it actually created a shadow effect that highlighted the hoof prints for a short time. Calling for retrieval, Allen took the lead over the radio to organize the deputies closer to town to search for horse tracks along FF. It didn't take another fifteen minutes and Deputy Carlisle and his trainee Sanders called all units to their location. Disturbingly, it was barely a block from the police station.

Nestled on a little street that dead-ended at the railroad tracks, sat a run of the mill, blue house from the early 2000's. It was designed from the ground up to be low-income housing for single mothers, but wasn't so displeasing to look at it would bring down property values. This unit had an attached garage and despite there being a Jeep Grand Cherokee in the driveway, it was obvious the occupant was using the garage as a stable for his horse. *In a post-plenty world, a horse actually made a lot of sense,* Ethan thought. Strangely, for someone who was an outdoorsman in his youth, Ethan wasn't a fan of horses. He likened them to vegan-dogs with the hipster-like smugness stereotypical of people with a chip on their shoulder about being vegan. However, being that he wasn't a moron, Ethan could see his department needing trained riders in the near future. He just wouldn't be one of them, executive privilege and all.

Once the majority of his men had gathered just out of sight of the suspect's house, Ethan called to apprise Lee of the situation. Against his wishes, Lee arrived with the M-1114 and the two largest men he could muster. This was the law's problem, not the military's, but now that he could see Lee just a parking lot away, Ethan felt bold enough to begin. He flipped on the lights to Carlisle's cruiser and illuminated the house.

Keying the mic, Ethan cleared his throat, "Attention.

Attention. This is Sheriff Ethan Kelly. Exit the house with your hands where we can see them." Someone peeked through the slits of the window blinds and Ethan repeated himself while curious neighbors watched from up the road, just beyond Lee's position. "This is your last warning," he tried again, but this time the barrel of a shotgun protruded from the bathroom window and took a potshot at the cops.

The buckshot went wild and hit no one, but the response was for Lee to have his gunner fire a burst from their turret mounted M-249 over the top of the house. Normally, this was a good enough trump card, gambling that nobody would seriously consider going up against a machine gun. This was generally a safe bet, except when you're trying to intimidate someone who has a *bigger* machine gun. Where the shotgun had been, a new barrel appeared, one that at first Ethan had trouble recognizing because of the shadows created by the blue and red LED lights from the cruisers. Lee, on the other hand, knew he'd been shown who had the bigger dick the moment he saw the length and girth of it.

A brief pause, where even the birds went silent, descended on the hillcrest and grassy nulls of gathered cops. Then the incredible *whump whump whump* of an M-240 shook everyone like the bass speakers at a concert, so hard you could feel it in your chest. A trail of dirt kicked up and walked directly toward the patrol car where it cut Deputy Carlisle almost in half long-ways and set his cruiser on fire with tracers. His trainee, a cop from Springfield who'd only joined the department earlier that week, was showered with glass and burning shrapnel and went down covering his eyes.

Mortified that he'd just seen his brother machine gunned in front of him, Lee rushed the scene with his M-4 blazing on three-round-burst. Everyone was shooting at the house in that instant. Thousands of rounds turned the cheap siding and foam insulation to confetti while Lee slid to a stop in the blood and gasoline-soaked mud where Ethan had been standing. Despite the crossfire, Lee just stood there, looking around like that poor bastard in *Saving Private Ryan,* searching for his severed arm. As the deputies and cavalrymen moved in, Lee spotted Ethan behind a parking bumper, desperately trying to cycle another shell through the Mossberg in the awkward position he was laying. Falling upon his brother like he was long-lost buried treasure, Lee embraced him under the red glare of the two-way tracers. Ethan was drenched in viscera, but it was from Carlisle and he was otherwise unharmed.

Taking the initiative, the Cavalrymen drove the armored Humvee straight through the single-story home's living room. The fight was effectively over, the enemy gun silenced and over Lee's radio they heard the all-clear. The deputies had somehow taken the assailant alive, albeit it seemed he'd "fallen down the stairs" on his way into captivity. This "falling" required the suspect to be hospitalized, but they were only a block away from that too. Though he had no real authority to do so, Lee ordered other deputies to ride in the ambulance with the suspect. Officially it was to prevent a conflict of interest, but really it was because Lee had an inkling the suspect wouldn't have been entirely safe in Ethan's sole custody.

It was awkward walking with Lee after such an event, but Ethan needed the time it took to secure the scene and hoof it to the hospital to detox from the adrenaline. He had the dubious task of informing the department that Deputies Ian Carlisle, a well-liked and hard-working officer, and notorious slacker Clyde Harper, were dead. This was assuming the rumor-mill hadn't already done that for him, but the weight of duty compelled him still.

This wasn't exactly the same situation as with Roberts back at Six Flags, but the guilt was just as bad. Ethan didn't know whether to wipe the blood off his face or not, it felt callous to do so, considering he'd at least known Ian for a few months. Though he was apparently adept at hiding it, the detox walk was just the newest version of Ethan's age-old enemy; *taking a deep breath and counting to ten.* For the hot-tempered youth, that was just ten more reasons to crack you in the face with a wiffle-ball bat.

Upon arriving at the hospital, Ethan was met by Rowe and Reynolds. The little round woman looked pissed, but that was to be expected when there'd been a two-way machine gun fight in the city-limits she was responsible for. To her credit, though, she didn't mention that when directing Ethan to the room where his attacker was being kept, feeling she could scold him later in private.

"Are you sure you don't want us to handle this?" Reynolds offered, possibly being the more rational of the bunch right then.

"Thanks, but no thanks, George. I can maintain," Ethan promised. He and Lee stepped inside the private room where the man's bandages were still being wrapped. Politely, they waited until the nurse left before flanking the bed. Pulling a seat up and leaning forward on the back as he sat, Ethan took a pen out of his pocket and started dragging it up and down the guy's bare feet like he was testing for brain function. This served two purposes, the first to make sure the suspect was aware and second to annoy the ever-loving piss out of him.

"Knock it off, fucker!" The man shouted, thrashing against his restraints.

"Oh good, you're lucid," Ethan scooted closer, making sure the legs of the chair dragged at the perfect angle to create that terrible scraping noise. "You were Mirandized at the scene, right? Because I can read you your rights now."

"Eat shit."

Ethan pretended to scribble that down on a blood-soaked notebook from his breast pocket, "...eat... shit... Got it. So, can you guess what my next question is?

"Why you?"

"Penny for the pretty lady."

The man glared, probably because he didn't get the admittedly obscure *Firefly* reference, but the tone was sarcastic enough. "Because you ain't the plucky-fuck hero you think you is. You and your doctor-fuck-buddy is killers. I was there, I seen whatchu did. The killin', the mayhem... it really were Helter Skelter, weren't it? Then I seen how you lit off like the pussies you is and just when the fight was only startin'. No one messes with awn outlaw MC!"

Ethan jabbed the pen into the man's arch and didn't let up despite his screams, "You're damned right I was there and I'd do it again and again and again." He twisted the pen each time he repeated *again* until Lee had to intervene. "Do you know why we stopped killing you bastards!?" Ethan maintained eye-contact without looking too strained. *"Because we ran out of fucking ammo!"* He shouted, showing his calm was just painted rust. Rowe and Reynolds both rushed in as the shouting from all parties intensified, but didn't it stop the sheriff from making an ass of himself. Luckily, the two pre-war cops were the only two besides his brother to see this most unprofessional meltdown.

Documents found in the house, which the man didn't own before the plague, suggested he was Dylon T. Cole, a trucker whose mailing address was the nearby hamlet of Steelville. None of that mattered to Ethan, though. To his mind he'd brought the perpetrator to justice. Until and if he was called to testify in court, his job was technically over. Taking the next couple of days off to fix his house, Ethan did notice a new shadow swinging from a purpose-built gallows in the parking lot outside Wilson's Jewelers on Main Street. Instead of looking up at the shadow's origins, though, Ethan simply went about the business of buying some new drywall and a few screws. All while the shadow swayed gently in the wind.

Chapter 15

The deep droning of a multi-engine aircraft roared close overhead, rattling glass and upsetting animals. Ethan, like most people, looked up because it wasn't everyday one heard a plane after the fall of civilization. The entire town was rewarded with a low-altitude view of a camouflage cargo plane descending through the smog, though one engine was coughing blackened exhaust.

"A C-130?" Keith voiced everyone's surprise, "Been a while since I heard one of those."

Ethan was just about to say something but was cut short by the clunking racket of an engine seizing and another one revving to compensate. Some of the clouds and weather systems were still dense with ash from a hundred thousand burning cities across seven continents, as if a chain of volcanoes had erupted. Were a plane to fly through these dense clouds at speed the particulate would virtually sand-blast more exposed parts while simultaneously accumulating in sensitive areas. The plane circled the town in a long arching left turn, lining itself up with the airfield. The Sullivan airport wasn't very big, but a C-130 could make a crash landing there if they were desperate enough. Sadly, the runway was clogged with Lee's cavalry company and their new base of operations. No one had even considered that a plane might land there again.

At the end of the loop, six parachutes floated down through the clouds toward the town. They looked like they'd be landing almost exactly on target for the airfield, except for the sixth, who would land on the highway because of a gust of wind. Ethan and Keith piled into his rapidly aging Crown Vic, not wanting to miss this action and raced toward the truck stop recently designated Liberty Outpost.

Ethan managed to jump into the Humvee that was headed down the highway to pick up the crewmember who'd gone astray. They could still hear the engines sputtering as the plane was getting farther away, so it was at least nice to have someone to ask what it was all about.

The truck came to a halt near a seldom seen refugee, who was also walking toward the town. He was helping the crewman to his feet, but Ethan got on the truck's PA system, "Step away from the airman. Quarantine of new arrivals pending medical examination is in effect."

Waddling up to the truck while still dragging his parachute, the airman looked relieved, if not mildly annoyed. The civilian could have helped him out of the rigging by now if nobody had interfered. "A little help here?" he said. Ethan ignored him and started giving his men orders regarding the refugee. Finally, he assigned one to help untangle the airman while patting him down personally.

The airman continued, "I'm Tech Sergeant Sam Lamont, 94th Texas AirLift Squadron, out of Amarillo. We were supposed to be airdropping supplies to the power plant, but we had bird-strikes, then had to reduce altitude. That fucking ass-soup up there sealed the deal on engine-four, so Captain Michaels redirected us here. The map says this is a green-zone," he gestured to the armed deputies, clearly not there for his protection.

"Is anyone still onboard your plane?"

"How many chutes?" Lamont asked while Ethan finished searching him, relieving the man of his M-9 without a fuss.

"Six including you," Ethan checked over the sidearm before stowing it behind his back. You could learn a lot about a serviceman by his sidearm, much like Forrest Gump's theory on shoes. This one was functionally clean, which meant the oil was dirty from carbon buildup, but still slick from having been recently used. He kept the ammo for now, but handed the gun back to Lamont, "Explain why this town was marked a green zone? Who marked it that way? Who knows we're still here?"

"Fucking bastards," Lamont stamped his foot, pointing at the now almost invisible plane. "Michaels and Saio are still onboard. Part of our cargo is munitions to the power plant's security detachment, lots of shit we don't want gangbangers to have, you know? High explosives and the like, so we have orders to destroy the aircraft and cargo should we have to abandon it. Ten to one those demented fucks are gonna try to ditch over the Mississippi."

"That's a long way from here. Why not just stall it, bail and let the fire take care of the cargo?" Ethan hurried Lamont towards the truck.

"The munitions containers are designed to be recovered from a land-crash, but not water, they sink as a safety measure."

"Enemy?" Ethan narrowed his eyes, "Who's enemy? You still haven't answered any of my questions."

"You seem like you used to be military, surely you know what I am and am not authorized to tell you out of hand," Lamont sighed.

Ethan nodded, "Fair enough. Did any of your officers make the jump if your pilots stayed onboard?"

"No."

"Great."

Back at Liberty Outpost, Lee was already waiting with the mucky-mucks, "What's your pilot's plan for retrieval?" he asked the group of newcomers when they'd gathered.

"Retrieval?" The crew chief scoffed, "*This* is retrieval, Sir. We're alive and with friendly locals. I hate to break it to you, but as orders stand, we're your charges until Texas can send a bird for us. You'll be compensated if you agree to keep us until then."

"That's all well and good," Lee said, "but how are your pilots getting back here?"

"We're given extreme-survival training, Sir," Lamont offered. "They'll ditch overland and make their way back along their last bearings to here. They'll be here in a couple weeks, I'm sure."

"I think we should go after them," Ethan shook his head. "It's a total unknown out there and I don't think their plan is a good one."

"I thought you were against leaving the wire, you know, because you're a *Fobbit**," Lee teased. He obviously wasn't concerned about the pilots if no one else was. (A Fobbit is a member of the military who is not regularly assigned missions that require their presence outside the confines of a protected Forward Operating Base, or FOB. Also see *POG*, Person Other than Grunt.)

Ethan's glare was icy, but accepting. He may not have signed up to kick-cages, but that was what the Army had made him do. Sadly, to do the job of a 'Corrections Specialist', you were relegated to being a *Fobbit* one way or the other. "Okay, if none of you are going to care about the pilots, I'll let it go."

Lee held his hands up for silence, "How's this, if they get into trouble we'll go get 'em. Okay? They have radios, they'll make contact eventually."

"Whatever," Ethan took his boonie cap off and ran his hands through his hair, now long enough to be out of Army-regs. "Rowe and Reynolds are at the Alamo for a training session with a new class of deputy-recruits. I said I'd check in at some point, might as well be now."

"By the way, have you seen Newton?" Lee asked, opening a stick of gum and sharing with some of the other guys.

"No, but I'll bet he's sick. Lots of people on his block have the flu."

Lee nodded, "Half my company has it. I have the guys who aren't sick sleeping in groups of five in different hangars, but it makes me paranoid to split them up like this. On the other hand, I can't have them all down at one time."

"I can assign a couple extra deputies to patrol the barracks area. It would make it easier if there was no reason to keep a fire-guard awake."

"Thanks, but no thanks," Lee was distracted, considering the numbers he had to work with. "The Fire-Guard system has, begrudgingly, worked for centuries. The standard patrols will do fine."

Ethan laughed at his brother's phrasing, "Your Jedi mind-tricks don't work on me, only money!" He quoted Watto from *The Phantom Menace*.

"God I hate you."

Rowe and Reynolds both showed up at the outpost in Reynold's favorite cruiser, procured from the State Troopers. Ethan checked the time and it was about when the class they were teaching would dismiss for lunch. Likely these two called it early on account of the newcomers and because they did not enjoy speaking to crowds the way Ethan did. For whatever reason he reveled it and the more eyes on him the more it excited him. "You guys saw the plane?"

"Yeah, what's going on?" Rowe added, "Mayor is real curious, I gotta tell ya."

"They're Texans. The entire crew except the pilots bailed over town. They're gonna ditch in the Mississippi and make their way back here."

Reynolds folded his arms, a new thing he could do after losing nearly fifty pounds since Ethan arrived. "Can they make it that far?"

"I think, maybe," Ethan changed the subject. "Had an actual refugee come through this morning. He's at the delousing station right now."

"Where from?"

"No clue. I tend to not debrief people when they're being deloused. I heard it makes them uncomfortable, what with taking two D's at the same time."

Rowe was becoming immune to Ethan's sarcasm and occasional sexual innuendos, "Alright, I'll go fetch His Highness, let him know we'll have visitors from Texas imminently."

Harrumphing, Reynolds washed his hands of it too, "Any idea what they're serving for lunch?" he asked Ethan.

Stepping inside the former *Flying-J*, Reynolds and the Sheriff made a B-Line for the restaurant attachment. The convenience store attachment was now a series of semi-private cubicles used by scavenging parties returning from the wild. It wasn't that they needed to be checked for bites, not with Invier-1's burn rate, but it was a good place to reorganize yourself and still be protected. While Reynolds started ordering food, Ethan noticed their refugee was just ending his medical workup.

"I'll take it from here," Ethan took the clipboard from the induction nurse. "The rest is of a non-medical nature anyhow, right?"

"Sure thing, Sheriff," she nodded politely, glad to be away from the refugee's unwashed aroma.

The refugee leaned back in his chair and smiled, "So you're the head-honcho, I take it?"

Ethan laughed, offering for the man to walk with him, "Hardly. I might be in charge of a rabble of deputized citizens, but even I answer to someone."

"That's good. I've been through four other towns since I escaped Chicago and not one of them has had a reliable law enforcer. The best you get is the local bully keeping his version of the peace, but always for a price."

"I wish I could say I'm surprised. I wasn't in the wild for very long and it nearly got me killed. I'd love to hear all about it when you've had a chance to rest. I'm Sheriff Ethan J. Kelly, by the way."

"Juan Berengar," he extended a grimy hand.

"Germanic surname, but Latin first?"

Juan nodded, but was interrupted by a waitress. Startled that anyone would be taking his order, he fumbled for a moment to realize the menu wasn't just trash someone had forgotten to remove, "I... I don't have any money," he admitted at last.

"Neither do we. It's all on a 3-meal ration system, hon," she handed him a flier that was kept in her apron meant to explain this very thing to the expected steady trickle of refugees that had never materialized. "Tips in the form of useful items are never unappreciated though," she smiled, offering to bring them both a cold Pepsi until they figured out their order. Again, Juan's mind was blown that there was soda to be had, let alone that it was chilled.

"How have you all gathered so many supplies?" Juan was stunned.

"We found a train while we were on a scouting mission. Total dumb-luck, but we also have gatherers that leave the wire under armed overwatch. That's how we've managed to find stuff that was overlooked during the Panic," Ethan cracked open the can of soda, though Juan was still seemingly studying it.

Finally, Juan opened his drink and held the can up to his nose like a fine vintage, "I didn't drink very much pop before The War, but this... this is... heavenly." He finished, sipping the froth that collected around the rim.

The waitress returned and took their order, Salsberry steak with fries, "You were explaining an odd name?" Ethan probed. He could see Lee's men guiding the Texans into the induction area and didn't want to be interrupted when they made it through. As curious as he was about Texas-today, he wasn't about to give up finding out what Juan knew about the outside world.

"All of my siblings are named after someone my parents befriended in each country they visited," Juan finished the Pepsi, equally delighted to see a glass of ice water replace it. "Claudet's namesake was from France, Jack's was from New Zealand and my doppelganger is somewhere in Tijuana." Their meals arrived and Juan tore into his, unapologetic at his lack of manners.

Ethan pressed the real questions he had, "So what's it like out there? Really? And how did you find us?"

"Mostly, like you'd say, it was dumb-luck. I skirted along the Illinois side of the Mississippi until I found a town where people were running a ferry across the river. That cost me my Fossil, but what good is time anymore, right?"

"You're rich, I take it?"

"No, but my parents are, or were," Juan trailed off for a moment, "and my brother and sister think they are too. I prefer making my own way, but that's not to say I didn't take advantage of the opportunities presented to me. I got my Master's degree at Berkeley, started teaching at a few rural community colleges in Illinois and Wisconsin. Just did it to piss the folks off by under-achieving, I guess. Best time of my life, though."

"Why didn't you just steal your own boat and cross? Wouldn't have lost your fancy watch."

"Fuck no, man. The Mississippi is a Red Zone from Lake Itaska to the Gulf. Like a log-flume of bloated ghouls, the ones who're done bloating sink again, so it's impossible to see 'em coming in the murky water. I've seen the aftermath, overturned boats, burned out hulks. As soon as a small boat would get near either shore, they'd just be capsized by an army of waterlogged dead."

The blood in Ethan's veins ran cold, "I fucking knew it wasn't safe," he muttered to himself, launching off from the table and running outside. The police cruiser Rowe had arrived in was gone and Keith had borrowed Ethan's car for his own assignments.

Thinking fast, Ethan ran up to a deputy who was just arriving for the day, "Dave, I need to borrow your car." Deputy Carpenter tossed his keys to the sheriff without hesitation and Ethan dived into what was essentially the same Grand Prix he had owned, but as a coupe instead of a sedan.

The passenger door opened and Tech-Sergeant Lamont flopped into the passenger seat, "Do you even know where they bailed out?" he cut Ethan off before he could protest. Lamont took his radio out and made contact with the plane's chief and then with Captain Saio, "You read me, Cap'm? It's Lamont, me and a local are comin' to get you guys, are you still ditching at LZ Bravo?

"Negative, the bird fell almost two klicks short, break, this is Red times fifty! You stay the hell away, Sergeant."

"I don't fucking think you heard me, Captain. I said we're coming to get you. Now shut up, sit down and stand by!"

"Do you always talk to your officers like that?"

"What's he gonna do, court martial me?" Lamont smirked.

Ethan deftly flew down the highway until they reached St. Clair, though with all the obstructions they barely averaged fifty miles per hour. Lamont got another call from his pilots once they were closer, now certain they were in a bedroom community called Pevely. It wasn't close, but it wasn't that far either.

"What's the next town?" Lamont checked an old-style GPS that had been hardened against an EMP. It had a green screen and no backlighting. Thankfully, nobody was slinging nukes at the undead, at least nobody on this continent.

"Cedar Hill, then we can catch 30 to 141, then to 55. Hopefully we'll be close enough for them to pinpoint their locations by then."

Lamont checked Ethan's directions against the GPS, "That should work."

"Okay, just keep watching the map and I'll watch the roads," Most of the towns along Highway 30 were either abandoned, or the residents didn't want anything to do with the speeding car. At the turn to Highway 141, Ethan noticed the road signs were wrong and looked like they were too low on the poles that held them. Highwaymen were trying to confuse people by turning signs pointing to FEMA camps the wrong way.

Lost in thought about the signs, Ethan side-swiped a parked car. Startled at the gunshot-like bang of losing the drivers-side mirror, he did slow down some. They couldn't rescue anyone if they were smoldering wreckage themselves.

For an agonizing hour they sat in silence, negotiating one traffic-snarl after another. Ethan wished he'd waited for a cruiser with a reinforced brush-guard on the nose, "Flight Four Six Six Leader, this is Four Six Six Echo. How copy?"

"*Copy Lima Charlie,*" a voice whispered back. "*Echo, this is Buckeye. Husky is KIA. Need retrieval now.*"

"*Fuck!*" Lamont slammed his fist against the roof of the car, "Captain Michaels is dead." Collecting himself, Lamont pushed the transmit button, "ETA is twenty-mikes, stay calm and stay hidden, Buckeye. We're coming for you."

"Approach with caution. LZ Bravo is heavy Red, like a bitch on her rag. Repeat, Heavy Red. Am holed up in an overgrown golf course, or park or some shit near the river. I'm gonna pop a smoke rocket when I see your vehicle. Over."

"Smoke Rocket?" Ethan hit the gas harder and the car passed the 100mph mark on a straight stretch.

"Ghouls'll go right for a smoke grenade, so now they're basically attached to a giant bottle rocket that leaves a smoke trail back to you, but lands and makes noise and light flashes about three hundred meters away. It's not a perfect system, mind you, but it's saved a lot of airmen."

Ethan perfectly understood, unsure why he'd just used his blinker when passing the wreckage of a charter bus, "We have something similar. They're a kid's tumble-ball, one of those battery powered ones-" Lamont knew the toy and nodded, "Stick a few Christmas bells on that with chicken-wire and you have a ready-made distraction that can last for hours if Zim doesn't accidentally hit the switch."

"Zim?"

"It's what we call the Infected because they turn green like *Invader Zim*. One of our town's deputy mayors thought it up back when he was just a cop," Ethan suddenly slammed the brakes and the car lurched to a stop. Pevely was no longer a rural town along the Mississippi River, but instead was a completely overrun hive of death, the hordes thick even outside of town. There were more undead residents now than people who'd live there before. They could see all sorts of burned out, half-sunken boats and barges wrecked against shores, teaming with the fetid flesh of the undead.

Ethan flexed his grip on the Pontiac's steering wheel, "Call him one more time and tell him to pop-smoke."

Lamont keyed the mic, "Buckeye, Echo. Pop-smoke, we're sitting on the north end of town." They watched and waited, seemingly forever, until finally a blue-hued rocket made it about twenty feet from a nondescript industrial building and started spiraling down into the unbelievable horde.

"Well that was anticlimactic," Ethan mocked.

"Wait for it..." Lamont had been counting in his head, then suddenly ten or more smaller charges sent flares in the opposite direction it had initially been fired from. "For the next five minutes daisy-chained charges will go off every thirty seconds or so," Lamont was incredibly proud of the invention.

Creeping forward, they didn't garner much attention. Thankfully, this Grand Prix didn't have the after-market exhaust Ethan had put on his, so it was still relatively quiet, "Must be nice having Texas' funding."

Lamont sighed, "It would be, in another world." Movement near the building the flare had been fired from caught their attention. Texan aircrews were issued a reversible hunting hat that could either be black, or fluorescent orange. Captain Saio's head bobbed through the uneven field like a traffic cone on the move.

Flooring it, Ethan took the car through the overgrown Teamster's Park. There were ruts and broken branches and maybe even a few low-lying Zims, but the sedan took it all like a champ. Breaking loose the ass-end of a car that wasn't supposed to be easy to slide, Ethan came to a stop less than five feet from Saio, who was considering jumping out of the way.

Saio leapt into the car and they were off before the adrenaline dump wore off. Around the corner and back toward Highway 55, they spotted Captain Michaels. He was jogging along Highway Z after having dumped his gear, a human-slinky of zombies shuffling along right behind him. It might have been comical if the Texan weren't in mortal danger should he slow down.

"I thought you were dead!" Saio hugged and then punched his pilot once they'd dragged him in through the car's open window so nobody had to slow down. "Just gonna go check around the corner my ass!"

"Gentlemen, this is Sheriff Ethan Kelly, from Sullivan. That's where we're heading now," Lamont reported.

"We owe you huge, Sheriff," said Saio, patting Ethan on the shoulder.

"Don't thank me yet, we're still a long way off."

Chapter 16

Finally safe in the vehicle, the two pilots all but fell asleep from exhaustion in the warm interior. Dave's taste in music was abysmal, twenty some-odd scratched up CDR's of *Insane Clown Posse* and *Twiztid*, plus all the worst *Offspring* hits with a touch of *Beastie Boys* to round out the ultra-annoying. The only song Ethan might have considered listening to on purpose was the *Beastie Boys* rendition of Tupoc's *"Boyz n the Hood,"* but that would only be for the comedic value and that track skipped.

Breaking the silence near Londell, Ethan had things to say. "Look, I'm former military, I know what classified means, but we know you weren't carrying just MREs and toilet paper to Labodie."

Captain Michaels lifted his head some, "I guess you should know, Sheriff, the coal's almost gone. Halliburton wants their people back and so do we. Nobody wants to be caught this far from home when the negotiations with the Feds break down again."

"Wait, there's still a-"

A concussive force, stronger than anything anyone had felt before, smacked the car along the front quarter panel. The vehicle was blown several feet into the air just beside a valley of farmland. A second thunderclap and crunch meant they had come back down, but they were still moving, sliding on the car's roof until it crashed through a rickety flatbed trailer that had been abandoned long ago. It was stacked with soggy, weather beaten household items that flew into the air and showered down on the car as they plowed through the wooden frame. The trailer and car went spinning over an embankment and into a mostly dried-up creek. The car hit trunk first and settled into an eerie silence where only the overheated motor could be heard ticking while it cooled.

Though he'd been aware through the entire crash, the shock of actually surviving it was enough to cause Ethan to lapse into momentary unconsciousness- *the nightmarish dreamscape that claimed him every night was waiting when he opened his eyes again. This time, though, he knew he was dreaming and that made all the difference. Instead of being hunted, or being singled out for expiation, Ethan went for his sidearm. When the Sergeant Major came storming around the concrete raid-shelter, he was going to empty the magazine in his scrawny, bird-like face... life was too short to suffer this.*

Gasping for air, Ethan came back to the world of the living first. He looked over at Tech Sergeant Lamont and met nothing but cold, glazed eyes. There weren't any puncture wounds, but with the angle his head was resting, Lamont definitely looked dead. Ethan tried to turn around in his seat, but his neck hurt. For that matter, his whole body hurt. The car's battery was disconnected, but since he'd owned one, just by feel Ethan managed to unlock his door by flipping the red plastic switch next to the handle. With little grace, he fell out onto a gravel bar and went into a coughing fit where he spat mucus and some blood. While rolling on the ground, he saw the car was ass-end down in the part of the creek that held an icy pool, but the passenger section was still dry. What disturbed him most was the sofa leg protruding from the Grand Prix's windshield. Had there been any more force from the crash he'd have been impaled. After drawing his weapon and checking their area quickly, despite his double vision, Ethan first pulled Captain Michaels from his seat. He was dazed, but at least kicked at the gravel to aid in dragging himself away from the wreck.

"Captain? Captain, are you okay?" Ethan clenched his eyes, still trying to recover from a probable concussion. Michaels pointed Saio, who was moving toward the open door with blood all over his hands.

"My leg is broken," Saio said back, taking short, shallow breaths. "Help..." The pain was searing and he could hardly think to speak, but his caring for his men didn't change and he tried to check on Lamont before helping himself. It took

Ethan some coaxing to get Saio to stop trying to take a pulse from him.

"I think he's dead, Sir," Ethan reached through and unbuckled Saio. "I'm sorry, but I'm gonna have to drag you out. It's going to hurt, a lot."

Saio nodded and braced himself for the pain as he helped push himself out of the car with his other leg. Captain Michaels was sitting in the gravel, slowly recollecting himself, but wary of zombies as he scanned the area with his pistol. There was the smell of burning oil and they worried the car would catch fire, but Ethan popped the hood and didn't see any signs of smoke. It must have been the shock of movement from opening the hood that brought him out of it, but Lamont was alive and started thrashing in pain, screaming bloody murder at the top of his lungs.

Ethan punched Lamont in the face as hard as he could, knocking him out cold. Michaels helped Saio get across the creek while Ethan carried Lamont. There was a house on a hill ahead and it seemed better than nothing, even if it was likely already broken into and looted out. They looked back at the car, taking stock and it was well and truly fragged. Everything else on the road was either rusted out, the tires flat, or parts were missing. They were stranded for now.

The door to the house was busted in and so was the sliding door to the porch from the kitchen. There was no smell of rotting flesh, though and no sign it had been inhabited by humans recently. Muddy footprints were everywhere, but all from animals, probably cats and dogs. Michaels limped to check the rooms on the first floor while Ethan cleared the massive living room and the upstairs. Once up the surprisingly noiseless staircase, Ethan found a baby-gate at the top where a dog had been kept. Beyond that, the carpet was dry and mostly undisturbed but for a few leaves.

With his flashlight Ethan signaled over the banister that he needed Michaels' attention while Saio babysat a still unconscious Lamont. The pilot slowly crept up the stairs too and made ready for the swarm of zombies the owner had likely locked in the only bedroom with the door still shut. Taking a deep breath, Ethan opened it. From within a wall of dust and rot assaulted their senses, but then abruptly went away. Turning their lights on again, they looked around an attic space above the garage. There was a lot of junk strewn about, but no cluster of zombies.

"Maybe an animal died in here," Michaels commented on the smell.

For no reason he could logically think of, Ethan reached back and flipped the light switch on. Something clicked, a solar-generator on the roof turned on and the lights in this one room did come back.

"Not gonna lie, that was just on an impulse," Ethan wasn't going to pretend he knew the generator was up there. In the far corner of a room they saw where the smell had come from and why there was none now.

The family who'd lived here was all dressed up in matching BDU camouflage, their child in between the skeletal remains of his mother and father, wearing a children's version of the uniform. They hadn't left a journal, but they did leave a note on a coffee table in a plastic folder with a handgun on top to weigh it down. Ethan moved the now rusted and useless snub-nose and took the note from its sleeve.

"Hey, I'm gonna shut the lights off so we don't waste energy. I think we should hold up here overnight," Michaels didn't give the impression he was asking Ethan's permission, not that he would have disagreed. Ethan started reading the letter aloud.

"To… Whomever,

Our goal was to survive together as a family. Obviously, that didn't work. We lost our little Erika to a car that didn't stop and then our son to this damned walking-plague. Deanna and I don't speak anymore, it's been weeks and she hasn't forgiven me for our babies…

So I shot her and then myself (obviously not until after this note.) I'm not asking you to bless our bodies or some other religious bullshit, just shove us out the window or use us for Halloween decoration, I don't give a damn, I was an atheist.

Sorry there's no Snicker's left in the candy drawer. I don't like Milky Way's, so there's lots of those nasty things. Don't give any to the dog if he comes back. He's a real beggar. I'll miss him.

~Trey"

Ethan stared at the note blankly, then at the bodies. Trey had lost his entire family as the world ended around him, could he really be blamed for throwing in the towel?

"Let's go get my crew," Michaels was feeling brave now, but then suddenly screamed a most unmanly scream and jumped several feet onto a pile of tote boxes. Ethan hit the light switch again and almost opened fire, but stopped when he looked down at the family's dog. There stood a scrawny, adolescent beagle, wagging his tail furiously in his excitement at seeing living people again.

"Hi, boy!" Ethan smiled broader than he expected, "Were these your people?" The dog sat, though looked impatient. Ethan knelt down and took a piece of deer jerky out of his pocket, since he was trying to use food to replace a chewing tobacco habit. He tore off a slice and handed it to the dog, which by his best estimate hadn't eaten in some time. After tearing up the rest of the jerky and leaving it on the floor, Ethan stood. "Let's get the family out of here first. Last thing Lamont needs is to wake up to the dead Simpsons." They did so, but only after the dog had gone up to his former masters, sniffed their remains and said his goodbyes silently. He backed away slowly to go and stand by Ethan, his puppy dog eyes completely irresistible.

"I think you have a new friend, Sheriff," Michaels joked as he slipped his gloves back on. First, they took the boy and then the mother and finally the father. The Clayborns had wasted away nearly to leather and bones and didn't weigh much. Somehow, the family's remains stayed cohesive long enough for Ethan and Michaels to utilize several half-collapsed graves the father had pre-dug, to lay the family to rest. Before shutting the doors once everyone was inside, Ethan called for the dog, who's tag read *Bogey*. He came running, abandoning his vigil over the graves of the dead where he'd stopped to lay down during the burial.

Saio pulled out his radio and, despite the pain in his leg, tried to make contact with town. Lamont's radio was nowhere to be seen and Michaels' was out of power. After a time with no luck he tucked it away, turning it off very slowly, as if the act were physically agonizing. There was always supposed to be a voice on the other end, but when he needed it most, there wasn't. Growing frustrated with the walkie and his own perceived failures as a pilot, Saio threw the brick next to where Lamont was sleeping.

Ethan wondered aloud if either pilot had ever lost a plane before and if that affected them like a captain losing his ship. To that question, the answer from both pilots was a resounding *Fuck No*. A plane, owned by the government, was surprisingly less special than any given personally owned vehicle, at least to most pilots. Michaels referred to that particular C-130 as "slightly newer than a B-17 and half as useful."

Finally regaining consciousness without much ceremony during the B-17 comment, Lamont first reached for his crotch. "Oh, thank God," he said, sitting upright despite some pretty severe bruises.

"Your dick would be the first thing you checked," Saio winced, trying to keep a brave face. It wasn't a compound fracture, but nobody was trained to reset it.

Lamont nodded, discovering he had a mild whip-lash, "Damn right, Sir."

Ethan started doing a check of Lamont's motor functions and vision while Michaels adjusted a makeshift splint on Saio. The Clayborns had stashed a lot of good stuff, including antibiotics, triage supplies like elastic gauze and tourniquets and prescription opioid pills aplenty. Securing the house with his new furry friend, Ethan made certain they'd be safe for the night while they licked their wounds.

"We're going to have to leave them," Ethan said while relieving Michaels for fireguard late into the night.

"What?"

"You and I are going to have to leave them for a few hours. We can head back to town and come back for them with an ambulance and an army to protect it."

"Why can't we just find another car? Saio's leg needs to be set and I think Sam has internal bleeding the way he keeps holding his abdomen. We can't leave them alone, one of us will have to stay and I say that's me," said Captain Michaels, standing a little taller than Ethan now. "I'm not leaving my crew, not again and definitely not like this... but I agree that someone does have to go for help. You can leave at your convenience, Sheriff Kelly. I'm not going to sleep tonight."

Not saying another word, Ethan grabbed a few bottles of water and two cans of spam. As he descended the staircase, the dog was right at his heels. He smiled, realizing there was no getting rid of this one. If he was lucky, Bogey might prove useful if he reacted the same way most dogs did when zombies were around.

A few Zims had arrived to investigate the wrecked car, but had just continued meandering in the direction they were already heading when there was nothing to eat. This gave Ethan and Bogey a chance to get to another house nearby without being detected, then on to the next one until they found a car or a motorcycle in a garage. At the fourth house a car was in the driveway, but its gas tank had been punctured and the fuel drained early in the apocalypse. By chance the house's garage was wide open and a bicycle was sitting in the only clear spot among the piles of weathered junk, a satchel strapped to a rack behind the seat with a bloody handprint on the side was ominous, though. Someone had been planning to bug-out and hadn't made it.

Normally, evidence of someone's death by zombie was not a cause for concern, but the blood was still red, some of it even dripping recently. Bogey must have been a hunter as a puppy, because the first thing he did was follow the blood trail into the laundry room behind the garage, assuming his new master could handle a few Zims. There were two undead in the oversized closet when Ethan finally dared look. One was a boy of about seven, wearing nothing but tattered superhero underwear and one house slipper. The other Zim was a much fresher looking elderly man wearing utility pants, a khaki explorer's shirt and a fishing vest whose pockets were bulging with all kinds of stuff a drifter might find valuable. The man had been trying to get away on the bike after looting this house when he'd been caught by Denis the Cannibal Menace.

Bogey started to bark and Ethan dispatched both Zims with his .45 ACP, then jumped on the bike knowing he'd alerted every ghoul in the area. He certainly wasn't much of a bicycler in daily life, but he did alright, even on the steep hills with the beagle at his wheels. Finally, at the bottom of a valley with an overgrown golf course on either side of the road, he had to stop and consider his next move. Between these two terrain features was a teaming horde of well-dressed Zim. With a gut-punch of loathing, Ethan realized these were one of the many church groups that committed mass-suicide during the final days of the Panic. Unfortunately for him as well, this group had believed the zombies were the literal embodiment of The Rapture and had seen fit to infect themselves en-masse. Something had also gotten them riled up recently, as few were holding still in what was colloquially known as "Zim-Coma." It had been miles since he shot Undead Dennis and Mr. Wilson, so there was no way these fuckers had heard it. The eerie feeling that he was being watched crept over Ethan like a haunting breeze, causing the hair on the nape of his neck to stand on end. Someone was nearby, getting these Zims excited.

"Well, Bogester," Ethan said to the dog, who looked up at him with an expression that said he too didn't like their odds, "we got two choices. We could turn around and look harder for a car I'm sure doesn't exist, or we could just go balls to the wall and hope for the best." The dog looked at him like he truly comprehended and maybe he did on some primal level.

With one heavy push of the pedal, Ethan started down the rest of the small hill and darted in between the undead cultists like they were traffic cones on an obstacle course. Most reached for him, but they were so weather-decayed their efforts seemed half-hearted at best. Once on the bridge, he saw it had been spared the Army's retreating demolitions teams by air-dropped ordnance that had then punched straight through the deck and sank into the river without detonating. Ethan stopped to catch his breath at the top of the bridge where it connected to a twenty-foot bluff above the Meramec. Some of the Zims were coming at him, but at a snail's pace after so many cold months inactive. After giving his companion a sip of water and another piece of jerky, they took off over the hill.

Atop the next crest someone had parked their minivan and then shot themselves next to a tree because, *fuck it*. Their body had lain mostly undisturbed since, save a few small predators picking at the remains of the head and exposed hands. While Bogey stood guard, Ethan searched the body for the keys to the nearest minivan. He found all sorts of knickknacks; an Epi-Pen, loose ammunition and a rusted pocket knife, before finding the keys, though there was a layer of soapy fat collecting on it by now. After a long winter and no maintenance, the van's tires were almost entirely deflated. The engine took a good long while to turn over, but it did start after a lot of struggling and nearly draining the last of the battery's power. Ethan grabbed the dog and they drove cautiously along Highway 30, back toward home. He hit several of the Cult-Zims that had followed him and Bogey barked furiously, apparently feeling safe and bold inside this rattle-wagon. The thought of going back for the airmen now crossed his mind, but it was just as likely the van would get there and break down completely, setting him back to square one and maybe costing someone their life.

The late 90's model Crysler Voyager coughed and sputtered, but thankfully it was holding its own up the winding road that would eventually come back through St. Clair proper. He was able to slip through two rusty looking traffic snarls and a defeated FEMA checkpoint from long ago, but the next intersection was an odd one. Located on a steep downward slope with thirty-foot drops on either side, it forced anyone turning left to crawl to a near stop and make a hair-pin turn while having a great deal of faith in the other drivers around you not to screw up the same maneuver. The turn was all but unnavigable in the road's condition today, covered in partially frozen leaves and twigs from storms. The van caught a large branch and one tire jumped it, ensuring there was no way to swerve back onto the road. This started an uncontrolled slide down the steepest embankment. Ethan cursed loudly as the van fell off the side, hit a tree stump and rolled over into a thicket of saplings, marking his second roll-over in less than twenty-four hours. *At least, though, he wasn't in a tree being hunted by dinosaurs.*

Bailing out of the van as it lay on its side, Ethan got his bearings while consoling a terrified beagle so he'd stop yelping. He could hear Zims moaning to his rear, but could also see flashlights and smoke from houses occupied by non-friendlies to the north. The only way to go was south, toward Sullivan on foot, which meant risking running into people who were looking to rob and possibly ransom him. Kenly wouldn't pay a ransom and Lee's reaction would be unadulterated violence.

Then it dawned on him, the local National Guard armory was just on the other side of the next row of trees near the Elks Lodge. Though such places were often heavily infested as refugees went there seeking help, Ethan couldn't see anyone outside the building, alive or undead. He and the dog ran for it and despite being completely out of breath, made it to the first row of anti-zombie defenses fairly quickly. Sullivan's raiding parties hadn't looted this side of St. Clair yet, which meant nobody knew what was inside the armory.

There could be tanks, weapons, food for months, or there could be nothing at all but a few dusty tables and broken ceiling tiles. Even if it was just a place to hide for a little while, it would be better than being exposed.

The second row of defenses were meant for living people, but it was only razor-wire and a serpentine clearly marked with white tape. Ethan carried Bogey, just to be safe. A few Zims were caught up in the wire, but they hadn't been shot or bludgeoned, which suggested the armory was abandoned because otherwise they'd have been euthanized per SOP.

Smashing open a window that turned out to belong to the female officer's latrine, Ethan grabbed the dog and tossed him inside before squeezing through himself. He'd been in this building before, in a lifetime he barely remembered now, his JROTC unit had conducted a drill competition here. Now it seemed, well, not empty, but definitely still. Junk was strewn everywhere and most of it was collecting dust. No lights were on anywhere and it smelled musty.

He guessed the truck dispatches were, in probability, in the same office as the supply area on the far side of the building. It was the only section the cadets hadn't been given free-reign to explore. If any of the trucks gathering moss on the armory's backyard would also start, he'd be good to go. Only problem was, once he opened the door to the main gymnasium the barrel of an M-249 SAW was just inches from his face.

"Get down on your knees and interlock your fingers over your head. You are trespassing on Government Property. If you make any sudden movements, I will kill you with extreme prejudice," the light shifted and he saw what looked like your stereotypical hard-ass *G.I. Jane* type, with close-cropped hair that might even have been shaved at one time, but that had started to grow out in all directions now.

"No problem, I'm putting my weapon down," Ethan shifted uncomfortably on his knees, the joints that already caused him the most pain. "My name's Sheriff Ethan Kelly, I'm from Sullivan, I promise we're on the same side."

"I don't care who you say you are, we're calling Higher and having them send an armed patrol to come and get you."

Ethan almost laughed, "How's that whole 'calling Higher' working out for ya?"

"Shut up! The call is already being made. I hear prison under Martial Law is a real shit-show," she said, holding the machine gun with a stillness Ethan respected.

"I imagine it would be scary, if there were any prisons left. Look, I know you're lying. I can still see the American flag on your uniform. If you had any government backing at this point, it'd be from Texas," Ethan relaxed. "Are you really even a soldier, or just some drifter that found a uniform?"

"What? Fuck you," the voice sounded something between annoyed and terrified. "We're U.S. Army soldiers, you yokel fuck!"

Ethan put his arms down and sat rather than continue to torture his knees, "Look, I was in the Army too and I too got left behind. I'm just trying to get back to Sullivan so I can get an ambulance and come back for my friends. They're airmen from Texas doing a supply run for the Labadie power plant, or did you not question why you still had power?" The sound of the weapon going to safe to fire made him stop antagonizing the woman, at least for now.

"I don't have time for this. Get out. I am authorized to shoot you if you don't comply."

"What the fuck are you doing?" another female voice came from a rear office, "Damn it, Tori, put the gun down. Can't you see he's a fucking cop?"

"Could be a trick, Sergeant."

"Yes and if it is a ruse, you can shoot him, I promise," there was something about the way she said the word *ruse* that reminded him of a friend from Basic Combat Training, almost ten years ago now.

"Sabrina?" he took a stab in the dark.

There was a pause while the second woman tried to comprehend what she was hearing, "What was your name again?"

"Ethan J. Kelly, Sheriff type," he smiled, recognizing one of his good friends from BCT. "Holey shit it is you, Sabrina fucking Johansen!"

The soldier holding the machine gun lowered it and for the first time Ethan realized the flashlight was meant to hide that the gun wasn't loaded. "You know this bozo, Sarn't?"

"Yes, I do!" Sabrina launched herself forward and bear-hugged Ethan, then kissed him on the forehead loudly, "I didn't think I'd ever see anyone I knew again."

Ethan let go when Bogey tried climbing them to get attention too, "What the fuck are you doing here? Why are you guarding this dump?"

"Final orders from Jeff-City," Sabrina explained, "We were supposed to be collected by helo two months ago."

"Two *months?*" Ethan looked around, noticing the pile of trash bags by the garage door and general lived-in look of the place now the lights weren't in his eyes. They couldn't throw the bags of trash outside, locals would notice and they couldn't burn it for largely the same reason. At least, from the smell, the plumbing was still working. Ethan couldn't deny, if there was any way to keep this building, Lee would certainly be excited to hear it.

"This is Specialist Tori Werner, by the way," Sabrina introduced her gunner, pronouncing the name with a proper German *V* pronunciation. Ethan reached out a hand, but a gunshot outside broke one of the windows from the kitchen. The armory's windows were not wire-mesh like schools, but just regular store-front pains, so without much effort that would be where the people pursuing Ethan would enter. If the machine gun were loaded, it would probably be able to stop them.

Ethan grabbed his .45 off the ground and fired three times from the window he'd entered, "I don't have time for this, I was on a mission to rescue downed Texan Airmen when our car hit what I think was an IED."

"So that explosion yesterday was you," Werner was

putting earlier events together. "We were hoping maybe some of the thugs in town had blown themselves up."

"Do you have a working vehicle? And do you have any ammo for that?" he pointed at the 249.

"Just one and that would be half the reason the gangs want this building," Sabrina pointed to a fiberglass-bodied training Humvee on the far end of the gymnasium behind a pallet of empty boxes. "It looks worse than it is, that's how I convinced them to leave it here. Oh and by the way, you're taking us with you," Johansen said quickly.

"What? We can't leave. Orders are to hold out until-"

Sabrina held Tori by the shoulders, "We have exactly two weeks of food at half rations. When was the last time we heard from Jefferson City? Wake the fuck up, Babe, I love you but I swear to God I will leave you hear if you don't put your gear on and get in that damned truck." Werner tossed the machine gun defiantly onto the concrete and walked back into the rear office where Johansen had come from.

"In case you're wondering, yes me and her, but no, I wasn't when you and I did that one thing that one time," she smiled at Ethan fondly. "And before you ask, no we can't come back here. As soon as we leave a militia of thug types will roll over this building like a swarm of retarded cavemen and we can't let them get all the munitions stored here. That's why Tori and I set *Serious-Puddy* charges three weeks ago."

Ethan choked back a snort-laugh, "Serious Putty?"

"Think about it," Sabrina said, "If Silly Putty is a toy, then what is Serious Putty, if not C-4."

"You shouldn't be allowed around children," Ethan side-hugged Sabrina. Knowing this escape plan was taking too much time, he didn't argue lest it take longer. He simply kept watch for whomever had shot the window out. Across the street, Ethan could see a few Zims and at least one person with a flashlight and a gun.

"C'mon! We gotta go!" Ethan leaned out the window of the truck. Two soldiers in full gear and weapons ran towards the Humvee from the locker rooms, struggling to hold it all together and still move quickly. Johansen jumped in the driver's seat and Werner in the turret while Ethan had the passenger seat with Bogey to navigate. They plowed through the gates and onto the street, smearing a Zim like it was so much soggy cardboard.

Werner kicked Ethan in the back. Looking down at him through the turret she said, "Cool guys don't look at explosions," and pushed a button on a cheap walky-talky. The delay was less than a second and a roof-mounted air-conditioner was sent skyward from the armory. Several more explosions caused the one-level drill floor and office space to implode on itself, all the while ringing the dinner bell for every Zim for miles.

True Story:

Cold, wet and weary for more than a week, Ethan's company was "in the field" on a training exercise "Spartan Focus." By now, there was a thriving black-market in chewing tobacco and cigarettes and naturally, Ethan was dick-deep running that racket. Late one afternoon his squad was assigned to patrol for Opposing Forces, or roadside bombs called IED's. Of course, these weren't real Improvised Explosive Devices, but typically Halloween bomb props. Some seen this rotation were cannon balls with comically large fuses, or bright red TNT sticks that held candy before someone ate it. A waste of time for sure, but this patrol would give some of Ethan's more reluctant customers a chance to sweat the $15 per-can price for the "last" of the much-maligned Cherry flavored Skole. Could he have stocked something people really liked? Sure, but it tickled him some to make the forgetful addicts pay triple for chewing tobacco that tasted like cough syrup.

While clearing what we'll call "Route Badidea," the patrol encountered the laziest, most obvious training IED that had ever existed. There had been one just like it at MP School at Fort Leonard Wood years earlier. Sitting on its side in the middle of the dirt road was a bright-white 155mm artillery shell. Since, to a squad of MP's who'd never spent time near artillery, the shell wasn't green and it therefore must be a training blank. Taking up station around it, Third Herd *proceeded to do everything by the book. The IED was called in to Explosive Ordnance Disposal, (or the sloppily dressed NCO from another platoon who would play EOD in this scenario,) and the waiting game began... then it got boring and then even more boring as the sun threatened to sink. For three hours the ten men and two women took turns telling stories, playing cards, searching for a nonexistent cell phone signal and finally posing for pictures with the IED-prop for their Myspaces, since this story is that old.*

Just before dark, as the last-call for hot chow was broadcast over the net, (meaning they'd missed it and would have to eat MRE's,) an open-top Humvee came barreling into the squad's perimeter. It had a white flag reading RANGE CONTROL *flapping overhead and they drove like they owned the place. As predicted, the men who exited the truck were not dressed to AR-670-1 standard. The jealousy seethed from the more strictly controlled Military Police. However, Ethan noticed these weren't just some paper pushers from another unit on an ego trip. The unit patch of a fat bomb surrounded by a representation of an explosion could denote no other group. Seemed their battalion's over-zealous Command Sergeant Major had actually harangued the seldom-seen Explosives Ordnance Disposal Technicians out from their cave and into the shitstorm of idiocracy that was* Spartan Focus; (*or more aptly,* Spartan Fuckus.)

Striding up to the "IED" while Ethan's squad leader gave them the obligatory rundown on the encounter, the Technician measured it with a yardstick. He then motioned for his protege to join him. He said something in a low tone Ethan didn't catch. He was packing his lip with Grizzly Wintergreen pouches from his private reserve and wasn't much interested in their little act in the first place.

"So, what are you planning to 'blow it up' with? A

smoke-grenade, a flair? Oooh, lemme guess... A balloon animal?" Ethan actually did the air-quotes with his fingers while joking with the lower ranking EOD Tech.

"Nah, we're gonna use C-4," the senior tech handed Ethan a bundle of wires before retrieving a gray block from an orange, padlocked case under the Humvee's canvas seat. *"That's a live 155 shell that fell short on an exercise last week. We've been looking all over for it, so good job keeping a safe perimeter, specialist."* He said with an honest tone. Clearly, he had no knowledge of the previous three hour's shenanigans.

"No problem, Sarn't... we train as we fight," Ethan stammered, several shades paler now. He and SSG Rodriguez got back in their truck and, while pulling 500 meters away to create a safety-parameter, had the rest of the men delete the last few pictures off their cameras. Shortly thereafter a powerful concussion shook the vehicles, followed by the boom itself that was barely muffled by the armored hulls. Debris rained down on the convoy of trucks for nearly a minute as the soldiers sat in stunned, embarrassed silence.

Chapter 17

"You know where you're going?" Ethan shouted over the engine.

"Yeah, I played an away-game in Sullivan in high school," Johansen shouted back. "Also, I have a living map," she patted Ethan's shoulder.

Werner slid down out of the turret and sat in between the seats where she'd been standing. "There'd bettered be a town where we're going, *Sheriff*, or I'll fucking kill you before anything else goes down," she whispered in Ethan's ear.

"I think you'll like my brother," Ethan laughed, "You'll make rank real fucking quick if you choose to stay." Werner raised an eyebrow, but for the most part continued to stare at Ethan the entire way to Sullivan, her hand not-so-secretly on her M-9. At the Far North Outpost, approximately a mile from town, they were stopped by Ethan's deputies. The lawmen were overjoyed to see their Sheriff alive and seemingly well and equally gracious in welcoming two new people, though they thought the approaching Humvee was Texan before Ethan stepped out. Within ten minutes Lee and an ambulance were on their way to the outpost. In the meantime, Ethan took his new four-legged friend inside to warm up.

"Hey, Whigg," Ethan motioned to the deputy in charge. "Make sure this guy gets a place to sleep, some food and water."

"He got a name, Sheriff?"

"I think the family who had him named him Bogey, but I was thinking something ridiculous, like *Electric Boogaloo*. Something that would have driven Nicole insane."

"Uh, sure. Maybe we can just stick with Bogey, Sheriff."

Ethan shrugged, "I guess." Lee walked in just then and Ethan turned his attention to his brother. "Did the Texans make contact yet?" he asked Lee, who really just wanted to slap his brother for being so reckless in the first place.

Lee nodded, "They're coming at first light, where are the airmen?"

"We crashed the car, someone set a boobytrap and it took us out around Londell. Saio has a broken leg, Lamont might have internal bleeding and Michaels is still a self-righteous ass who demanded he stay to watch over them. I had to leave them at a house along 30, but they're safe enough for now," Ethan chugged a Gatorade one of the deputies handed him, glad to see Whigg inside the building feeding Bogey.

Sabrina peeled away from where Tori was unloading their personal effects and came to thank Ethan again, "I can't thank you enough for finding us."

"Who's this?" Lee wanted to know.

"Sabrina Johansen, meet my *little* brother, Lee."

"The one who got the ROTC scholarship?" She impressed herself by remembering such a mundane detail about a person she'd never actually met.

"Yup, he was a first lieutenant with 10th Mountain before all this shit."

Sabrina's next question was only logical, "If you were stationed at Fort Drum, what are you doing here, Sir?"

"That is a long story," Lee sighed, shaking Sabrina's hand, "I take it by the uniforms you've been isolated since about mid-summer?"

"...yeah. So, we lost the war then..." Sabrina ultimately wasn't that surprised, but it wasn't the news she wanted to hear.

Lee looked at Ethan, then took the lead, "We were hoping it wasn't true too, but the only functioning government we've heard of is in Texas, maybe even still in Alaska too. There's surely holdouts overseas, but nobody knows for sure."

Sabrina gave the U.S. Flag patch on her right shoulder a forlorn look, "So it's all over then?"

"Hardly," Ethan seemed more optimistic than he felt comfortable with in reality. "We just have to wait out the winter, most Zims will be too degraded to be a threat by then. After that, Lee and I can mount an expedition to the

Oklahoma FEMA camp, it's where our family was sent. There have to be answers there.

"Wow, so this has to be your big brother," Tori had just joined the group and was teasing Ethan, her perceived competition for Sabrina's attention. "I knew there had to be an Alpha-Male version of you out there somewhere and a fine specimen he is."

Swatting Tori's hand down as she felt Lee's bicep muscles, Sabrina seemed every bit as embarrassed as Lee, "Enough," she hissed. "Can we sit out the rescue mission? I... we, need a shower."

Lee was impressed, "You're not my soldiers to command and nobody is going to force you to do anything here. Welcome to our humble slice of paradise." The town's only up-armored Humvee and one of the two large cargo trucks called LMTV's pulled up to the outpost with now *Captain* Keith Brewer hanging out the window like a happy dog. He was training a new medical team for the Cavalry and rescuing the three injured Airmen would be a perfect first mission for the mixed-aged recruits. Before getting into the Humvee as the navigator, Ethan hugged his friend Sabrina one more time, agreeing that she did, in fact, need a shower.

The drive to St. Clair was uneventful but a raging fire of tires and trash, mostly destroyed trailers and cheap FEMA housing, blocked the exit Ethan had taken when originally heading out on his rescue mission. The gang Sabrina claimed were the Crips had rightly suspected someone would be coming back, but they hadn't expected what amounted to a four-wheeled tank and its fatter big brother full of soldiers. Upon sighting the two heavily armored vehicles the light resistance scattered without a shot being fired from either side.

Once they made it to the wreck site, Ethan saw the car had caught fire during the hours he was gone, which made him concerned the St. Clair gangs might have come out this way. He drove up the hill to the Clayborn house and was the first inside, not even bothering to draw his sidearm. Ethan shouted to Michaels, hurrying up the steps and opened a door he only just realized should have been secured from the inside. He was greeted with a scene of horror and gore that would not have been out of place in the movie *House of a Thousand Corpses*. Ethan found himself staring at a reanimated Tech Sergeant Lamont, who had had a piece of Michaels' throat in his mouth until he swallowed it. Blood from Captain Saio's hands were smeared down an eviscerated Lamont, telling a grizzly story of struggle and death, but one that Ethan was too stunned to comprehend at first. He froze at exactly the worst time and Michaels' corpse lunged for him, gnashing his teeth hard enough to audibly crack the molars.

Sensing his brother's hesitation, Lee pulled Ethan back by his shirt and let loose on the zombies with his own sidearm, an Hk P30L he'd found in a holster being worn by a zombie who didn't need it anymore. The ear-splitting pops of 9mm snapped Ethan out of it and he too fired into the men he'd thought he'd come to save. His Colt .45 held only about half the number of rounds as Lee's and he actually ran out first.

"Fuck! *Fuck fuck fuck!*" Ethan shouted, throwing his empty weapon at Lamont's lifeless body. He kicked a box of supplies, this one full of kids coloring books and it came tumbling down, burying most of Michaels' lower torso. Lee shot all three of them in the head again, just to be safe. Ethan collapsed to the floor and tried to catch his breath, his mind swimming as if he were drunk. He didn't enjoy adrenaline-dumps, or anxiety attacks and this was both. The Texans were coming, time-now and he had nothing to show for his efforts. Not only that, but the barriers had been in place when he entered, how had they become infected? Who had been the idiot who'd gone outside and who'd been dumb enough to let him back in? *Stupid sheltered Flyboys*, Ethan thought. *Didn't know how much danger they were still in.*

The Cavalry medics followed Keith upstairs, but after seeing the carnage stepped outside into the hall as there was nothing they could do. Lee stepped outside with them and began discussing their next steps while Ethan just stared at the men he'd risked everything to save.

The rest of the ride home Ethan didn't speak. He couldn't. He'd taken the turret of the Humvee because he didn't want to hear what anyone below was saying. Riding in open air is like being in a roller coaster that you had a degree of control over and on any other day it might have been fun. The other saving grace of being a gunner was that, without a headset, it did leave you alone with your thoughts. Before crossing the Meramec again, the convoy stayed to wipe out the Cult Zombies, which gave Ethan plenty of chances to take out his anger on them.

The defeated men pulled up to the Liberty Outpost an hour later. The crew of the C-130 was devastated by the news of the death of their pilots and crew chief and so were the leaders of the convoy of Texas National Guardsmen detailed with retrieving their stranded men. At least they had half the crew back and were able to make contact with the survivors of Sullivan.

"Sorry we couldn't bring them back," Ethan said to the Texan CO when their paths crossed unloading Saio's body. "We were too late, Zim got in."

"Your brother told me. I appreciate your efforts, Sheriff," the major sighed. "I lost the cargo *and* the pilots, but my investigator made the jump. The way your mayor speaks of you, the two of you might become good friends," he pointed to a group of Texans mingling with the Sullivan Cavalrymen. "Short brunette."

Ethan's head was still swimming, because it didn't occur to him to ask why these guys would need a civilian cop flown to their location. Rather than go talk to her, though, he more or less stumbled inside the truck-stop restaurant. A waitress came up to him to take his order, but he didn't have the wherewithal to say anything. Eventually he dazed off, unaware that anyone had brought him a cold beer, or that someone was sitting in front of him now.

"... Sheriff, can you hear me?"

Ethan snapped out of his malaise, thankful he hadn't fully gone to sleep. Surely the dead men in the attic would be added to his nightly regiment of horrific visions of a cold and lonely hellscape. A small woman in her mid-twenties was sitting across from him with an all-weather notebook, already looking impatient. She could have been of Mediterranean descent, or maybe even South American, Ethan was a terrible judge of ethnicity, but her skin was a lovely golden color, like fresh baked bread. In fact, everything about her was lovely, including the flecks of gold that surrounded her hazel eyes. At the same time, he noticed his cold beer was now warm. How long had he been sitting there? It was daylight now, so that was telling.

The woman sighed heavily, "Ya know, typically, unwashed, Yankee stoners don't trip my trigger, so you can stop staring at my tits whenever."

"I'm sorry, who the fuck are you?" Ethan realized he had been staring in what she might consider the direction of her breasts. Now that she'd pointed them out, though, he kinda liked those too.

"Detective Mary Guiterez, on loan from the Texas Rangers," she said, though she didn't reach to shake Ethan's hand. "Sheriff, I want you to take me to that abandoned hotel where you found the naked body. Your investigation was more thorough than I should have expected, but it left some glaring gaps."

"Gaps?"

"Your men put remarkably little effort in finding your assailant, for starters."

Ethan shrugged, "It was a different time."

"It was four months ago."

"And since then I've been put in charge of a hundred and fifty people, been nearly shot up by an M-240, I've been blown the fuck up and have rolled two cars in one night," Ethan laughed. "I'm sorry if I'm the classic Millennial disappointment, but we're all just barely holding on here. I mean, I'm not in charge of a proper sheriff's department so much as the principal's staff at a school where nobody is forced to be there and everyone has a gun."

Guiterez backpedaled before her local liaison stopped liaising, "Sorry, I didn't mean to imply-"

"Whatever, I've had nastier things said to me by people whose opinions meant a lot more to me than some out of work detective Halliburton hired to do... what again? I mean, I'm not saying I'm beyond insult, but you gotta do better than implying I'm not a very good sheriff by Old World standards, because *fucking duh*."

A wry smile crossed Mary's face, "I don't know why, but I like you."

"You and the mayor both," Ethan shook his head, sipping his cold beer.

"I'm impressed, actually. None of the other towns I've been sent to, since Texas went independent, have had a regulated police force. Let alone a small military that is accountable to civilian leadership."

"I've heard."

"Why is that, do you think?"

Ethan had never considered the question, "That we followed civilian leadership and didn't take over? That is the million-dollar question. I'd hate to suggest I or my brother are outright 'the good guys' lacking in any selfish motivations, but we're not the bad guys either. A better question, in my opinion, is what's Texas' stake in all this? I get Halliburton was contracted to run the power plants before the collapse of the Federal government, but why is Texas honoring that deal? Also, why would they send a cop to investigate anything, let alone *my* cases?"

"I told you, people have been disappearing-"

"I genuinely wasn't listening, for that I'm sorry. Are they your people, or mine?" Ethan patted the stack of papers she had on the table next to her, "because this looks suspiciously like our records, I'd assume Mayor Kenly gave them to you on the likelihood I didn't come back alive... Where are your files then?"

"Those are classified."

Ethan scoffed, "Then get the fuck back on the truck with Major Square-Jaw and be gone with you. Either you spill your guts or I make the case to the mayor to lock the gates and never let you back in."

Mary hesitated, "The political climate back home is... paranoid. There are powerful elements who don't believe we should be keeping the hydroelectric and coal plants running north of Texan soil."

"Then this conversation is a non-starter," Ethan started to stand. "You can make yourself at home, but I'm going-"

"Six Halliburton workers and a two-man Army scout team have gone missing from various mission locations since last October."

This time Ethan did laugh, "Yeah, there's zombies, or didn't you hear? There are a million ways to buy it in the wilderness, not including the undead."

"They all disappeared within two miles of your town's farthest patrolled parameter."

Ethan stopped, "Now that is new information."

"I need access to your refugee records. You have an induction area, but virtually no one to in-process."

"We've noticed, but there isn't much north of here anymore, or south for that matter. The original evacuations were fairly comprehensive and most people in St. Louis or north of there, were sent to green zones near the Great Lakes. The only reason we had any population here at all is because this was the last flight-line for FEMA out of St. Louis and they never came back for their final run."

Considering Ethan's interpretation of events, Mary ran it by her own thoughts, "That might be true, but there has to be a hundred small cities between St. Louis and Chicago, each one with at least two hundred original holdouts who refused evacuation..." Mary's eyes darted around while she did the mental math, or "guestimation" for the sake of saving time. Ethan thought it was kinda cute that he could almost make out her eyes darting from invisible formula to invisible formula in the air, "The rate of newcomers to your town should be still be like the other townships that've held out. Take for instance your closest neighbor, the colony at the Bagnell Dam at Lake of the Ozarks. They have one quarter of your current population, but their intake of refugees has remained steady at about eighty-percent that of yours. If the rate keep up, their population will exceed yours by mid-summer."

"Eighty percent?" Ethan motioned for the detective to follow him outside to the parking lot. Keith had brought his car back during the previous day, but he'd messed with the seat settings and Ethan couldn't reach the pedals properly, since his friend was a solid three inches taller. He felt silly as the painfully slow electric motor pushed the seat forward until his boots touched the gas pedal.

Mary wasn't impressed with Ethan's beat up Crown Vic, "I guess I pegged you for a sports-car type, a Camero or something with only two doors and too much power."

Checking under the sun visor, he found a joint meant for his drive home the day before. The reality that the night before had been his ill-fated mission made time dilate for long moments he couldn't later account for. They saw that the mayor's car was taking up both handicapped spots again, not that a '59 Eldorado was capable of fitting in a regular sized parking space in the first place. It was becoming Kelly's signature move, though, which entertained some folks. The good news was, he was over whatever flu had kept him down only days prior. The bad news, he was well enough to be in a mood.

"Guten morgen, meine Sheriff!" Allen pretended to snap to attention with a heavy click of his boots. Today he was imitating Sergeant Schultz from *Hogan's Heroes*, "However, Oberst-Bürgermeister Kenly is not having a guten morgen. Naturally, I know *nothzzzing!*"

"Stay out of my DVD's, shithead," Ethan made the sign that he was watching Allen and headed for the main office.

He knocked three times and heard Kenly shout something obscene before he entered, "I heard you're 'in a mood', Sir."

"Shut the fuck up, Kelly," Kenly slapped a mug full of pens off the desk with his sausage fingers. "Do you know what it takes to run a town?"

"I'm afraid I'd need to download the cliff-notes, Sir," Ethan sat in a chair at the edge of the room under a trophy-set of antlers. Reynolds, Rowe and Lee didn't even look back at him. Apparently, this had been a long meeting already and Ethan was just walking into the latest shit-storm with no time to take a breather from the last.

"*Boy...*" A massive vein popped out of Kelly's forehead as he wrapped his beefy hands around a snow globe, ready to launch into his underling. "All of you, find Newton. I don't give a shit if he's hiding in his basement smearing feces on the walls, or if he got eaten by a fucking zoo lion. You find him, you bring him back here so I can fucking kill him *myself!* This is the fourth shift he has failed to show up for and I don't have time for it, Goddamnit!" Froth was starting to form at the edges of Kenly's mouth. He noticed and tried to calm himself before it got worse.

"Did anyone consider maybe he just left?" Everyone turned to glare at Ethan. "No, seriously. I can't be the only one who's thought about just wandering off into the great beyond. Maybe he just beat the rest of us to it," he said, motioning for Kenly to toss him the snow globe. It didn't happen.

"I've served with Newt' for six years," Rowe was incredulous. "He doesn't have an adventurous bone in his body. He doesn't like to camp, or even stay in hotels. I can't imagine him just 'wandering off' into this mess. He's too clean."

"It was just a suggestion," Ethan shrugged. The verbal abuse from Mayor Kenly went on for another grueling twenty minutes and in that time, Ethan realized Detective Guiterez had stayed outside. Whether or not she thought she had to, he didn't know, but he envied her for it.

Before the end of the meeting, the Texan's senior officer made an appearance. Apparently, the TNG had adopted a deep brown Stetson as its standard headgear and whatever aging Army uniform the individual could muster. This man wore the style of desert camo the Army fielded until its unnecessary rivalry with the Marine Corps ended in a uniform change to gray pixels. Eventually internal supplies would filter down the chain and they'd all wear pixelated forest camouflage, but that was far from now. The ten-gallon hat rivaled Mayor Kenly's for ostentatiousness by any standard and he made no effort to take it off before addressing Sullivan's leadership. How strange that his accent was definitely not Texan, maybe east coast above Georgia.

"Ladies and gentlemen, my name is Major Kyle Donovan." the major shifted his weight, unsure how to address the people gathered. "On behalf of the Governor, I'd like to officially extend my apologies for simply dropping in on you like this."

"Literally," Rowe quipped.

The major took that one in stride, "I've been authorized to extend an offer to officially bring you into the fold. I'm sorry that, for now, you're limited to what can be air-dropped in, but the day will come when a supply train might make it here. It seems dark right now, but the infection will burn through its current population of hosts in less than a year and if we don't give it fresh bodies, it cannot last beyond that."

Kenly ashed a cigar, "Any word about the President?"

The Major was silent for a minute while he considered his words, "There are no lines of diplomacy between the Cheyenne Mountain Complex and Texas."

"What the fuck is a Cheyenne Mountain Complex?" Rowe wanted to know.

"Seriously?" Ethan scoffed. "It was all over the news for a month before the virus broke quarantine at Nogales."

Rowe shrugged, "I watched Netflix, not TV." Ethan rolled his eyes.

Major Donovan continued, "We receive radio

transmissions from the Complex routinely, but they're clearly not for our benefit and they're coded with a cypher we've yet to break. Since the last day the Administration was active, the emergency beacon at the center of the CMC has been encoded. There appears to be no civilian radio traffic within a hundred miles of the complex in any direction. Most analysts think it's because they've gone into full lockdown and are jamming any potential foreign interference."

"Well that's just ridiculous."

"I agree, Sheriff, but wondering what happened to all the HAM operating civvies in the Four Corners isn't something I give much thought to." The major pulled out a thumb-drive and plugged it into the TV Mayor Kenly kept in his office. There was an adapter that ran out the back of the flat-screen to a VCR and a dozen worn looking cassettes, because Kenly didn't like change. "Higher has given me a list of tasks to complete in order to give Sullivan protectorate status..." At this point Ethan stopped paying much attention, as most of it had little to nothing to do with local law enforcement. It was all about shared labor and supplies, not that Sullivan had any of the latter to trade with, but the fact remained. Lee suggested the town could be a Green Zone for the power plant's workers and defenders to come and take a few days off and that seemed to please the Texans to no end, especially since they'd have a jumping off point for salvaging resources from the St. Louis area. Sadly, the coal-powered plant was all but done for, but there were infinite uses for a town like Sullivan.

It was past lunch when the meeting adjourned, Detective Guiterez was still in the office area chatting with the deputies, or more accurately passively interrogating them. Ethan knew a shakedown for information when he saw one, having run afoul of people who were arguably better at eliciting Freudian-slips than her.

Rather than allow her to gather information even he wasn't privy to, Ethan suggested they take a drive so he could show her the town before he decided whether or not to take her on a tour of the greater murder spots of this new Sullivan. The best way to get to know her, he felt, was to share a meal, so he drove them to the hilltop fortress in Meramec State Park. At the now infamous "FOB Alamo" they got in line for chow with the regular contingent of men. Ethan and Mary stood and chatted about things not related to the job. She found out Ethan was actually a rabid *Evanescence* fan and he discovered she hadn't heard any of their music beyond one played-to-death single. This, he vowed to change, much to her chagrin.

"I read the After-Action Report on the raid against the gang," she said, changing the subject so Ethan would stop ranting about a bunch of songs she'd never heard. At least he was passionate about something besides drinking.

Ethan bit into his pulled-pork sandwich. It was rich and juicy and in dire need of some original flavored *Lays*. "That's funny," he said between bites, "because I don't remember writing one."

"Your buddy Captain Brewer did."

"Right. I guess someone had to."

Mary cocked her head to the side, "You're not the bad-guy in that story, Sheriff."

"Never thought I was, but I can't say I'm proud of it either. Just had to be done." Ethan set his pork down and shoved a few potato chips in his mouth, "If you'd seen what they did to those girls... they weren't people anymore and I wasn't a sheriff yet, so no laws to uphold, no examples to set."

"And the incident with the machine gun?"

Ethan nodded, swallowing his perfect mixture, "Which one? Because they were both related."

"The last one, I guess. Officer Rowe took responsibility for the incident at the northern outpost before you were sheriff."

"I was still there, though. It was all the same gang, so in reality most of our problems have been a series of semi-coordinated gang attacks. As for Dylon Cole, he sneaked into town and acted like one of us until he could figure out how to take me out and make it look like an accident."

"But he failed."

"Spectacularly, but also only just. He might have been caught, but Cole still could have killed more than just one deputy." Ethan cracked open the root beer he'd gotten with his rations, "Carlisle was a good man... didn't deserve to die like that, but thank God it wasn't Keith or Paula."

Now Mary made a suggestion that Ethan didn't really like, "What if you didn't get their leadership, though? What if Cole was taking orders, not just acting alone for the sake of revenge?"

Ethan couldn't let himself forget the truth, no white-washing it with false statements this time. "No, I shot them myself. First one through the chest, his second in command through the neck and there ain't no coming back from that. The girls who came to town described these fuckers to a T. We got the right guys."

Mary took a chip off of Ethan's plate, "Imagine, though, that you took out their senior enlisted, but their commanding officer, well, he might still be out there."

"... robbing and killing refugees..." Ethan started to connect the dots, his heart sinking that he could have failed to see the bigger picture like this. "I've been so worried about what I can see, I never considered what I couldn't."

The accusation of incompetence, even if he was his own accuser, actually bothered Ethan on a deeply personal level. Catching on that she might have struck a chord, Mary decided to back off and change the subject again. For whatever reason, she sympathized with this yokel. He was holding down a job he was barely qualified for and was woefully in over his head at this point.

"It's okay, Sheriff. You're not failing by any means, you're keeping order in a lawless land. A little bit of a *shoot-out at the OK Corral* was probably justified."

"Yeah, maybe one day they'll give both the massacres I've been involved in a catchy name."

"What is you call them, the *BK Kids Club Biker Gang?*"

Ethan's manic laugh burst out a little, drawing everyone else's attention for a moment, "Sadly I can't claim credit for that one. That was all Newton."

"Who's Newton?"

"One of the cops who stayed in town. He's the one Kenly is always yelling about missing work. If you ask me, he just took a walk, if you know what I mean."

The wheels in Mary's head were turning, "Does that happen often?"

"Not these days, really, but in the beginning, sure," Ethan really wished he could figure out where Mary was going with this. "There've been a few, though. People just packing up and leaving to find family. I almost did, but Lee came back and talked me down. I was really hot to trot to get to the OKC FEMA camp, lemme tell ya."

Mary froze mid-chew, unsure how to move forward. She tried to play it off, but the sheriff wasn't stupid and she'd tipped her hand. "I think we should go back to the station and-" Ethan reached out and grabbed Mary's hand gently, but firmly by the wrist. He tried, but couldn't speak. His eyes pleaded for it not to be true, or at least not to be as bad as he imagined.

"Ethan, please..."

"No... tell me now," he was actually trembling, something he couldn't remember having ever happened to him outside of being cold.

Taking a deep breath, Mary tried to sugar coat it, "It was early in the last days of the evacuations, someone forgot to secure a sewer access and-"

"Did anyone..." Ethan almost threw up, his head swimming "did anyone get out?"

"Maybe," Mary shook her head in a doubtful manner, "anyone who was near the helipads, or on the other side of the sally-port when it started. The flight-line was empty when we got there, but the birds never came to Texas. There were no itineraries left behind either, most sensitive items went up in a fire from the fighting... I'm sorry, Ethan. I really am."

Standing up so quickly he almost knocked the table over, the sheriff straightened his uniform in an attempt to compose himself and made a B-line for his car. The aging Crown Vic roared to life and he spun the tires in a half-donut before catching traction and taking off to parts unknown. Mary immediately got the nearest Cavalryman to radio to the police station.

Chapter 18

Kenly was the first to find Ethan and even though it would have saved a few man-hours if he'd called it in first, he didn't. The Crown Vic the sheriff drove was parked lazily in the center of a turnaround in the city park that was meant probably for service vehicles. Kenly followed the trail into the woods where the young sheriff was already aware of his mayor's approach and already had a cold one waiting for him. Most of the authorities the Texan woman had alerted to Ethan's disappearance focused their attention on his home. Some of them went to look at the south gates, but being an old law enforcer himself, Aaron Kenly had suspected the defender of the town wouldn't go very far.

"Never would have known this was here," Kenly remarked as he approached.

"Kinda the point," Ethan tossed another glass bottle down a small waterfall. It had formed over time at the end of a drain culvert from the artificial dam above and judging by the graffiti was a popular place for youths to be delinquent. Of course, Ethan Kelly knew where it was.

Kenly struggled to sit on a large slab of sandstone, finally resorting to letting Ethan help him down to the same level. "This was not an ideal way for you to find out."

"Did you know?"

"Not until their detective radioed that you'd gone all bibbledy over it," Kenly reached and took his beer.

"And you would have behaved better?" Ethan didn't buy it.

Kenly chuckled, "I was raised by my grandmother. When I was drafted into the Corps, she wrote to me every day. There were so many letters I had to send a bunch of them back in a box, cost a month's pay."

"Nicole did the same," Ethan was already fighting back the tears. "There's still perfume on them..."

That detail actually struck a chord with Kenly, not

expecting to feel as much sympathy as he did. "My point is, they cut off mail a month before we go home. In that time there was a clerical error and she got a telegram that I was missing in action. It was meant for a boy in a neighboring city, but our service numbers were mixed up by the IBM machine."

"Oh shit. What happened, a heart attack?" Ethan guessed. It was a logical assumption, after all.

"No, car accident on her way to church a few days later. Probably to pray it was all a big mistake," Aaron sighed, it had been twenty years since he'd recalled this story to anyone. She'd been gone since 1970 and still he missed his grandma. "What bothered me the most, was that she died assuming I was dead too," Kenly tossed the empty bottle. It went significantly farther than any of Ethan's and exploded on a stump.

Wiping away a few tears, but still not the torrent to come, Ethan helped the aging Mayor to his feet. "I'll handle my shit, Sir... I think I should be with my brother right now though. Permission to disappear for a little while longer?"

"Granted, but I'm driving you home," Kenly gestured to the two six packs Ethan had already killed. No need to point out that that had barely gotten him tipsy yet.

Lee met Ethan in the driveway as the massive golden-tan tail fins of Kenly's Eldorado were just pulling away. Detective Guiterez, Keith and Paula were all waiting in the living room too. The brothers embraced and the rest of the night became a blur of alcohol, mourning and stories commiserating the dearly departed.

Just after dawn, Ethan rolled out of the bed in his loft and found he was still too drunk to walk. Using a beaten up looking *bokken* training sword as a walking stick, he stumbled into the bathroom he'd been installing since the break-in months earlier. The project was as much practical, as it was to keep him occupied when he was off work. Thank God he'd made it functional before beautiful. After violently punishing the toilet and the small trash can, sometimes simultaneously, Ethan crawled back toward bed, feeling much better. It was then that the hours before dawn came flooding back, a torrent of naked bodies and sweat, as dizzying as it was intense. To an outsider it might be nothing more than sympathy sex, but for the person who needed it most it was a reason to keep going... except these flashbacks weren't with the right woman.

His eyes flashed to the bed. Still asleep and on Nicole's side, was Mary Guiterez, an empty pint of Southern Comfort loosely gripped in her hand. With his vision still swimming, Ethan tried imagining maybe she was still fully clothed and that his bed, in his loft, was simply the safest place for her to spend the night. Needing to know the answer, he pulled the covers down a little, exposing one of her breasts. Though the sight of it sounded the clarion call of the angels and a beam of light descended from heaven to celebrate earthly perfection, he covered her back up and collapsed into an old armchair in despair and self-loathing.

Mary had to remember to breathe slowly, but deeply in order to pretend she was still asleep. She hadn't expected Ethan to react this way. Not being nearly as drunk as he was, the idea had been to keep Ethan's mind off his family's grizzly fate, if only for one night. Now, it seemed he was hellbent on punishing himself for taking comfort in another woman's arms. Though surely Nicole had been dead for months, Mary realized that to Ethan she might only have been *genuinely* gone for mere hours. *That was very stupid*, she scolded herself.

On the bright side, Mary now knew that Ethan wasn't the type to feel-up a sleeping woman and that gave her some amount of comfort while the pretending continued. Eventually Ethan fell asleep in his chair, unwilling to come back to bed. After Mary was certain he was out, she sneaked from the loft bedroom and used the landline to call for someone to come and get her. Until the sheriff had time to process his grievous loss, she would need to carry the investigation for him.

To his credit, Captain Kelly was a little more collected in his response to the news than his brother. That wasn't to say he didn't care, because he left his XO, Captain Brewer, in charge while he slept off a hangover that might have rivaled only Ethan's. His men would understand, but Lee didn't need to be at work right now.

"Mornin'," Brewer's feet were up on the desk when Mary's investigation brought her to the Cavalry barracks. Keith had been watching, with some satisfaction, a lower ranking soldier dig a one-man fighting position behind the office. Mary assumed the police academy and the military weren't that dissimilar and so almost certainly this kid had screwed up and gotten caught.

Mary poured herself a coffee from the pot Brewer's wife had set before her arrival. Paula was swelling and unlike Mary's overworked mother of nine, glowing with maternal warmth. "I guess both Kelly boys will be playing hooky today," she made small talk, "wouldn't want to be at work if I were either of them... hell, I don't think I really want to be at work," she admitted.

"Better than sitting around, pretending to console Ethan, Detective," Keith confirmed that he knew what she'd done. Mary practically choked on her coffee, bit maintained. "No matter, what can I do for you, Detective Guiterez?"

"I need to see the hotel where Sheriff Kelly was attacked, I was hoping you could provide an escort."

Keith didn't understand why she'd want to see a building they'd already picked clean for evidence, but then again he really didn't have to, "Sure thing. I'll arrange an armored escort for this afternoon."

"Thanks," she turned to leave, "By the way, Captain, did anyone find that third officer on the mayor's staff?"

Unsure, Keith opened the window to his office so that the sergeant overseeing the young soldier's punishment could hear him. "Hey, Anthony!"

"Yessir?"

"Tell fucknuts to take five and get in here."

"Aye, Sir!" As the sergeant jogged inside, the kid in the foxhole practically collapsed into it with sheer exhaustion.

Mary shook her head, "Fine, I'll take the bait, what did that guy do?"

Keith shrugged, pointing to the captain's bars on his collar, "No clue and also, not my problem."

"You were an E-5, before the collapse of Federal authority?" Mary prodded.

The young captain nodded, "Sure was."

"Hell of a promotion, straight to captain."

Keith was fairly uninterested in the Texan's presence in the first place, so answering any of their questions about himself seemed like a waste of time. Thankfully, Sergeant Clevenger walked through the chow hall and into the adjacent row of offices where Keith and Mary sat.

Clevenger snapped to attention and saluted, "Reporting as ordered, Sir."

"Your team was on perimeter-patrol last night, you hear anything about Deputy Mayor Newton being located?"

"No, Sir. Nothing but the obligatory teenagers shagging in the vacant houses. The sheriff's department took those calls though, so maybe they know more, but I doubt it."

Keith lazily swiveled his chair back toward Mary, "You heard the man."

"Fair enough. Before I go, though, what did that guy do in the first place, Sergeant?" Mary pointed to the soldier in the super-deep foxhole.

"Habitual masturbator, ma'am. That dumb-shit gets caught choking-the-chicken in the porta-shitters on the reg, Captain Kelly's fucking tired of it."

Mary wished she hadn't asked, "Hasn't he figured out how to lock the shitters?"

"I wish," Clevenger folded his arms, glaring at the bane of his existence taking a smoke-break in what should have been his own grave. "He's a moaner."

"Gross." Mary turned her attention back to Captain Brewer, "I guess I'll go wait for the escort then."

"They'll collect you from the police station at thirteen-fifteen," Keith said, returning the dismissal salute for his subordinate to leave the room. "What gets me," he said, turning to watch the punishment continue, "is there's a brothel on the far side of town. Why not just avail yourself of their services?"

Cocking her head to one side, Mary stopped, "A brothel, you say?"

"Yup. It's a Libertarian government here. Each *Worker* is over twenty-one and has had an STD screening."

"How does a married man know so much about whores?"

"They prefer the title 'Bonafide Companion,' but who do you think did their medical workups?"

Mary nodded, "Fair enough. I'll see your men at one-ish, then."

Outside of the admin building, Mary ran into another one of the Texan Airmen who'd made the jump with her. AFC Marino was a radio operator and likely tasked with upgrading Sullivan's tech for direct communication with Austin. They hadn't talked much before now, but a familiar face was nice to see so far from home.

"Howdy, 'Tective," his southern drawl was more Louisiana than Texas, but Mary could forgive him for that. "You find anything interesting?"

"Interesting, yes. Relevant... not yet."

Emilio Marino shrugged, pointing to the two bored looking deputies that were following from the safety of their patrol car. "We got escorts wherever we go, even to the shitter. Makes a guy feel a little unwelcome."

"They're here for your protection, I promise. They're escorting their own people around too, so it's not personal."

"That sure is a load off," Emilio unscrewed a bottle of Powerade. "They got walls, so what's the danger? Federals again?"

Mary's eyes lit up and darted around to make sure they were out of anyone else's earshot. "Remember your OpSec, airman. You're not authorized to discuss the current political climate with locals."

"My bad, ma'am. You're right." Most military personnel she encountered treated her with the deference of a commissioned officer, though she was well outside their normal chain of command. Likely, they just didn't know how else to work with her.

Marino's face looked like he'd accidentally kicked a puppy, but Mary got over it quick, "You're fine, airman, but I think it would be best if those of us from Texas traveled in pairs from now on. Makes us harder to disappear."

"You think these people would do that?"

That was a loaded question, "Not these people, but someone besides Dead Zed is taking out targets of opportunity. Don't be a soft target, is all."

"Yes, ma'am. Also, if you need to, I should be able to get you a direct line to Austin in about an hour."

"I don't have anyone special to call, but it's good to know," Mary patted Marino on the shoulder and went about exploring the quaint, midwestern town of Sullivan. It reminded her of the Old West section of Disney World, as every store had been commandeered by new owners to serve the needs of a besieged city. In its haste and lack of neon-signs, the scene really sold the feel of yesteryear. Food markets were just the tip of the iceberg, too. Weapons sales were a big thing, winter clothing and "Zim-Proof" outfits made of thick denim or vinyl with protective sports gear sewn into strategic places, were all high-ticket items. A blacksmith forged a steady stream of sturdy melee weapons and custom-fit iron bars over low-lying windows and vehicles. Many of these same retro jobs were sprouting up back home, but that someone here had actually designed a logo to sell their protective clothing, really tickled her. If she could find something to trade, she'd definitely purchase some of their wares.

Back at the police station, which was being packed up for a planned move to the aged Town Hall nearer the center of the city-proper, Mary just tried to stay out of the way of the organized chaos. In the early 2000's, Sullivan was expected to grow at a steady pace for the next several years and so putting the police station on the outskirts of town made sense as in-fill would far surpass the station's location in a decade or two. Now, it was just barely inside the walls and not at all in a strategic location.

Mary approached Ethan's protégé, Allen Broadwick. He was lurking about, looking for something to do besides help, as most teenagers will, so she obliged. "Deputy Broadwick, right?" he nodded, "Do you still have case files at this location, or have they been moved?"

"Case files labeled Alpha through November have been moved, the rest will make the trip after the drivers get back from lunch," Allen was visibly saddened that this line of questioning was also dull as dirt. Overseeing the moving of a bunch of office equipment and the three mouthy drunks who were doing their community service, was hardly what a young deputy wanted to do with his Saturday.

Mary was about to move on, but Allen wasn't done with her now that the movers were out of earshot, "We need Ethan Kelly functional and relatively sober, Miss Detective. He was getting there and then you dropped a bombshell on him."

"I didn't mean to, I-"

"No one ever does, but we're cool, Detective. I get it. Good intentions, the road to hell and all that jazz," Allen signed a clipboard when another deputy brought it to him. They then began the process of moving the town's malcontents into a plain white cargo van with bold MDOC in vinyl lettering on the sides. It had been on loan from the nearest prison because of the early cases of Invier Plague and was simply never retrieved. It was hardened with a bite-proof cage in lieu of traditional seats, making it a horrible experience for anyone with claustrophobia, but anyone inside was safe from Zim.

"With as little attention as the designers gave to ventilating that cage, these three should get to taste each other's rancid flatulence the whole ride." Allen changed the subject as the inmates were walked away. Mary's expression disapproved. "Don't feel sorry for them, Detective. The two big ones were wife-beaters and that one that looks like Malibu Ken with crows-feet was a Fox Network executive... I mean, that last part wasn't relevant to why he got arrested, but it does remove the element of sympathy."

"Can I ask you about your thoughts on the bodies?" Mary returned the conversation to something resembling professional.

"You mean the naked guy? Yeah, that was super weird," the DoC van left the parking lot and headed into the center of town. Mary caught Deputy Broadwick giving the finger to one of the inmates, who'd flipped him off first. "I know the tox-screen was negative, but then the guy who ate a man's face had no 'bath salt' related drugs in his system, either, so where does that leave us? I do admit, it is harder to explain the GSW to the chest."

"In your opinion, there's no way it could have been a suicide?"

Allen laughed, "I heard you were funny. Look, we grid-searched the area, no weapons or cartridges were found and Ethan has a video of the crime scene on his phone from the moment we realized there was a fucking dead naked dude in a parking lot."

"Wait, there's footage? I need to see it asap, Deputy, if you would."

"We have a copy of it, but I don't know what the file name is. It might take a minute to find. If it got packed already, you're looking at waiting overnight."

Mary sighed, "I have an appointment to be escorted to the crime scene at One."

"I'm coming with you," Allen wasn't asking. "Last time there was a Randy-Rando in the hotel we never saw, gave Ethan quite the shiner. It was freaky, but there was no evidence to suggest the assailant even knew there was a dead man outside. Likely, we just stumbled into his hiding place and it was fight or flight."

"And what do you make of Sheriff Kelly's claim to have seen a tiger?"

"Claim? Lady, I was there and so was a large zoo-cat. I can't tell you what species specifically, but I saw the shadow moving in the reeds, it was going to attack us. I've had my parents and little brother stay inside and away from tall grass, make sure we take our trash to a dumpster away from the house, that sort of thing."

Though unlikely, Mary did have to concede it wasn't entirely outside the realm of possibility that someone might have failed to euthanize a large cat. "Sheriff Kelly did mention something about a Tiger last night, but I thought he was just drunk."

Allen shrugged, "Well, Ethan is usually drunk, so it's not like you're wrong. He probably called it a Liger, though, right?"

"Yes."

"There's some early reports from refugees, before we got the Department up and running," Allen started rummaging through a box labeled *Reorganization Period*. Taking it off the dolly, he tossed a few evidence bags on the floor and finally snatched the one he was looking for. Mary read the hand-written reports, wishing they'd been converted to type, but grateful anything existed at all. Together they collated a timeline of sightings before they simply stopped at the Sheriff's own report. It was hard to deny, but several refugees had seen a white cat that resembled a tiger, but with more hair around the neck than a tiger should have.

When the Cavalry's Humvee arrived, Allen made himself comfortable behind the driver's seat. Mary had never actually ridden in a Humvee before, let alone an up-armored version and true to description it sucked. Her knees barely fit in the bucket area and she had to wear a helmet in case the truck shook her so violently she hit her head. It was like a SWAT vehicle, but more cramped and utterly lacking in creature comforts. The three-inch thick windows were weird to look through, but there probably wasn't a safer place to be in the world.

The corporal and private-first-class assigned to escort Mary were friendly enough, but maybe not the cream of the crop. Corporal Lebedev had just turned twenty and hadn't graduated high school because he admittedly was a recovering coke-head. His story was he'd barricaded himself in the factory where he was on work-release when the Panic hit its apex. He survived off of the break-area's snack machines for two months before scavenging parties from Sullivan found him while looking for extra acetylene tanks. Seth Lebedev liked being in the Cavalry and professed to have not touched so much as a joint since being rescued. PFC Tanner, on the other hand, was a forty-year-old local handyman with an active drinking problem that had left him somewhat braindead, though ultimately useful as a warm-body. *Among such gems, how could Ethan and Lee not shine?* Mary tried not to think such things about these men, but as a cop it was hard not to dissect the motivations of people in a hurry.

A short trip down the service road later, as nobody used the interstate anymore for a variety of reasons, they arrived at the abandoned hotel before Mary could fully collect her thoughts. Allen climbed out and scanned the area with his M-4, even though Tanner was in the turret with a machine gun. Relying on *him* to spot danger was a danger in itself. Lebedev went about helping secure the area, but his true mission seemed to be pumping Mary for trivial, personal information. Surely, he was trying to flirt.

Mary checked her notes, "So the body was here?"

Allen nodded, "Splayed out like that drawing, you know, the guy in the circle?"

"The Vitruvian Man," PFC Tanner said, shocking everyone. Their expressions clearly said as much while he lit a cigarette with nonchalance, "What? I have other interests outside of daytime drinking and watching game-shows."

"You just keep on-the-swivel, let the Detective detect shit," Lebedev threatened.

"Did it look ritualistic to you?" Mary was spit-balling ideas, holding up a crime-scene photo and comparing it to the derelict hotel.

"I dunno," Allen put his hands on his hips like the Kelly brothers did. "It was sure as fuck weird, though."

"Did either of you hear the gunshot?"

"Nah. There was no spatter either and the M.E. said his liver was hours-cold."

The next question seemed logical, if you were assuming the rumors about the big cats were true, "Feeding time... do you think you guys interrupted feeding time?"

"That's... drastic," the color in Allen's skin drained some. "No wonder it didn't attack us, it was hoping we'd leave so it could have the body."

"We should do a cursory search of the property, just to be sure." A storm was on the horizon, threatening freezing rain and snow.

"I disagree, Detective," Allen pointed to a thrift store and another dilapidated strip-motel across the highway. "If I were a sick fuck feeding people to zoo animals and my feeding area were compromised by local law, I'd move it. However, I'd still want to keep it within a similar range so that I don't have to alter my routine too much."

Mary was only teasing when she repeated, "*If* I were a sick fuck?"

"Why you gotta piss in my Cheerios?" Allen took it in stride.

"Maybe we should start where the zoo was. Might be some answers there." Everyone turned to look at Tanner, apparently blown away that he'd have an idea, let alone a good one. Just as quickly as his spark of intelligence had appeared though, it was snuffed out when he plugged one nostril and blew a snot-rocket from the other onto the hood of the Humvee.

Lebedev sighed, turning his attention to Allen, "Deputy Broadwick, would you drive? I don't know this area very well yet."

"After we've had a look here," Allen tossed an empty soda can. "Honesty, we should just burn this place down and leave one of those shelters Hodgkin is designing."

"Who?" Mary asked, absentmindedly trying to imagine a day when this road-side motel had been a vibrant business. It seemed too far from anything important, but that was probably just a modern take on a world where Route-66 had lost some of its importance.

"One of the deputies, he likes to weld. It's basically just a horse-trailer with a radio beacon that tells us someone is occupying it and needs rescue."

Texas hadn't come up with that idea yet and it was a good one. Of course, roaming bands of horse-mounted citizens with guns and nets was also an effective way of keeping the number of undead in check. This Hodgkin guy had the makings of a millionaire though, if he lived that long.

As most of them had suspected, the rotting old motel yielded no answers. It was water-damaged, moldy and smelled like there had been a few meth-labs in it over the years. Hypodermic needles and scorched pieces of glass pipes were everywhere, except in a loading bay for the upstairs kitchen. The smell of ammonia, most commonly associated with cat-urine, was pungent there and Mary wanted to examine it closer.

"Does this floor look swept to you?" She asked Allen, who was packing a wad of tobacco in his lip.

"Maybe, but refugees have stayed here, we know that for a fact."

"So recently that there's no new accumulation of dust?" Mary wiped her fingers across the floor, "It's almost clean."

Allen's brow furrowed, "Okay, you have my attention." He turned his high-intensity flashlight on and started searching the random kitchen implements that were scattered about in varying stages of decay.

"There!" Mary pointed to an area Allen had just illuminated. "Go back a few inches, then under that folding table." Her own light still used a comparatively weak incandescent bulb, which didn't help much.

Tipping the table over, Allen revealed a partial print. In his youth, before the virus, Allen Broadwick and his two brothers were avid hunters. Their preferred quarry was wild boar, an invasive and destructive species that had no season and most importantly no limit. Not to mention, boars were little shits that just so happened to be made out of delicious bacon. This, however, wasn't a hoof print and it was huge.

Mary just came out and said what they were both thinking, "If this is what I think it is... Ethan is never going to let any of us forget it."

"I know, damnit."

Chapter 19

The last dog to live in this house was Nicole's St. Bernard Mia, and Mia was mostly an outdoor animal. She also wasn't a licker. Bogey, on the other hand, thought the best cure for a hangover was to lick every inch of Ethan's face and exposed fingers. He then went pee on the rug nearest the bathroom.

"...nooooo..." Ethan moaned through his whole-body-ache, "Bad dog..."

A knock at the front door almost sent him into a panic, but then he remembered zombies don't knock. It was Newton, dressed in civvies and holding a six-pack of home-brewed beer. Before he said anything, Ethan took two and popped the caps before chugging one in its entirety.

John smiled so wide it parted his thick cop-mustache, "Good to see Yossarian is still himself."

Ethan rolled his eyes, ignoring the reference to the main character of the classic novel *Catch -22*, letting John into the house, "You know the Mayor's looking for you. Pretty sure he wants to fire you."

Newton made himself comfortable on the couch, "Had he the authority, I'm sure. I was hired to protect this town long before he moved into that ramshackle safety-hazard he calls a house. I just needed... a break from it all, I guess."

Ethan toasted to the air with his bottle, "Preachin' to the choir, man."

"I heard. About OKC, I mean," Newton offered Ethan another beer. They weren't really cold, but then that was how Ethan liked them.

Bogey ran and jumped into his master's lap. Though Newton offered, the beagle wouldn't have anything to do with him. Ethan scratched behind the dog's ears while he talked, "It's a lot to process."

"Have you seen your brother yet?"

"No."

Newton sighed, "Lee's gonna need you right now."

Ethan changed the subject, "So where have you been, man?"

"Fishing trip."

"During the zombie apocalypse?"

Shrugging, Newton offered little in the way of an answer, "I have a cabin down the river a ways. A guy I knew before Zim owned it."

"I'm a little jealous."

"I'll take you there sometime, but for now, I think you need to go see your brother. Maybe the two of you should take a break, ya know? It's done wonders for me."

Finishing his beer, Ethan added, "If you run into that Texan detective, Mary, don't tell her where I am."

Newton fell silent for a moment, "A detective?"

Heading into the kitchen to make an omelet, Ethan continued talking, "Yeah, the unit at the power plant called for a detective to help figure out what happened to some of their people."

"It's the end of the world," John's point being that the Texan's measures seemed to be a little extreme. "People disappear all the time, just look at me."

Ethan chuckled, "Right. She thinks some of the bodies you and I found in the early days are connected to the hiker gang."

Newton lit a cigarette, "Well that's a dead end, because they're all dead."

"Thank you, that's what I said." Ethan set a bowl of food on the floor for Bogey, but the dog wasn't interested and eventually went into another room, "Strange, he's always hungry. Anyway, I'd just as soon not see her for a little while."

Newton had never known Ethan to shy away from anyone, "Did you fuck her?"

"Something like that," Ethan responded after a time.

"Well that didn't take long."

Ethan rolled his eyes, "Shut up."

Checking for coffee, John was disappointed to see that was the one thing the sheriff didn't keep stocked. "Alright, I'm going to head out, maybe have a chat with that detective you're avoiding."

Waving as he tossed an eggshell in the trash, Ethan said, "Don't be a stranger." He was almost done eating before Bogey came back and started on his food. "What's the matter, boy, you don't like the smell of cigarettes?" A whiff of ammonia hit Ethan's nostrils and he glared at the dog, "Did you pee?" he checked every room after throwing his plate in the trash (it wasn't paper,) but didn't find anything. Finally, he assumed the smell must have been Newton. Smokers didn't smell great, this was true, but that daffy fuck had obviously stopped dealing with his cat's litter, or bathing.

Before noon, Lee showed up at the house, negating the need for Ethan to leave. Not being a couple of teenage girls, they didn't chat or catch up, but rather tinkered with their grandmother's old Crown Vic and drank all the Budweiser left. Finally, Ethan brought the last two beers from the six-pack Newton had left for him.

"What brand are these?" Lee asked, holding the car's air filter up to the light after cracking open the bottle.

"Newt' dropped by this morning, left 'em here."

Lee paused, "John Newton?" Ethan nodded absentmindedly. "Damn. I thought for sure he was dead."

"Me too, but no, he just went fishing or some shit."

"Nice," Lee laughed until he realized his walky-talky was chirping at him. Apparently, the Texans had made good their promise to get repeaters up and running. "This is Alamo Six, go ahead."

"*Alamo Six, this is Alamo Blue,*" Keith's voice was a little quieter than usual, "*I need you to make-a-meet-at-mine.*" Meaning he was being called into the office.

"Alamo Blue, you know I'm on bereavement-leave today."

"Negative. Get Ghost Rider Six and bring him with orders from on-high."

Lee sighed, shoving the air filter back in its slot, "Maybe they found your Ligers."

"Shut up," Ethan was tired of hearing about it. He'd officially given up on the theory. There were better things to do on any given Tuesday.

At Cavalry HQ, the joke was on Lee, though. At first, hearing that there was indeed evidence of a big cat from the Stanton zoo didn't sink in for either brother. Detective Guiterez had to confirm what Allen was saying and Mayor Kenly finally nodded his head in sad acceptance that this was in fact not a joke. Lastly, they all braced for the inevitable.

"I told you," Ethan smacked his hands together and pointed at Lee. "And I told you and I told you and you and you were there too!" He finished by pointing at Rowe and Reynolds. Everyone, to a man, was rolling their eyes as hard as they could.

Mary could barely take the display she was witnessing, "Wow, this is a really petty side of you and I don't know that I like it."

Ethan laughed, "I'll live."

Mary remained the adult in the room, "Moving right along... were this *just* a big-cat problem, I'd have Major Donovan's men comb the area until we killed it. However, someone, probably a former zookeeper, is feeding at least one animal."

"Feeding them what?" Kenly already wished he hadn't asked before he was even done asking it.

"Refugees," Ethan was suddenly somber. "That's why we haven't been getting a steady influx from the north. Anyone who makes it this far ends up fucking cat-food." No one spoke for a moment after that. The realization of their own staggering incompetence slapped every man and woman in that room like a leather glove filled with rocks.

Not letting a good silence go to waste, Kenly chose to galvanize his men, rather than berate them for a failure he was ultimately responsible for. "Captain Kelly, organize all of your able-bodied men and prepare to engage a living enemy, cats be damned."

"I'll double the watches," Ethan took a deep breath, "Detective Guiterez, would you please report your findings to Major Donovan?" Mary nodded.

"I thought we got them all," Keith shared a significant look with Ethan, both men realizing their mission to destroy the gang had only pushed them underground. It put, very clearly, into perspective how unimportant the incident with Cole was. In all likelihood he had taken orders from someone en-high and simply failed at his mission.

As disturbing as this revelation was, life had to go on. Kenly ordered this meeting classified, nobody outside the room could know for now. Later in the evening, Ethan joined Lee at the airfield to commiserate their loss in private and to get shitty drunk.

Private Fuck-knuckles was finally done digging his own grave and allowed to get some sleep, for in the morning, he'd have the honor of filling it in again. The sentries rotated and night shift conducted PT by force-marching around the parameter. Thanks to Lee, the abandoned airfield had started to actually look like a real military base.

Drinking until they couldn't see straight, Lee started a one-man karaoke of *Bon Jovi's* greatest hits. Unable to stand the sound of baritone caterwauling, Ethan wandered away from the HQ building to maybe find a spare rack to pass out in. He loved Lee dearly, but the guy was probably tone-deaf.

Just as he was considering calling a deputy to drive him home, Ethan found his people having a small party in his promised land. A dozen enlisted were grilling on a small spit that was obscured by quonset huts, the aroma of hotdogs and smores a change from the livestock in town. The commodities from the old world wouldn't last, so it was best to enjoy them now, Ethan reasoned.

Joining the group with the offer of some of Lee's apple-pie moonshine, pilfered straight from the source, the sheriff finally felt like he belonged somewhere. He was raised to be "an officer and a gentleman," but Ethan had never felt at ease around the gentry-types that pervaded the officer corps. Did a slightly lengthier training period and a fancy title really make a man modern aristocracy? Something seemed fundamentally wrong with that thinking, especially in this day and age, but Ethan could hardly articulate the whole argument himself.

"So, what did you do before the Apoc, Sheriff?" A sergeant handed the moonshine back to Ethan on his sip-sip-pass turn.

"Oh fuck, it's the sheriff! Run!" Another, incredibly drunk cavalryman shouted, falling backwards out of his lawn chair.

Everyone had a good laugh at that, "Okay, he's cut off," Ethan teased, but not really. The young man was skipped over for the next round and given a bottle of water.

"I was a security guard," Ethan answered the cavalryman once the drunkard was taken care of. "I know, huge stretch from what I do now."

"And where's your girlfriend?"

Shooting a murderous glare at the lady who asked, Ethan had to calm himself for a moment and clarify, "Detective Guiterez is not my girlfriend."

"No, no. The other girl, the one with the Irish face."

Now Ethan recognized this woman. She was a local and had worked at Walmart before the first cases of *Inviere*. He was less upset now and luckily the glow of the embers hid how red his face had gotten with anger. "She's gone."

"So's my husband," the woman took a shot of whiskey. "He was a good husband."

"And she would have been a... well, she was kind of a bitch, actually." Everyone laughed and Ethan felt horrible, but he was truth-serum-drunk now and just let it spill. "She was going to leave me. I know she'd been cheating on me with some fat-fuck that, I swear, used to stalk her in high school, but I couldn't let go... should have let go."

Nobody was laughing now, "Wow, that's... pretty fucked

up, Sheriff."

Ethan shrugged, "C'est la vie. Any of you got any weed?"

"Nah, Cap won't let us smoke."

Rolling his eyes, Ethan pulled a couple joints out of a rigid cigarette case he hadn't previously intended to share, "What he don't know won't hurt him. He'll be singing *One Wild Night* on repeat for another couple hours still, so we're safe." The sarcasm about someone they all looked to as a leader went over pretty well. Every now and then, you just have to blow off some steam about management.

"I have a question for you, Sheriff," another cavalryman spoke up. "Do you think the Texans are here to-" his question was cut short when another figure stepped out of the darkness toward the fire and grabbed the man's arm in an icy death-grip. Before anyone could grasp that there was a zombie in their midst, the corpse bit down on the guy's arm and came away with a huge chunk of bloodied flesh and tendons pulled from its meat.

Shouts of terror and surprise were followed by the clattering of beer cans and glass bottles as everyone sprang to their feet. A female cavalryman grabbed a spiked club that was never too far away and impaled Zim in his occipital lobe. Another cavalryman tore into his nearby med-kit and retrieved a tourniquet, applying it to their fallen comrade while a sharp blade was located. Ethan suddenly felt very naked, having taken his sidearm off to be a responsible drinker. *That*, he thought, *was now officially Old World Thinking.* Instead he had little to do but hold the wounded man's legs while the others tried to save him.

A man went running toward Lee's HQ building, hoping to find the soldier on Staff Duty who'd have emergency supplies and weapons. He was just as suddenly tackled by another, much fresher zombie, raising the fear there could be more hidden in the shadows cast by the lamps. The yelp the runner let out when the breath was knocked from his was chilling, but he was too far away to be helped. Nobody in the group had a gun because they were supposed to be guarded by the roaming patrols and lookout towers, another bothersome procedure from a garrison Army that maybe didn't make sense anymore.

With nothing more than a folding chair, Ethan sprinted toward the tackled soldier, but it was too late to save him. Swinging the chair, the Sheriff actually managed to knock the zombie down... if only he'd been a few seconds sooner. Through his cries for a mercy that wouldn't come in time, the dying soldier was already starting to succumb to infection, spitting blood and coughing on every breath and forcefully gnashing his teeth.

"I need help!" Ethan shouted to the others, but they were already well into the process of hacking their buddy's arm off with a kukri-style blade. Seeing no alternative Ethan tackled the rage-monster by the ankles just as he was getting up.

For a moment there seemed to be some kind of recognition in the man's eyes as to what had happened, but that surely was just the virus realizing it had a much closer host to infect than the people by the fire. Also coming to the conclusion that he'd fucked up royally, Ethan let go and reached for anything he might use as a weapon. He found a wiffle-ball bat the drunks had been using in a party-game and did the best he could with what he had. After only a couple of good whacks, the flimsy plastic bat broke and now he had two pieces of useless plastic instead of one. The rage-zombie snarled at Ethan and gave chase, possibly aware that his prey was virtually defenseless.

Meanwhile, with the high-drama unfolding outside, Lee had finally changed songs and this one was a little quieter for a moment. The one moment no one was shouting, of course and the music picked up again. Had he looked back behind the couch, he would have seen his brother running like a chase-scene in Scooby-Doo between rows of training targets on the quad. Finally, as Lee was shadow-boxing an imaginary assailant, enjoying the song, Ethan tripped over a spare propeller for a light aircraft the men used while weight lifting. He fell face first into a drainage ditch that still had ice around the edges, certain he would feel the agony of the death-bite any time.

Sure enough, the zombie tripped too, but unlike Ethan it made no effort to arrest its fall and plunged head-first into the crick, just inches from its target. The water turned red and Ethan realized Zim had cracked his head on a ceramic drain pipe hidden by the grass. Despite the freezing temperatures, Ethan collapsed into the water, huffing cold air and watching the steam rise above him. For whatever reason he thought of the scene from the movie *Titanic*, where Rose looks up into the night sky after the ship sinks. Had he *really* just survived yet *another* attempt by fate to kill him? *This shit was starting to become episodic.*

Chapter 20

The damage to the fence that surrounded Fort Sullivan was more substantial than anyone had expected. An unknown attacker had driven a U-Haul over the concertina wire and opened the door to release three zombies. One immediately became entangled in the wire and was still there when Lee's patrol found it, but the other two had made a B-line for the lights and noise of the men's social gathering.

Calling the entire base to high alert, flood lights reallocated from the local car dealership illuminated every inch of the facility like high noon. Supposedly, FOB Alamo was doing the same, but they didn't have any heavy weapons besides a single M-249 and claymore mines. With every vehicle running, the men started two counter-rotating search grids, weapons hot, though they had no idea who their target might be. The frenzy of activity got even more heated when reports from dispatch of an attack at the hotel where the Texans were billeted came across in the open. A deputy came to get Ethan and even though he was soaking wet he drove out of sheer anxiety to get to be in control of at least something.

At first the Texas Guard wouldn't let them in, a matter of trust perhaps, but Ethan's star changed their minds. The ranking Texan present was a lieutenant and her report to the sheriff was blood curdling. A man dressed as a local cop walked in and asked the soldier at the desk where Mary's room was, under the auspices of official business. He then assaulted her and tied her up and shot the two men who came to her aid with a suppressed pistol. On his way out he shot the desk clerk too, but she'd lived and was already at the hospital.

Before Ethan could panic too much, Allen pulled up in his cruiser and ran straight to his sheriff, "You need to see this-"

"Someone's taken Mary," Ethan said in shock, trying to

gather his wits.

"I know," Allen handed over a set of keys attached to a large, gaudy keychain that boldly read MERAMEC CAVERNS ZIP LINE. "It's from the U-Haul, Lee's already on the way there with QRF and he doesn't know about this. There was writing inside the cargo area, it's about the Detective."

"What?"

Allen opened up the gallery app on his phone. They might not have signal, but they weren't entirely useless. It read: HA HA, I HAVE THE TEXAS WHORE, YOSSARIAN WAS TOO LATE, but Ethan was in shock and the obvious wasn't registering. "I can't raise the convoy. Lee must have ordered radio silence over broadband." Shoving his protégé back into his cruiser, Ethan took the wheel and started back down I-44 toward Stanton. His mind was racing with possibilities, but as Allen explained the mini-manifesto he only became more confused and angry, too many thoughts competing for attention.

"But who is it!?" Ethan gritted his teeth, the cruiser breaking eighty.

"I..." Allen didn't want to say it, but Ethan couldn't see it. He'd had his suspicions for a while and now they'd been confirmed. "I think it's Newton."

Ethan's foot almost fell off the gas, "What?"

"I don't know why, or how, but he's involved in all of this."

Grabbing the radio, Ethan tried to call Lee again, "Alamo Six, this is Ghostrider, respond. This is Ghost Rider calling any Alamo element, please respond." Nothing. Throwing the radio down in frustration, Ethan charged forward.

Lee, unfortunately, never heard his brother because of the signal jamming emanating from somewhere in Stanton. What had been a minor inconvenience was now clearly sinister, but why? What did whoever this was gain from messing with their radios this far from town? The two horse-mounted troopers he had were scouting ahead of the convoy of gun trucks, but their radios weren't on the police band. They'd cleared the rental cabins at the top of the hill and were moving down toward Meramec Caverns, where the hills were beginning to mess with their signal too. Several sentries had reported seeing an all-black Dodge Charger leaving the town out a service gate barely minutes after the time the attack on the airfield had begun. Since he was a betting man, he felt that was their best chance to uncover their culprit. They'd actually lost the trail for a time, but disturbed leaves in the width and pattern of tire tracks were visible even at night and the convoy had followed them to this deserted little berg.

"You okay, Sir?" First Sergeant Alverez asked, handing Lee a bag of coffee he'd brewed from an MRE. Every once in a while, stashing those packets of coffee and chemical heaters paid dividends.

"No," Lee said almost too quickly. He was becoming un-drunk quickly, but not fast enough to suit his own unreasonably high personal expectations. "I should have known this wasn't over." There was a tap at the door. Lee looked out the LMTV's window at one of the signalmen from the truck behind him. Cracking the window, he motioned for the soldier to speak.

"Sir, Ghostrider Six is trying to contact you on *all* the bands. He's saying something about this being a trap, Sir," the signalman tried to hand the mic to Lee, but he didn't take it.

"Maintain radio silence over the town's net. Use our private line to recall Miles and Matheson, I don't want to risk-"

Lee's "private" radio started squawking so loudly he had to turn it down, Corporal Miles was shouting into the receiver and he was impossible to understand. Waiting for the line to clear, Lee tried to calm his soldier, "What's your location, Alamo Scout?"

"*-at the b- where the sign- eated from caves... The smell!*"

Alverez shrugged when Lee looked at him for clarification. He was a Gulf War Veteran and didn't hear so well anymore. "Alamo Scout, remember your bearing. Take a deep breath and repeat what you just told me."

Lee was about to get an answer, but he didn't hear it because he was too busy watching from the far side of the Stanton overpass as his brother's police cruiser went flying broadside up the ramp and down the service road toward the caverns. The flashing lights disappeared over the hill and Lee motioned for his convoy to start engines and move out. He then broke radio silence to warn Ethan of the horses ahead, but doubted the call would go through.

Ethan skidded to a halt before melding a horse into the front end of his cruiser, no warning over the radio ever having reached him. The beast reared back, but his handler calmed him while the other rider staggered up to Ethan, still visibly shaken.

"What's happening, Corporal?" Ethan asked quickly.

At first Miles tried to answer, but his words failed him and he vomited instead. "There's bodies... all of them... the refugees..."

Ethan got out of the car to keep Cpl. Miles from falling over, "Are you wounded? Where's my brother?"

"There's bodies everywhere beyond the camp ground. We couldn't get anywhere near the cave itself, the horses ain't having it! But Sheriff, I saw a light. Someone is there."

"Where?"

"The caves, Sir!" Matheson seemed as upset as his mount.

Pushing Allen out of the cruiser, Ethan locked the doors and took off without him. If this really was Newton, if he had Mary, there was no reason to risk Allen's life too. Chances were, Ethan was about to die confronting Newton, as the man was definitely waiting for him. Coming over a small rise that acted as a berm to protect a six-room motel, the first skeletal bodies appeared in the cruiser's headlights. Similar to the FEMA triage points the news just had to broadcast around the world, bodies were laid out in rows, organized as best as they could be in their dismembered state. It was impossible not to run some of them over, but then whomever was doing this was also just driving through the mess like these weren't once living people. The bodies closer to the outskirts of the cavern's parking lot were fresher than the ones closer to the visitor's center. The tarps that covered the larger collections, or maybe family groups, were tattered and faded, leaves and twigs from storms drifting up against them.

The reflective tail lights of the blacked-out Charger shone in Ethan's headlights, but the car itself was off. Aiming his searchlight at it, he saw steam was still rising from the tailpipes and hood. Part of Ethan's mind didn't want to accept that this man, whom he'd grown somewhat fond of as a coworker, was really the mastermind of... well, anything. The guy was a doofus, uncoordinated and awkward, far from the pride of any force. How the hell had he not seen this coming? There had to have been warning signs.

Drawing his sidearm and exiting the cruiser, the smell of all smells assailed Ethan and he almost fell back inside the car. The only descriptor his mind could find was what soldiers of the Great War had said of the smell of No Man's Land. Bodies bloating and rotting in the shelled-out hellscape, their blood and entrails running in small rivers when it rained. All that gore pooling in the trenches around their living comrade's feet as they huddled for warmth with nothing but the shelling and fleas for comfort.

His heart pounding, Ethan walked carefully up to the visitor's entrance, the door propped open with a tall ashcan. A swarm of blow-flies were buzzing in and out of the foyer, landing inside Ethan's ears and nose. The husks of their larvae and the bodies of those who'd lived their life-cycle crunched under his boots. Grime covered the glass partitions that separated the gift shop and dining areas from the hallway, hand-prints in blood were smeared eerily across one and the acrid stink of feces and cat urine started getting stronger.

"Newton!" Ethan shouted into the empty cavern. "Show yourself... You've been trying to kill me for some time now, why not just step out into the light and do it yourself?" The gift shop, Ethan saw, was where Newton had kept his victims before butchering them in the kitchen. The refrigerator would be found to be stocked full of the tastiest choice cuts of Long Pig, but that was just a gruesome fact they'd learn later. "Your car's here, you have nowhere left to go, John," Ethan's grip on his M-9 tightened and he thumbed the safety to make certain it was off.

The PA system from overhead speakers screeched. There was heavy breathing at first, but then yes, it was the voice of the most contemptible man alive. "I hadn't expected you so soon, Yossarian. Tell me, are any of the rest of this plucky cast nearby?"

"Nope. It's just you and me," Ethan couldn't tell where the voice was, but he'd find the Wizard of Oz and shove that microphone down his throat. "You know I've only read like the first two chapters of that book, right? Your references are lost on me, John. Why not just come out and face me like a man? It's the best death you're going to get."

A light flickered on in the far recesses of the kitchen, revealing a slender figure behind the plexiglass ordering screen that Ethan instantly recognized. He was smoking a cigarette and leaning against a doorsill, "If you really think you're ready for that."

Ethan raised his gun, but another light in the center chamber of the cave where visitors gather to begin their guided tour stole his attention. Unsure what he was seeing at first, he began to recognize an artificial berm where an authentic moonshiner's shack had been relocated for tourists to gawk at. Mary Guiterez was bound and gagged in harnesses meant for violent inmates, propped up against the hundred-year-old wooden structure.

"So that's your plan? Distract me with a damsel in distress so you can run?" Ethan's fingers wrapped around the pistol again to vent some of the heat that made his palm so sweaty. He could take the shot, but the plexiglass meant to keep guests from sneezing on the food could easily distort the bullet's trajectory.

Finally, a face emerged from the shadows of dim lamps in the stocking room. Newton's face was no longer that of a simple man with simple thoughts and desires, always lost in daydreams. This was someone else, someone new entirely. His normally gray eyes were black and shark-like, his features gaunt and menacing with accentuated shadows

"No, Yossarian. I'm going to give you the choice: Take me, I'll even go without a fight, but the Detective dies. Or, you could try to save her and while you're both dying, I will, in fact, make good my escape." Newton paced, admiring his gruesome work in replacing the menu above the malt-machines with human hides, meticulously arranged into a hideous mural, "It's a pity, I really would have liked to have added those pilots. The Asian man would have truly completed the darker regions."

Enraged, Ethan belted out five shots, shattering the plexiglass and showering Newton with the fragments. Sprinting as best he could in combat boots, Ethan ran up the gently sloping ramp to Mary and took position between her and the only way Newton could get to them. Not seeing any sign of pursuit at first, the sheriff began to reach for his handcuff keys when he saw Mary's eyes dart to his left and just behind. Fearing Newton was there, he turned just in time to see a Siberian tiger crouching to attack. Flopping backward out of instinct, he just avoided being snatched by the cat's outstretched claws by a few inches when the whole cave was plunged into near darkness but for the emergency exit signs.

A bullet zinged over his head and hit the farthest wall of the cave. The tiger retreated and Ethan scrambled to get back on his feet. He'd dropped his primary weapon when he tumbled and now all he had left was his grandfather's 1903 Colt Hammerless. It held nine rounds, including one in the chamber, but he didn't have another magazine for it, since it was a secondary. He saw what he thought was a human figure in a shadow and fired twice, but it was just a dissected geode in a display case.

Newton, however, took the bait and emptied his weapon at Ethan while he scrambled away again. Realizing he could even the odds some, the sheriff took his flashlight and quickly put it on top of the wooden podium used to collect tour tickets, then scuttled away to the other side of the cave, reasoning by the debris on the floor that the tiger couldn't reach this far. In fact, he'd probably been in no danger while trying to help Mary, but how should he have known that in the moment? Again, the deranged cop shot up the podium with half a dozen rounds. By now, Ethan had a pretty good idea where Newton was, but he was still out of effective range and it was too dark to see more than a slight silhouette. From behind him, the tiger roared and clanked its chains, frightened by the gunfight in an echo chamber.

"You know you're a broken toy, John," Ethan said, knowing the cave would distort the sound if he said it toward the ceiling. "People who aren't fucked in the head don't feed other people to tigers."

"I did what I had to do! Don't you understand!? These beasts-" and now Ethan knew there were two tigers instead of one, "They were our last line of defense! They were our patrons, don't you see? As long as we kept them fed, they staved off the inevitable, but now you've gone and ruined everything!" Newton shot up another shadow, but in his muzzle flashes had seen Ethan and redirected fire.

Firing back twice, Ethan low-crawled toward a rare Foucault Pendulum, or at least a scaled recreation of one, that had been installed by a student decades ago. Kicking it, he rolled away and let his enemy fire several more shots at the swinging metal ball. A bullet ricocheted off of it, but that was seemingly the end of Newton's ammunition, at least for his primary.

Trying not to give Newton enough time to reach for his ankle-carry, Ethan jumped up from the edge of the cave's wall and fired too many times at Newton, keeping his head down. The antique pistol locked back, empty, but Ethan had closed the distance and gave his foe the pistol-whipping of all pistol-whippings. It was so hard, in fact, the slide would never fit perfectly on its rails again.

Spitting blood, Newton whipped out his baton and tried to hit Ethan, but he was dazed and could barely see straight. Having left most of his gear at home, because just an hour ago he had been getting stoned while chilling with his brother, Ethan searched for anything else he might use as a weapon. Wouldn't you know it, but a display case of Civil War memorabilia held an authentic Confederate officer's saber. Throwing his empty pistol at the case, Ethan rushed over to it while Newton was still recovering, but he wasn't fast enough.

Plunging a pocket knife into Ethan's left leg, just above the boot, Newton dropped him on his face, chipping a tooth. Still in shock and somehow not believing he'd been stabbed, Ethan could do practically nothing as the pressure took over inside his head like when he'd been hit with the rifle. Newton pulled the knife out and started clawing his way up his next victim with his bare hands. Screaming like a little girl now, as that is the appropriate reaction to being repeatedly stabbed in the leg, Ethan was now all but helpless. Struggling in the slippery blood and cat-piss laden floor, there was no getting out from under Newton. He grabbed Ethan by the collar and started smashing his head against the concrete while babbling about something unintelligible, since he was also spitting blood and maybe a tooth of his own into Ethan's ear.

His breath smelled like cigarettes and coffee and Ethan genuinely feared this would be the last thing he smelled in this life before suddenly Newton's body-heat was gone from him, the abject terror lifted before it claimed him. Confused even more than concussed, he looked around through swimming vision and saw one of the tigers was loose. She had slammed Newton bodily against a display case and was now happily mauling him while he wailed in visceral pain.

Looking back at the way the tiger had to have come, Ethan saw Mary illuminated in red by an emergency exit sign. She ticked off the last of her chains and picked up the M-9 he'd dropped when he fell away from the tiger. She ran to him and bear hugged him, helping Ethan to his feet while the beast toyed with Newton's shredded body. He was still alive though and as Ethan and Mary slipped by the scene of carnage, he reached out to them with trembling, bloody fingers, one perhaps already missing. There was a sickening crunch as the tiger sank her fangs into his ribs for the dozenth time.

Ethan flipped him off.

The last time anyone saw John Newton he was being dragged back to where the other tiger was chained up, whimpering the entire way.

Epilogue

"Well," said Ethan, "We're back."

To be continued ...

About the Author

Author and Comic Strip Artist J.K. Robinson lives in rural Missouri and served in the U.S. Army in Iraq during Operation Iraqi Freedom V. He hated every moment of it, and that has largely tempered his view of the military in fiction. He likes Star Trek and temperamental old Pontiacs and is navigating the waters of raising a young daughter.

If you enjoyed this book, please check out Irregular Scout Team One by J.F. Holmes. A parallel series to The Thin Dead Line, IST-1 follows the adventures of a mixed Team of military and civilian scouts as they advance back across a devastated America. Contains the Dragon Award Finalist novel, "Falling".

For even more great Military Science Fiction check out:

Fallen Empire

What's a soldier to do when the war is over? When he's only known conflict his whole life? Since time immemorial the solution has been to find another war, this time for pay. Whoever has the credits and wins the high bid gets the experienced fighter. Sometimes, though, the credits aren't enough to over the price.

Empires rise, but Empires also fall. The Terran Union has spent five centuries under the control of the alien Grausians, like a barbarian tribe under the thumb of Rome. Now, after almost two decades of civil war and succession struggles, the formerly subject races have settled back in their ancient territories to lick their wounds and rearm, leaving hundreds of settled planets to exist in a political vacuum. Into that space steps the free companies, mercenary units that fight for gold, honor, power and glory. Veterans who can't get the wars out of their souls, new recruits looking for adventure, corporations with their own agenda.

Join us in a 27th Century that echoes history.

An ancient enemy invades Earth, returning to claim their home world. The men and women of the U.S. Military find themselves matching technology against magic as cities burn and armies clash.